Vladimir's Diary

By the author

THE COUNTDOWN INSTALMENTS:

The Kiss Of The Mandarins
The Warehouse
Never Go Back

ORIGIN TALES:

The Brotherhood
Rise of the ACF

OTHER WORKS:

Red Empire
Vladimir's Diary
Fifty Years to Paradise

Vladimir's Diary

Martin M. McShane

The Book Guild Ltd

First published in Great Britain in 2019 by
The Book Guild Ltd
9 Priory Business Park
Wistow Road, Kibworth
Leicestershire, LE8 0RX
Freephone: 0800 999 2982
www.bookguild.co.uk
Email: info@bookguild.co.uk
Twitter: @bookguild

Typeset in Adobe Garamond Pro

Printed and bound in the UK by TJ International, Padstow, Cornwall

ISBN 978 1912881 659

British Library Cataloguing in Publication Data.
A catalogue record for this book is available from the British Library.

FSC www.fsc.org MIX Paper from responsible sources FSC® C013056

Contents

Prologue

Lenin had an ambition that every country in the world would be run as a communist state. He wrote a treatise about it: '*Communism In Many Countries*'. He never realised his ambition.

After Lenin's untimely, some say suspicious, death in 1924, Joseph Stalin seized power and set about exterminating all his rivals.

Stalin too believed in '*Communism In Many Countries*' but could see no way of achieving it. Then events put a tremendous opportunity his way; World War II. Stalin's plan was to let the opposing Axis and Allied forces fight themselves to a standstill and then, while they were in a weakened state, conquer them all. His plan was ruined when the Nazis invaded Russia in the summer of 1941 dragging the Soviet Union into the war. Stalin believed his chance had gone.

At the end of WWII Stalin, Churchill and President Truman attended a so-called peace conference held in Potsdam. Stalin had the leaders of the free world in the palm of his hand while millions of his Red Army Soldiers were less than a day's march away. It was the opportunity he had been waiting for. Stalin seized Truman and Churchill and ordered his Red Army to march on Europe and begin his quest for Communism In Many Countries.

There is no avoiding revolution.
When postponed it is
to the advantage
of others.

The Telegram and its Aftermath

Diplomatic communique handed to former vice president Henry A Wallace by an unnamed Soviet agent.

Potsdam July 26th 1945.

Documents in my possession make it clear that Winston Churchill conspired with renegade American politicians to drop an Atomic Bomb on Moscow with the intent of murdering me and my Central Committee. Accordingly, as at 1400 today, a state of war exists between the Soviet Union and Great Britain.

Winston Churchill and his legation have been arrested and are being held in Berlin. President Truman and his legation are under my protection and will be handed over to American forces at the earliest possible opportunity.

To avoid accidental conflict between our two great nations I hereby serve the United States of America notice that my Red Army will immediately march through the low countries into northern France. I have no desire for war with my loyal allies and so advise that the United States military do not engage with Red Army forces.

I strongly urge American politicians and the American people to consider their position carefully to avoid getting involved in yet another unpopular and unnecessary European war.

J Stalin – General Secretary of the Soviet Union.

On the Polish border four million Red Army Soldiers were marching west backed up by thousands of tanks and planes. The Soviet navy weighed anchor at Murmansk; destination unknown.

President Truman was held for four days before being handed over to American forces. He never once spoke of what happened to him during his captivity.

★

The Red Army marched through the Netherlands and Belgium and on into northern France, depositing large numbers of Red Army Soldiers along their route as forces of occupation. Hundreds of thousands of civilians were rounded up and transported east by train to be herded into concentration camps around Moscow and Leningrad to deter America from using the Atomic Bomb against their ally.

Under Stalin, the Soviet Union had become expert in the mass transportation of people as he regularly ordered the relocation of entire populations, including mass removals of ethnic groups to the various desolate hinterlands of the Soviet Union. Many Soviet Soldiers returning home after the war found their families had been '*relocated*', often to Siberia. Arriving at their Siberian destinations the displaced had to fend for themselves as the homes they had been promised were seldom ever even built. Money paid for house building ended up in the pockets of corrupt officials. Those that were built were ferociously fought over by desperate people in their frantic struggle for survival.

★

On its march to northern France, the Red Army engaged in several ferocious battles with British forces. Due to vastly superior numbers of men, tanks, cannon and planes the Red Army easily defeated the British Army which they slaughtered to a man, being under orders not to take any prisoners.

While the former allies in arms battled it out, American forces were under orders not to get involved. Behind the scenes American politicians were trying for a diplomatic solution. This strategy was futile as appeasement is never successful when dealing with tyrants such as Stalin. By the time the Americans accepted that diplomacy was not going to work it was too late. The Atomic Bombs that could have blasted Stalin to the negotiation table could not be used as to do so would wipe out millions of innocent Dutch, Belgian and French citizens who were housed in concentration camps around Moscow and Leningrad. As powerful as it was, the Atom Bomb was useless in such circumstances.

After enduring five years under wartime conditions, the people of Great Britain were soon starving as the Soviets set up a blockade to prevent food and fuel from reaching them. With most of its forces already wiped out, Great Britain was at the mercy of the Hammer and Sickle and on 3rd of October 1945 the Red Army mounted its invasion. Due to the Soviet Union's overwhelming forces the invasion of Great Britain was little more than a series of skirmishes. The instrument of unconditional surrender was signed on the 5th of November 1945 by Clement Attlee. The number of dead was estimated at over four million after the Political Commissars achieved their quotas on those deemed to be '*Politically Unreliable*'.

The politically unreliable executed by the Political Commissars included; class enemies, class traitors, potential opponents of the Soviet regime, those previously designated as '*politically unreliable*', the aristocracy, land owners [*including allotment holders*], the rich, the upper-classes, the middle-classes, managers, agricultural workers [*through the forced introduction of his Agrarian Policies Stalin discovered that agricultural workers were fundamentally counter-revolutionary*], intellectuals, all military above the rank of Corporal, the police, artists, poets, musicians, writers – including Eric Blair, imperialists, fascists, socialists, those the Political Commissars did not like the look of, those killed to satisfy the vendettas of Soviet collaborators, Nazi sympathisers, anybody with a strong community following and anybody who '*might be trouble*'.

Political Commissars concentrated their attentions on those areas reputed to be hotbeds of political activism, trade-unionism, religious devotion and general attitudinal belligerence. Most of which were concentrated in the north. Consequently, the populations in those areas were decimated.

★

The Red Army reserve numbered as many as the Red Army itself and while the main force occupied northern France, the reserve force marched south to Greece. After which it turned west, attacking and occupying Austria, Switzerland, Italy, Southern France, Spain and Portugal. Now unable to respond either politically or militarily, the Americans stood by as Soviet style Terror was conducted on the very peoples whom Churchill had predicted would suffer under the communists unless an Atom Bomb was dropped on Moscow. How right he had been.

★

Terror, religious and secular, has been used against populations throughout time. Soviet style Terror had its beginnings in Lenin's time. He believed Terror was a vital instrument to keep the spirit of the revolution alive. He advocated and practised Terror right up until his death. Lenin's Terror was responsible for the slaughter of millions of ordinary citizens but would be as nothing when compared with the Terror enacted by his successor, Joseph Stalin.

Stalin's Terror was on an altogether different scale to Lenin's Terror, or anybody else's for that matter. It truly was in a league of its own. The backbone of Stalin's Terror were his Secret Policemen, of which there were many types, including the notorious People's

Head Commissariat for Internal Affairs, commonly known as the NKVD. Stalin demanded that the leaders of local Soviets throughout Russia enacted Terror on the citizens in their regions or face Terror themselves. Many leaders of local Soviets carried out their Terror with great enthusiasm and became rich and powerful as a result, until other instruments of Stalin's Terror caught up with them; denunciations for example.

Denunciations were a key part of Stalin's Terror. Anybody denounced would be doomed to die or sent to the Gulag; which, in reality, meant a death sentence but while doing something useful for the state before perishing at its hands. Denunciations caught the imagination of the population. They could be used for anything from revenging unrequited love to getting rid of one's boss. Children, particularly through the Pioneer programme, were a central part of denunciations. They were encouraged to spy on their parents, relatives and friends; listening to what they said and reporting it to their school's Political Commissar or the local KGB. The entire population of the Soviet Union lived in fear of being denounced.

A major instrument of state Terror was '*targets*'. For example, those failing to achieve production targets could be executed, along with their entire family. Targets were a key component of Stalin's infamous Five Year Plans and many citizens charged with responsibility for them ended up dead. There were also targets for executing enemies of the state. According to Stalin, and Lenin before him, it was '*logical*' that there must be a certain number of Soviet citizens who were '*wreckers, saboteurs, counter-revolutionaries or guilty of anti-Soviet activities*'. It was the job of '*responsible workers*', such as the Central Committee, to root out these elements and destroy them. Death lists were signed by the Central Committee as authority for others to do the killing while they sat in the '*comfort*' of the Kremlin. It was mass slaughter by proxy.

The Soviets perfected Terror between 1936 and 1938 when the Central Committee oversaw the annihilation of tens of millions of innocent people. This became known as the Great Terror. Stalin used the Great Terror to rid himself of his political enemies. Other victims of the Great Terror included vast numbers of Communist Party members, Government officials, former Tsarist Officers, Peasants, Kulaks and those identified through widespread surveillance as counter-revolutionaries. To demonstrate loyalty, those responsible for carrying out the Great Terror regularly executed far greater numbers of unfortunates than was on their lists. Over performing in this way often earned the executioner more enemies than friends. They inevitably ended up on somebody else's death list. There was no such thing as a safe place in Stalin's Soviet Union.

Each of the conquered nations of western Europe, especially so the British Isles, were subjected to round after round of Terror. Millions upon millions of ordinary people were slaughtered. Industry and agriculture virtually ground to a halt because all the experts had been executed or sent to the Gulag. The people were starving. To address the Terror-decimated skills shortage in the conquered nations Stalin decreed that all conquered nations should be, like the Soviet republics before them, Russified. That is to say, large numbers of ethnic Russians were ordered to live in the conquered nations. In support of this policy, university graduates had to live and work in the conquered nations for at least ten years following graduation. Many graduates remained after this time as they assimilated into the general population through marriage and so on.

In an effort not to totally turn the peoples of the occupied nations against the state their institutions were left intact. Initially so at least. Then Stalin's methods were used against them. It was always the same; the state would set up identical institutions imitating those of the occupied nations; they would then become affiliated, then assimilated, then exterminated. The new institutions were, of course, owned and operated by the state. China too adopted this model. The USA necessarily adopted it to fight off, so it claimed, stealth communism.

★

Seeing what the USSR was doing, China, not wanting to be left behind, embarked on its own campaign, conquering Japan, Mongolia, the countries south of Turkmenistan and the Arabian peninsula. Shortly thereafter, India, south east Asia, Indonesia, the Philippines and Australasia fell to China. They all became China, no other country names were allowed. The survivors became Chinese citizens but none could ever be card carrying party members. By comparison with what happened to citizens in the Soviet Union the new Chinese suffered very little Terror.

★

Conquered nations were integrated into the workers' paradises of both communist regimes. Lenin claims to have coined the phrase *'workers' paradise'* to give the Proletariat the illusion of living in a paradise meant only for them. Soviet Proles were told that they were the new bosses and they held the fate of their nation in their hands. The Bolshevik leadership sold the dream but it turned out to be a nightmare as those at the top were largely incapable of running a sweetie shop let alone the industries of the world's largest country. The suffering of the people under Communism was far worse than it had ever been under the Tsars. But the new Tsars learned quickly and nobody could even have guessed at the enormousness of Stalin's organisational talents. He would have made an outstanding CEO.

Not everybody was welcome in the workers' paradise of the Soviet Union. Stalin declared the peoples of neutral nations as cowards and politically unreliable and came down on them very hard indeed, particularly so the Irlandtsy. He ordered that the people of Irlandiya be removed to various, particularly harsh, Gulags in the furthest and coldest reaches of the USSR. All were given life terms; men, women, children, the aged, the infirm, the crippled. The 1961 pan-Soviet census showed there were no people of Irlandtsy ancestry alive in the USSR. Irlandiya itself became the Soviet Union's western frontline outpost against America and off limits to all except military personnel.

By the summer of 1948 all of Africa was under Soviet rule. Latin America was abandoned as unruly warring countries left to be run either by former Nazis or graduates of Stalin's communist training academies. Canada remained independent, largely because nobody was interested in it. The Soviet Union petitioned the USA to return Alaska to it, claiming that there were indigenous Soviet descendants living there who were demanding Alaska become a Soviet Republic. This debate was maintained for years to and for the amusement of bureaucrats on both sides.

In that same year, Stalin embarked on his scheme to control his new super-sized Soviet Union. He did this by expanding the instruments of State Terror. First, he approved a programme to create a network of Lubyankas. A competition was held to design a model Lubyanka which was won by a twelve year old in Perm; her design came with four sub-levels below ground and eight levels above. Lubyankas were prefabricated in the Urals and transported around the Soviet Union. They became home bases for local KGB. Second, the Gulag was expanded to all the conquered nations. These became the home bases of the NKVD. Third, Stalin commissioned the expansion of the Kremlin. The new Kremlin ran for over a mile along the banks of the Moskva river on either side of the original citadel. The extensions were built in Stalin's gaudy Soviet Empire style with eight floors above ground and four below. Areas below ground were connected by labyrinthine corridors. Holes were knocked between corridors in some of the lower floors to access torture cells, interrogation suites and administration departments. Over time some corridors were modified into makeshift offices which, in the 1980s, were tiled and converted into execution rooms for dispensing the summary justice of the so-called law courts across Red Square.

★

To all intents and purposes, after 1948, there were only three nations; the USA, the USSR and China. Each possessed sufficient natural resources to be self-sufficient. They were able to satisfy their own internal markets, though a certain amount of barter-trade went on, particularly between China and the USSR. Gold was the only internationally recognised currency when sides failed to reach a barter-agreement. It was a short lived boom for American commodity brokers.

There was so very little trade between the three great nations that innovation and technological advancement ground to a halt. There was no commercial imperative nor was there funding to create new products. Small scale consumerism carried on in America, Canada and Mexico but nowhere else.

★

Soon, the secrets behind America's Atomic Bomb were possessed by the Soviet Union and China. With all three major nations possessing '*The Bomb*' a state of mutually assured destruction ensured peace. It was not long after getting the bomb that the first nuclear reactors were built. It seemed as if mankind's energy needs were met and exceeded overnight. The Soviets still had their old '*five year plan*' mentality and instead of working out all the kinks they went ahead and built the world's first nuclear reactor as a prelude to the world's first nuclear reactor disaster. Millions died and continued to do so for years and years from radioactive fallout.

Typical of Soviet mentality, the Central Committee ordered a witch hunt to uncover the anti-Soviet, counter-revolutionary wreckers and saboteurs responsible for the disaster. Not for a single second did they consider Soviet methods to be at fault. Thousands were put on trial, all were found guilty and executed within minutes of their sentences being handed down. They had Stalin to thank for this swift delivery of justice as he did not believe in appeals, *"appeals are a waste of time, everybody knows that... the guilty are guilty."* Below every Soviet court house are basement cells. When defendants are found guilty they are taken below and told to stand on one side of a yellow line or the other. One line of prisoners are taken to the nearest railhead to be transported to the Gulag while the other line of prisoners is taken, one at a time, into a tiled chamber, ordered to kneel down and shot in the back of the head, usually by junior NKVD or KGB Officers to '*blood*' them.

Velikobritania, Bolshoi Britanski as it was known by its inhabitants, was the testing ground for type one nuclear reactors. By the mid sixties all type one's were failing, with several blowing up completely. Through trial and error the Soviets built a '*safe*' nuclear reactor which was installed right across the USSR. Everybody was assured that type two reactors were safe. They were not. It was rumoured that type three nuclear reactors were designed and built in China and '*sold*' to the Soviet Union. It was further rumoured that the Chinese nuclear reactors were in fact American.

★

Throughout the Soviet Union, the only language that was permitted to be spoken, written or taught was Russian. The only exception to this rule being those who were employed by the Ministry of Nationalities, the KGB, the NKVD, the Red Army Intelligence Corps, certain Red Army Officers and students attending the University of Nationalities in Moscow. Most foreign language speakers only learnt the two common foreign languages; American and Mandarin. Agents working for state security services, and certain students attending the University of Nationalities, could learn as many languages as they needed to perform their duties for the glory of the Union of Soviet Socialist Republics.

A Soviet life was all the generations born there after 1950 knew and most Soviet citizens were content with it. There was enough work to keep citizens occupied, some leisure time, good wages, good entertainments and cultural events and lots of marches; especially '*workers days marches*' – these were invariably held on Sundays, the only day of rest for workers, which annoyed many of them.

The Soviet Union was big on state-controlled-mass-entertainment so there were resident ballet companies and circuses in every city and large town. On the flip side of the coin, hundreds of millions of citizens went hungry at least twice a week despite the efficiencies promised by agricultural collectivisation. Farmers unhappy with collectivisation were sent to political re-education centres. Nobody ever got to find out how things worked out for them as none of them was ever seen again. Rumours circulated that there was no such thing as political re-education centres and the farmers were just sent to the Gulag to be worked to death.

Everybody in the Soviet Union was taught that all citizens were equal and many genuinely felt that they were indeed equal. But even in the most equal societies, inequality is never far away and as the population of the Soviet Union grew, and productive employment became less and less, more and more work and more and more production and more and more bureaucratic administration was drawn into the centre; that is to say Russia and that is to say western Russia, and that is to say the environs of Moscow, Leningrad and Nizhny Novgorod. This became known as the Work Relocation Programme, WRP. Across the vastness of the Soviet Union, hundreds of millions of citizens suddenly found themselves, to all intents and purposes, jobless. WRP caused misery and chaos, which turned into protests, rioting and widespread civil unrest. To combat this, the Central Committee introduced the

Workshare Programme; a form of job-loading, job-splitting and job-sharing; the aim of which was to over-resource jobs to keep citizens in employment. Whereas under WRP one job was carried out by one person, under the Workshare Programme one job was carried out by two people... then three... then four and then up to eight or ten by the beginning of the twenty first century. In reality, a job was still done by one person, the others were covert Political Commissars there to report on the worker and their colleagues. The Workshare Programme resulted in the NKVD becoming the largest Commissariat in the Soviet Union, employing over fifty percent of the '*working*' population.

A strategy used by the state to control the Proles following WRP was '*redistribution of citizens*' to '*match resources with output*'. Rumours circulated that tens of millions of redistributed Soviet citizens were sold to China while others ended up in the Gulag. "*These rumours make no sense*," preached Political Commissars at factories, offices and farms, "*What does China need more citizens for? They have enough workers. Now! all of you, get back to your work!*"

After several years of WRP and Workshare, rioting, civil disobedience and social unrest returned. Whenever the masses were brought to the brink of revolution orders were passed by the Central Committee for workers to receive bonuses, which were paid in Vodka. The Vodka bonuses added fuel to the fire of alcoholism already endemic amongst the workers of the Soviet Union; but alcoholism brought increased employment so it was not all bad.

These measures were successful for a little while but things soon slid back. Somehow, from nobody quite knew where, an elite class of citizen emerged from out of the chaos. It was with their appearance that Terror was once more visited on the citizens of the Soviet Union.

★

By 1984, nearly all disaffection amongst the citizens of the USSR had been eliminated after wave upon wave of mass Terror was carried out; nation by nation, republic by republic, until all those remaining were considered '*politically reliable*'. Tens of millions of citizens were massacred or sent to the Gulag to be worked to death. To ensure there would be a sufficient number of politically reliable workers children born after 1984 became wards of the state. They were educated by the state, fed by the state and brain-washed by the state for the first eighteen years of their lives.

For the three months of their summer and winter breaks every citizen-child between the ages of seven and eighteen went off to Pioneer Camp for immersive indoctrination. Surrounded day and night by party officials, Pioneer Camp Counsellors, Political Commissars and Communist activists, they were told tales of the Great and Glorious Revolution by people who were there and then by people who claimed they were there and then by people who claimed to have known people who had been there. Pioneer Camps made each and every young Pioneer feel deeply honoured to be a citizen of the workers' paradise of the Soviet Union.

At the age of eighteen each citizen-child was assessed for political reliability. Those failing the assessment were transported to the Gulag.

★

By 1999, and this despite the Soviet Union having been in decline for decades, Soviet life remained bearable for the majority of Soviet citizens. According to surveys carried out by the KGB's Citizens Information Unit, Soviet citizens were better off than their American or Citizens of the People's Republic of China counterparts. The statistics from the '*Citizens Information Unit*' only fooled those who wanted to be fooled into still believing in the workers' paradise of the Soviet Union. "*Citizens Information Unit? Citizens Disinformation Unit more like!*" Speaking such words got you carted off to the Gulag.

From their vantage point in Moscow, the Central Committee could see that the whole fabric of the Soviet Union was disintegrating. *"What is to be done?"* They asked in echo of Lenin's seminal treatise. In Stalin's day, the Central Committee controlled the Proletariat through Terror. It was Terror that kept them in line, it was Terror that kept them compliant, it was Terror that kept them obedient and in perpetual fear of the Soviet State Machine. It seemed logical, therefore, to the current Central Committee, that the answer to the Soviet Union's woes of the twenty first century was to bring back Terror; after all, was it not Lenin himself who had said, *"Terror is essential to keep the spirit of revolution alive."* It was time to bring back Terror.

Localised Terror campaigns aimed at supressing pockets of unrest in the odd Republic or occupied nation apart, it had been four decades since the Soviet Union had witnessed large scale Terror. In Stalin's day, it was Russia who was first to suffer state sponsored Terror, followed by the republics and then the conquered nations. In those days Terror was a progressive, piecemeal, affair seldom having to deal with more than a couple of tens of millions of people at a time. Terrorising the entire Soviet Union of the twenty first century, with its population of nearly one and a half billion, required Terror on an unprecedented scale. Stalin's Terror in the 1930s wiped out over twenty million people. An equivalent scale of Terror in the modern Soviet Union would put over two hundred million of its citizens through the process. Such an enterprise was going to need some serious resources and planning to make it successful; the Central Committee knew revolution would be the price of failure.

The Central Committee's readiness to carry out Terror was impacted by the fact that none of them had any experience of, or expertise in, carrying out mass Terror. So, where to begin, should they have a practice Terror first? No; if Terror started in one nation then the other nations would rise up in revolt. What should they do? How should they go about it? Then, unexpectedly, Central Committee member, Nikolai Karev, volunteered to put the Terror plan together.

'*Nobody volunteers for anything in the Soviet Union, everybody knows that.*' Anybody doing so are regarded as dangerous self-promoting career climbers. Karev's card was marked by his Central Committee peers. As soon as he slipped up, and slip up he would, everybody does, they would get him.

Nikolai Karev knew the risk he was taking in volunteering to put the Terror plan together. The sensible, life preserving, thing to have done would have been to ask open questions about how the Central Committee thought the Terror might be carried out; '*what does the Central Committee think needs to be done?*' and so forth. Such interest would, in all likelihood, have led to him being appointed by the Central Committee to put the Terror plan together which, under false-protest, he could have graciously accepted; saying he would do his best to reward their trust in him. Such words would save his life if, or rather when, things went wrong. The Central Committee raised its hands and voted for comrade Karev as being responsible for producing and executing the plan to enact Terror on the citizens of the Soviet Union. Naturally, it would be a five year plan. Everything in the Soviet Union was a five year plan.

Predictably, and in typical Soviet fashion, the five year plan failed, mainly due to it being an impossibly large and complex task to complete in five years without alerting the Proles to what was going on. The Central Committee voted in favour of embarking on a second five year Terror plan, after first executing all those responsible, in its opinion, for the failure of the first five year Terror plan, starting with Nikolai Karev. Maxim Kirilenko, General Secretary of the Soviet Union, decided that the Terror was to coincide with the centenary celebrations of the Great and Glorious Revolution which were being held in 2017. This gave the Central Committee time, so it thought, to get things right and ready. None of them lasted a month after the execution of Nikolai Karev. Maxim Kirilenko, the perennial survivor, appointed a new Central Committee and kept knowledge of the Terror plan from them until he thought that the time was right to let them in on the secret.

★

The first leaflets started appearing shortly after the 2016 results of the KGB's Annual Soviet Worker's Satisfaction Survey were published in Pravda. The leaflets told of the misery, poverty and suffering of Soviet citizens. They called for '*Great and Glorious Revolution*' to rid their beloved Soviet Union of the incompetent and corrupt officials running the state along with the hated NKVD and KGB. The leaflets told of the ways, workings and gangsterism of the Central Committee; how they behaved and how they and their families lived their lives in luxury while ordinary citizens starved. They told of the new elite, the '*Untouchables*', who were bleeding the USSR dry. They called for the creation a '*New Workers' Paradise*.'

The leaflets were signed by somebody called Lev in the name of a revolutionary group born over a hundred years previous; Narodnaya Volya – The People's Will. Groups of workers standing and reading the leaflets spontaneously chorused:

Long live Lev.
Long live Narodnaya Volya.
Long live the revolution.
Long live Lev.
Long live Narodnaya Volya.
Long live the revolution.
Long live…

Vladimir Goes to Moscow

Hello. My name is Vladimir Vladimirovich Vakhnenko. I was born and raised in the hero city of Budyonovsk, a seaport in northwest Velikobritania on the westernmost borders of the Soviet Union. From the age of seven to eighteen I attended school number eight in the Leninski Distrikt. I was never remarkable but I always felt myself lucky. I came from a '*good family*' which in Soviet terms meant we were politically reliable. It is important to be politically reliable in the Soviet Union, political reliability is everything. My mother is a card carrying member of the communist party. Not everybody gets a party card. They are, and have always been, your ticket to privileges in the Soviet Union.

At the age of four I contracted pneumonia which left me partially deaf. My deafness impacted on my social and educational development which in turn affected my behaviour, singling me out as different to other kids. Relatives said I was "*not right in the head*" and "*a bit slow*". They did not lower their voices when they said these things and I was not so deaf that I could not hear what they said about me; plus I am pretty good at lip reading. They said I was a child of the radiation, which, for me, meant I did not blink or cry tears. Other children of the radiation had far more severe conditions than just not being able to blink or cry tears. For some reason the things people said about me did not bother me, I just went about my life in my own happy little world, oblivious to all that went on around me. This led people to describe me as '*happy go lucky*'. I heard them say that too and I was happy with that description; '*happy go lucky*', that was me.

My mother, Lyudmila, was an ethnic Russian who, after graduating from Archangelsk university in economics, was ordered to live in Budyonovsk for her post-university-ten-year-assignment. Introduced by Stalin, university graduates had to live where the state sent them '*to balance the skills required in local populations to meet the production targets of the Soviet Union*'. This was because he massacred all the people who knew how to do the jobs necessary to make cities work. Mum was fortunate, she could have been sent to a city in the baking jungles of Afriski or the bitter cold of Siberia. On the other hand there were better post graduate assignments than Budyonovsk as it was considered to be a hotbed of subversives, revolutionaries, anarchists, trade-unionists and so on. Budyonovskites have a reputation for a certain kind of madness which makes them antagonistic, confrontational and difficult to deal with but to one another they are good, kind and loyal to a fault.

Though post-university assignments are supposed to be for ten years they are invariably longer, oftentimes for life, as many assignmentees marry locals or their bosses simply refuse to sign the paperwork permitting them to travel back to their home.

My father had an old Engliski name, Patrik. He met Mum on a worker's day march for accountants one sunny Sunday. They fell in love and married within a month as is the Soviet custom. He died of radiation sickness when I was eight, my little brother six and my sister four. It was unusual for Soviet families to have three children but my father's ancestors were originally from Irlandia where it was traditional to have a large family. Our family unit was not so large when compared with the families of my father's siblings. In all I had over fifty first cousins. Collectively we were known as the fighting Vakhnenkos.

We had everything a Soviet family could ever want or need; a four room apartment on the first floor; the latest Malenkytel with a fourteen inch screen, it was a black and white set though there were rumours of colour Malenkytels; a ten year old Yugo – we seldom used it as fuel was hard to come by but we washed the dust, grime and dirt off it every Saturday evening and polished the chromium until it shone. We did not share our kitchen with another family even though it was a full size 3 by 3 Khrushchev kitchen and not one of those useless 2 by 2 Malenkov kitchens.

After my father died things became difficult for Mum. Raising such a large family on one income was not easy for her despite her having a good job. She was the Personal Economic Assistant to a Regional Head Commissar. Like almost everybody in the Soviet Union at the time, my mother shared her job with three others but as she was the only one qualified to carry out the work the other three women just sat around chatting and scheming. "*Idle hands are the workshop of the Devil*," Mum used to say. I think she got that saying from Dad.

I had no concept of rich and poor or of being poor. Everybody, more or less, had much of the same so there was little to compare things to; except the size of one's Malenkytel that is and whether one had a Yugo or not. I occasionally saw cars that were not Yugos. They were black and shiny and polished and long and had blacked out windows so you couldn't see who was riding inside them. Most of them had the name '*Merkov*' in silver letters on the front of the bonnet and on the boot lid. People said that they were the cars party officials used when going about official business. Whenever a Merkov passed us in the street we would stand on the pavement and wave and cheer and salute the '*hard working party officials going about important party business*'. One day a Merkov stopped outside my school and all us children ran to the windows to get a better look at it. Unusually, it was silver, not black. None of us had ever seen a silver car before. An argument broke out as to whether the car was painted or not. Several children argued that there was no such thing as silver paint; "*Do not be so stupid there is no such thing as silver paint, how could there be?*" The driver opened the rear door of the Merkov. He wore a grey suit, white shirt, black tie and a grey hat with black piping and a little round badge on the front. A man in a suit got out of the rear of the car and walked into the school. The man in the grey uniform bent and spoke to somebody inside the car. The passenger pushed the door wide open. It was a beautiful young woman. She was wearing such clothes as we had never seen before. Even I could tell they were beautiful. Comrade females went into a huddle and drew the young woman's clothes, saying that they were going to make the exact same clothes for themselves. They pooled their meagre resources and made a good attempt at reproducing the clothes they saw the beautiful young woman wearing.

Other than that, school was uneventful that year.

It might have been a coincidence but disappearances increased after the visit to the school by the man in the silver Merkov. Small numbers of people, say a couple of hundred a year, went missing between my neighbourhood and my school but after the visit by the man in the silver Merkov it doubled. There were lots of official reasons given for the disappearances; '*they have been promoted*'; '*they have been transferred with their jobs*'; '*they have gone to live with relatives*'; '*they have…*' The old Proles likened the situation to the days of the Terror. They said this was how it started; a few people disappeared, then more and more until eventually snatch squads operated openly on the streets. Mum told us not to get involved in discussions about the disappeared because such talk might get us denounced, "*such talk will call our political reliability into question.*" Mum said she would lose her job and her party card if she was denounced and we understood what that would mean for us all. So, we kept our mouths shut and our eyes closed and said nothing to anybody about anything to do with disappearances… or anything else on the list that mum gave us.

★

I was in the kitchen trying to cook breakfast, the power had gone out three times already that morning and it was not even seven o'clock. I lit the last of the candles for light, its flame being totally inadequate for cooking kasha. My brother, Sergei, took the candle into the bathroom. I sat alone in the dark waiting for the post to arrive, hopefully with good news about my application to attend the University of Nationalities in Moscow. At nine thirty the post arrived. A brown envelope marked State Education Head Commissariat flopped onto the linoleum floor. It looked thin to me. I ripped the envelope open and removed a single sheet of paper. It was good news. I had done well enough in my exams to win a place at the University of Nationalities. I left for Moscow the next day as the train journey would take at least two weeks.

★

"*At last*!" I yelled as I arrived in the outskirts of Moscow. I had never seen anything like it. I had read about Moscow of course and seen pictures, photographs and films about it but to see it for real was incredible. Never in my wildest dreams did I ever think that an ordinary citizen like me from Budyonovsk would ever actually get to visit Moscow. Not only visit but to study, to stay, to live in Moscow. I felt my dad would have been proud of me.

I ensured that I had a window seat for the final leg of my journey. Once the train entered Moscow's suburbs it slowed down to a speed slower than a Budyonovsk trolley bus. It took over two hours to reach the centre but I did not mind, I was taking in all the sights. We passed by so many buildings; so, so, so, many buildings. The apartment blocks were twice as high and ten times as wide as anything in Budyonovsk. There were office blocks everywhere; factories of every type; power stations... and so many parks. So many people too. They looked like lines of marching Army Ants walking along the streets and crossing over bridges. There were faces in every window of every apartment, shop and office block.

As the train passed into the densely populated inner city areas of Moscow the buildings were older, smaller and decrepit. They looked as though they were going to fall down at any minute. Every building seemed to be in urgent need of renovation… and painting! they all badly needed painting! The closer we got to the centre, the more shabby and dilapidated everything was. Everything that is except for the state run entertainments and government buildings. In Moscow's suburbs I counted eight State Circus Palaces and four Opera Houses, which are used as much for ballet as they are for opera. The closer we got to the centre of Moscow the more State Circus Palaces there were and there seemed to be an Opera House on every second corner. From the window of my carriage I saw a poster for my favourite ballet, Swan Lake. The great Irina Petrova was dancing the lead. I had never heard of the man dancing the part of Prince Siegfried, which was disappointing. I recalled from my history classes that after the Great Patriotic War there were calls to change the Prince's name to a Russian sounding name but Stalin would not hear of it.

My journey ended at the Kievsky Rail Terminal in the south central zone of Moscow's city centre. When I stepped out of the railway station the noise and the bustle hit me like… like a train.

★

When registering my arrival with the Moscow State Security Police my USSR internal passport was inspected as were my travel documents. They brought a laugh from the Security Officer. He called his comrades over for them to have a good laugh too. After the laughing was over I was told to report immediately to the Security Section at the University of Nationalities. I was ordered not to deviate on my way there otherwise I would be arrested and sent to the Gulag. The Security Officer laughed after saying this so I think he was trying to make a joke. I did not laugh.

★

The University of Nationalities was housed in a campus built in 1933 in the classic Soviet style; often referred to as Socialist Classicism Architecture. Despite the buildings having been renovated in the 1960s and the 1980s many of my fellow students described them as '*retro*' to sound western and cool. I called it something else for which I was reported to my course leader. This got me loss of privileges for a day. Privileges? What privileges? What a joke! there were no privileges. Then I got to thinking; "Only a day's loss of privileges?" Back in school number eight it would have been at least six months loss of privileges for such a derogatory remark about a revered Soviet building and institution.

It was not so bad losing privileges as the building's amenities were far less than I was used to back home in Budyonovsk. But never mind, here I was in Moscow, the centre of the Soviet Empire. I briefly wondered what my old school friends were doing right then and where they were but the thought did not stay in my head for very long.

When I checked in with the Security Section that first day I was handed a list of rules. I wondered why I had been given them as I have lived by the rules every day of my life. Out of a sense of curiosity I read the list expecting to tear it up and throw it away as soon as I was out of sight of the security guard. On reading the list, however, I concluded that things at the centre were a lot more relaxed than in the provinces.

★

The next day at the 0700 Assembly, which started at 0800, with students sauntering in up until 0830, there were no morning readings from the approved writings, no reaffirmations of oaths and pledges, no denunciations, no filing past under the watchful eyes of the KGB '*guard of honour*' before starting the day's study. All forms of religious activity and symbolism were banned throughout the USSR but here were students openly crossing themselves, counting with prayer beads and muttering prayers and devotions before beginning their day. Wanting to fit in, and curious to see what it was all about, I imitated my fellow students. I was okay with the bowed head part and the crossing myself part but my devotional mumblings and bead handling, the first day I used a set of keys, needed working on. Afterwards though I felt calm and warm inside which surprised and comforted me.

At lunch on the fourth day I sat at a table with students I knew to be '*Religniks*'. I joined in with their prayers before eating. A student from my class whispered to me from out of the side of her mouth.

"Comrade, you need to learn the words to our holy prayers. Everybody knows you just mumble nonsense. Some think it is funny but some think you are a KGB spy put amongst us to report back to your handler on our religious activities."

"What do you think?"

"I think you need to decide what you are and then tell everybody otherwise… well, you know, something might happen to you."

"Will I get loss of privileges?" I asked. She laughed. Then I laughed.

"My name is Svetlana."

"I know… I mean… I am not spying on you… my name is Vladimir Vakhnenko…" I said all in a rush of panic.

"It is okay. Stop talking." She laughed again. Her laugh caught the attention of the others at our table and it seemed to reassure them. I felt I had overcome a hurdle of acceptance and the danger of me being attacked evaporated. My luck was holding.

⋆

Svetlana was a classic Urals beauty but it turned out she was from Petrozavodsk, the administration centre and capital of Karelia. Her family, along with most of their neighbours in Perm, had been ordered to move to Petrozavodsk two generations earlier as part of a Stalin-style resettlement programme. There was a large indigenous Finnish population in Karelia at the time so hundreds of thousands of Russians were sent there to Russify the population. At the same time tens of thousands of Karelians of Finnish extraction were resettled east. Which meant Siberia. Few survived their first winter due to there being insufficient shelter, food or fuel. It takes something for such hardy people to die in their thousands as they did.

Similar scenes had been played out in the conquered nations. In Budyonovsk, for example, forty percent of the population who survived the Terror were sent to live in various remote parts of Russia while twice that number of ethnic Russians were sent to live in Budyonovsk. Like the Irlandtsy immigrants a hundred years previous, the Russian immigrants settled into the particular, some say peculiar, ways of that city. Over time they came to be regarded by party Head Commissars as being as politically suspect as the indigenous Budyonovites. Being politically suspect is one of the reasons why there are few Budyonovites who are card carrying communist party members.

★

After lunch I walked with Svetlana toward the exit of the canteen. She turned and asked me if I would like some fruit and pointed to a table which was laden with all kinds of fruit. I assumed they were all fruits as I did not recognise most of them. I asked her if they were all fruits. She laughed. I adored her laugh. She asked me where I was from and when I told her she looked shocked.

"Budyonovsk? Really? I have heard so many terrible things about that place... and its people."

"Like what? Budyonovsk is a great place."

"I have heard it is where they send people when they want to… it is the last place before the Atlantic… and America. They say Americans put things in the ocean which end up at Budyonovsk and that is why the people there are so… crazy." She did not mean crazy but she was scared to say what she really meant as we were recent acquaintances.

"I have never heard anything like that before." I replied defending the honour of my city.

"I have read that nobody there is politically reliable or has a party card." She looked down at her feet in shame for me.

"That is nonsense. My mother is a card carrying party member." Svetlana looked startled and uncertain. "What is wrong? All I said was…"

"I know what you said but I have read all about Budyonovsk and it says in all the books that everybody in Budyonovsk is politically unreliable and nobody there has a party card."

"Well, my mother does."

"Do you have a card?"

"No, but that is normal, I am a student."

"So am I but I have one." Svetlana fished inside her purse and pulled out her party card. It was green with a yellow border. I had never seen a party card with a yellow border before. The surrounding students stared at her. "What is wrong? Don't any of you have a party card?" Nobody replied, they just turned their backs and walked away.

"I am sorry. I should not have…"

"I am so surprised. I am shocked actually. Everybody I know has a party card."

"Not me. And going by their reactions, not any of them either." Though most did have a party card but wanted to appear cool in front of their new friends by pretending not to be part of the establishment. A short, slightly tubby man approached us.

"I too have a party card. Let me introduce myself, my name is Grigori Andreivich Rabinovich. How do you do? My father is the chief Head Commissar at Narodni Vagon."

"I am Svetlana and this is Vlad."

"Vladimir, my name is Vladimir, not Vlad." I held out my hand for Grigori to take and shake but the offer was ignored.

"I call him Vlad." This was news to me. "We are taking the same languages classes. I am hoping to earn a place on the special multi-lingual course so I can learn all the foreign languages." One did not speak about what it took to earn such a place as '*rewards*' of that kind were usually sponsored by the KGB and their like.

"I am a day or two late for the start of the term, there were a few family matters I had to attend to. Did I miss much?" said Grigori. Without waiting for a reply he pointed a manicured finger at the fruit table. "Oh look, Mangos. Lovely. Do you know what a Mango is Vladimir?" I took an instant dislike to Comrade Rabinovich.

That conversation set the tone for my relationship with Svetlana, who I adored, and Grigori, who I did not care for but I did not hate. Things got tense between us after I was awarded a place on the special multi-lingual course despite not having sold my soul to the state-clandestine-security-services-Devil. I was advanced through my abilities. Svetlana came round pretty quickly and apologised for her behaviour toward me but it suited Grigori's purposes to bear a grudge.

★

After the end of year exams I wanted to go home for the summer break but there were no free student places available on the trains and I could not afford to pay for a trip all the way back to Velikobritania. Svetlana offered to make me a loan but I refused. Besides, it was a round trip of about a month and I was not prepared to do that. Grigori offered to buy the train ticket for me but I refused for obvious reasons. He just wanted me out of the way. I stayed in my student accommodation all summer and got some '*black-work*' with a builder who paid me in Vodka and some cash. I sold the Vodka despite knowing that I could be sent to the Gulag for doing so. I wondered why Grigori did not report me to the authorities. I supposed he did not want to give Svetlana any reason not to like him.

During the summer break I occasionally met up with Svetlana and Grigori for study sessions and river swims on hot days. During one river swim day, as we lay on the riverbank after a race, I learned that Svetlana and Grigori had been to university together in Leningrad before being accepted at the University of Nationalities. It was then that I realised they had known one another long before that day in the cafeteria and that they were at least two years older than me. At the time I could not imagine why they kept something like that from me.

The Irregular Society

At the beginning of my second year at the University of Nationalities I was determined to get to the bottom of why Svetlana and Grigori had pretended not to know one another and how they were allowed to take a second degree. That was against the rules. I resolved to stay close to them both, particularly Svetlana, who I had developed a thing for. Even if she did not ever reciprocate, I thought she could definitely do better than Grigori.

University life in Moscow was wonderful and much more relaxed, Bohemian even, when compared with my former life in Budyonovsk, which I began to hate.

What a drag that place seemed to me now. '*What a drag*' was one of the new phrases I picked up from my fellow students. When I asked where the phrases came from I was met with blank looks. One student actually accused me of trying to get him to admit to subversive, anti-Soviet, counter-revolutionary, activities. '*What a dork!*' That was another of my new phrases. '*Subversive, anti-Soviet, counter-revolutionary, activities*'? The language of the party and state is so stylised. That was another of my new phrases; '*so stylised*'. I was looking forward to trying them out in Budyonovsk to see how they went down there. One day, Svetlana asked me where I thought the new American phrases came from and when I replied that I did not know she punched me in the chest. It actually hurt a lot. That girl could punch!

*

During the language students statutory site tour of the Kremlin, Svetlana grabbed my arm and pulled me away from the group. We walked out of the Kremlin and across Red Square where we found Grigori waiting for us. I was not pleased to see him, I had hoped Svetlana had finally given in to my charms and wanted me all to herself. This was one of my many joke-wishes. As we approached Grigori he flicked his head toward Nikolskaya Ulitsa and walked on ahead of us toward Lubyanka Ploshad. I wanted to hold Svetlana's hand while we walked behind Grigori but it refused to reach out to hers. Entering Lubyanka Ploshad Grigori slowed his pace for us to catch him up. It was then that I saw the dreaded Lubyanka, the one and only original Lubyanka. I had heard so many terrifying stories about that place, we even learned about it in our history lessons at school number eight. I found myself staring at it, mesmerised. I wanted to take my eyes from it but I could not help myself, I had to look. Svetlana dragged me back to reality with a yank on my coat sleeve. Grigori flicked his head again and we started walking toward the building itself. "*Where the hell does he think he is going?*" I asked myself.

We entered the Lubyanka in single file through a glass and stainless steel security door. Once in the '*air lock*' we passed through a metal detector tunnel, after which we were frisk-searched. We then passed through a massive double door similar to the outer security door. As we entered the reception area I felt a cold shiver go through to the marrow of my bones. The inside of the Lubyanka was just as I believed I imagined it to be; all polished marble, glass and stainless steel with lots of armed guards. '*What were they doing there?*' '*What were they guarding against?*' '*Only a fool would come inside this building.*' These thoughts ceased when I caught my reflection in a glass panel.

Grigori went up to the security desk and asked the guard to call his uncle's office as he was expected. The guard punched a series of numbers on the pad of a '*state-of-the-art*' [another of my new phrases] white plastic telephone. He looked uncomfortable, distrustful of the device. Until recently he probably used a wire and plug phone system.

★

According to translation work I carried out on '*Technical Documents*' at the University these phones used some sort of new technology. With it, according to what I read, hundreds of phone lines could be automatically handled through a single switchboard. Rumours going round had it that in America everybody had a telephone in their home and their telephone systems could handle thousands of calls through a single switchboard. The rumours did not stop there. It was rumoured that nearly all American homes had colour Malenkytels with 32 inch screens, some homes had more than one! so the rumours had it.

★

The guard informed Grigori that his uncle was still in a meeting and told us to take a seat at the far end of the reception area. Our steps were amplified by the acoustics in the marble, glass and stainless steel reception area. The racket caused all the guards' heads to swivel in unison at us. '*Why are they wearing sunglasses indoors*?' My head was in a spin. For some reason, Grigori told us that nowadays the Lubyanka was simply the KGB's administrative centre and prisoners were no longer held there. I was not convinced by this, it was a very big building.

After twenty minutes waiting, Colonel Vasily Zaytsev of the KGB's Special Security Section came rushing out of a lift and ushered us back through the doors of the Lubyanka. I was glad to be outside in the fresh air. Grigori's uncle, Dyadya Vasya, had the appearance of a typical KGB agent or a party official; smart suit, shiny shoes, white shirt, dark tie, manicured nails, regulation haircut. His complexion was pallid and his forehead sweaty. He had that medical condition which made his eyes bulge; they were shiny and wet looking like a fish on a slab. His pockmarked jowls had the consistency of week old porridge. Grigori told us later that his Dyadya Vasya had not always looked that way. His wife blamed the pressure of his job but the drugs, long days, late nights and alcohol played their parts too. The Soviet Union, particularly Russia, was a hard drinking hard playing place and Moscow more so for career climbers like Colonel Vasily Zaytsev of the KGB. We went to a restaurant right next door to the Lubyanka. Grigori looked disappointed.

"I am sorry Grigori, I cannot stay long. I have to…" Colonel Zaytsev looked at me and stopped himself from what it was he was about to say, "How are you Grigori? You look well, you too Svetlana, it has been too long since we last…"

"I am very well Dyadya Vasya… you look very well too." There followed an uncomfortable silence.

"We both know that is a great big lie," laughed the KGB Colonel. "I am… I am getting better. I think I am more healthy. You should have seen me last year! Tyetyenka Olga thought she would have to bury me." He laughed again and we tried to join in. "Well, nephew, introduce me to your friend."

"I did introduce him to you Dyadya, in the…"

"Ah yes, I apologise, I am very distracted at the moment, I have a lot on my mind. There is a… well, you know, I am not allowed to say. Let me see if I can recall your friend's name; Vladimir? Yes?"

"Well done Dyadya."

"My memory is still excellent!"

Colonel Zaytsev grabbed a menu and we did likewise. I had never seen anything like it. There were pages and pages of meals, most of which I had never heard of before. A bottle of Vodka arrived at the table housed in a stainless steel cube. Grigori poured us all a shot of the water of life and made a toast to his uncle. We emptied our glasses in one and then it was Svetlana's turn to fill them and make a toast. Toasting in this manner is a tradition from old Russia which all parts of the Soviet Union adopted with zeal. After downing two large shots of Vodka my toast rambled on for far too long, only ending when Svetlana put a finger across my lips and laughed. I laughed too. Grigori did not look happy. I learned later that he had not wanted me to come along but Svetlana had insisted and when she insisted Grigori obeyed. He wanted her to himself but she was playing a game with him and would only be his when she thought he had suffered enough.

"I suppose it cannot hurt to tell you…" said Dyadya Vasya out of the blue, '*did I want to hear this?*' "I have great news." Often when somebody says that it means they have been demoted or posted to some far off place… usually a war zone. "I am being promoted…" '*Here it comes*,' I thought, "to Head Commissar of the Western Frontier Gulags." '*Christ, it was a promotion!*' Even I understood the importance of such a role. He would be responsible for the Gulag in the whole of the region west of Warsaw; laying roads, digging tunnels and canals, smashing boulders into rubble, coal mining and all the types of jobs which limit life expectancy.

"Congratulations Dyadya Vasya, well done, you deserve it." Grigori drained his glass and we did likewise, "Where will you be posted?"

"That is the bad part… Velikobritania."

"Bolshoi Britanski!" I loudly blurted out in my semi-drunken state while clapping my hands wildly. Thank goodness they all laughed. They were laughing at me not with me but I did not mind.

"Now, let us order our food. I must get back to the office soon to carry on with the handover of my duties to my replacements. Four of them! Four of them! It will take four to do my job after I am gone! One of them is a bumpkin from Bishkek, he is an idiot!"

I cannot speak for China or America but this is how things are in the Soviet Union. Job dilution through loading, splitting, sharing keeps employment high. So much so that there were now more than four workers where there was once one. Before I left for Moscow my mum shared her job with six or seven others, none of which knew anything about accountancy. She said that they were really KGB and were reporting on her as well as each other. So, four people were going to do Dyadya Vasya's job in future. With his job being in the Special Security Section of the KGB that would mean four times the misery for the people at the receiving end of the KGB's attention.

★

At the beginning of the third week of my second year at university, Svetlana '*suggested*' I join the Translation Society which offered government departments free translation services.

Afterwards Svetlana told me to call her Lana and Grigori asked me to call him Greg. She sometimes went by the name of Vesna... 'a *beautiful name for a beautiful...*' I had to stop thinking about her like that. I found out that Svetlana was a twin, though looking at photographs of her sister they were not in the least alike apart from their silken blonde hair. Svetlana said that families desperate to have well-bred children paid maternity nurses to swap their babies for those of parents with high IQs. She said that even if there was a test that could show Mara was not her twin it would not matter because they loved one another as sisters.

As I was leaving a meeting of the very boring Translation Society, Grigori asked me to follow him. He walked on ahead of me to a wing of the University used by the sporty types to do weight training. Greg said that if I used the facilities there once in a while I might not look so scrawny. I told him I was lean but strong enough to do whatever I needed to do. He shook his head. Taking a key from behind a locker Greg opened a door which had the words Pest Control sign written on the wire reinforced window beneath a symbol of a skull. We passed through the room and entered a cupboard at its far end which led to another room. Inside the other room were about twenty people, including Svetlana and four professors. They were sitting in rows facing a blackboard. There was a machine on a desk in front of a young female.

"Are you sure about him?" asked a professor.

"Yes. He is okay, even if he is from Budyonovsk."

"Budyonovsk? That is good enough credentials for me. Welcome friend. There are no comrades here, just friends. I understand you met…"

"No, not yet," interjected Svetlana.

"How so? If he is here then he is here as one of us."

"There are some changes I need to tell you about. After that we can decide who to tell. These are dangerous times."

"Take a seat friend," said the professor. I sat in between Svetlana and Grigori. "Welcome everybody to this meeting of our Irregular Society." And with those words the lines of my destiny crossed with those of many others in what would become dangerous times.

The meeting of the Irregular Society was as boring as the meeting I had just come from until I learned where everybody got their new American phrases from. The machine sitting on the desk was something called an electronic brain by one of the professors and a computer by the pretty young operator. It looked like a Malenkytel that had been forced to breed with a typewriter. I was told by the operator that there were many others like it, especially in the hands of the military and the KGB. After she switched on the computer a little green line flashed for about a minute in the top left hand corner of the screen before travelling down and leaving behind writing saying, "HELLO MOSCOW" in American. The operator put a plastic disc into a slot in the front of the computer; she called it a disc even though it was square, then the machine hummed and the Malenkytel lit up. She said the Malenkytel was called a screen.

A list appeared on the screen, lines of which could be selected by pressing buttons with directional arrows on them. The operator said they were called arrow keys, which made sense. Pressing the return key selected the highlighted line. She chose '*American Dictionary*' and then '*Popular Phrases*'. It all made sense where the new American phrases came from.

"Look, Vladimir, see… you can type words… or even write letters to your family back home… or a book… and then save them in an electronic file."

"How?"

"It all goes onto the disc… unless it is full, then…"

"Full?"

"Yes, the disc can get full but you can check to see how much space you have left on it," Irina pointed at some numbers on the screen, "if it is full then you just put in another disc. I am not explaining it very well but if you want to know more ask Svetlana, she is the expert."

The computer was incredible. It seemed to know everything. The operator said it just needed the right commands and it could do all sorts of things. She told me that the discs came from the Network but that was all she knew, how they arrived or who or what the Network was she did not know. It seemed to me she was letting me know how little she knew in case I was a spy.

Who would have thought that the twenty first century would turn out something so wondrous as an electronic brain?

The evening at the Irregular Society flew by and it was well after midnight before it was over. As I walked along the corridor toward my room I came across Grigori and Svetlana kissing. It was no ordinary kiss. It was an extremely passionate kiss of the type that leads to more than kissing. I tried to creep past them but Lana spotted me even though she had her eyes closed when I first spotted them. She asked me if I was okay to which I replied, "*Why would I not be okay?*" I had a gut-wrenching ache in my stomach seeing them like that and I wanted to cry or scream but I knew it must have been like that between them. Grigori did not care how I felt he just wanted to carry on kissing Lana followed by some *more and more amour*. I smiled at my Frussian. I should not have been upset at seeing them like that, they had been dating for a long time and it was obvious that they were from the same level and I was just a shit-kicker from Budyonovsk. I started to feel sorry for myself before my mother's voice entered my head telling me not to be so childish. I think she would really have used the word foolish not childish.

★

When I woke the following morning I felt much better in myself about Grigori and Svetlana. During breakfast I think Svetlana sensed this, she smiled at me and stroked my arm. At the 0700 assembly, which started at 0800 as usual, we were informed that fifteen hundred students were required to volunteer as Counsellors for the upcoming winter Pioneer Camps. I was barely older than the senior Pioneers but nevertheless Svetlana put my name down on the volunteer's list, saying it would look good on my university record, adding that I needed to join at least another four societies. I asked her about the electronic brain. She snorted and corrected me, "*Computer!*" and then promised she would tell me all what she knew about it if I signed up to four more societies.

"Last night at the meeting, Greg told me to be careful what I said when I am in my room."

"What? I would have thought you would have known that already."

"Known what?"

"Everywhere is bugged! They listen in on everything everybody says. They record it too."

"What, everything everybody says? That is impossible."

"We need to talk but not here. Let us take a walk together after lunch. You really are a… Vlad, you need to think hard about everything you have said in the so-called privacy of your room. You really are a… words fail me." She shook her head and glared at me in such a way that I felt ashamed, alarmed and foolish all at the same time.

At first I worried about what Svetlana had said but put it down to her spinning one of her stories to make the Budyonovsk bumpkin feel stupid.

⋆

On the way to my rendezvous with Svetlana I saw her crossing the road ahead of me. She was carrying lots of bags, most of which she passed to a man in a grey uniform who put them on the back seat of a black Merkov. Up to that point I had never really thought much about it but Svetlana always dressed well and she always seemed to have everything she needed; nice clothes, two good winter coats, four pairs of good winter boots, jewellery, shampoo, leather bags, nice shoes, though Moscow girls always seemed to have nice shoes, and her hair always looked nice… and perfume, she always smelled nice. I loved the smell of her perfume especially when it rose from the warmness of her neck. I was definitely in love with her and I wanted her to be in love with me but Greg was in the way. I shouted "*Svetlana!*" She looked at her watch and shouted back that I was early. She beckoned me to join her in the park and handed me four shopping bags to carry on our promenade. I asked her what was inside them. Instead of answering she dragged me down onto the grass, kissed me hard on the lips and told me to mind my own business. I went to peek inside one of them but just a look from her stopped me from doing so. She laughed and said, "*Go on, have a look if you are so curious.*" When I looked inside the bags I was dumbfounded.

"Where did you get these?" I asked holding up a pair of jeans. She dragged them off me, stuffed them back into the bag and told me that I could look but not touch. I immediately recognised the metaphor in her words.

"I got them from a shop on the Romanov Gallery."

"You must have had so many coupons… and had to queue for ages and have…"

"Coupons? Queue?" She laughed. "Darling Vlad, I do not queue for anything… or save coupons. I bought the jeans and all the other things with money."

"Of course, but you still need…"

"No, I do not. It is time for our talk. I have grown fond of you Vlad and I do not want you disappearing into one of the KGB's holiday camps because you do not understand what not to say, where not to say it or who not to say it to." She proceeded to talk, or rather lecture me, nonstop for almost two hours. The longer she talked the more wide eyed I became.

Our talk started with a history lesson. I thought I knew everything about the history of the Soviet Union but all I knew was the Soviet version. She said "*the victors write the history books*" and I understood what she meant after hearing her version of our history.

She said the Bolshevik revolution was recorded as a popular uprising but it was driven by the ambitions of the have-nots who wanted to be the haves. They did not have power, they wanted it, so they took it. "*Ironically*," she said, "*to keep the revolution alive, many people had to die in state sponsored Terror, carried out on the orders of Lenin and then Stalin.*" She said although Lenin began Terror, Stalin made an art out of it. It was state sponsored Terror that kept people looking around at one another instead of looking at what the leadership was doing. Party leaders, the Central Committee and others, such as Sovnarkom delegates, all led the high life. The Bolsheviks replaced hereditary Tsardom with their own brand of it. Dachas, great wealth and power to do anything to anybody; everything was wolfed down by those revolving around Stalin's star. She said it was not easy staying alive around Stalin but those who did became the new ruling elite, especially so following his death.

Svetlana told me about Stalin's methods, claiming they were still in use today. "*For example,*" she said, "*before becoming General Secretary, Stalin ran what the Americans call the HR department for the Bolshevik party.*" Cunningly, according to Svetlana, he placed those who were loyal to him into key political positions. He set up the first mass surveillance programme, eventually building it up to fifteen thousand telephone operators whose job it was to listen in on party and CC members' conversations, making a record of anything anti-Stalin, anti-State or anti-Soviet they said... plus anything else of interest, which usually meant sexual deviancy. "*Stalin expanded his surveillance programme throughout the Soviet Union and it is still in use today.*" Svetlana was convinced, and she convinced me too, that every government department, university, school, party office, shop, railway station, hotel room, trades-unions building, etcetera, was bugged. She said Stalin increased his control over the state by creating shadow organisations, which he used to replace real organisations overnight. If they were politically reliable, the workers of the original organisations were recruited into Stalin's agencies but all managers were shot. Svetlana believed the programmes were still running today but with much bigger numbers.

Then Svetlana told me about what was currently happening. I was shocked to learn of the civil unrest and uprisings in the provinces, republics and some of the conquered nations. I asked her why nothing about this was reported in the news. She said I was listening to the wrong news. She claimed that for the past decade the NKVD had been fighting ferocious battles within the Soviet Union's borders. She said the Soviet Union "*was falling apart, as all Empires eventually do*" and Work sharing and WRP was killing the economy. "*Four people to do a job that can be done by half a person? Having no real work is the main reason why there is so much alcoholism in the Soviet Union!*" She continued, "*On top of everything there are food and other shortages, wages are not being paid on time, particularly so with Red Army Soldiers, then there is the endless brutality.*"

"*Look,*" she said, "*look at our Workers' Days Parades, what use are they?*" I told her that I liked going and watching the Workers' Days Parades, to see them celebrating the work they did for the glory of the Soviet Union. I said I was looking forward to joining in with them when I became affiliated or employed. She asked me why. I replied that it was normal for workers to want to join comrade workers from other parts of one's city or region and march together with them, knowing that your workers' march was being replicated all over the Soviet Union by other workers. I told Svetlana how, every year, I looked forward to watching my mother's Accountancy Workers' Day march on the news programme after I had watched it from the streets. I told her that I saw my mother in the background on four occasions on the news; "*one time she was actually interviewed!*"

"Okay, I do not think you understood the question. What use are they? What purpose do they serve?"

"I do not understand the question."

"They do not have a use but they have a purpose. Their purpose is to occupy the time of workers when they are not at work. If you are not marching, you are watching other workers march. Plus, it takes a lot of organisation and planning and getting permissions and making new banners and so on and so forth; it is all designed to occupy the time of workers so they do not have time to think about anything else. Ask yourself, if we did not have workers' days what would everybody do on Sundays? Why are they held on the only day of the week that is free from work? There is no need for you to attempt an answer. The answer is to keep the people occupied. It is a form of oppression."

"Perhaps, but they are fun." I wanted to reach out and hold Svetlana's hand but resisted the temptation.

"What do people want?" Svetlana asked me after a brief contemplation of the clouds.

"They want… they want…" I had lots of answers in my head but I instinctively knew they were not the right ones for Svetlana, "okay, what do they want?"

"They want more. That is what people want and they are not getting it."

"More what?"

"Just more. More of everything. They want what the leaders get; what the elite get; what card carriers get; what Americans get every day."

"That sounds like the type of talk that gets people denounced."

"Are you going to denounce me Vladimir Vakhnenko?" I shook my head in shame. "Say what you really mean Vlad; this is the type of talk that gets people put in front of a firing squad. Look Vlad, I know you are scared by all this but believe me there is more to life than you are getting and to get it you have to fight for it."

"But I am happy with what I have. Why would I… what would I…"

"Happy? Look inside those bags. That is happiness Vlad." Svetlana smiled, "We must get back to the university soon otherwise we will miss the curfew. Before we go though I want to tell you about the future and what we can expect unless we do something about it."

Svetlana's vision-story of the future terrified me. It was a future full of Bolshevik Terror enacted again and again against ordinary citizens right across the Soviet Union. She said the party was planning to bring mass Terror to the Proles because it was losing control. But, she said, that was all to the good because it would motivate them to rise up in revolution against the state.

"We are the vanguard, the new revolutionaries. Universities are hotbeds for revolution and that is why we are allowed so much freedom. They want students to relax, talk freely, so they can observe us, record us, monitor us, study us, categorise us, bend us to their purposes. But we are wise to their game. We play their game but we do our best work in the shadows. Let them think they have got us where they want us. Let them think they know us. Let them think we are just a bunch of intellectuals holding silly secret meetings to study American words." Svetlana looked at her watch. "We must be going otherwise you will get into trouble."

On our way back to the university I asked Svetlana if Grigori was of the same mind as her. She said he was the leader of their revolutionary cell and that was the reason why she loved him. '*She loved him.*' When she said the actual words they cut through me. I did not hear anything else for the next few minutes. I asked her if she had any other reasons for loving him; I was in a self-destructive mood. She replied that he had everything to lose and he was prepared to lose it and she loved him for that. I could not hold my tongue, I had to let her know how I felt about her, I told her I loved her. "*Of course you do,*" she replied, "*everybody loves me.*" She laughed. It was not an unkind or taunting laugh, it was a laugh to break an awkward situation. In that moment I found her wonderful laugh not so wonderful, I found it irritating. I asked her why she had told me what she had told me and if she was afraid I might go to the authorities and report her. Her reply froze the blood in my veins.

"You have been chosen to join us because of your language and computer skills. At the moment you are only on the bottom rung of the ladder. You do not know anything other than there is a society of intellectuals who meet to discuss American words and phrases. Such meetings are banned. If our meetings are raided then we would know you for a traitor and you would have to be killed." The coldness in her voice convinced me she meant what she said.

"Who would do it?" I hoped she was not going to say Grigori.

"Me because I introduced you to the society. We have to clean up our own messes, it is the rules." She was so matter of fact about the act of killing me that I was turned on. I asked her if she would kiss me one more time.

"One more time? Why? Are you going somewhere? Look Vlad, I like you and if you like me and would like to have sex with me then just say. It is like that with us revolutionaries. Well?" I thought for a few moments and decided I did not want it to be like that with her.

"No thank you Lana."

"Are you… you know… a boy-lover?"

"No!" I sputter-choke-laughed.

"It is okay if you are… we do not condemn people for… but as you say you are not I will introduce you to a couple of girls from the Irregular Society who said they think you are attractive."

"Attractive? Is that all? Just attractive?" I joked trying to sound confident. She kissed me hard again and said she would tell the Irregular Society girls what a great kisser I was. As an afterthought she hit me hard in the stomach. That girl could punch.

Narodnaya Volya – The People's Will

In the months leading up to the winter Pioneer Camps, student, Military veteran, party member and Trades Union member disappearances increased dramatically. In response, Narodnaya Volya increased its anti-state activities. The state hit back with mass arrests under the Soviet Union's extensive anti-anarchy laws, to which Narodnaya Volya retaliated by carrying out some '*disappearances*' of their own. Some of the disappeared turned up when one side or the other wanted to demonstrate how terrible it was to be taken. It was a vicious circle. Hundreds of thousands were disappeared from both sides in just a few months.

★

An old custom from Stalin's time was to outperform one's predecessor to demonstrate that they had not been doing their job properly. To counter this, those leaving their jobs, if they were lucky enough to do so while still living, would ensure that they were replaced by more than one person or by a department if they could get away with it. Colonel Vasily Zaytsev of Moscow KGB's Special Security Section understood this and so ensured that four people replaced him when he left to take up his position of Head Commissar of the Western Frontier Gulags.

Extract from Colonel Vasily Zaytsev's leaving speech taken from the official surveillance recordings of his last day in his Lubyanka office:

> "I have long said that what is needed in this section was at least four extra staff to root out traitors, wreckers, saboteurs and other anti-Soviet elements. We all know that they are everywhere. The number of traitors on the execution lists bears testimony to the size of the problem. I am hopeful that the four Officers selected to replace me will be successful in their careers as I have left them a solid foundation from which they can go forward. We can only hope that they work as hard and as diligently as I did by bringing four times as many traitors, wreckers and saboteurs to justice."

"That will put pressure on them!" Muttered the KGB Colonel loud enough for Luka Bazanov, Commissar of the KGB, and his cronies to hear him. "If they do a bad job I am sure I can accommodate them in the Western Gulag." This snide remark brought raucous laughter and clapping loud enough to send the needles of the recording level indicators off the scale. Colonel Zaytsev's speech continued for another forty minutes. In it he made sure to thank all those who should be thanked; his superiors, Luka Bazanov and the Central Committee, and put down those he'd always wanted to stick it to; his subordinates, those who had stolen his thunder and those who had not made him look good. They would have to be very lucky if they were to survive.

It was due to Grigori's Dyadya Vasya's replacements that so many students, veterans, party and Trades Union members were disappeared. The four wanted to outperform their predecessor and so divvied up former Colonel Zaytsev's duties to bring in at least four times as many wreckers, saboteurs and anti-Soviet elements than he had. The University of Nationalities was now under the eye of a former KGB Captain from Bishkek. The one who Dyadya Vasya had referred to as a bumpkin.

★

Greg and Lana were still friendly toward me but I had the feeling they were distancing themselves from me. We still went to Irregular Society meetings together but… but there was something going on that they did not want me knowing about. I could feel it.

During a typically dreary Translation Society meeting I felt a hand touch mine before it pushed a piece of paper into my open palm. I went to look at it but the paper-pusher tugged at my wrist to stop me. I turned around and saw a student from the second stream called Sergei staring at me. He shook his head almost imperceptibly, it was enough to let me know I should look at the piece of paper in private. When I turned to face front again a number of students had turned to look at me before facing forward again. I could hardly wait to look at the piece of paper so I left the meeting and headed to the toilet. Inside the first cubicle I unfolded the piece of paper. It read:

> Take good care friend. Be careful, they are watching you. Do nothing to attract attention to yourself otherwise you will be next. Do not do anything or go anywhere which might call your political reliability or loyalty to the state into question. Do not mention this note to anybody. Destroy it right now by eating it.
>
> Power to the People.
>
> Narodnaya Volya

I ate the note immediately, flushed the toilet and returned to the auditorium. It was empty, it appeared that the meeting of the Translation Society had finished early. '*But it still had thirty minutes to go.*' I thought. As usual there was a meeting of the Irregular Society immediately afterwards so I made my way to go there. "*Should I go?*" I asked myself recalling the warning note. I did not want to do anything which could put my loyalty to the state in question so I slumped off back to my room. Lying on my bed, I weighed up the risks of going to the Irregular Society meeting. I concluded that my safety and the safety of others around me was more important than my hoping to eventually have sex with Irina or Marina. '*I was getting on so well with them too*!' At least I thought I was. I put all thoughts of Irina, Marina and the Irregular Society out of my head. I could never go to their meetings again.

It was still early but I was not in the mood to do any studying so I just continued lying on my regulation size single bed and began a mammoth self-pity session. As I lay there I heard people passing my door. Some were chatting. Some were laughing. Some were silent. There is a feeling that some people get when something is not right. It is as though their internal instincts, a sixth sense, picks up on something but they are not conscious of exactly what it is, they just sense that something is not right. All noise in the corridor had stopped. I was not conscious of that fact, I sensed it. I had the feeling people get when somebody is watching them or is in close proximity; for example, when somebody is standing on the other side of a door. The microsecond that thought passed through my head the door to my room burst open and four men wearing Camo-balaclavas and toting matt black machine pistols stormed in.

A fifth, eyeless, Camo-balaclava was forced over my head. I was dragged to my feet and frog marched down the hall. I sensed no doors opening along the dormitory corridor. My fellow students knew better than to be witnesses to something like this.

★

Hauled along corridors by my thumbs and with my head forcibly held down I kept smashing into walls. After each collision I was struck with batons. Every so often my abductors spun me around, disorientating me completely. We must have marched for ten minutes, or so it seemed to me, up and down stairwells and along winding vinyl floored corridors typical of state institutions; doors opening ahead and slamming shut behind. I believed we were still inside the university building as I had not breathed any fresh air or heard outside noises. Suddenly we came to a halt. I was force-sat on a metal chair and my eyeless Camo-balaclava was ripped from my head. The room was in near total darkness. It still took a minute for my vision to fully adjust to the gloom. In front of me were, I assumed, my inquisitors. They sat like crows in a row on a bench behind a tubular metal table. Each was leaning on their elbows with their hands clasped together staring intensely at me through hood covered eyes. The female sitting in the middle of the bench, who I took to be the foreman, sat back and studied some papers by candlelight, which I could see included photographs of me and hand written notes. I was asked to state my name.

"My name is Vladimir Vladimirovich Vakhnenko. I am politically reliable." I wanted to ask my inquisitor her name but decided that would be inappropriate.

"Do you know why you are here Citizen Vakhnenko?" '*Citizen Vakhnenko*?' Who were these people? I had no idea what was going on but this was not normal KGB interrogation language.

"No comrade, I do not know why I am here. I..." A door opened to my right, admitting a ray of yellow light and two people, one of them in chains. I could only see their silhouettes and so did not recognise them.

"Do you recognise this person?" asked the Madame Foreman pointing to the shape shuffling towards me. On closer inspection I recognised the person in question.

"Yes comrade, yes I do. His name is Sergei Ivanov, he is a second stream student in the same year as me. He..."

"Is there anything you can tell us about Comrade Ivanov?" Madame Foreman leaned forward, her hooded figure gave the appearance of a crow of ill omen.

"Yes comrade, Comrade Ivanov is an excellent footballer, though he favours his right foot far too much." Sergei grunted his disagreement of my assessment of his footballing limitation.

"Do not play games with me Citizen Vakhnenko, you know what I mean."

"I do not know what you are referring to comrade." I began shaking uncontrollably. Shock was setting in. Even though I was seated my knees turned to jelly. '*Had I been drugged*?'

"Citizen Vakhnenko, if you do not cooperate fully with this tribunal, not only will it not go well for you but it will not go well for your family back in Budyonovsk. I understand your mother is a card carrying party member? A rare thing in Budyonovsk. Can you imagine the shame? The fall from grace? The humiliation? The suffering? Having to shop in the same places as the Proles who despise her? Your little brother will not be so fortunate. I wonder if he can survive in the Gulag? Your little sister will be sent to a state orphanage."

"Comrade, please, my family have always been loyal servants of the party. My mother is the Personal Assistant to the Chief Head Commissar of the Budyonovsk region. My little brother..."

"Personal Assistant to Chief Head Commissar of the Budyonovsk region?" spat an inquisitor mockingly, "Is that what she told you she is? Is that what you think she is? Citizen Vakhnenko, your mother is his whore, cCtizen Vakhnenko, his whore. She performs whatever services she is required to perform whenever Chief Head Commissar Nabatov visits Budyonovsk." I wanted to pull out the tongue of the person who had just called my mother a whore and feed it to her.

"Cowards! Pull back your hoods you cowards! Let me see your faces!" I screamed raising myself from my seat. As I did so a huge pair of hands grabbed my throat from behind and started choking the life out of me.

Try as I might I could not break free of my strangler. I cursed my puny physique and lack of strength. A voice told my strangler to let go of my throat and chain me to the chair. Until then I had not noticed that the metal chair I was sitting on was bolted to the floor. This was my introduction to Lubyanka bracelets. With my wrists and ankles chained to the chair I was beaten by two men who took turns punching me in the stomach, back, legs, arms and chest. I prayed for them to hit my head and render me unconscious but they knew their work too well for that.

I must have eventually lost consciousness because I woke to find my chin resting on my chest. I was dribbling drool and blood from my mouth. I looked up. The two men who had beaten me were standing right in front of me. I could see the Madame Foreman through the gap between them.

"If you do anything so foolish again things will be cut off, do you understand, Citizen Vakhnenko?"

"Yes, I understand. What do you want? I do not know anything."

"Ah yes, denial. The next stage is bargaining. We will not be having any of either from you. Do you understand? Now, what can you tell me about Citizen Ivanov that you know I want to hear?"

"Please comrade, you must have me confused with somebody else. I am just an ordinary, hardworking, student looking forward to graduating and using the skills the state has provided me with to serve it as a loyal…"

"I now understand why you are studying languages, Citizen Vakhnenko, you are quite the word-smith." It was a surprise to hear the Madame Foreman use a rare Americanism. "Prepare him."

At that command the two goons who had beaten me up ripped off my shirt and from behind I heard the squeaking of wheels. Next I heard the noise made by a switch, followed by the hum of an electrical transformer and guessed what was coming next. Since my early school, I had heard horror stories about how the KGB used electricity to torture people. I guessed that was what was about to happen to me, I was not looking forward to the experience.

The person who had wheeled the electrical equipment in

attached electrodes to my body. I did not struggle as I knew it would be worse for me if I did. '*Worse? It cannot get much worse; can it? At least they were not cutting things off.*' Then I thought, '*Yes, it can get worse, much worse.*'

The cables from the electrocution machine were terminated in saw-toothed bulldog clips. They cut into my skin as they were attached to my body. Blood trickled from the site of each attachment. The bulldog-clipper looked toward the Committee Bench and pointed to my nipples. The Madame Foreman nodded. Then he pointed to my groin, "*Not yet. Let him contemplate what it would be like to have a wire inserted into his urethra and a metal torpedo plug in his anus.*" I nearly passed out at the first zap of electricity.

"Citizen Vakhnenko, you are too feeble to withstand prolonged interrogation of this nature. Tell me what I want to know."

"I do not…" I lost control of my bladder at the second, much more powerful, zap from the electrocution machine.

"Citizen Vakhnenko, tell me about the note Citizen Ivanov handed to you. The one you took to the toilet to read. What did it say? You must realise that Citizen Ivanov has already been broken?"

"Please comrade, no more… no more… please. It was a love letter, he is a boy-lover and is in love with me. I destroyed the note to save him punishment."

"What do you have to say now Citizen Ivanov?"

"He is a liar. The note I passed to Citizen Vakhnenko warned him that he is being watched and that he is to be careful. The last line ordered him to eat the note, which he did, proving he is an agent of Narodnaya Volya." I had no idea what Comrade Ivanov was talking about though I had read about Narodnaya Volya in history lessons.

"Do you wish to change your story Citizen Vakhnenko?"

"Comrade Ivanov is ashamed and will say anything to save himself and his place in the university." I turned to Sergei and said, "I forgive you Serge." The lights came on.

"Very good comrade, well done. You stuck to your story," said the Madame Foreman, "It is most vital that you always stick to your story and never change it. Not even by a little bit. Keep it simple and that way you cannot screw it up." I recognised another Americanism. The bulldog clips were removed and the electrocution machine was wheeled away. What was happening? Was it a KGB trick? The Madame Foreman spoke again. "You did well. You turned the tables on Sergei just in case he was being manipulated but did not expose him to too much danger. Very clever. The unnatural sexual deviancy element was excellent. It plays to their prejudices. I will add it to the manual. By the way, we do not persecute sexual deviants nor anybody on the grounds of religion, colour, ethnicity or… or anything. We only persecute and sometimes execute those in the NKVD, KGB and the party." A man standing in the shadows shouted something like '*get a move on.*'

"Okay everybody, back into your places… you… you and you… go with Stan and grab the next one. Citizen Vakhnenko, follow Citizen Ivanov." We were ushered out of a door at the back of the room. The guard handed me a jar of soothing antiseptic salve as I was in great pain.

★

Sergei and I walked along corridors, down stairwells, along some more corridors and through subterranean halls, before finally emerging into a vast underground auditorium. I was astonished at its size. I wondered at how the ceiling had not collapsed into this vast open space.

I estimated that we must have descended at least two hundred feet. I learned later that the auditorium was constructed in the 1950s when the Soviet Union was preparing a pre-emptive nuclear strike against the USA and China. They wanted Soviet life to continue after the inevitable nuclear counter-attack. Why the button was not pressed is not known. Perhaps the party leaders saw the futility in it all.

The auditorium looked like a lecture or concert hall with seating in the form of deep, broad, steps in a massive curve. Around the perimeter were dozens of doors half-glazed with wire woven obscured security glass. Some doors had writing on them. Some were lit while others were dark; others were illuminated by flickering lights which made me think that films were showing behind them.

Distracted by the massiveness of the Auditorium, I did not register the general hubbub, which rose and fell according to the shushing of debaters and group leaders. There must have been five thousand people there. Some were stood around blackboards; pointing, discussing, rubbing out, re-drawing. Others were arguing over documents, getting up and walking around agitatedly before re-joining their cluster. Some were printing pamphlets. In the far corner, people sat at computers, probably to minimise interruptions. It seemed as though they had a fenceless exclusion zone around them. Most of them were just drinking coffee and smoking. Svetlana walked toward me with Grigori in tow. Seeing them there I understood some of what might be going on.

"Am I on the second rung of the ladder now?" I asked Svetlana while ignoring Grigori's wave of greeting.

"No Vlad, we are all on the top rung now. Follow me. We are in Greg's group."

"What about the torture? What was that all about?"

"We use their methods so you will know all about them when your time comes… and come it will comrade." Svetlana looked sad when she spoke those words, I had never seen her look anything other than dazzling and happy but now she looked sad.

"Lana, what would have happened to me had I not passed the torture test?"

"I was confident that you would pass otherwise I would not have put your name forward." I realised Svetlana had not answered my question but I was scared of what the answer might be so I let it go.

"We must give you a code name… a nom de guerre, just like in the old days."

"Why?"

"Because you are a member of Narodnaya Volya now… they are hunting us down, so to confuse and make things difficult for them we all have secret names… just like in the old days." I liked the thought of having a secret name.

"What about Orel?"

"No, sorry Vlad, that name is taken." I expected that such a cool nom de guerre had already been taken but by the way Lana spoke it was as though she did not see me as an Eagle.

"Yastreb?"

"No!" I expected that such a cool nom de guerre had likewise already been taken but the sharpness of Lana's reply was as if she did not see me as a Hawk either.

"What then?"

"Let me think." Svetlana looked to the ceiling for inspiration, "My nom de guerre is Molniya… Mol for short. Greg's is Grom… his nom de guerre is short enough as it is." She was struggling for what to suggest. "We three should have stormy weather names. Yours should be Uragan… Ura for short."

"I like it," I lied. I was fed up with secret name giving, I just wanted to get on with things as I felt this was the kind of place where things were got on with.

In Greg's group I learned why I had been promoted to the top rung of the ladder along with thousands of others that week. According to Narodnaya Volya, the Central Committee was about to unleash mass Terror to combat unrest in the Provinces, Republics and Conquered Nations. They were going to turn back the clock to the time of denunciations, death lists, internment camps, torture houses, ethnic concentration camps, mass-relocations, mass-disappearances, Gulag slave labour camps and so on.

"What can we do to stop all this from happening?" ssked one of the group.

"Revolution, comrade… only revolution can prevent the Terror from happening!" came a shout from the back of the group.

"Our operatives inside the Kremlin have told us that the Five Year Plan for Terror is almost complete," added Greg.

"Why did they not say something sooner?"

"Who is to say they did not?"

★

In the Soviet Union, large scale programmes, such as transforming Russia from a peasant based agrarian economy to an industrial economy, are carried out under Five Year Plans. Each Five Year Plan had targets and were used for everything from increasing grain production to the number of tractors and tractor plants built. Career climbers would aim to exceed their targets in order to get noticed by the Central Committee. Getting noticed in the Soviet Union was invariably a bad thing. Career climbers would bring back more grain to the centre than demanded, even though the centre did not need it; this left the Provinces and Republics at the point of starvation. Career climbers would exceed their quota of executions by adding names to death lists. This was carried out with help from local or regional Soviet administrators, often to satisfy personal vendettas or land-grabs or to own the possessions of the denounced. The '*logic*' behind the numbers for death-list quotas was simple; '*there had to be a certain percentage of wreckers, saboteurs, counter-revolutionaries and anti-Soviet elements inside the workers' paradise of the Soviet Union and they had to be dealt with swiftly and severely.*'

Method: estimate death-list numbers based on the political reliability index of the target areas; then add ten percent to be certain of cutting out the whole lump. Next, send NKVD Soldiers under the command of '*Responsible Workers*', usually overambitious political climbers willing to do anything to advance themselves, to execute those named on the lists. Next; increase the numbers on death lists by adding names to them given up under interrogation, torture, vendetta-satisfaction, the local Soviet administration or otherwise. Next, execute all those whose names appear on the list. Finally, send the completed lists of the deceased to the Central Committee for review, totting up and signature of approval. In lengthy execution lists, Central Committee members would sign alongside the first victim's name and ditto mark against all the other names. It was not uncommon for execution lists to have in excess of two thousand ditto marks on them. Undercover Narodnaya Volya operatives working inside the Kremlin would often replace names on death lists with the names of NVs enemies or even entire Regional Soviet Administrations. Sometimes they just threw whole bundles of death lists into waste paper baskets.

A death-list interrogation conducted in the field by a junior KGB Officer.

"I can see in your eyes that you are a wrecker, confess!"

"No comrade Lieutenant, I am not a wrecker but look at Oleg's eyes. He is obviously guilty."

"I am not guilty, I am loyal to the party and a hard worker."

"I heard Irina's grandfather was a Kulak sympathiser."

"Liar!"

"Names! All of you, I want names!"

"No, comrade Lieutenant, please spare us." They each cried.

"It is obvious to me that you are all in it together and you have simply chosen some of your treacherous cell to sacrifice in order to take attention away from others. Write down your names and those of your family, relatives and anybody else you can name as being guilty." This was an opportunity for the condemned to settle old scores. They were dead anyway, '*so why not?*' they thought. The victims themselves did most of the NKVD's list building dirty work for them. Not only were those executed who had been directly accused but also most, if not all, of their families too. It was the easiest way of exceeding quotas and to get noticed.

In the old Soviet Union in particular it was hard keeping the ground you had gained. Many list-builders names appeared, or were added, on the lists of other list-builders. Trumping up charges in the USSR was always a piece of cake. Most victims immediately pleaded guilty in the hope that some of their family might be spared. Whenever party officials were scooped up in death-list trawls they were usually left in a room with a Mauser and a bottle of Vodka, '*to do the right thing.*' Doing so, they hoped their families stood some chance of survival. Afterwards, the state could say anything it wanted to about the '*sad and tragic loss of [fill in name]. He/she will always be remembered as a good comrade, a loyal servant of our glorious Soviet Union and a leading… blah, blah, blah.*'

★

Just when I thought I had heard everything I glanced over at the group next to ours. They were sitting at a blackboard discussing a map pinned on it. It was a map of the whole of the Soviet Union. Simply possessing such a map was punishable by ten years in the Gulag. Everything, it seemed, was punishable by either ten years in the Gulag or death. Death, for many, was the preferred option as life in the Gulag was terrible, though death comes sooner or later in those places and the state at least gets some free labour out of their victims before they pass from this life. Pinned over one corner of the map was a map of Velikobritania and on the opposite corner was a map of Vladivostok Oblast. There were red dots and crosses dotted all over both these maps.

I hiss-whispered to the nearest person in the other group asking why a map of Bolshoi Britanski was pinned to the blackboard. An annoyed sounding female replied saying Velikobritania and Vladivostok were going to be the first victims of the Terror. Then she said something like, "*That is where they will rehearse.*"

"What do you mean?"

"It has been a long time since the last Terror and nobody wants to make any mistakes. You know what it is like in the Soviet Union, mistakes are punishable by death… or the Gulag. So, they are going to start small, like a practice, then grow big."

"That is not right," said a voice joining in the discussion, "the plan is to start at either end of the Soviet Union and work in toward the middle. Velikobritania is the perfect location in the west and Vladivostok in the east. Besides, they have been making trouble there for a long time."

"I am from Velikobritania," I replied indignantly.

"Then you know what I am talking about. Northern Velikobritania, especially the Shotlandiya region, have particularly bad reputations."

"I am from the north… Budyonovsk."

"Well brother, now you have something to fight for," said an old man shaking me by the hand. Somebody wearing a badge with Group Commander printed on it was listening to our conversation and joined in.

"There are in fact a number of reasons why Velikobritania was chosen as the western launch point for the Terror. The Central Committee could have decided to start on the mainland… Frantsiya for example, so why Velikobritania? It is true that Velikobritania has a certain reputation for being troublesome but that alone is not enough of a reason to start the Terror there. There is a great deal of risk involved in bringing Terror to more than a billion and a half people… it might be two billion… who knows?

"So, what is the case for Velikobritania over Frantsiya? Firstly, Velikobritania is an island, making it difficult for anybody to escape from the Terror. Being an island it is isolated from the rest of the Soviet Union, no prying eyes to spread the word so to speak. Secondly, Velikobritania is situated right next to the Red Army bases in Irlandia, meaning that the Terror can be backed up by millions of Red Army Soldiers if necessary; to subdue a mass uprising for example. Thirdly, many inhabitants of Velikobritania, particularly those from places such as Budyonovsk and Shotlandiya, are regarded as politically unreliable and therefore need to be subdued in the early days of the Terror for obvious reasons. Fourth, Velikobritania is the nearest landfall across the Atlantic from America. US agents use VB as a staging post to drop off and pick up returning agents. It is common knowledge that items dropped into the Atlantic by the American secret services are carried by the ocean currents to VB. Everybody knows that most American contraband comes through VB."

"I did not know that."

"It is a fact. And fifth and finally, the Central Committee has hated Velikobritania and its inhabitants since Stalin's time. Those are the reasons why Velikobritania has been chosen ahead of Frantsiya as the western launching point for the Terror."

"When will the Terror begin?"

"According to NV agents working inside the Kremlin, forty NKVD battalions are preparing to depart for Velikobritania and another forty for Vladivostok. Their information is that the Terror will begin in two to three months' time. So that the Terror does not unsettle the rest of the island, it will start in Shotlandiya and work its way south. Forty battalions will be nowhere near enough once things get going, many more will follow. Undercover NV operatives report that the Red Army will cleanse areas after the NKVD have moved on. Local leaders will be transported to Irlandia for questioning." I stared at the Commander. "They will be tortured and killed."

"I am from Budyonovsk, my family are there. When will the Terror get to Budyonovsk?"

"We do not know exactly but it will be soon after they have cleansed Shotlandiya. The NKVD will do their work quickly and move on before they can be blamed for anything."

"What do you mean by, '*blamed for anything*'?"

"It is the Soviet way; '*never be the last person touching* anything'. If, for example, following the NKVD's actions in Shotlandiya there's an explosion here in Moscow, investigators will link the bombing to Shotlandiyan dissidents. If the NKVD has moved on then the Red Army will be blamed and its Officers executed. Somebody has to die. It is the rules. That is the way things are."

"Can I warn my family?"

"Of course you can warn your family. Warn everybody! As you are from Budyonovsk they will believe you and not think it is a

KGB plot to stir up trouble and then arrest the trouble-makers to meet their quotas. Tell as many people as you like, the more people we reach the more recruits we will get. Tell you what comrade, you should join our group, citizens of Budyonovsk are always welcome, they have a fine tradition of sedition and of converting Soviet minds." The commander laughed.

"If I warn the people back home, will the NV comrades working in the Kremlin be in any danger of exposure?"

"I doubt it. There are tens of thousands of people working in the Kremlin. Even if they suspect anybody of passing information they will not shoot any of them because they are like a family. There would be internal rebellion and the whole house of cards would collapse. Nobody messes with the Bureaucrats!" The commander laughed again. I failed to see what was so funny.

I had mixed feelings about joining the Commander's group, mostly brought about by thoughts of leaving Lana behind. I wanted to be around her just in case anything happened to Greg. '*I could be a shoulder for her to cry on.*' I felt mildly disgusted with myself for having such a thought. Then she laughed at something Greg said. I loved her laugh. My eyes met Greg's and we looked away at the same moment. Putting my family and my country ahead of my lust for Svetlana I agreed to join the Commander's group and received lots of slaps on my back from my new Comrades-in-Arms. I think it was an initiation ceremony.

Suddenly, silence passed like a wave over the noise of the Auditorium. Wherever the wave of silence touched people stood and stared. I climbed up a couple of steps and looked over heads to see what was going on. I felt a shove between my shoulder blades and turning round Svetlana told me that Lev had entered the room.

"Who is Lev?"

"He is our leader of course!" Svetlana shook her head at me and my ignorance. I did not know how I would have known that this

Lev was our leader. "Those people walking behind him are his inner council. Something must be going on. I have never seen them all together like this before."

A chorus of "Lev, Lev, Lev. Long live Lev. Long live Narodnaya Volya. Viva la revolucion," spontaneously sprang up. At least I thought it was spontaneous until I observed that the chorus was led by some of Lev's flunkies.

> "Lev, Lev, Lev. Long live Lev. Long live Narodnaya Volya. Viva la revolucion."
> "Lev, Lev, Lev. Long live Lev. Long live Narodnaya Volya. Viva la revolucion."
> "Lev, Lev, Lev. Long live Lev. Long live Narodnaya Volya. Viva la revolucion."
> "Lev, Lev, Lev. Long live Lev. Long live Narodnaya Volya. Viva la revolucion."
> "Lev, Lev, Lev. Long live Lev. Long live Narodnaya Volya. Viva la revolucion."
> "Lev, Lev, Lev. Long live Lev. Long live Narodnaya Volya…"

Lev raised his arms in acknowledgement of the chanting then called for it to stop. The Commander walked forward with outstretched arms and greeted Lev like an old friend. They hugged, "*Good to see you again Koba.*" Said Lev. Before the Commander could reply, Lev walked on to a microphone in the middle of the stage. He looked like a groom on a bride-less wedding cake. When I got a full view of Lev I was surprised at just how short he was. He was shorter than me by a head but he had a dynamic presence. He held up the open palms of his hands to quiet the noise in the auditorium. Lev's inner council came to stand in front of him, forming a barrier between him and his audience. They faced us like a line of warlords. Before Lev began speaking he took the time to look about the room. He nodded and smiled here and there and those he recognised stood proud, broadened their shoulders, puffed out their chests and raised themselves to their full heights. Some even stood on tip toes.

"Comrades," began Lev, what a voice he had, I had never heard such a voice, "comrades, our time is upon us. We have grown many and mighty over the past ten years…" Lev certainly knew how to give a speech. It was very rousing and went on for over two hours and he would have continued had he not received some whispered communique which caused him to leave the stage in a hurry. One of Lev's inner council walked to the microphone and apologised for Lev's swift departure, assuring us that it was to attend to urgent NV business.

Lev spoke to us about the coming Terror and the need to fight against it. He said he prayed for a bloodless revolution but revolution there had to be. It was inevitable according to him. He told of the many millions of NV followers who were ready to do battle and of his vision for the future of the Soviet Union. He said he would create a workers' paradise fit for all Soviet citizens. Despite everybody having heard those words before they sounded different coming from Lev. They sounded believable. I believed him and I believed in him. As Lev left the auditorium I joined in the thunderous applause for our great leader, I clapped so hard that my hands felt like they were on fire.

"Lev, Lev, Lev. Long live Lev."
"Lev, Lev, Lev. Long live Lev."
"Lev, Lev, Lev. Long live Lev."
"Lev, Lev, Lev. Long live Lev."
"Lev, Lev, Lev. Long live Lev."
"Lev, Lev, Lev. Long live Lev."
Lev, Lev, etcetera, etcetera.

Our chanting was accompanied by the stamping of feet in time with the words. Its volume increased by the wooden floor. We carried on our adulatory chanting in honour of Lev The Great until just about everybody in the audience was hoarse. Before I returned to my room, I was introduced to a woman called Oksana. She told me that she and the Commander were lovers. I do not know why she gave me that information.

*

While lying in my bed, too awake with excitement to sleep, my body really started to ache from the beating and electrocutions I had suffered earlier. I put my bedside lamp on and looked at the time, 0500. I got out of bed, went to the communal facilities and ran a hot bath. While lying there, with the room filled with steam, only then did I fully comprehend the importance of what I had heard in the auditorium. Lev's words swirled around in my head, they were hypnotic.

I woke with a jolt at the sound of Lana's wonderful laugh echoing around the bathroom. It was 0525. I felt terrible after having twenty minutes' sleep, more so than if I had not slept at all. What was Svetlana laughing at? Who knew? But that laugh saved me from drowning or, worse, waking up in a bath of freezing cold water. Then I heard a deep male grunt echoing around the bathroom and realised what was going on. "*Hello, do not mind me, you carry on. I am going now anyway.*" I got out of the bath, quickly dried myself and made my way back along the freezing cold corridor to my room. Just before I reached my door I passed Greg and wondered who Lana was with. I was so tired that I just did not care but I did feel hurt. I do not know why as Svetlana had offered me sex that day in the park but I turned her down. What a fool I felt now, what an idiot I felt now.

Operation Zima

Maxim Kirilenko, General Secretary of the Soviet Union, had ambitions to be Dictator of the Soviet Union. He was tired of governing through the Central Committee, the Politbureau, the Supreme Soviet and Sovnarkom. In the early years following the Great and Glorious Revolution there had been a great many more political bodies but Stalin put pay to them with most of their members ending up in the Gulag or the torture cells below the Lubyanka. Comrade Kirilenko wanted the same thing for the present lot.

★

A top secret meeting of the Central Committee was convened in the Lenin Chamber of the Kremlin on the afternoon following Lev's rally in the auditorium beneath the University of Nationalities. All CC members were in attendance but eager to get on with business as most were about to start their winter break.

★

The Winter Break is divided into three one month blocks. Workers are allocated to one month of the three available. The same applies to the Summer Break. The number and type of Worker in the month groups was calculated to ensure the USSR did not grind to a halt due to there being insufficient Workers to keep the Empire running. If an assigned month did not suit a Worker then it was up to the individual concerned to find somebody to swap with. This required the posting of cards around the workplace, neighbourhood, party office, shopping and community centres etcetera. The main rule was that the swap had to be with someone within the same work-type designation; for example a factory worker from zone A could only swap with another factory worker from zone A, preferably from within the same factory and on the same shift. For most managers this effort was all too much, unless it concerned them, and they invariably turned down swap requests, unless there was something in it for them. Agricultural Workers were responsible for timing their breaks with harvesting, planting and other essential food production work. Central Committee and other 'Responsible Workers' chose which four weeks they took for their breaks. As nobody watches over them they invariably abused this privilege and took as many weeks as they could. In order to ensure Central Committee business was not impacted by breaks, the rule was that votes could be taken so long as there was a quorum. Some CC members only ever put in an appearance for important CC business, such as today's '*top secret*' meeting. As far as CC members were concerned the less time they spent in the Kremlin the better their chances of staying alive.

There are also two one week breaks taken between the Winter and Summer Breaks which are spread over a four week period with the same rules applying to them as to the longer breaks. In all, Soviet citizens had ten weeks' break per annum plus celebration and commemoration days such as Lenin's and Stalin's birth and death days. As there were so many holidays, little wonder then that the USSR was in dire economic straits. American workers were only given two weeks' holiday in summer, two days in winter [over their Christmas period], one for New Year, one for Thanksgiving, one for Independence Day and three other days spread throughout the year. China had only four single day national holidays during the entire year. Nobody was happy with their holiday entitlements.

Children Citizens between the ages of seven and eighteen had to attend Pioneer Camps for the entire three month duration of each

Winter and Summer Break. Parents could travel to the Pioneer Camps to see their children though many chose not to, preferring to enjoy their month long breaks without them. Not having denouncing offspring around for six months of the year meant they could talk freely plus it saved them lots of ration coupons, meaning they could acquire a few little luxuries of life. All citizens were supposed to shop in state shops but citizens such as Svetlana's and Grigori's parents were from the new elite and they shopped where there was no queuing, no shortages and no need for coupons; all transactions were in cash, usually American dollars. The existence of these shops was hotly denied by the state and hotly disputed by NV. Most Prolcs though refused to believe there were such places or in people who had more than they did. They still had faith in the revolution and, a century on, remained committed to it and the party. It is incredible what can be accomplished laundromatting young minds at Pioneer camps.

★

The Central Committee sat facing Maxim Kirilenko's ormolu decorated desk in two rows of plush red velvet covered chairs. The desk itself, which had once belonged to Napoleon III, was fitted with various devices to protect the General Secretary, including a popup bullet proof screen and a brace of Markovs clipped underneath the desk, both ready for use with a round in the chamber. Behind the desk was a quick-drop floor panel that worked like a stage trapdoor to remove First Citizen Kirilenko, in an instant, to the room below the Lenin Chamber. If a pre-emptive strike was necessary each of the plush red velvet chairs was fitted with a shaped explosive charge designed to send multiple poly-spiked projectiles into the undercarriages of the Central Committee.

Senior Central Committee members sat in the first row of seats, they were the ones running Commissariats, including Luka Bazanov, feared Commissar of the KGB. Even First Citizen Kirilenko was scared of Comrade Bazanov. Other CC members, those without portfolio, sat in the second row. These were the CC members Maxim Kirilenko planned to use against the '*big six*', chief among them Luka Bazanov. Nobody other than Maxim Kirilenko and the Kremlin Guard were allowed to be armed inside the Lenin Chamber but everybody suspected Bazanov was armed, as were the '*advisors*' he never went anywhere without, but nobody was prepared to challenge them to a search. Maxim Kirilenko hated Luka Bazanov with a passion, the feeling was mutual.

A trumpeted fanfare announced the arrival of First Citizen Maxim Kirilenko, General Secretary of the Soviet Union, into the Lenin Chamber. He arrived like an Emperor at the head of his Kremlin Guard. As Comrade Kirilenko sat down, the Kremlin Guard dispersed around the Lenin Chamber to keep an eye on the Central Committee and Bazanov's advisors.

Comrade Kirilenko hammered his gavel on the well-dented spot on the corner of the ormolu decorated desk to bring the meeting to order. Without even attempting to disguise the contempt he felt for the CC, General Secretary Kirilenko remarked with great sarcasm how good it was to see so many members present. The '*newbies*' with careers, and possibly their lives, hanging by a thread, shifted uncomfortably on their seats. Most thought, especially so more recently, that they should have backed Kirilenko's schemes but it was too late for that now.

The Recorder for the meeting was, as usual, Comrade Kirilenko's Chef de Cabinet, the impressive Alexander Orlov. He stood and politely requested silence in order for Comrade Kirilenko to address the Central Committee. Comrade Orlov normally read the agenda out aloud before asking if there were any AOBs before starting the meeting but not today.

★

Comrade Kirilenko hated being ambushed by AOBs so he ordered that they must be declared at the beginning of meetings. That would give him time to prepare his answers. If he could not come up with an answer he would announce that time had run out and the AOB would be added to the agenda for the next meeting. If the AOB was on a difficult topic, Comrade Kirilenko would have his Chef de Cabinet convince the AOB raiser to withdraw it. This was achieved by a balance somewhere between bribery and threats, such as being handed a dead-end Committee job, or worse, responsibility for delivering an impossible Five Year Plan. First Citizen Kirilenko yearned to be a Dictator. Dictators did not stand for any AOB nonsense!

★

General Secretary Kirilenko took to his feet, adjusted his standard Soviet issue steel rimmed spectacles, arranged his papers on top of his desk and leaned forward onto his hairy knuckles. This was unusual, he normally sat during CC meetings. His predator posture created a state of apprehension in the audience; everybody in the Soviet Union got apprehensive whenever something different happened because it was usually a harbinger of some doom or other. They were all expecting the worst, even the big six.

Taking a deep breath, Comrade Kirilenko slowly, deliberately, surveyed the faces of the CC. His loathing for them was palpable. He hated having to deal with, having to negotiate with, such scheming vermin. He would have had them all killed except for the fact that they ran the KGB, the NKVD, the Red Army, the Ministry of Production, the Ministry of Communication and the Ministry of Nationalities. They were the power and he was merely the orchestra leader; according to them that was.

If the CC united against Kirilenko they could have easily overthrown him but what would be the point? Another General

Secretary would be appointed and the cycle of scheming, intriguing and treachery would start all over again. No, better to stay with what they had, what they knew, no need to train another monkey. A factor in Kirilenko's favour was that CC members were perpetually suspicious of, and schemed against, each other. Power grabs were commonplace and when uncovered they were greeted by looks of surprise and shock; "*Really comrade? I had no idea that was going on. I will ensure that those involved are severely punished.*" And severely punished they were for being so inept as to be discovered carrying out their skulduggery.

"Insurrection!" roared Comrade Kirilenko. "Rioting on the streets. Open civil disobedience!" He raised his arms high above his head and waved them about wildly. "What next… revolution? And what are you doing about it?" He blasted at Luka Bazanov. Ever the actor for the big stage, Maxim Kirilenko turned his back on the CC and slowly strode to look out of a window overlooking Red Square. He let his words and the way he had delivered them hang in the air. He resumed in a more conciliatory tone. "Our beloved motherland is lying broken on her knees." Comrade Kirilenko withdrew a handkerchief from his pocket and wiped behind his glasses.

"Comrades… the time for action is upon us." If the audience did not like the introduction, they especially did not like the '*us*' word as that meant somebody was going to be handed responsibility for something and if it went wrong it would mean their death. There was no Gulag option for Central Committee members, only death. "As you all know, over past decades, unrest, riots, civil disobedience and uprisings have increased throughout our beloved Union of Soviet Socialist Republics. The Proletariat do not appreciate that I have created for them a workers' paradise here on Earth." Comrade Kirilenko paused to take everybody in the chamber into an icy cold gaze before continuing. "What is to be done?" Asked Comrade Kirilenko in an echo of Lenin's words.

"We should exterminate them Comrade Kirilenko, teach them a lesson they will never forget… we should smash each and every one of them, the ungrateful..." The speaker stopped speaking after realising she had used the '*we*' word. Her fellow CC members smiled at her. "What I meant to say, Comrade Kirilenko, was..." she stuttered, trying to recover her spoken mistake. Comrade Kirilenko held up his hand to stop her from continuing her embarrassing of herself.

"I agree with you comrade, I agree with you. The vermin must be crushed. I am sure you all realise that it is a big task and not one easily accomplished... and we must each bear the burden of responsibility for the success of Operation Zima."

"Operation Zima?" chorused the audience slightly out of time with one another.

"Yes comrades, Operation Zima," repeated comrade Kirilenko looking pleased with himself. "Operation Zima heralds perpetual winter for those who seek to overturn the state." By '*overturn the state*' Comrade Kirilenko was really only referring to himself. "Two years ago, Comrade Dobrovski took over as head of a special project after his predecessor failed to complete it on time." On hearing that the hated Jew had been given responsibility for a '*special project*' the CC thought it would, hopefully, bring about his end when it went wrong as things always seemed to in the Soviet Union. None of them gave a moment's thought to who the predecessor was or what had happened to him or her. Key to survival in the CC was dodging responsibility for anything and everything as, by doing nothing, they could not be held to account for it going wrong. In the case of Operation Zima, mistakes would be down to the '*incompetence*' of Comrade Dobrovski.

"Perhaps Comrade Dobrovski might update the Central Committee about Operation Zima..." interjected Luka Bazanov eager to understand where all this was going.

"All in good time, Comrade Bazanov... all in good time." The second '*all in good time*' was delivered in a tone of voice laced with hatred. "Before Comrade Dobrovski provides an update, I am going to tell you about Operation Zima, the success of which you will all shoulder responsibility for." Once again, Comrade Kirilenko paused to take the audience into his icy cold gaze before continuing. "There is a part for each of you to play." This revelation did not go down well with the CC. "Operation Zima will wipe out, once and for all, the wreckers, the saboteurs, the anti-Soviet and counter-revolutionary elements and the politically unreliable… by bringing Terror to them all." The CC sat pale-faced and still at what they had just heard.

"Comrade Kirilenko, is it…" Comrade Kirilenko raised an open palmed hand to silence the speaker.

"For the past two years Comrade Dobrovski has been putting the final pieces in place for the commencement of Operation Zima." The CC looked around the room until their eyes locked onto Vasily Dobrovski. "It will strike simultaneously in Velikobritania and Vladivostok in approximately three months' time. After cleansing both those places our glorious NKVD forces will proceed east from Vladivostok and west from Velikobritania until they meet in the middle and annihilate any remaining pockets of resistance…" There followed feigned cheering and thigh slapping celebration at the announcement, nobody wanted to be seen to be against Operation Zima while they were sitting in front of its sponsor.

"Going by the expressions on your faces, security around Operation Zima has been good so far." Kirilenko allowed himself a slight smile. "Dissident groups, such as Narodnaya Volya, have been fed disinformation about the Terror. They think it is a small local action to crush rebels in Shotlandiya and so they will focus their resources in the west where the Red Army is strongest and will be annihilated. I will not say what other disinformation Narodnaya Volya has been fed but it will bring about the end of them and their ambitions. You will receive updates about Operation Zima as well as the parts you will play in it direct from Comrade Dobrovski. That is all. This meeting of the Central Committee is over." Comrade Kirilenko fast-walked from the Lenin Chamber surrounded by his Kremlin Guard. The Central Committee stood and applauded their approval of Operation Zima, with each of them checking who was faking it.

★

The Presidium members of Operation Zima arrived in the Lenin Chamber accompanied by Maxim Kirilenko and Vasily Dobrovski.

"Pull up chairs and sit down around my desk. Let us get down to business." Comrade Kirilenko turned to his right. "Comrade Dobrovski, give us your progress report." Dobrovski cleared his throat, shuffled his papers, downed a cup of Vodka and began.

"Comrade General Secretary, preparations for Operation Zima are proceeding well," he said trying to sound as confident as possible, "and…"

"Vasily, my friend," when the Comrade General Secretary called you as his friend you were in trouble, "I have sat in this seat long enough to know when I smell horse shit and I smell it now. What is going on?" The other Presidium members relaxed, some even smiled, knowing that while Vasily Dobrovski was on the hook they were safe from Kirilenko.

"Comrade General Secretary, I apologise, I misspoke. Preparations, though highly advanced, are slightly behind schedule. It is not by much. I am certain the time can be caught up. I did not want to concern you over such petty matters."

"I will decide if a matter is petty or not. Proceed with your report… and no more misspeaking."

"Certainly Comrade General Secretary. I shall begin with logistics, personnel, distribution and special assignments…"

Comrade Dobrovski continued his progress report to the Presidium without faltering further. He purposely understated the advanced status of certain elements of Operation Zima so as not to appear too capable. People who are too capable are gotten rid of by higher ranking less capable people.

There was more to Comrade Vasily Dobrovski though than met the eye. He was, in fact, extremely capable, politically astute and fox-like in his cunning. He constantly played mind games, just as he had with the Presidium of Operation Zima. In fact, he had everything under control but being a cautious comrade, Dobrovski did not want to show all of his cards. He had seen what happened to people who were talented. They would be found with things or found doing things that were anti-Soviet and then it was all over for them. No help was ever given to those on the way down in case they dragged others down with them. It is always best to steer well clear of people on the way down.

Vasily Dobrovski was smart enough to know he had to distance himself from Operation Zima as soon as he possibly could. A key part of his plan was to quickly hand over operational responsibility for Zima to the NKVD. Then it would be their heads on the block, not his. If asked why he had delegated operational responsibility to the NKVD, he would offhandedly reply that they were best placed to make on-the-ground decisions; '*That is what everybody is crying out for*', he would say. If asked how lessons learned from the campaign could be taken to ensure better success in future, he would reply he had no mandate to do that. If the merest hint of a suggestion of such a mandate was ever in the air he would put his plan B into action; create a storm in a Commissariat teacup and claim it demanded his entire attention... and then slaughter those trying to stitch him up.

★

The plan was for those rounded up in Zima actions to be transported to Irlandia for interrogation and, when found guilty by a military court, executed. In some cases it would be '*if found guilty*' as they would have been identified as potential collaborators. A certain number of them would be transported to the Gulag for a slow death. None would be allowed to return to Shotlandiya.

After cleansing Shotlandiya, the NKVD would travel south to Englia to start Zima against the northern regions, especially Budyonovsk and Chelovekski. The Red Army would follow in the wake of the NKVD to remove prisoners to Irlandia and occupy cleansed areas.

The Generals in charge of the occupation knew that if they messed up they would be called to Moscow to account for themselves and would, in all likelihood, never be seen again. After a brief hearing they would be removed to the labyrinthine passages beneath the Kremlin to stand in one of two lines along with hundreds of other unfortunate souls. The left hand line leads to lifts which emerge in an inner courtyard of the Kremlin where the prisoners are loaded onto covered trucks and driven away to the Gulag. Some might reappear years later in Siberian exile but most would not. Those in the right hand line would be taken into small, dimly lit, roughly tiled rooms to receive summary execution.

The entrance to each room was a crude gap smashed through a corridor wall. The exit was a similar gap in the opposite wall. Rooms were fitted with gutters and drains at the end of a sloping concrete floor. Inside each room two junior KGB or NKVD Officers waited with Mausers for the next customer. The poor soul, man, woman, child, able-bodied or otherwise, would be forced to kneel on a canvas sack. The sack was not there to spare the knees of the condemned, it was there to soak up blood as the Officers were responsible for cleaning up before they handed over to the next shift.

As those in the left hand line made their way to the lifts they did so to the sound of continuous single pistol shots. Shot after shot, one after the other, some overlapping the short echoes of other shots.

★

Until the launch date, Operation Zima was the responsibility of Vasily Dobrovski. He used the intervening time to entice those he wanted rid of into Zima's web with promises of power. With such promises his victims would be reluctant to wriggle free despite warnings they might receive. This was his opportunity to satisfy personal vendettas. Thoughts of what was going to happen to his enemies excited and dizzied him. This made him feel extremely horny. Standing on the verge of a great undertaking does that to people. Vasily once had a marriage of convenience but his real, one and only true love, was Andrei. He touched himself at thoughts of Andrei's image running in the video inside his head.

They had met while at University. Showing any feelings whatsoever to a member of the same sex was a risky business in the USSR but it was never difficult recognising somebody with the same needs, drives, predilections and desires. Had they been found out, Comrade Dobrovski would have been killed and Andrei sent to the Gulag. Vasily's execution would be staged as an unfortunate accident. It was incredible how many prominent Soviet officials fell out of tenth storey windows. The same thing would happen to his so-called wife if her true nature were ever uncovered. To keep everybody safe she had decided to remain celibate but sometimes her urges were just too great and so she occasionally took risks in certain parks, clubs and bars.

Despite him having signed death lists in the thousands and despite his instinct for survival at all costs, Comrade Dobrovski was deeply uncomfortable with Operation Zima. Since the Presidium meeting, he had once again run the numbers. They were so large they were mind bogglingly unreal. He checked them over a further four times. There was no mistake. As a direct result of Operation Zima at least one hundred million people would die with even bigger numbers sent to the Gulag. The stage was set. Hundreds of new Commissars, including Grigori's Dyadya Vasya, had been appointed in preparation for Operation Zima. It was just waiting for somebody to light the blue touch paper.

★

Vasily Dobrovski closed his Operation Zima files for the day, locked them in his wall safe, put on his good winter coat, gloves and hat and left his office. Where was his official car and bodyguard detail? This was the sort of thing that happened right before they picked you up and took you in for interrogation. A dozen scenarios ran through Vasily's head. '*What would he be accused of? Who was behind it? Did they know about him and Andrei?*' He was so frightened he almost lost control of his bladder. He looked up and down the street but nobody was showing the slightest bit of interest in him. He began walking toward the entrance to the underground carpark. '*Maybe his bodyguards were playing cards in the back of his limousine*?' He was hopeful that they had forgotten what time he was leaving today. He would give them an earful. He was looking forward to it when four slightly built but tough looking men settled in alongside him. The closest put his arm across Dobrovski's chest, halting him.

"Do not be alarmed, Comrade Dobrovski, we are not going to harm you."

"Does that mean I am in no danger?"

"That all depends on you…" The man looked around, "Follow me."

"Where to?"

"Your questions will be answered but not here… follow me." At this second '*follow me*' a 9 mil was shoved hard into Vasily's back just above his left kidney. It hurt like hell.

"That is much more like it." He said, "That is more like the KGB we all know."

"KGB? Do not be so stupid… if we were KGB we would not…" The man looked irritated at Vasily, "follow me… now!" At the '*now*' the 9 mil was shoved harder into Vasily's back.

Alone on the dark deserted wintry streets of Moscow, Vasily had no option but to comply. The man's companions formed a guard in case he tried to make a break for it. The group hugged the shadows of tall buildings as they walked along the street. After a few hundred yards they turned into the driveway of an underground carpark of an office building just four blocks down from Vasily's office.

The men shoved Vasily down the sloping driveway and into the underground carpark. He hoped his kidnapping had been witnessed and was being reported to the Security Services, '*with any luck the KGB will rescue me*.'

In a dark corner at the far end of the carpark was a door, its edges illuminated by whatever light was beyond it. Dobrovski's only comfort was the sway of the 9 mil in his shoulder holster as it thumped against his chest while he walked. He had never shot, or even shot at, anybody in his life. As the moment came Dobrovski's heart nearly beat out of his chest. His head was pounding with the blood coursing through his brain. Just as he was about to reach for his gun a hand was placed on each of his shoulders accompanied by the word '*stop*'. The leader asked Dobrovski if he was armed. If they patted him down and found his 9 mil he imagined they would not be pleased, so he admitted to being armed.

"Where is it?"

"In my shoulder holster. No… the other side." Comrade Dobrovski was a southpaw.

"Nice little stopper," said the guard ejecting the clip. "Look boss, dum dum load. Nasty!"

"You never know when you need something like that," replied the leader with a smirk.

"Enough…" uttered Dobrovski defiantly, "I demand to know what are you going to do with me."

"Relax. You have been so good up until now it would be a shame to spoil it by acting up. We only have a little while to go and then all your questions will be answered."

"Who by? Who will answer my questions?"

"Relax," the leader repeated. "We are all on the same side. We have the same bosses." Comrade Dobrovski prayed the man was not referring to the KGB.

Instead of using a lift the group made for the stairs. Each floor was gained by ascending two half-flights of stairs. They climbed to the fourteenth floor. Dobrovski said that had he known they were going to climb mount Elbrus he would have brought oxygen. The guards wheezed as they laughed.

"We are here. Once on the other side of this door you will not speak unless you are spoken to." '*This was a fine way to treat a Presidium member of Operation Zima,*' thought Comrade Dobrovski. "You will be taken to a waiting area. I cannot say how long your wait will be."

"Shall we wait too?" asked one of the three man escort team.

"No, you can all go. Do not leave the building together and leave at least four minutes between each departure. If you are picked up do not worry, we will know about it..." The leader hesitated, "You know what will happen. Go now, we will meet soon." The men slapped one another across the shoulders and departed.

An hour passed before Comrade Dobrovski was invited to enter '*Conference Room 1*'.

The room was in almost total darkness. At its far end was a desk with an angle poise lamp pointed straight ahead rendering the person sitting behind it a silhouette. Comrade Dobrovski could tell by the silhouette's shape that it was a man. A large man. A gloved hand extended into the cone from the light from the angle poise lamp, inviting Comrade Dobrovski to sit. As he sat, a pack of cigarettes, American, was pushed across the desk followed by a gold cigarette lighter, Dunhill. Dobrovski had cut his smoking down drastically at Andrei's request but he took a cigarette from the offered pack and lit it. The taste was much smoother and milder than he was used to. '*American cigarettes. Hmmmmm. Smooth.*'

"I apologise for keeping you waiting Mister Dobrovski, it was unavoidable with all that is going on. I am sure you understand because you are involved in it." Said the silhouette in American, his voice raspy as though speaking through a broken loudspeaker… but different.

"How do you know I can understand what you are saying?" Dobrovski replied in Russian.

"Please, Mister Dobrovski, I know everything about you. May I call you Vasily? I have had you brought here today because you need to make some changes to the plan you are working on."

"What plan are you referring to?"

"You know the plan I am referring to, Vasily… but first let me tell you some more about the organisation we both work for." Dobrovski put on an exaggerated expression of puzzlement. "You know what I am referring to so no looks of puzzlement Vasily… please… you are embarrassing yourself." Dobrovski shrugged his shoulders. He thought he was being led into a trap by his CC enemies or the KGB or both.

"I think you have me confused with somebody else… comrade? I did not catch your name."

"Vasily, there is no confusion… as for my name, you know me as The Director." Dobrovski knew the name well and it changed everything.

The Director described aspects of Dobrovski's life, focussing particularly on his relationship with Andrei. Comrade Vasily Dobrovski was at the total mercy of the silhouette sitting opposite him.

"You appear to know a good deal about me but I know almost nothing about you… not even your real name."

"What you do not know you cannot give away under interrogation or torture… or even give away freely in some dirty deal to save yourself if it comes to that."

"You do not trust me?"

"Of course not. What a stupid question."

"But there is no reason for you not to trust me."

"We are wasting time. I will get straight to the point as I am running late for my next meeting."

"Do not let me keep you, comrade." Dobrovski's sarcasm was ignored by the Director.

"Vasily, we are on the same side, we want the same things."

"What do you want?"

"We want you to alter…"

"Who is this '*we*'?"

"You are being irritating, Vasily. The '*we*' is The Network of course… I think you knew that. You are in the final stages of planning Operation Zima. It will take us back to the bad old days of Stalinism and we cannot allow that to happen."

"Why are you telling me this?"

"Because the Terror must fail and for that to happen, Vasily, you must make changes to the plan for Operation Zima."

"If the Terror fails then that will be the end of me."

"No, it will not. We have influential people, many of whom are Red Army Generals, who are with us. You must change the plan before the Terror begins."

"How will I do that?"

"You are a clever man, Vasily. You will think of something. An intermediary will act as go between for you to make your reports."

"How will I make contact…"

"The agent will give you one of these." The Director threw a small black button across the table. "Goodbye and good luck." Then, after a pause, "If you betray us, Vasily, Andrei will pay the price. You will watch him die and you will live." Above his anger at the threat to Andrei's life, a cold shaking-shiver raced through Vasily's body. He felt like jumping into the darkness and grabbing the silhouette by his throat. As though reading Dobrovski's mind the silhouette showed the tip of a pistol in the cone of light.

"Vasily, go, before you do something you will regret. You will be escorted from the building… go!"

As soon as the door to Conference Room 1 closed behind him, Vasily was greeted by a female pointing a Mauser at him. She ordered him to follow her.

Pioneer Camp

Throughout the Soviet Union, university students '*freely*' volunteer their time as Pioneer Camp Counsellors for winter and summer camps. It was good for their careers as well as for improving their chances of getting a party card. Their role at Pioneer Camp was to help bend malleable young minds to the Soviet system, just as their minds had been bent when they attended Pioneer Camp.

Some Pioneer Camp Counsellors' names were permanently on the list of volunteers. This meant they were '*highly*' politically reliable. This was code-speak for a child of the elite. Just becoming an everyday Pioneer Camp Counsellor was going to be a problem for Vladimir because he was from Budyonovsk. Despite Svetlana and Grigori coaching him for days he failed the selection interview even though he got higher marks than ninety nine percent of first time applicants. The fact that he came from Budyonovsk was considered too risky for the Political Commissars to give him a placement. They did not want to suffer the consequences should this potential trouble-maker make actual trouble. They knew that if they made any mistakes in the selection process they would end up in the Gulag. Their underlings prayed that they would make a mistake so they could gain promotion into their shoes.

Neither Svetlana nor Grigori sat selection because they were children of the elite. Vladimir had wanted to warn his family about the Terror instead of going to Pioneer Camp but had been assured that NV was warning everybody about it and leaflets had already been sent to Velikobritania which would be pasted on every factory wall in the land.

★

In anticipation of problems obtaining a travel permit, I made my way at first light to the Ministry of Travel. When I arrived there I found a very long queue. It was a freezing cold morning, everybody in the queue was doing all they could to keep warm; jumping on the spot, banging their gloved hands together and rubbing each other's backs, shoulders and upper arms; some were even doing star jumps; that uses too much energy in my opinion. The queue stretched all along the front of the building and around two corners. It was well known that this building was a hotspot for KGB surveillance. After queuing for over three hours I neared the entrance to the building. A young man came and stood in front of me in the queue.

"Hey comrade, no cutting in the line!" I shouted. Nobody paid a blind bit of attention.

"Comrade, you are mistaken, I am not cutting in the line, I paid this fellow here to keep a place for me." The man the stranger referred to shrugged his shoulders, the line-cutter was not cutting in front of him so what did he care?

"Look, he does not know what you are talking about!"

"Am I supposed to pay you too?" asked the stranger. "Here. Take it. It will help you with your trip." He shoved a piece of paper into my hand and then turned his back on me. I was about to punch him in the back of his head but thought better of it as our conversation had caught the attention of a couple of NKVD guards. The stranger whispered to me, "*Comrade, I suggest you read it quickly,*" out of the side of his mouth.

I unfolded the piece of paper and what was written on it froze the blood in my veins.

Attention comrade. You are being watched. Do not enter the building, you will not leave it alive. NV has been betrayed. There have been many arrests and your name is on the list. Do not speak with me, just make an excuse to leave the line and walk away. Once you are out of sight then run. Do not stop running. Ever. Good luck comrade. If we do not meet again in this life, please God we will meet in the next.

Long live Lev.
Long live The People's Will.

The stranger sniffed twice to attract my attention and then scratched his backside. In doing so he made an NV sign to show he was genuine. The line shuffled forward. I was now only five people from the entrance. I started patting my jacket as though it was on fire. Then my trousers. Then I looked inside my canvas bag. I hit myself with the flat of my hand on my forehead and exclaimed how stupid I was, "*I have left my papers, my passport, my travel coupons and my money in my room back at the university. Comrade,*" I said to the woman standing behind me, "*keep my place for me please, I will be back in five minutes.*" I left the line. Before I made ten feet one of the NKVD guards shouted for me to come back. As I walked toward her the stranger shouted something in a strange language, pulled out a revolver and shot it into the air. The queue immediately scattered in all directions. This worked well for us to make our escape. '*Moving at the speed of the herd is the best way to stay hidden in plain sight.*' I had no idea where that thought came from.

"I am Hyram," shouted the stranger. "It is good to meet you at last… I just want to say what an honour it is to…"

"Hello, I am Vladimir." I shouted back.

"Who?"

"Vladimir, I am…"

"Not Dmitri?"

"No, Vladimir!"

"But you understood the NV sign."

"Should we be talking about NV? Is it safe? You could be a…"

"So could you… Vladimir! If that is even your name! Shit, where the hell is Dmitri?"

"How should I know? I have no idea who he is… or who you are for that matter."

"Do not worry about me comrade. At least everybody in the queue dispersed so the real Dmitri should be safe."

"Where are we going?"

"Keep up because I will not stop for you."

As we ran bullets zinged through the air just above our heads. We weaved in and out of service alleys in the maze of Moscow's back streets. Just as we ran out of breath we reached an NV safe house. Hyram gave a series of knocks on the back door. Once inside we were pushed to the floor, guns were put to our heads and we were interrogated. After passing the interrogation we were given a change of clothes. After resting for a minute we casually walked out the front door. We looked just like two ordinary Muscovites going about our business. If we were stopped I was told to say I was a student on winter break. '*Wait a minute, I am a student on winter break.*' This seemed very amateurish to me. As we walked along Moscow's bustling city centre streets two people sidled up alongside of us and matched our pace. I instinctively knew they were NV.

"Who is this?" asked the man.

"Long story," answered Hyram.

"Hello, I am Vladimir."

"Where is Dmitri?" asked the woman.

"Same long story."

"What the hell have you done Hyram?" They chorused with obvious irritation in their voices.

"As I said, it is a long story but at least Dmitri got away… at least I think he got away… if he was still standing in the queue when the shots were fired."

"Shots?"

"Yes shots, but in my defence…"

"In your defence? This story is getting worse by the minute."

Shouts of '*there they are*' rang out followed by shooting. Not wanting to hang around to see who the NKVD Soldiers were shooting at we ran. Two minutes later we were inside the next safe house in the chain.

*

While Vladimir and his NV compatriots were running for their lives, Svetlana and Grigori were arriving at Vladivostok. They had gotten lucky, as if luck has anything to do with children of the elite receiving unasked for privileges, and were assigned a private compartment on the Trans-Siberian express. They could have flown but Svetlana said the train would be '*romantic*'. The journey brought them much closer together philosophically, emotionally and physically. Deeply in love they had made an oath to die rather than be separated by the state. They even made a suicide pact should they be exposed as NV. In truth they were being over-dramatic but their feelings for one another were genuine nevertheless.

Waiting to take the children of the elite to the Pioneer Camp was a fleet of black Merkovs. All others had to wait in the freezing cold for buses to take them to the camp.

*

When the fleet of Merkovs pulled into the Pioneer Camp a solitary guard directed them to an enclosed area at the rear of the Camp Commandant's offices. This, as far as the passengers were concerned, was normal procedure so the Proles did not witness their luxurious arrival. It had just started snowing again. Due to the strength of the wind it was a blizzard that the passengers emerged into from the warmth of their cars. Standing before them in full winter combat gear was a KGB Major. '*This was not good*,' they each thought. Until recently the KGB Major had been based in

Bishkek and was promoted after taking up his new role as Deputy Security Commissar for Universities, Trades Unions and Veterans Associations. He was one of four KGB Officers who took over when Grigori's uncle moved to Velikobritania with his new job.

The new arrivals were ordered to stand where they were and not to move. One of them spoke up saying who she was, who her father was and how dare they make her stand in a blizzard without her good coat to keep her warm. She was hit to the ground by one of the KGB Officers surrounding the Major. He held up his hand to prevent further punishment. The girl's friend picked her up and they held each other close for warmth. Another female asked what was going on and why were they being made to stand in the open, '*freezing to death*'. The KGB Major ordered her to remove her clothes. She refused and was kicked to the ground and then dragged away, leaving a red trail in the snow all the way to the Adjustment Block. Svetlana and Grigori looked at one another and almost imperceptibly each shook their heads. They knew from their NV training to keep a low profile. Not to attract attention. Be humble. Cooperative. That was the quickest way for it to be over.

After ten minutes the new arrivals were chilled to the marrow of their bones. The KGB Major looked at his watch and then ordered the guards to take the prisoners to the stockade. "*Light the furnace and place the interrogation irons in it.*" Shouted a KGB Officer. The Soldiers were relishing the opportunity of getting at the children of the elite. Some were not so sure it was such a good idea and planned to hold back on their mistreatment, believing that they might be shown some small mercy should the parents of the elite children come down on them.

Inside the stockade was a metal interrogation desk. Behind the desk was a wooden chair with a cushion on it and in front of the desk was a metal chair which was bolted to the floor. Next to the metal chair was a bank of batteries connected to a device for delivering electric shocks. Saw-toothed bulldog clips, thick with dried blood, were attached to the ends of the electric leads. On the other side of the metal chair was a portable furnace with an electric fan forcing air into its coals. It had eight white hot irons in it. The room smelt like a Smithy.

Eighteen students in various stages of undress, distress and terror were dragged from their cells to where the KGB Major had set up his interrogation desk. They stood in silence but were unable to control the involuntarily swaying motions their bodies were making. The first student from the left was force-sat on the metal chair and restrained with Lubyanka bracelets. Saw-toothed bulldog clips were attached to various parts of her body. She screamed as they crunched into her flesh. A junior KGB Officer pointed to her vagina. The KGB Major shook his head saying she could look forward to that later. The female looked at him through bulging, bloodshot, eyes and asked, in an unnervingly calm voice, why she was being treated this way.

"You are a member of Narodnaya Volya, a banned organisation concerned with plotting violent revolution against the state and of threatening the lives of the Central Committee of the Soviet Union. These are crimes punishable by death and you will beg for death before this day is over."

"I am not a member of any such organisation… or any organisation. I am a student studying…"

"I know what you are studying. I know what you all are studying." The KGB Major held each of the students in a fiery glare. He raised himself to his full height before continuing, "I am KGB Major Artur Arsenovich Popov, Deputy Security Commissar for Universities, Trades Unions and Veterans Associations." The KGB Major paused to let his impressive title sink in. "I am here to find out what you know about a certain Mr Hyram Malkovich and a certain Mr Vladimir Vakhnenko. They are…"

"I know you," Grigori called out. A guard made to strike Grigori but was screamed at not to do so by Major Popov. "My uncle is Vasily Zaytsev. He was a KGB Colonel in the Special Security Section. When he was promoted to Head Commissar of the Western Frontier

Gulags it took four people to replace him at the Moscow Lubyanka. I believe you are one of them." The KGB Major's forehead broke out into a sweat. Svetlana stared at Grigori hoping he was right.

"What is your name, good comrade?" enquired Major Popov cringingly.

"Grigori Andreivich Rabinovich."

"A bloody Jew," muttered one of the KGB crew.

"You understand young sir that I must do my job. If I do not..."

"My uncle, Dyadya Vasya, Vasily Zaytsev, so named after a hero of the great patriotic war, did your job and the work of three others without resorting to the torturing of students freely volunteering their time for the glory of the party and the state." He could thread a good speech together when he wanted to could Grigori. "Acting in the way you are, you are implying that my uncle, a highly decorated KGB Colonel, did not know how to do his job." The Major took a deep breath but before he could speak Grigori continued, "I think I would like to speak with my Dyadya Vasya."

"It is very early in the morning in Velikobritania. No need to wake the Head Commissar with this little misunderstanding. I will contact Moscow later today for guidance."

Which of course the Major never did for to do so would attract the wrong kind of attention from his boss. Instead, KGB Major Artur Arsenovich Popov reported that he had carried out a thorough investigation and found no connection between the terrorist runaways and the Counsellors at the Vladivostok Pioneer Camp.

"That was lucky."

"It was," replied Grigori.

"Look at me, I am still shaking."

"What has Vladimir been up to? Idiot!"

"We must find out."

Entering their dormitory Grigori made the sign for a bugged room. Svetlana nodded her agreement. They needed to talk but not at the moment as they were late for duty. Each grabbed a piece of dried fish from their stockpiles, donned their Pioneer Camp winter uniform and ran to the parade ground.

Svetlana and Grigori were concerned about what was going on with Vladimir but could not talk about him until they were confident they were not being listened in on. The dormitory was indeed bugged as was every room in the camp and much of the surrounding area. "*Record everything Rabinovich says and his girlfriend too. I want to get to the bottom of what he knows about Vladimir Vakhnenko.*"

⋆

Svetlana, Grigori, and a few other stragglers who had been entertained by the KGB Major, fell in with their Counsellor comrades. All heads turned to look at the late arrivers. The Camp Commandant gave them a cold look before announcing that as they were late they could take the Pioneers on their morning run; ten kilometres through knee deep snow. Grigori thanked the Camp Commandant for the opportunity to get to know the Pioneers at such an early stage, then introduced himself using his uncle's credentials. The Camp Commandant whispered something to himself like, "*It is about time he showed up.*" Svetlana gave Grigori a dig in the ribs and told the Camp Commandant that they were to be treated like any other Pioneer Counsellors. "*Will you stop using your uncle's name!*" Hiss-whispered Svetlana giving Grigori another dig in the ribs. They were then both pulled from the line, along with half a dozen other Counsellors, and ordered to report to the Security Section for duty assignment. "*Security Section! We're going to be spying on the Pioneers! I wanted to do some skiing, shooting and wilderness trekking... but now...*" Svetlana was incandescent with rage.

The Security Section building was huge, consisting of four storeys above ground and four below. The entrance was guarded 24/7 by heavily armed NKVD Soldiers and a machine gun bunker. '*Why*?' It was unlikely to be attacked being in the middle of a Pioneer Camp in the middle of nowhere and surrounded by over six thousand committed communists. But that is what those in charge do in case something does happen and they are accused of '*inaction*'. Like most crimes in the Soviet Union, inaction was regarded as a crime against the state and therefore punishable by death or the Gulag which was the same thing in the long run.

Standing inside the Security Section building was Major Popov. He stared in disbelief as the line of students entered the building and sat outside the administration office waiting for their security passes to be issued. He was about to speak when Grigori informed him that they had all been assigned to the Security Section by the Camp Commandant. A slight smile passed across Grigori's face when he said this. Once again, the former Bishkek Captain felt the stab of injustice cut into his fragile ego. '*Why, was life always so unfair to him?*' He asked himself. '*Why were these lazy, feckless, over-privileged students given so many advantages in life when they were so undeserving of them? Why?*' Popov vowed to get even with them all but especially with Grigori Andreivich Rabinovich. He mused on how he would like Grigori all to himself in a sound proof torture cell in the Lubyanka.

After receiving their security passes the new Security Section Pioneer Camp Counsellors piled into a conference room for induction. The Officer carrying out the induction made the KGB Major seem like a pussycat. He had a pockmarked face and the neck of a bull. He did not smile and his voice was like sandpaper. It was he who assigned '*newbies*' their tasks.

"You two are assigned to me. The rest of you will find your duties posted on the notice board by the security desk. Dismissed." Grigori was about to introduce himself when Svetlana got in first.

"Comrade Lieutenant, I am…"

"I am Lieutenant Mikhail Mikhailovich Kozlov of the Red Army Security Service, RASS, on assignment to root out wreckers, saboteurs, traitors and those forming counter-revolutionary centres. Introduce yourselves."

"My name is Svetlana Panshina. I am the daughter of…"

"I am not interested who your father is or who your mother is. While you are here they are nothing. Do you understand?"

"Yes." The Lieutenant stared and waited, "Yes, Lieutenant Kozlov." He continued staring and waiting. "Yes sir."

"That is more like it. Carry on." Svetlana gave a short introduction of herself, careful not to mention anything she thought the Lieutenant might not like hearing. She did not want to make him any angrier than he already appeared to be. Grigori spoke as soon as she finished.

"My name is Grigori Andreivich Rabinovich. I am studying languages at the University of Nationalities in Moscow…" Grigori spoke widely about himself and his family for ten minutes.

"Why did you mention your uncle's position? Do you expect special treatment because of who he is?"

"No, I…"

"Do not lie to me, boy!" Anger raged through the Lieutenant's eyes.

"I am not ashamed of my family." Which he sometimes was. "I will not hide them or their achievements from you or anybody else. My family connections do have their advantages; I do not ask for them but I do not refuse them. Why should I? If people are in awe then let them be in awe." Grigori held the Lieutenant in a solid defiant stare. The Lieutenant laughed.

"You are alright comrade. I thought you would fold and try to worm your way into my good books but you did not." Lieutenant Kozlov slapped Grigori hard on his back and indicated for him and Svetlana to follow him.

After a day introducing Svetlana and Grigori to surveillance techniques, Lieutenant Kozlov told them to report for duty to the fourth sub-level. They each thought that knowing about surveillance and how the state carried it out could be useful to them one day.

*

As Svetlana and Grigori exited the lift on the fourth sub-level they were pinned to the wall by four armed guards demanding to see their passes. Svetlana made to open her bag when it was snatched from her and she was shoved hard against the closing lift doors. Grigori did not protest her rough treatment as they both knew the score. Another guard asked Grigori for his pass, he expected the same treatment as Svetlana but as Grigori reached inside his jacket pocket to retrieve his pass the guard could not care less. He was preoccupied watching Svetlana bending over retrieving her belongings from the floor. Grigori snapped his fingers in front of the guard's eyes, held his pass up and then bent down and pulled Svetlana's pass from under the other guard's boot. As Grigori stood up he expected to be knocked to the floor but instead they were just pointed in the direction of the security section.

"Did the guards give you the first day treatment? You know, rough you up?" asked Alexei, the senior camp surveillance supervisor.

"Yes they…"

"They do that sort of thing all the time. I think it makes them feel big… feel important. Did they give her a hard time?" asked Alexei pointing at Svetlana. "They are especially jealous of females. They see them doing interesting work while they just stand there for hours every day doing nothing."

"Maybe they do the things they do out of boredom?"

"Do not bother trying to psychoanalyse their situation. Do not pity them. Do not sympathise with them. They are basic Proles, end of story."

"Maybe they should be given more to do than just stand around…"

"What? I can see you are going to be trouble," said Alexei laughing. "Take my advice, do not get attached to the monkeys. It only gives them hope." Alexei jumped in the air and clicked his heels together. They both liked Alexei's warped sense of humour and zany behaviour.

On entering the security section Svetlana and Grigori audibly gasped. They had never seen anything like it. It was a different world.

"Somebody took a big risk assigning you two to this operation."

"It was the Camp Commandant."

"I doubt that, you must have an Angel somewhere… or a Devil. Somebody wants you here. Perhaps they have something in mind for you," suggested Alexei knowingly. "Everything you see and do in here must never go beyond these four walls." Alexei winked as he said this. "I am supposed to give you some big speech now but it is boring and I have forgotten much of it. Let me introduce you to everybody. Actually, that is a lot of names." Alexei then clapped his hands together and shouted, "Everybody. Listen. This is Svetlana." He said pointing at Grigori.

"Hi Svetlana," everybody droned in reply.

"And this is Grigori," he said pointing at Svetlana.

"Hi Grigori," everybody droned again.

"They are going to be with us for a couple of weeks…"

"May we ask questions?"

"Of course but I may have to shoot you if you… do not worry, I am only joking. I will of course answer any questions so long as you have the correct security clearance for the answers." Alexei inspected their security passes. "I see from your passes you have full security clearance."

"Is that unusual?"

"No, we all have full security clearance here, you cannot enter this room without it." Svetlana and Grigori looked puzzled, "Do not worry, you will get used to me… eventually." As Alexei said this several people sitting behind him shook their heads as if to say '*no you will not*'.

"Can you tell us about these machines, they look like…"

There were over four hundred personnel in the room. It was one of three similar sized rooms separated by office dividers along their length. Individual sections handled different types of security work. Alexei was in overall charge of the operation. Everything was lit by rows of fluorescent light fittings of the type that makes white skin appear translucent. Everybody sat at long desks designed for three people. In front of each person was a small, white, what looked like, computer. Svetlana asked if they were computers. Alexei replied that the devices were not actually computers but screens connected to the latest Colossus Mk XIV mainframe. Grigori asked what a Colossus Mk XIV mainframe was. Alexei replied that it was a colossal computer which every terminal in the camp was connected to… plus some in Moscow, Leningrad and a few places he did not want to elaborate on. He said the mainframe had just been upgraded and could now handle over two thousand terminals, "*but*," he said, "*in theory, it can support sixty four thousand terminals.*" Alexei believed with that many terminals connected it would probably stop working.

Alexei asked Svetlana if they were interested in computers and had they ever operated one. They were unsure how to reply. Should they tell the truth and risk everything or should they lie? But how could they have simply guessed the word '*computer*' and related it to the machines on the desks. They opted for the truth which was wise of them. They told Alexei about the Irregular Society and the work it did using computers to assist them in their language studies. Alexei asked them where the computers came from. They replied that all they knew was they came from something called The Network. This seemed to resonate with Alexei. He said he now understood why they had been selected for this assignment and wanted to know more about the Irregular Society's computers. Svetlana described the computers to Alexei and it was all he could do to hold in his laughter. They were not pleased by his reaction until he told them that if they were impressed by their Irregular Society's computers they were going to be really impressed with what he had to show them next.

Alexei directed the pair to a red door on their left. Grigori pushed against it but it would not open. There was no handle to gain entry. Alexei waved his security pass over a small box at the side of the door frame. It made a clicking sound and the door opened. "*The door locks using a strong electromagnet which is deactivated by waving your security pass over the box there.*" He told Grigori to give it a try. He waved his pass over the box on the wall and the door opened.

Inside the room were twenty four people. Alexei pointed out that the devices on their desks were computers not terminals, but they too were connected to the Colossus Mk XIV mainframe. Svetlana was about to ask a question when Alexei whispered into the ears of the two closest computer operators. They stood up and made to leave the room. Alexei announced to the staff of Red 3 Section that they had been transferred to blue section. Everybody applauded and wished their now ex-colleagues the very best of luck. Alexei muttered something like, "*That is the last of the KGB spies gone... good riddance.*"

"Svetlana... Grigori, take a seat. No, not there... there. Only joking. Sit anywhere you like. Well, not anywhere, just one of the two desks available." Several computer operators shook their heads behind Alexei's back. He knew this and told them to stop shaking their heads behind his back. The reason he knew they were shaking their heads behind his back was because everywhere in the Pioneer Camp was covered by CCTV and he had studied the tapes. Few people in the Soviet Union even knew what CCTV was. Svetlana looked around the room.

"This is..." she said slowly, unsure of the words she should use.

"This is what? Great? Amazing? Fantastical? You will get tired of it sooner than you think. Allow me to introduce you to the latest thing in computing. The Americans call them personal computers. According to certain sources, about fifty percent of Americans have one of these things at work as well as in their homes. Well, not one of these things exactly but something like one of these things but better… so I hear. These computers have no external disc drives so you cannot remove data… you understand my meaning?" They both nodded though they did not really get Alexei's meaning. "You will notice the screens. They are polychrome, not monochrome. You will notice the device sitting on the desk next to the computer? Move it. See how when you move it a small arrow… called a pointer… moves around the screen. When the arrow is on something you want to use press the left hand button of the controller. Go and sit with the operators over there, they will demonstrate the computer to you." Alexei checked his watch, "I must go… I am late for… this piece of junk is meant to be an alarm watch… Chinese rubbish." Alexei shook his head. "I will leave you in Alina and Galina's hands, they will show you what needs to be filled in and how to do it… everything…" Alexei exited the room leaving Svetlana and Grigori sitting with the operators.

"Hello, my name is Alina and this is Galina." They all shook hands. "We are the surveillance agents responsible for monitoring the activities of Pioneers and Camp Counsellors. I will remove your names from the camp roll of Counsellors. Nobody in Red Section is monitored. I will make a report to say why I removed your names. We must report all our actions. Here is a list of things that must be reported."

Alina remarked how surprised she was that people like them had been handed such an assignment. Svetlana asked what she meant. Alina replied that they did not fit the profile. They were not serving or ex-military, nor were they ex-KGB, nor ex-NKVD and they were obviously not spooks. "*You must have powerful sponsors.*" Svetlana and Grigori again tried to insist that "*the Camp Commandant had assigned us.*" Alina stopped them, "*that is extremely unlikely.*" After a long silence Alina said it was possible that NV was preparing them for a mission… or perhaps the KGB was setting them up, *"it could be somebody wants rid of your parents. Simply possessing the information you now have is enough for the KGB to execute your family… or perhaps turn them to the purposes of the state."* Svetlana and Grigori made scoffing noises. Alina's theorising as to why they had been chosen extended to themselves, being children of the elite, needing to prove themselves ahead of the coming conflict. The scoffing was repeated. Then Alina told them that they were not the first strangers to be put through Red Section; "*I think they were sent because they were young and understood how computers work… old people just do not get it.*" Galina spoke for the first time, "*Alina is usually right. I would be careful if I were you.*"

Svetlana and Grigori wanted to ask about the strangers who had been through Red Section but instinctively they held their tongues. Better to stay silent until they learned how surveillance was carried out in the camp then they could talk without fear of being listened in on.

Cell NV4K

All the fuss and commotion had died down by the time we reached the next safe house. Safe house? It was right next door to where it had all started, the Ministry of Travel.

Hyram's NV associate, or whatever she was, pushed me into a small room and ordered me to wait inside. I asked what was going on and she told me that if I kept my mouth shut and if I was '*reliable*' then I might survive. As all those in the house were armed I thought it best to take the advice and just sit quietly in the room. '*I must get my story straight otherwise I could be in big trouble,*' I thought.

I deliberated on how I had ended up here. I concluded that I was in the wrong place at the right time. Hyram, if that really was his name, had made the mother of blunders by mistaking me for somebody else. Somebody who was obviously a member of NV and in imminent danger of arrest. Now I said it in my head it sounded far-fetched. What were the chances? I did not have time to ponder my situation any further as the door burst open and standing there was Irina Shushonova from the Irregular Society. She threw her arms around my neck and said how glad she was to see me safe… and alive. '*And alive*?' Now I really started to worry. Who was I in death-danger from? The state? Hyram's associates? NV?

"Do you know him?" asked Diana, Hyram's NV associate.

"Yes, I know him very well, his name is Vladimir Vakhnenko. We are on the same course at the University of Nationalities."

"What level is he?"

"Top level. He has permission to study all languages and has open access to the university."

"Open access? Excellent. I have a job for him before he goes on the run."

"On the run!" I exclaimed.

"Shut up, we are still deciding about you!" Through Diana's tone of voice I appreciated my predicament was serious but I was not going to go quietly.

"I will not shut up! I want to know what is going on. I have a right to know what you…"

"You are lucky to still be alive. Your resemblance to…" Diana hesitated.

"Dmitri? The person you mentioned when we first met? Dmitri?"

"Yes, Dmitri. Your resemblance to my brother has put you both in danger."

"Dmitri is your brother? This is too much! Look, I am not him so how am I in danger, I only…"

"Because, Comrade Vakhnenko, my brother is on a death list and so probably are you by now. If they had arrested you they would have found out that you are not Dmitri and released you… but you ran. You would have been allowed to get on with your life as a student… but you ran. Unfortunately, Hyram mistook you for Dmitri and handed you the warning note. At least you are NV so there is no reason to shoot you." I looked for a sign in Diana's eyes that she was not serious but received no such reassurance.

"I am NV… right? So we are all in this…"

"You do not know what we are in. Things are about to start. It is time for war." Did I hear her right? '*War*?' War with who? The Americans? China?

"War?"

"Very soon, a great Terror will be unleashed on all the Soviet Union. The Central Committee has ordered it to stop the coming revolution. Millions will die unless we do something to stop them."

"Why would the Central Committee… that is crazy."

"Is it? Terror has been used to control the Proletariat since Lenin's time… which you would know if our history books told the truth." Diana was handed a note. "You will join a briefing in half an hour to learn what part you will play. There is no going back for you now Comrade Vakhnenko."

My situation looked hopeless. In Irina's opinion I should immediately go into self-imposed exile. "*Get out of Russia… go into hiding for a while… go to Velikobritania.*" I was not convinced that was such a good idea and considered handing myself over to the authorities and pleading with them that I had been abducted against my will because I supposedly resembled somebody they were looking for.

Within minutes of the start of the briefing thoughts of my throwing myself on the mercy of the authorities were washed away as I learned that those who were warning Velikobritania of the coming Terror had been captured, tortured and executed. Instead of feeling sorry for them I could only think about what information they gave away to the KGB. Then somebody in the meeting yelled out exactly the same concern. He received black looks and curses from those around him but I am certain that many of them harboured the same thoughts and their condemnation of the man was more from a sense of their own shame than any disgust or anger they felt for him. The man apologised, begged everyone's forgiveness, and then led a prayer for the martyrs and their families. The scene touched me and along with most other people in the room I cried. Then I thought about my family back in Budyonovsk and what was coming their way. I had to find a way to warn them… '*for all the good it would do,*' I thought.

"*Death to the party. Death to the Central Committee. Death to the revolution.*" Was the prayer-mantra that emerged from the meeting. It rang out louder and louder like a gathering storm as it was echoed by those in the corridor. The chant changed to, "*Long live Lev. Long live Narodnaya Volya. Long live la revolucion.*" This chant went on and on, increasing all the while in volume and fervour… right next door to the Ministry of Travel. I hoped what I had been told about every building in the Soviet Union being bugged was untrue.

As the meeting broke up I thought I had been forgotten about in all the commotion and so made my way to leave the safe house. The only thing on my mind was finding a way of returning home to warn my family about the Terror. Thoughts of handing myself in to the authorities and taking my chances with them came back. I thought, '*They might send me back home and then I could warn my family.*' I did not know exactly when the Terror would start so I needed to get on my way as quickly as possible. A hand grabbed my shoulder.

"There you are Comrade Vakhnenko. Not thinking of leaving were you?"

"No, I was just…"

"Good. Come with me. It is time you found out the part you will play." Diana's brusque manner aroused me. Even for a Russian she was blunt and direct and I had always found such women attractive.

All around me I sensed the activity level had gone up a few notches and that it had not yet peaked. People making their way to the main door were holding exit slips. Thoughts of where I might acquire one of these entered my head. As though reading my mind Diana turned and told me that I would not be allowed to leave the building without an exit slip. Ten paces later we entered a room. The door was slammed shut behind us. I turned and saw Lev, the leader of NV. I was in a state of shock and awe seeing him there like that just a few feet from me.

"Good evening comrade, let me introduce myself…"

"No introductions are necessary comrade, I saw you at…" This was a mistake. I later learned just how much Lev liked to speak, especially about himself, and how he disliked being interrupted. He cleared his throat and looked in Diana's direction before continuing.

"Comrade Sokolov has a couple of jobs for you and now we have no Dmitri I need you to travel to Tula with a message for the resistance fighters there about the Terror. Dmitri was meant to… but… never mind, we have you. I can see how Hyram made the mistake… there is a resemblance."

"Some see it, I cannot."

"You must return here to Moscow with any messages the Tula cell has for me. That is if I am still here… if not you will be told where to find me. You must give the messages to me and me only. Is that clear?"

"Yes Comrade Lev. Please, Comrade Lev, with our agents in Velikobritania dead who will warn the people there about the Terror? They will need to know…"

"They will be warned, I promise."

"Can somebody else go to Tula so I can go home to warn my family?"

"An international travel ban is now in place so you will not be allowed to travel to Velikobritania. I am sorry. You have a job to do here and it is a very important one and one which your family can be proud of."

I wondered why Lev simply did not make a phone call to the Tula cell. It would be much quicker and simpler, not to mention risk free for me. A question jumped into my head, '*Why me?*' I understood I was supposed to look like this Dmitri person and that he was supposed to go on the mission but I was not trained for this sort of thing. Then the word '*dispensable*' jumped into my head.

The jobs Diana had for me were simple enough. So simple in fact that I assumed they were a test to see how reliable, daring and competent I was. All I had to do was enter the university, no problem for me as I was a student there, light a small fire in the west wing, set the fire alarm off and leave a couple of fire doors open for NV people to… she did not say exactly what they were going to do now I come to think about it. I was preoccupied fantasising about her… about us… together, instead of listening while she was speaking. '*I must pay proper attention in future!*'

⋆

The following day I met up with three NV agents. One of them handed me my new ID and Soviet travel passport. As the authorities were on the lookout for Vladimir Vakhnenko, I was now Mikhail Morozov.

It was midday and the line in front of the Ministry of Travel was longer than ever despite the international travel ban. At the front of the queue were four people who were allowing others to pass in front of them. They gave an NV signal and we took their places in the line. Nobody uttered a word of protest. All we had to do now was work our way through the half kilometre of hidden line inside the building. Everything went smoothly. Two hours later we emerged with our travel permits. '*Could it be that easy*?' I felt that we were purposely left alone.

Then a taxi, I had never been in a taxi before, pulled up next to us half a kilometre from the Ministry of Travel and we all got in. Up until then I had not had the opportunity of speaking with my new compatriots and as I went to do so they put their fingers to their lips as a sign not to talk. I was bursting with questions so it was not easy keeping my mouth shut. During the journey the taxi driver pointed out various places of interest along the way. I later learned this running commentary was to keep up a pretence of normalcy for the benefit of the KGB listeners.

I noticed from the road signs that we were heading for the airport and not the railway station. As we neared our destination the taxi driver handed us travel tickets. I had never flown before. I was very…

excited… nervous?… apprehensive? Yes, apprehensive, given the crash rate of Soviet planes. There were rumours that the number of plane crashes was far greater than was reported in Pravda. I believed the higher number to be true, '*after all,*' I thought, '*it is not natural for something man-made to remain in the air for so long.*' Once inside the terminal building our leader spoke to us. She said, "It is okay for us to speak now. They do not monitor anything in here for obvious reasons but let us save our conversation until after we have checked in." '*Checked in?*' I just followed what the others did.

"Where is your luggage?" Growled the huge NKVD Officer sitting behind the check-in desk.

"He has no luggage."

"I have no luggage."

"He is travelling to Tula, his clothes are there."

"I am travelling to…"

"Where is your luggage?"

"None of us has any luggage. If you check our travel warrants you will see that we are assigned to a TS1 project and therefore…"

"I know all about TS1 projects." Snapped the huge NKVD Officer though there was no such thing as a TS1 project. '*Was there?*' I was not sure of anything anymore. The NKVD Officer stamped our passports and papers like he was trying to punch holes through them and then waved us through with the back of his hand.

We made our way to '*Security*' where we were frisk-searched. Once through security we were directed to the left while most other travellers went to the right. From the signs above they were going to private lounges while we went to the public lounge.

The Khrushchev Lounge, as it was named, was massive… and almost empty. In one corner was a Vodka bar and in another a coffee bar that sold cake. We sat in the centre of the lounge as far away from anybody else as we possibly could.

According to our leader, Olga, there was no monitoring of conversations at the airport, so I told her that I needed to travel to Budyonovsk to warn my family about the Terror. She said I had to complete this mission first as we were responsible for taking Lev's message to NV in Tula and I had to go as I was deputising for Dmitri. I asked, "*Why did Lev not just call them*?" Olga looked to the ceiling, tutted and said that such missions were always carried out this way. I wanted to know if she could tell us more about the mission: "*You cannot give away under interrogation or torture what you do not know.*" I snort-laughed in derision and said I wanted more information if I was expected to take such risks. Olga replied that it was they who were taking the risk as I was not known to them.

After our briefing, a cleaner came close and made the sign of NV. Olga hiss-whispered to him, "It is about time you showed up." The cleaner changed the bag in the nearby waste bin and then '*accidentally*' spilled its contents onto the floor. Taking a small brush and scoop he cleaned up the mess he had made. As he kneeled he slipped an envelope under our bench and walked away cursing aloud in case he was being watched.

Waiting five minutes Olga retrieved the envelope. Inside it were four sheets of paper with combinations of words and numbers on them. She said they were the orders from Lev to the Tula cell and that they had all to be delivered for the message to be readable. She handed us one sheet of paper each, telling us that if we were compromised we must destroy our sheet. The taller of my compatriots, Vitaly, said he would swallow his. Olga said that was a great idea, "*as a last resort.*" I asked what she meant by that. She said the paper was impregnated with a deadly fast-acting neurotoxin. Eating it would result in death within four minutes; adding that, as far as she had been told, handling the paper was okay because the amount of neurotoxin that could be picked up on our hands was not enough to do us any harm, "*but I would not go licking my fingers if I were you.*" She smiled. I was alarmed. Olga's final piece of advice was, "*Do not lose your piece of the puzzle. If you do then do not return to Moscow.*"

Our flight was still showing as delayed. Bored, I asked Olga why we were able to talk openly in the Khrushchev Lounge. She replied that monitoring was not allowed in airports, "*for obvious reasons.*" I asked what she meant by that. Olga explained about '*dead zones*', such as airport lounges, saying the KGB were not allowed to monitor conversations held in them by order of Comrade Kirilenko, according to NV operatives inside the Kremlin. "*Other than dead zones,*" added Olga, "*everywhere else is bugged.*" I said that was impossible. "*You cannot bug 'everywhere', it is impossible!*"

An announcement went out over the PA system informing us that our flight was now ready for boarding.

Red Section

Svetlana and Grigori's instruction began straightaway. They were to learn all they needed to know to play their part in a raid on KGB HQ in Moscow. Those who had gone through Red Section before them had been taken or were dead and Svetlana and Grigori's replacements were in the pipeline should they share the same fate. NV had long realised they had traitors in their ranks but so far had failed to expose them. To some it seemed as if they did not want to.

"These are the computers Alexei told you about this morning," said Alina, "they are connected to the Colossus Mk XIV mainframe…"

"Which is in KGB headquarters in Moscow," added a smiling Galina enthusiastically.

"Thank you Galina," responded Alina with an icy glare. "Each computer can operate independently of Colossus as well as acting as a terminal. All activity is monitored and logged by the system."

"What do you mean?"

"Whenever you log onto a computer everything is recorded; who you are, when you were logged on, what you did and so on. Some activities are reported direct to KGB HQ in Moscow." Svetlana and Grigori gave Alina a look of disbelief about the computers being connected to Moscow… over five and a half thousand miles away. She picked up on their scepticism and advised them not to underestimate the power of the new computers and that they would be astounded by what they would learn over the coming days.

"What is that?" asked Svetlana pointing to a large screen hanging on the far wall.

"It is a sector map of the camp. It operates in real time. It also covers areas used by Pioneers when they are outside the camp. All you have to do is press this key on the computer and… there you have it." The image on the map changed to show the area beyond the security fence.

"How does it work?"

"It shows the location of everybody in the camp by sector. You will notice the colouring of the different areas. The darker the colour the greater the density of people."

"What is it used for?"

"It identifies activity zones and contact patterns for us so we can carry out our surveillance effectively. The system records every conversation that takes place and films meetings of groups as well as people of special interest. We call those groups we monitor conspiracy clusters. The surveillance files are sent to Moscow every night at midnight."

Svetlana asked what the grey areas on the map were. Alina replied that they were safe zones, saying that, as far as she knew, they were free of all surveillance. "*They were Alexei's idea, he wanted somewhere for NV activists to go if they needed to talk and not be overheard.*" Svetlana and Grigori made mental notes of the locations of the safe zones so they could talk in private. Guessing their thoughts, Alina handed them maps of the safe zone locations. "*You should know, there is no surveillance anywhere in this building. It is not allowed.*" The pair shook their heads imperceptibly, they did not want to risk speaking openly around people they hardly knew.

Svetlana wanted to know if Alina was a member of NV, the answer she gave surprised both her and Grigori. "*NV? There are many more organisations than just NV you know.*" Svetlana asked about the other organisations. Grigori shook his head. "*Not now,*" he whispered while taking in the room, though nobody was paying them the slightest attention.

"Are you interested in knowing about the computers and what they are used for or do you have any more questions?"

"We are interested in knowing about the computers… and our jobs too," said Grigori. For caution's sake he did not want to discuss anything else for the time being.

Time dragged for Svetlana and Grigori as their thoughts were on getting to a safety zone so they could talk freely. Before the day was out they were handed lists of those they were responsible for targeting for surveillance and told to memorise them. They wanted to take the lists back to their dormitory to study them but were ordered to lock them in their desks and not talk to anybody about the lists, not even each other. As soon as their shift was over, Svetlana and Grigori raced back to their dormitory, showered and changed. They were so preoccupied that they did not even contemplate having shower sex, they just soaped one another's backs, got dried, got dressed and hightailed it to the safe zone closest to their dormitory.

"What if Alina was lying and there are no such things as safe zones?"

"I do not think we have a choice, we have to trust her… and Alexei too. Besides, we have already said enough to get us both executed. First… Vladimir. Why do you think Major Popov wanted to know if we knew him?"

"I cannot imagine. I would have thought that he is far too much of a goody two shoes to do anything that would interest the KGB."

"But he knows us and might say something incriminating. How can we find out if he has been arrested… they might be torturing him as we speak. We cannot take the chance of calling Moscow… writing is out of the question. We must return to Moscow and find out what is going on. We need to find out if we are safe. Do you agree?"

"Soon nowhere will be safe for us. I have a feeling that the revolution has already started." Grigori was startled by Svetlana's words.

"If you are right then we must get back to Moscow without delay." Svetlana and Grigori planned their next moves while others listened in.

Back in Red Section, Alexei and Galina were handing Alina her winnings from their bet.

"I told you they would go to the nearest safe zone and talk their heads off. They are fools and do not deserve…"

"At least it proves that they are genuine and not here to spy on us."

"I am glad they are not spies… or traitors. I like them. I think they are in love with one another."

"Shut up Galina."

"You are just jealous because they have been chosen to…"

"Jealous? What do I have to be jealous of? I do have a question though. Why them? Of all those who have passed through this place, why them?"

"It is obvious," replied Alexei, confident he knew what Alina did not.

"Well? Tell me, why them? If you know something then say it." Alexei was not going to tell Alina that all those who had passed through Red Section had been taken or killed.

"Alina, it is they and their kind who will lead the revolution and will rule us all afterwards. They are the chosen ones… chosen by the network to…" Alina had heard enough and changed the subject.

"It is our job to turn them into agents. Alexei, I am putting you in charge of their training."

"Thank you boss," replied Alexei sarcastically.

"And Galina," whispered Alina, "not a word of warning to them, okay? We are all expendable and should be happy to die for the cause."

"Okay, I promise. Not a word. But save them if you can. Promise?"

"I promise," whispered a smiling Alina but Galina knew from experience that Alina smiled when she lied.

Alina went to her communications room to make her progress report to Moscow. The Director was very pleased with how things were going and while he was in a good mood Alina asked him for a transfer to active duty. He said he would think about it and changed the subject. She interrupted, saying that she deserved a chance to show what she could do and being stuck in Vladivostok was not the best use of her or her skills. The Director thought for a moment and asked Alina if she knew anything about being a PA. Though she did not know the first thing about PAing she claimed to be an expert. "*In which case I have an assignment for you. You are going to be the PA for a Presidium member of Operation Zima. Congratulations. Your tickets to Moscow will be waiting for you at the airport. Do not disappoint me or let the Network down… or give me any cause to regret my decision.*" Alina said she would rather die than do either and hung up the call. She smiled and lit a cigarette to spite the sign prohibiting smoking.

⋆

Arriving for their afternoon shift, Svetlana and Grigori were surprised to see somebody they did not recognise sat in Alina's seat. Galina informed them that Alina had left to take care of a sick uncle, then gave them a knowing wink and a quick smile. She gestured for Svetlana to sit next to her and told Grigori to sit next to Irina, Alina's replacement. Grigori said he thought he recognised Irina from the previous day. She said she had been sitting under the sector map screen when they were looking at it and that was probably where he recognised her from. They were both certain Irina was lying but could not figure out why.

Alexei appeared at six o'clock, asked how things were going and handed Svetlana and Grigori coded messages on two sheets of paper.

"What is this?" asked Grigori.

"I have been ordered to prepare you. I am responsible for turning you into competent agents."

"What are you talking about?"

"You are already reasonably competent with computers, for amateurs, but now you have to acquire the skills necessary for a critical mission in case you are chosen." Before Svetlana and Grigori could open their mouths to speak Alexei held up his hand to stop them. "Just accept what I am saying for now so we can get on with it. Time is short."

"Can we ask questions?"

"Yes. But not now," smiled Alexei in his weird way. "You will need these," said Alexei handing them the cypher keys. "You are not expected to break cyphers, just be accurate in decrypting them. Both pages must be read in conjunction to understand the message. Go! You have two minutes."

The pair were shocked by what they read. They asked Alexei what he meant by giving them such a message, possession of which would mean death for them both. He told them not to be so dramatic, saying that if they were captured they could eat the special quick dissolving paper in seconds, adding that they should only do so as a last resort as it was impregnated with a fast-acting neurotoxin which would kill them in minutes. Svetlana looked at her hands but was assured by Alexei that, as far as he knew, the neurotoxin could not be absorbed through handling but recommended she did not lick her fingers. "*You should both wash your hands,*" he said. Alexei looked down at his own hands and joined the pair in the bathroom.

The documents Alexei had handed to Svetlana and Grigori were details of a mission to mount an attack on a building in Moscow, incapacitate the guards; "*that is a nice way of saying kill them,*" said Alexei, and take over the computer system. "*To what purpose?*" asked Svetlana. Alexei said the less they knew the better because what they did not know they could not give away under torture… or worse. Grigori asked what was worse than torture. Alexei replied, "*Watching somebody you love being tortured to death right in front of your eyes.*"

Reliving memories, Alexei left the room. Galina took over. She asked if there were "*any questions so far*?" adding that they could not ask her about the coded message.

"What is this mission about Galina?" asked Svetlana.

"Please do not ask me. I cannot say. I do not know."

"I do not believe you…"

"Please, do not ask me anything further… please!"

"Is it something to do with the revolution?" Galina's look told Svetlana that her guess was correct.

"But we know nothing about breaking into buildings… killing guards… taking over computer systems," sputtered Grigori.

"They have faith in you," smiled Galina putting an arm around Grigori. Then she added, "You will not be alone, there is a team."

"You are talking as if we have already been chosen."

"There is not a lot of time left. We must hurry your training."

"Does that mean we have already been chosen?… will we be?…"

"Please, do not ask me anything else."

"You have said too much comrade," whispered Irina menacingly.

⋆

Alexei returned to Red Section after Svetlana and Grigori had left after finishing their shift.

"Did you talk about the mission?"

"She did."

"I did."

"How did they take it?"

"They…"

"Galina must answer."

"Grigori panicked but Svetlana seemed to take the news well."

"Good, well done. They will make for a safe zone, record every word they say. They might whisper so use a directional microphone too."

"I do not trust them. Why have they been chosen? Why not us? Good people… good Russian people. They are just…"

"They have been chosen because of what they represent. If we are successful they and their kind will be running the Soviet Union."

"Then why are we doing all this?"

"Enough! They have been chosen and that is all there is to it. Get on with your work. There is a lot to do."

★

Svetlana and Grigori trudged through the newly fallen snow back to their dormitory. As they reached the door Svetlana grabbed Grigori's arm and dragged him to the safe zone.

"What shall we do my love? Run away?" Grigori thought before giving a croaking reply.

"We will do our duty," he said with emotion in his voice. "Many have sacrificed themselves for the cause and now it is our turn. The Proles will want to see what we are made of; are we sofa-sitting-revolutionaries? Are we all talk or can we fight? You were right, my love, revolution is here. It is not coming, it is here. There is nowhere left to run to so there is nowhere to hide. The time has come to fight and we must do our best even if our best is only to die." Svetlana felt so proud of her Grigori at that moment. She kissed him so hard their teeth clashed.

After talking for ten more minutes, the pair kissed again and then made their way back to their dormitory and went straight to bed. The danger they felt made them feel closer than ever. Though the dormitory was shared by thirty people, nobody paid any attention to their love making. Everybody had their own thoughts to deal with in the darkness.

★

Svetlana and Grigori's conversation was recorded and sent to Moscow.

"I said they were the right choice. I was sure of them all along. I told you. I told you all. They will complete the Tula cell."

"Yes comrade, you told us, you told us all."

"Big deal, so you told us. They have not done anything yet. They might still turn and run away. The first thing Comrade Panshina suggested was they run away."

"It was not a suggestion, it was a question. You could tell by the intonation in her voice."

"They are adventurists looking to salve their pseudo-socialist consciences… typical children of the elite, rebelling against their parents, that is all they are doing. They do not feel the revolution in their hearts as we do."

"Why are we talking about them in this way? They are loyal to the cause."

"I do not doubt they are sincere but are they really loyal? That is the question we should be asking ourselves."

"There has never been any question over their loyalty so why are we discussing it now?" Lev spoke next.

"We are discussing it because the time for action is here… we are facing our moment of truth and we must be sure of everybody. You all talk of things about which you have no knowledge or experience. You are nervous… frightened, I understand that, it is natural. You are concerned for your own safety and that of your families but you must remain strong… strong for the cause. If you show any sign of weakness, or have a moment of doubt, it will spread like wildfire through the ranks. It will be disastrous. We will be defeated before we have even begun. The wheels are in motion comrades and we must trust in those we have chosen to deliver the revolution!"

"Comrade Lev, why did we leave it to the last minute to tell them about the mission?" asked Bogdan. The members of Lev's Revolutionary Council stared at him in disbelief.

"Has it escaped your attention, comrade, that all the others who passed through the Red Channel have been arrested and executed? It is clear that we have a traitor in our midst. Leaving things to the last minute was our best hope that they would make it to join the others in Tula."

"I think it is Alexei who is our traitor," said Valeri.

"Keep such opinions to yourself. Alexei has proven himself many times and besides, he is the only one who knows about what needs to be done with the computers. Without him we are lost." The Revolutionary Council considered Lev's words.

"Comrade Lev, we must ensure that the Tula cell arrives safely in Moscow after they have completed their training."

"That is your job comrade," snapped Lev. "Just make sure you do your job well. The future of our beloved Soviet Union depends on us all doing our jobs well." Lev stood and downed a tumbler of Vodka. "*Long live The People's Will,*" was the toast. "*Long live Lev. Long live The People's Will. Long live la revolucion,*" chorused the Revolutionary Council and downed their tumblers of Vodka. Lev raised his eyes to the ceiling, he was weary of this fad of mixing languages. After the toast the meeting was over and as everybody dispersed Lev turned to Volk and whispered to him to stay close to Bogdan. "*If there are any problems with Comrade Bogdan you know what to do.*" Copying Stalin's methods, Lev always gave ambiguous orders in such matters. If Volk did something that could later be deemed a bad decision then Lev could justify sanctioning him.

Later, when he was alone, Lev sent a coded message to Lieutenant Kozlov at the Vladivostok Pioneer Camp saying it was time to kill the traitor as Svetlana and Grigori had been confirmed as the final members of the Tula cell.

Tula

The flight from Moscow to Tula was short but was the most exciting event of my life up to that point as I had yet to have sex. I often wondered what it would be like when it did eventually happen… that was if it ever happened. I had to keep such thoughts from entering my head otherwise it would… I did not know exactly what it would do but I knew I had to think more positively about my prospects of having sex one day.

I was astounded to be served food, Vodka and beer while flying high in the sky. Olga hiss-whispered that I should stop drinking but I ignored her. Who can resist free Vodka? After four Vodkas I looked across at Olga and noticed how attractive she was. A film was being shown but there was no sound. I noticed some passengers were using earphones to listen to the film. I asked the attendant for earphones. He brought some and asked me for four roubles. I protested at this outrageous price. He replied that if I did not want to pay for extras I should have flown second class. I thought his demeanour effeminate and when I looked across at Olga she smiled and flipped her hand downwards as though she had no bones in her wrist. I got the message.

Through a gap in the curtain at the side of the movie screen I could see into the next compartment, which, I assumed, was second class, and at the front of that compartment was another curtain. Was there a first class? I did not really care, I was drunk-happy.

★

I woke when the plane thumped the ground. It thumped the ground so hard that the passengers let out a chorused scream followed by applause for a safe landing after the bouncing around finished. I knew no different and did likewise. This earned me a black look from Olga. She hiss-whispered that I needed to pull myself together soon as we would be going through airport security and needed to blend in. I had no idea what she was talking about and nor did I care.

I saw through the now open curtains separating the compartments that the passengers from second class were disembarking. After they had all gone the attendant stood to one side and let us through. Standing by the exit were four NKVD Soldiers carrying matt black machine pistols. As I got next to them they pushed me to one side, raised their firearms and shouted for my three companions to lie on the floor. The other passengers panicked but were calmed by the cabin attendant shrieking at them to remain calm. I was shoved out of the plane's door along with the other passengers and told to go to a waiting bus. Walking down the stairs I turned to look back. The NKVD Soldiers were putting Olga and the others in handcuffs. They were not interested in me. I stepped onto the bus and the doors closed with a pneumatic hiss. All the passengers were looking back at the plane, all except me that is, I knew what was going on. It was obvious that we had been betrayed, they were waiting for us, we were expected. But why had they let us come this far? they could have taken us in Moscow. Panic set in. What should I do next? Where shall I go? I decided to follow the other passengers, do what they do, and once out of the airport make my way to… to where? I needed to return to Moscow.

★

Olga, Sergei and Vitaly were dragged down the steps leading from the plane by their hair and thrown into the back of an Armoured Personnel Carrier surrounded by eight black Merkovs with blacked out windows. Inside the APC they were pinned to the floor by eight pairs of boots. All through the forty minute journey they were punched, kicked and beaten with batons on their bodies, arms, legs and genitals but not the head.

The beatings stopped when the APC came to a halt. Olga and the others were dragged out by their hair. After face planting the ground they were kicked to their feet. They crashed through doors as they made their way along corridors. Then everything went silent. To the three the silence seemed worse than the beating. They tensed their bodies awaiting an onslaught of baton blows but nonesuch came. Lines of fluorescent lights flashed on as their hoods were removed. The sight that greeted them terrified them. They were in a tiled room as big as a warehouse. There were cages around the perimeter and metal hoops fixed into the walls… chains… pulleys… metal hawsers. In the middle of the room were stainless steel tables, about forty of them. Next to each table were stainless steel glass fronted cabinets, some housing scalpels, saws, knives, cavity spreaders, secateurs, electric saws, electric drills and hammers of various sizes and head shapes, some were ice-picks. In the smaller cabinets was a selection of syringes and glass bottles, most containing clear liquids but some were coloured. Hoods were forced back over the heads of Olga's compatriots. She noticed movement behind a dark green curtain.

"Where is the fourth member of the cell?" The question was followed by the sound of metal baton on bone. A groan came from behind Olga. She recognised the voice and tried to call out through her gag.

"Remove her gag," ordered the KGB Colonel. Olga twisted round to see Dmitri. He was in bad shape. He had obviously been through what she and her compatriots were about to go through.

"Dmitri," Olga whispered tearfully, "what have they done to you my Angel?… why have they done this?"

"You know why. Do not play games comrade," said an Officer calmly.

"Why would you do this to…" Olga choked on her words.

"To who?"

"To good Russian people… people fighting for freedom… everybody's freedom, including yours."

"Oh, I see. So, you are a freedom fighter?" said the Officer sarcastically. "I thought you were a member of a banned political group calling itself Narodnaya Volya?"

"I have nothing more to say."

"We shall see about that. You do know that NV has been allowed to exist to concentrate all the traitors in one place so we can destroy them? Do you think that you were so clever as to fool us when your headquarters is right next to the Ministry of Travel? You expect us not to know what goes on there and in the underground auditorium at the university? We have been listening in ever since you began… Narodnaya Volya; The People's Will. Ha!" Mock-laughed the KGB Colonel to taunt Olga. He was letting her and the others know how much he already knew in the hope that they would break more quickly. Time was of the essence. "The People's Will indeed. Could you not think up an original name? Naming yourselves after a long dead movement. Pathetic."

"I do not believe you. You are just trying to get us to open up." Olga was not fooled by the KGB Colonel's tactics.

"Where is the fourth member of your cell? Did he travel with you? Where is he? Was he on the same flight as you? How did we miss him? Is it a he? Or a she?" Olga shook her head. "Ah, it is a she. Did she travel with you? Or did she travel on ahead? Is she yet to arrive? Who is she? Name her! Who is the fourth member of your cell?"

"I do not know her identity. You know the protocol, we do not know what we do not need to know…"

"She is lying Comrade Colonel," said an Officer stood behind Vitaly.

"Of course she is lying," screamed the KGB Colonel, exasperated at the ineptitude of his subordinate. "Tell me where she is otherwise you and your… take their hoods off." The remaining hoods were removed. "Ah, Sergei… Vitaly. May I still call you Serge, Sergei?"

Sergei mumbled a reply through his gag. "Leave it on for now, I can guess his reply. Now comrade, as I was saying, tell me where she is otherwise you and your comrades will go to the tables." Said the KGB Colonel pointing at the stainless steel tables and their companion cabinets. Olga's throat dried at the thought of being strapped to a table and interrogated.

"I do not know who she is. She was to make contact with us. You know how it works, we cannot tell you what we do not know."

"What is your mission here in Tula?"

"Mission? If by mission you mean the conference we were to attend for the furthering of..."

"Where is the message you are carrying?"

"Message? There is no message, we were to be..."

"Liar!" The KGB Colonel nodded to an NKVD Soldier. He punched Olga in the stomach so hard that she vomited.

"Bring their luggage to me."

"Comrade Colonel, they did not have any luggage with them. It must still be at the airport."

"Have you searched them?"

"Yes Comrade Colonel, they only had these few possessions on them." A KGB Lieutenant tipped a motley collection of items onto an interrogation table.

"The messages must still be in their luggage. Unless we locate the fourth person we will never decode the message. She must be found." The KGB Colonel ordered a dozen KGB and NKVD Officers to accompany him to the airport to search for the prisoners' luggage. "Bring Dmitri in case he can identify the missing target. In the meantime take Olga and her friends to the tables. Get the cypher out of their heads."

Olga, Sergei and Vitaly were picked up and slammed onto stainless steel tables. They were strapped down using heavy-duty, brass-bound, leather straps and injected with a psychotropic cocktail specially designed to enhance the horrors they were about to experience. Behind them they heard the high pitched whine of a bone saw coming closer.

"Comrade Colonel, did the prisoner tell you the identity of the female we are looking for?" Asked an NKVD Officer.

"Female? Olga gave that away far too readily. We are probably looking for a male and he was most likely travelling with the other three. Somehow your men missed him on the plane. Check the tapes as soon as we arrive at the airport. With any luck our missing NV operative will have been met at the airport. We might bag more rats than we thought we would. Come on, drive faster! We have no time to lose."

⋆

It felt as though everybody in the airport was watching me. Every time I looked up my eyes seemed to meet other eyes which quickly darted away. Following along behind the other passengers I scanned all around the baggage hall to see if anybody was paying attention to what I was doing. Not properly looking where I was going I bumped into an old man, "*That hurt. Look where you are going*!" I apologised and helped the old man with his baggage. We walked through security control together and then I left him to the care of his family.

I went to a café bar on the upper gallery and watched as people made their way to I knew not where. I felt truly alone. Panic gripped me. What should I do? Give myself up to the authorities and tell them some sad tale about… abduction? I could not think of a story that would not lead to me being arrested and then what? Tortured? Executed? I regretted ever getting involved in this foolish adventure. As I looked across to the other side of the arrivals hall I noticed two men and a woman. Were they looking at me? They were looking at me! I looked away. The next time I looked they were gone. Before I could stand to leave the café bar the female I had seen came and sat at my table.

"Do not cause a fuss. We do not want to attract attention, do we?" I shook my head. The two men I had spied sauntered over to the table and mumbled to the female.

"As far as we can tell he was not being watched."

"That is lucky for you. We have to get you out of here."

"I just thought the same thing."

"Vladimir," the woman knew my name! "you need to tell us what happened to the others in your cell… but not here. Keep thinking while we make our getaway." I was highly suspicious of the woman and her two companions. What if they were KGB? At that thought the woman made a sign for NV.

"How do you know anything happened?" I asked as nonchalantly as I could.

"A couple of the other passengers are NV. They told us about Olga and the others being taken. I wonder why you were not? Until I am satisfied that you are clean you will be treated as a traitor. In case you are thinking of making a break for it there are more of us concealed around the airport, you will not make it."

★

I was driven away from the airport in the back of a van. I heard one of the men say to the female that I looked a bit like Dmitri and he wondered if I was a relative of his. The female asked me if I was one of Dmitri's relatives. I said I was not but Lev had asked the same thing. At the mention of Lev's name everybody turned and stared at me. The female asked if I had really met Lev and I told her that it was Lev himself who gave me this mission. She gave me a look as if to say, '*tell me another one*'. I told them about the events from when Hyram mistook me for Dmitri in the line outside the Ministry of Travel to meeting Diana, "*Dmitri's sister?*" the female butted in. "*Yes, the very same,*" I replied and continued my tale, telling how I had been given this mission by Lev and the discussion with Olga in Moscow airport and… the female said that was enough and removed my handcuffs.

"Hand it over."

"Hand what over?"

"This is not the time to play games Mister Vakhnenko," said the female in American. "You obviously still have it so hand it over."

I removed a small plastic bag taped to my armpit, wiped it down and handed it to the female. She took it from me with the very-most extended tips of her fingers and shook the sheet of paper from the plastic bag. I asked her what her name was. She said, "*Alice*" then warned me against trying to retrieve the sheet of paper, saying it was covered in a neurotoxin solution and I would die an agonising death if I ate it. Olga had not mentioned '*agonising*' in her little speech about eating the document.

The female scanned the lines of the message and then asked me if I knew what had happened to the other three sheets of paper. I said that they must still be with Olga and the others. She reckoned that they had most likely been taken to a KGB facility on the outskirts of Tula, about a forty minute drive from the airport.

By the time we reached the safe house I had everything crystal clear in my head until Alice began questioning me. She was like a machine gun. Question after question after question. How could she ask so many questions about such a small number of events? A messenger arrived and told Alice that the KGB had returned to the airport with Dmitri in tow. The messenger said he looked in bad shape. Alice deduced that they were probably looking for the sheets of paper. She asked me again about luggage. I confirmed that we had none, "*not even hand luggage.*" Alice surmised that Olga and the others must still have the documents on them otherwise the KGB would not have gone to the airport. "*Having Dmitri with them means they are looking to identify the fourth member of the cell.*" That made sense to me.

⋆

The KGB Colonel was incandescent with rage after no luggage for the prisoners was found at the airport and even more angry when it was confirmed from Moscow airport that they had no luggage with them. Then it hit him. Olga and the others must have either hidden the documents on their bodies, "*but Comrade Colonel, we searched them all thoroughly and found nothing*," or they had disposed of them at their moment of capture. He knew they could not have eaten them as they were still alive.

"At least, Comrade Colonel, we know that the fourth member of the cell looks like Dmitri so he should not be hard to spot on the surveillance recordings." The KGB Colonel was frantic. He knew the price he would pay for failure.

"Where is the plane they arrived on?"

"It is on its way back to Moscow comrade…"

"Get it back here, now! And you, Comrade Sokolov, why did you not tell me that your brother was the fourth member of the cell." To save his family from arrest, torture and death, Dmitri gave Vladimir away.

"Comrade Colonel, I swear that the man on the recording is not my brother. I have never met him or seen him before in my life. Check the records, that man is not my brother."

What seem like small, seemingly insignificant, pieces of information have value. Dmitri's information stopped the KGB Colonel from pursuing a dead-end line of enquiry and set pursuers on Vladimir's trail. Had Dmitri played along, the KGB would eventually have found out that the fourth member of the cell was not his brother. This would have bought the mission valuable time. But Dmitri had suffered greatly and did not want his family to go through the same thing so he did what he did and would die with that on his conscience.

★

Having established that none of us travelled with luggage, and I had picked my portion of the message out of my armpit, Alice asked the obvious question and I replied that I had no idea where the others had hidden their sheets of paper. She thought for a moment.

"It will not be long before the other sheets are discovered. We must go to the Smirnovsk complex and…"

"And what? What will we do, Alice? Smirnovsk is a fortified torture house full of…"

"A what?" I asked as if I had not heard the words I had clearly heard.

"A torture house! They are all over the place. There are about a hundred in the Tula region alone. They are getting ready for something."

"I think I know what it is they are getting ready for and I think that is what the message is about… I think."

"So, Mister Vakhnenko, what is it all about?"

"Terror is about to be unleashed on the people of the Soviet Union. Lev told us that the Central Committee is losing control and they are going to use old style Terror to regain it. They believe Terror is the only way to make the USSR great again."

"Are they crazy? Or are you crazy?"

"No, he is not crazy, it makes sense and if something makes sense then it is right. We have to retrieve the messages from the others."

"How?"

"We will mount an assault on the torture house at Smirnovsk to rescue Olga and the others."

"That is suicide! There are dozens of guards there… they are Spetsnaz. Every one of them is a trained killer."

"Spetsnaz? Rubbish! You do not know what you are talking about. What would Spetsnaz be doing guarding a KGB operation? You are just trying to spread panic because you are a coward."

"Shut up both of you. If Olga and her team are still in possession of the documents then we have no choice we have to go. If what

Mister Vakhnenko says is true we will be amongst the first to go so we have no choice."

"May I suggest something?" asked a slightly built female who had been listening from the side-lines.

"Sure, why not."

"As Mister Vakhnenko supposedly looks like Dmitri we could dress him up like Dmitri and see if that gets us past the guards at the main gate. It is only a small building so there cannot be that many guards inside it. If it does not work we would be close enough to them to overpower them with the element of surprise."

"Petra, you are not just a pretty face, you are a genius."

"Genius? It is a crazy idea! They will not fall for it!" barked Mikhail.

"It is not your decision Mikhail, I am the leader of this cell and I say we go."

"How about we put it to a vote?"

"We are not communards, Mikhail, we are an NV cell and I am its Commander. So what I say goes and we go in five minutes."

Petra handed me a selection of clothes and recommended which I should wear to most look like Dmitri. I checked myself in a mirror. I was not convinced. The clothes were a terrible fit. They were too big for me. Petra pinched the jacket at the back and put safety pins all down the bunched seam, she pinned me too. She recalled Dmitri was taller than me and suggested I walk on tip toes. While I was practising my '*walk as tall as possible to look like Dmitri walk*' Petra brought Alice and the others into the room. They creased up laughing at the sight and I realised Petra had played a joke on me. "*Very funny, this is serious!*" When I returned to the main room everybody was walking around on tip toes and laughing. The laughter lightened my mood and took away the fear of what we were about to do.

*

The van we used to travel to the Smirnovsk torture house in was, I was assured, identical to the vans used by the KGB when they disappeared people. I sat in the front passenger seat, the driver looked every inch KGB, especially the haircut. The rest of Alice's cell were hiding in the cargo compartment, Markovs cocked and at the ready.

The torture house was accessed by a thin strip of winding road enclosed on either side by a twenty foot high electrified barbed wire fence. It is impossible to turn a vehicle around in them. At the far end of the road was a concrete bunker with a slot cut into it which had a large calibre machine gun muzzle sticking out of it. There was an armoured machine gun nest on top of the guard post roof. We pulled up alongside the window and a guard asked us for our IDs. The driver produced a KGB Lieutenant's ID and pointed at me. I leaned forward to show my face. The guard nodded her head in the direction of the barrier and we proceeded on through. We were in.

We parked inside the loading bay and closed the metal roller doors behind us. I opened the back door of the van and was startled by eight Markovs pointing at my face. Inside my head I heard them fire. It was like a firing squad. I never shook the thought that it might be a premonition. It could be my fate.

The building was well signposted. We followed the signs to the '*Interrogation Centre*'. We walked down four corridors separated by swing doors. When we reached the Interrogation Centre we hid in the darkness of its perimeter. The middle of the room was lit by cones of yellowish light from angle poise lamps attached to the stainless steel tables; next to which were cabinets containing stainless steel instruments. The horrors in that room froze me.

Olga, Sergei and Vitaly were connected to shiny metal machines that 'beeped' to their individual rhythms. Intravenous liquids of various hues hung above them, their tubes inserted into necks, stomachs, legs and arms. Next to each of them was an electric shock machine, their red lights indicating they were fully charged and ready to use.

Alice whispered for me to walk toward the people interrogating Olga. As I approached, a white-coated assistant from another table looked at me, looked away, and then looked at me again. It was clear that she was not taken in by my Dmitri disguise. In response to the assistant's reaction to me Alice raised her Markov and shot her twice in the head. "*Double tap, it is the only way to be sure*," was the instruction given to me before we set off. I went for my gun but by the time I held it up to shoot somebody the torturers were all dead. I remembered something else, "*Aim for the middle as that way if you miss by a little you will hit something.*" Looking at the bodies lying on the floor they had all been shot in the head. So much for the advice I had been given.

When I looked around at what had been a merry group I fell to my knees and sobbed deep shoulder shuddering tear filled sobs; my comrades were all past saving. I looked at Alice. She knew what I was thinking. She nodded to me once in the direction of Olga.

"Say your goodbyes."

"Olga," I whispered in her ear, my trembling lips brushing her cheek. Olga turned her head toward me with empty eye sockets. "We came as quickly as we could." I could not look back at her.

"What are you doing here Vladimir?" Olga's voice was croaky-dry. I gave her a sip of water. "Why have you come? Dmitri, they have my Dmitri!"

"We know." Alice said just loud enough to be heard.

"They cannot read the message without your part. Destroy it Vladimir. Destroy it now."

"Alice has it." I called her over.

"Olga, the KGB is checking luggage at the airport. You travelled without luggage so where are the other parts of the message?"

"They took them," replied Olga, nodding in the direction of the deceased torturers. "Destroy Vladimir's part… if they find out what the message is about… we are lost… we are all lost!"

"I need the other parts of the message. Where did they take them?"

"I do not know."

"Olga, please… give me the cypher."

"No, if they capture you…"

"Olga, please give Alice the cypher… it is important that she has it." Olga looked toward the ceiling and then turned her head back towards us.

"What are you going to do about us?"

"We cannot take you with us."

"I understand." Olga took several deep breaths before she was able to continue. "The cypher is alternate prime numbers between one and nine hundred and ninety seven. The key is one hundred and thirty one. The second level cypher is the unused prime numbers and the key is three hundred and thirty one." Olga paused for a moment before continuing. "Who will do it?"

"I will," replied Alice matter-of-factly.

"What about Vladimir? What will happen to him?"

"We will take him in. He can join the fight here in Tula."

"I may as well fight here as anywhere."

"Vladimir," Olga gasped. I moved close.

"I am here, Olga."

"Listen to me carefully comrade. If you want to stay alive keep a low profile… do not go looking for glory. If you get caught remember this; under interrogation or torture, no matter what the evidence against you, deny everything at all times. Always stick to your story. Never change it; ever. That is your best chance for survival. Remember, most of all, if you want to stay alive keep a low profile," she repeated. "Do not go looking for glory… it will be your downfall. Now leave me with Alice, we have things to discuss." I was not fooled, I knew what she meant. I kissed Olga on the cheek and went to say my goodbyes to Sergei and Vitaly.

A thought entered my head, I could not prevent it manifesting. I did not want it but I was powerless to stop it; '*my luck is holding out.*' I was disgusted with myself for having this thought. I wanted to take a knife and cut it from existence. Alice asked me what was wrong. I replied that nothing was wrong. She said that we all have thoughts we cannot help having.

Alice's cell searched the torturers and found the remaining three parts of the message. They cut them up and distributed them between themselves. The chances of us all being taken and all parts of the message being retrieved was now zero so Lev's message was safe.

★

After sitting in the van for ten minutes Alice emerged into the loading bay from the door that led to the Interrogation Centre. She said we had five minutes to make our getaway before the explosives went off. Banging the side of the van she shouted, "Time to go." Ully drove out of the loading bay and toward the security station. As she got close, she flashed the van's headlights and indicated with upward movements of the back of her hand for the guard to open the barrier, which she did. She saluted us as we drove past.

We parked the van around a nearby bend and waited for the explosion. The whole site had to be destroyed because we could not afford for the KGB to find evidence of our visit. If the device was discovered or it failed to go off we would have to attack the building and destroy everything. Alice checked her watch and counted down from ten to zero. Nothing. As we sat staring at one another there was a massive explosion. Ully and two others left the van to check the aftermath of the blast. When they returned Ully reported that the whole building had been flattened and she had destroyed what had remained of the guard post with RPGs. She was confident there were no survivors. With everything gone the KGB would never even know we were ever there. We left the scene in sombre mood at the loss of our comrades. Five miles down the road we passed a convoy of KGB vehicles heading toward the torture house.

A Short Course in Espionage

Svetlana and Grigori noticed there were twice as many KGB Officers and four times as many NKVD Soldiers in the Pioneer Camp that morning. When they were ten yards from the Security Section building Major Popov of the KGB shouted for them to stop where they were. When they turned to face him they saw dozens of trucks pulling onto the main parade ground. Popov looked incredibly pleased with himself after he told them that they were coming with him. He ordered them both onto the back of one of the trucks which were rapidly being filled with Camp Counsellors and Pioneers of all ages. Four floors below the parade ground, on Red Section's large surveillance screen, Alexei saw what was happening and ran to get help.

Within a minute of Alexei's warning, Lieutenant Kozlov burst through the doors of the Security Section building accompanied by a dozen Spetsnaz geared up in black balaclavas and toting machine pistols. They spread out either side of the Lieutenant as twenty more Spetsnaz emerged on rooftops around the parade ground. Though the Spetsnaz were heavily outnumbered, nobody fancied taking them on.

"Major Popov, by order of the Vladivostok Revolutionary Council you are ordered to release your prisoners and you and those with you are ordered to leave this Pioneer Camp immediately and never return." As the Lieutenant finished speaking the clicks of the Spetsnaz's machine pistols echoed around the parade ground.

"Lieutenant Kozlov," responded Major Popov in confident voice, "I will do no such thing." Then the Major looked around at his forces expecting them to likewise cock their weapons. They stood frozen like statues, fearful of moving a muscle in case all Spetsnaz hell broke loose. "Cowards!" screamed the Major and thought for the briefest of moments about removing his pistol from its holster but decided, wisely, to leave it where it was.

"All of you! I order you to stand down!" Shouted Lieutenant Kozlov to the Major's forces. "Release the prisoners!" The prisoners jumped down from the trucks and ran for cover. "You now have a choice. You can return to your homes or you can remain here for the fight ahead." The Spetsnaz beckoned those who wanted to join the fight. "Major Popov, take your trucks and your troops and leave while you can." At this, many of the troops walked across the parade ground and joined the Spetsnaz. A loud cheer greeted them. They had made their decision. KGB Major Popov jumped into his staff car and ordered his driver to take him to the airport.

"Who the hell are the Vladivostok Revolutionary Council?" asked Alexei.

"Anybody who wants to join the fight."

"What fight?"

"Alexei, please, do not act the innocent with me. Do you think I do not know what goes on here? War is coming and I have chosen my side. I hope I chose well comrade." With that the Lieutenant left to speak with '*The Pride and the Glory of The Revolution*', as he now referred to the Spetsnaz.

Entering the Security Section building, Alexei told Svetlana and Grigori to follow him, '*they had four days to prepare for their mission.*' They took the lift down to the second level to commence their training.

★

Four days was not enough time for Svetlana and Grigori to absorb a tenth of what they would need to know for their mission but Lieutenant Kozlov promised them that he would prepare them as best he could for what lay ahead. The Lieutenant then introduced them to a Spetsnaz instructor. None of the Spetsnaz wore anything denoting their rank but as other Spetsnaz deferred to her the pair assumed she was an Officer.

First on the agenda was buildings entry. In the civilian world this is breaking and entering. The Spetsnaz trainer was a wiry male of five foot ten called Mikhail. He could pick locks in seconds, climbed like a circus performer and could wriggle through impossibly small spaces. Just to prove it could be done he scrambled through the entire air ducting system in the ceiling cavity, including six right angles. Svetlana poked her head inside an air duct vent and said, "*This is not for you Grigori.*" A shiver shook down her spine at the thought of being confined in such a small dark space.

The pair were provided with lock picking kits and under Mikhail's instruction they learned to crack a whole variety of locks. Grigori complained that the kits were incomplete and was told that they had belonged to somebody who had given his life for the cause. Svetlana felt Grigori's shame.

Next was scaling walls and crossing open spaces by rope. Firing the air powered gun that sent a grapple over a wall set Svetlana on her backside, to the amusement of Grigori who ended up in the same position when it was his turn to try it. Resisting the kick of the air powered grappling launcher took them some getting used to.

When the day was over they were ordered to the far end of an obstacle course where they were met by a Spetsnaz who introduced herself as Mikhail. Then they got it, names could be given away under torture so they were all Mikhail. This Mikhail was an expert in self-defence. She knew they were tired and so just taught them basic throws, rolls and elbow cracks against the joint.

"You were too easy on them," commented the Spetsnaz Officer.

"They are tired and weak. They will do better tomorrow."

"What do you think of them?"

"Svetlana shows promise. Grigori?… I am not sure about him yet."

★

Day two began where day one left off, self-defence, but this time it was hand to hand armed combat. They each had their own instructor called Mikhail. The first exercise was to defend themselves against assailants armed with knives. "*Is there any need to use real knives?*" Moaned Grigori. Svetlana raised her eyes to the ceiling and asked the instructors to ignore her boyfriend. "*Boyfriend? We did not know you two were in a relationship. That could compromise the mission.*" The instructors sought advice but were ordered to just get on with it, there was no time for substitutions. Once again Svetlana shone brightest and even had her instructor tapping out of the arm holds she put him in. Grigori claimed that Svetlana's instructor was going easy on her because she was a female. Mikhail walked away shaking his head.

The evening session of day two was safe cracking and saw the return of the first Mikhail. He told them that he had learned his safe cracking from an American special services operative who had been converted in the 90s. "*Safe cracking is fun. The easiest safe to crack is one manufactured by Sovsafe.*" There was nothing to choose between Svetlana and Grigori as to which was best.

★

Day three concentrated on killing people, '*assassinating*' them as the Spetsnaz Officer referred to it as. She was stealthy and deadly with a Kommando dagger. The methods they were being trained in were all silent. They were only to use their supressed Markov's as a last resort. "*Killing somebody is not like you see in the films. If you shoot somebody they do not magically die the next second. The only sure kill shot is a head shot... even then they might live long enough to raise the alarm. So, the only way to be certain is to be close to your target and by close I mean touching close. Let us consider the garrotte...*" Mikhail moved like lightning, grabbed Grigori, pulled him to the floor and somehow, while carrying out the manoeuvre, she slipped a garrotte round his throat and locked it. Grigori's eyes were bulging before Mikhail released him.

Svetlana showed to be the best with the garrotte. She was much more physically gifted than she realised, which surprised her as she had never fought with her hands before.

★

Day four. The Spetsnaz Officer announced. "*Today, Alexei will be teaching you about breaking into computers. The two who should have been doing this committed suicide rather than let the KGB find out what was in their heads.*" The pair looked at one another; this was real, this was serious. What was expected of them now? Alexei spoke next.

"You were chosen because you are familiar with computers and could follow operating instructions without getting confused and that is why you were placed in Red Section. Mikhail and I will go over what you need to do once you are inside the target building."

"We already know a lot about computers. We used them before we came here and I even programmed one of them for the Irregular Society."

"Svetlana... Grigori, the computer you will be gaining access to is very different to the ones you are familiar with... including those you have used here..." Svetlana and Grigori looked sceptical.

"If something goes wrong we will need a backup."

"We have a backup in Tula."

Alexei tutored Svetlana while Grigori was tutored by Mikhail. He was very unhappy at this as he did not like the way Alexei looked at Svetlana. Grigori noticed that whenever Svetlana was distracted Alexei took the opportunity to stare lustfully at her. For the time being though he had to push his jealousy to the back of his mind, there was a job to do. Then Alina's words of doubt about their sponsorship came back to him. It was all just too much of a coincidence for this to happen the way it had. Somebody had to be behind it.

Svetlana was the star pupil with the computer lessons and it was agreed that she would take the lead once they were inside the target building.

It was important for the success of the mission to put everything they had learned into practise by demonstrating their competence. They were ordered to break into the Camp Commandant's office, pick the lock on his desk drawer, remove his Soviet travel passport and place it in his wall safe. Then they were to start his computer, load a disc Alexei had given them and follow the instructions that came up on the screen. If they completed this last part successfully a message would be sent to Alexei's computer. Svetlana and Grigori were filmed while they went about their B&E of the Camp Commandant's office. When they returned to the Security Section and reported how the mission had gone the Spetsnaz Soldiers congratulated them with hard slaps on their backs and tumblers of Vodka. They had passed the espionage course.

Alexei had good news. The NV Commanders in Moscow had seen the footage of the pair in action and were very impressed. Alexei shook their hands so earnestly he almost broke Svetlana's wrist.

★

As Svetlana and Grigori entered Red Section to say their goodbyes, they were grabbed from behind, hooded, handcuffed, gagged and dragged away at pace. Those in the open area of the fourth level wondered what was going on but in those places nobody asked any questions. They just bent their heads to their desks and carried on with their work, assuming it was the KGB going about its work and the people they were taking away were traitors, wreckers, saboteurs, guilty of anti-Soviet activities or whatever. Each silently prayed that it would never be them in the sacking hoods.

The door to the stairwell banged shut. Svetlana and Grigori were dragged up flights of stairs and catapulted through a door which slammed hard shut behind them. They guessed they were on the third underground level.

"Remove their hoods and handcuffs. Welcome to your final training session. We have a little surprise for you. Today we are going to cover resistance to interrogation techniques. You are going to learn how to stay alive in enemy hands while not giving anything away." When their eyes adjusted to the light they saw Lieutenant Kozlov standing in front of them, by his side was a bank of batteries and pairs of electric leads terminated in saw-toothed bulldog clips.

Before the session began, Svetlana and Grigori were given tuition on how best to act during interrogation to try to avoid torture by appearing to be compliant and cooperative. They were advised never to be confrontational and always stick to whatever cover story you had been given no matter how ridiculous it was or how much evidence the KGB had that the cover story was a lie. "*In America*," the Spetsnaz Officer said, "*this was called the FBI defence; deny everything at all times no matter what the weight of evidence is against you.*"

After being given their cover story and IDs, the session began with a few simple questions; their names, their ages; they had been given obviously incorrect ages; their schools, they had been given schools that were single sex schools and each was the wrong gender for the school they had given. "*Keep up the lie no matter what*," were their instructions. When asked about their ages, Grigori, who was clearly not forty, claimed he was cursed with "*youthful looks*", giving his interrogators stories about being old enough to do things but did not appear to be so, "*I was not allowed to take driving lessons until I produced my birth certificate and then they accused me of forgery.*" Svetlana thanked her interrogators for the compliment, she said it was important for Soviet women to always look young and attractive for their husbands. The way they handled being the wrong gender for their schools was equally creative. Then they were told they would have to keep up their stories under torture. The interrogators said that they would not torture them too severely but they had to know what to expect. They both stuck to their stories even after Grigori bit off the end of his tongue while being electrocuted. After an hour they were told that the resistance to interrogation session was over. Grigori thought they were being lulled into a false sense of security and said so to Svetlana. She agreed with him.

Lieutenant Kozlov ordered Svetlana and Grigori to follow him. They entered a large room brightly lit by rows of end to end fluorescent light fittings of the type that makes pale skin look translucent. Their eyes locked onto the weapons lying on a trestle table. On the opposite side of the room sat four bound, gagged, and hooded figures, each secured on a metal chair with Lubyanka bracelets.

The Lieutenant drew his Markov 9 mil from his holster and attached a silencer to the business end. He then cocked the Markov, putting a round in the chamber. The hooded figures reacted to the sound of the Markov being cocked by making frantic mumbling noises. One sounded like she was praying. The Lieutenant said that the prisoners had been interrogated but so far they had refused to speak. He said he wanted to find out which of them had attempted to sell out Svetlana and Grigori by passing a film of the burglary of the Camp Commandant's office to the KGB. The pair thought it was all a game and that they were probably going to be asked to find out '*who did it*'. Svetlana smiled and made to walk toward the prisoners but was stopped by a Spetsnaz with such force that Grigori made a move towards him but was cut down from behind by a blow to his head.

By the time Grigori came to his senses Lieutenant Kozlov was standing in front of one of the prisoners, his Markov inches from the man's face. The Lieutenant asked the prisoner to give him the name of the person he had attempted to sell the footage of the burglary to. The prisoner mumbled an answer which the Lieutenant did not like. He screamed that he was sick of having his time wasted and shot the prisoner point blank in the chest. The man's body keeled over sideways, still on his chair, onto the floor. The Lieutenant said to Svetlana that he was not one hundred percent certain that the man he had just killed was the traitor. He ordered her to choose a weapon from the table and continue the interrogation.

Without a moment's hesitation, Svetlana picked up a Markov 9 mil from the table, fitted a silencer to it, cocked it and walked across the room toward the prisoners, shouting, "If any of you wants to confess about selling me out to the KGB you should speak now!" The three remaining prisoners stayed silent and motionless. Lieutenant Kozlov whispered to Svetlana that he now believed that it was probably the middle prisoner of the remaining three who was the traitor. He ordered her to shoot him in the head. Without questioning the order, Svetlana went to stand in front of the hooded, gagged and bound prisoner, raised her Markov and squeezed the trigger. The muzzle flash from the pistol caused the prisoner to shout out, "*Shit, she burned my nose. Get some water.*"

The guards laughed, pulled the smoking hood off Mikhail's head and doused his nose with water. The Lieutenant told them it was a test and that the weapons on the table were loaded with blanks. Svetlana said she guessed as much. Lieutenant Kozlov said, "*Somebody did try to sell the footage of the burglary to the KGB.*" Svetlana asked if it was Alexei. A voice from beneath the first hood from the left shouted that he had never felt so insulted. Grigori laughed and said his money would have been on Alexei too. He still had it in for Alexei for the way he looked at Svetlana while her head was turned.

After untying Alexei and the Spetsnaz volunteers everybody shook hands to show there were no hard feelings and made to leave the room. Svetlana turned and pointed to the slumped figure still on the floor and asked, "*What about him? Is he not coming too*?" The Lieutenant replied that the man was dead, "*He was the traitor.*" Neither Svetlana nor Grigori fully took in what the Lieutenant had said for a few seconds. They had never witnessed an execution before and were in a state of shock. A hand placed around their shoulders guided them from the room. "*Okay, that is resistance to interrogation done… and how to deal with traitors. Now comrades, you must leave straightaway. News has reached us that the KGB has moved against NV and Lev has fled Moscow and gone into hiding.*"

Lieutenant Kozlov did not tell Svetlana and Grigori that the traitor had in fact sold the footage of the burglary to his KGB handler before the local NV cell apprehended him. He would only tell them if he failed to locate the footage and destroy it; in the meantime they did not need to know anything more about it, they had enough on their minds.

*

Over the previous four years, Alexei had been breaking into the computer systems of the Red Army, the KGB and the NKVD and altered records. For months on end tens of millions of citizens were not paid a kopek and when they finally received their back-pay they were paid too little or too much, sometimes a lot too much or a lot too little. Overpayments had to be repaid but in most cases the money was already spent. These errors caused a lot of anger amongst the ordinary Soldiers of the Red Army and low-level administrators of the KGB and NKVD. Alexei never messed up the Officers' pay.

NV let everybody know that Officers never had any problems with their pay; "*it goes into their banks as regular as clockwork every month without* fail" and "*bonuses are paid to them for unknown reasons.*" The spread of this information caused a massive rift between grunts and Officers, administrators and agents. Each group historically distrusted the other and this boiled over into outright hatred after NV stirred the pot.

Through this method, NV had recruited a great many supporters for their cause in the Soviet Union's armed forces as well as its secret services. Some were plants of course but even they started to believe in NV after learning what they stood for. They wanted to see change and NV appeared to be the best way of bringing change about.

★

Shortly after Svetlana and Grigori left for Tula, Alexei was summoned by Lev to join him and his Revolutionary War Council in hiding.

Everybody Wins

Alexander Orlov's winter break this year was more a working holiday than a vacation. He had even left his beautiful young wife, Vronika, back in Moscow, much to her chagrin. Officially, Comrade Orlov was in the USA at the direction of Maxim Kirilenko to meet with his American counterparts. He had proven very useful to Comrade Kirilenko on numerous occasions in the past and he expected to benefit from his Chef de Cabinet's American trip. It being so close to the start of the Terror, Kirilenko was desperate to find out what the Americans knew about it and if they were planning to intervene by inciting righteous revolution instead of the one he had prepared. Comrade Kirilenko was desperate that his Chef de Cabinet return to Moscow as soon as possible with news of what was happening in America.

On the morning of the penultimate day of his US trip, Alexander Orlov woke later than usual and ate a large brunch at his leisure. Having no official business that day he planned to do some shopping; he had an extensive list of '*must haves*' from his wife. It was a long list, proportional to her displeasure with him for not taking her to the USA. With what he had to arrange how could he have brought her along given her propensity to blab his secrets to her friends?

★

Comrade Orlov had held some degree of power since his early twenties serving several General Secretaries of the USSR but he never had any love in his life until he met his Vronika. He saw that women are attracted to powerful men but not so him with the way he looked. He lusted after Vronika from the moment he met her and pestered her for two years before she finally relented and agreed to marry him. He had tried everything to snare her, even contemplating threatening her family to convince her to marry him on threat of being sent to the Lubyanka. He was not an easy man to love, not least due to his partially deformed body but also his manner which was unattractive too plus he was rather malodourous and boring. His face, with its Neanderthal brow, was no oil painting and his hair sprouted rather than grew. Orlov's fingers were like fat, greasy, Russian sausages. He knew what everybody who looked at him thought of his features and he used his power to make them suffer for their stares. He even had a blind woman taken to the Lubyanka for recoiling from him after she had felt his facial features during a veterans' day visit to the Kremlin; how the Central Committee and Kremlin Guard laughed at that one.

For some reason Comrade Orlov could not explain, people in America hardly ever stared at him. It was as though they accepted him for what he was. Nor, it seemed, did they pity him, they just dealt with him on whatever level whenever he interacted with them. It was not as though it was the people he had to work with who behaved this way, it was everybody in every walk of life; waiters, bartenders, shop assistants, even the barber he visited during his trips to New York. Comrade Orlov's KGB bodyguards too noticed this behaviour, or lack of it. For their part, they were happy to let him go about his business, often unguarded, so they could enjoy the delights of America. America was the land of opportunity for them too. While going about their business, official or otherwise, the KGB guards well knew that they were being watched by the American Secret Service who, of course, could not afford to have anything happen to Alexander Orlov, Chef de Cabinet to Maxim Kirilenko, General Secretary of the Soviet Union, on American soil. This situation suited Comrade Orlov and his KGB guards down to the ground. He was a little concerned about the American Secret

Service following him to his meetings with '*The 400*' but as they were in the guise of a consortium of financiers interested in funding projects in the Soviet Union such meetings would not arouse suspicion given the state of the USSR's finances.

*

After brunch, he loved what the Americans had done in creating that word, Alexander asked the concierge about a new menswear store he had seen advertised in the hotel's lobby. Could he recommend it? Had he been there? and so forth. The concierge said he had heard from other guests that it was excellent but expensive, even for Fifth Avenue. Alexander said it sounded like it was the store for him and, without his asking, the concierge ordered a taxi and it was waiting outside for him by the time he exited the revolving doors with his KGB bodyguards in tow. He could not get away from them all the time, especially as they knew his habits and therefore they knew, with it being Comrade Orlov's second to last day, he was going shopping.

The so-called taxis which always seemed to be on hand for Comrade Orlov were obviously bullet proofed and therefore obviously supplied by the American Secret Service. He and his KGB minders were always careful what they said in taxis, their rooms, restaurants and anywhere else they might be overheard. They were even careful to speak in code when talking in parks or on streets. Sometimes they just spoke gibberish to confuse any would-be eavesdroppers.

When the trio got into the taxi, Nikolai, the head bodyguard, saw it had an in-car telephone in it. He asked the driver about it and she said it had just been installed. He asked where it could call to. She said anywhere he wanted. He asked her if he could use it to make a call. "*Sure, go right ahead.*" Before dialling the hotel's number, Nikolai stared in amazement at the phone for some ten seconds.

When the hotel answered the call he just laughed and hung up after saying he did not need to speak with anybody. He loved America. They all loved America.

★

Arriving at the store, Alexander's KGB bodyguards made to accompany him inside. He told them he preferred to shop alone. They needed no second invitation and went to the information boards at the foot of the nearest escalators and descended to the sportswear department like two excited children while Alexander went up two floors to Formalwear.

Now free to wander the store at will, Alexander approached a straight backed young man who was standing under a sign which read '*Personal Shoppers, we're here to help you.*'

"Hi, I'm Sam. I'll be your personal shopper today and will be happy to help you to find the clothes that are just perfect for you," spoke Sam in what Alexander considered a camp effeminate voice.

"Hey Sam, it's your break. I'll take over this one," said a man who appeared from behind a column.

"No… I'm on until three."

"Joe told me to tell you it's time for your break."

"Joe?"

"Yeah, Joe!"

"Who's Joe and who are you?"

"I'm Tony, I'm the new personal shopper in Formalwear."

"What? They told me I was…"

"Yeah, they say a lot of things, now go take your break. Don't worry, I'll look after your client for you… honest." As Sam briskly stomped away in a tight-trousered buttock-clenching flounce, Tony turned to Alexander, "This way sir, we'll start in our Outdoor Wear department. You'll look terrific in a sports jacket."

Alexander and Tony ascended the escalators to the fourth floor. The Outdoor Wear department was situated to the rear of the building. Tony selected four jackets for Alexander to try on. They were all taken from the far ends of the rails so Alexander surmised that was the end the larger sizes were hung, suitable for builds such as his. He liked the look of the jackets and was eager to try them on.

"Where can I try them on?"

"This way, sir, follow me." They entered a large mahogany panelled room with comfortable leather seating, brass fittings and cheval mirrors. "I suggest you try this one on first."

As Tony held the jacket open at Alexander's back he glided into it. It fitted like a glove. He had never had anything that fitted like a glove before. He asked Tony to wrap it. As far as Alexander was concerned the shopping expedition was a success and he wanted to move on but Tony persuaded him to try the other jackets too. They all fitted wonderfully and Alexander looked and felt like a different man in them. The question was, could he afford to buy them all and still have enough money to buy everything on his beautiful young wife's shopping list? "*I need a business suit, a smart business suit so people will take me seriously.*"

"Tony, I need a smart business suit and then I need to buy my wife some gifts… but it has been an expensive trip and I do not know if I can afford everything so I will have to decide which I keep and which I…"

"Say no more, sir. I can arrange credit for you if you wish?"

"You do not understand, I am visiting your country from the Soviet Union and I will be leaving New York tomorrow and do not know when I shall return."

"That's perfectly okay sir, we can't have our man looking like… I don't know what… now can we sir?"

"What? What did you say? Our man?"

"Just a moment sir, there's somebody here to see you." Tony unlocked the changing room door and a female and a male entered the room. "Let me introduce you. This is Special Agent Smith and this is Director Jones."

"Their real names?"

"Not important," interjected Director Jones. "We need to have a discussion with you about some of the people you have been meeting with. We know them to be members of an organisation calling itself The 400." Alexander made as if to speak, "Please, sir, if you don't mind letting me finish? As I was saying…"

After letting Alexander know that she knew everything about his meetings with The 400, Director Jones handed him her business card. Alexander laughed a little internal laugh, it read ASS Director Jones. The meeting was brief because neither wanted Alexander's KGB bodyguards raising the alarm over a missing boss. Director Jones said she would provide Alexander with all the resources necessary to do the job.

"The job?"

"Yes, the job, Mister Orlov. My meaning might be clearer if I told you that we're The Network." Alexander became light headed on hearing that. He was confused. "Yes, Alexander, it's been us all along who've been providing, among other items, computer equipment to the Soviet government, its military, its spy networks, Narodnaya Volya and organisations such as the Irregular Society."

"You want me to be your spy?" Alexander was still confused.

"No Mister Orlov, we want you to be successful. You need to be asking yourself, '*after it is all over where do I want to be*?' Do you want to be running with the herd or do you want to be sitting at the top table of the Soviet Union?" Alexander was shocked at the idea even though he had dreamed of such a thing many times. "We need to terminate this meeting in case your goons are looking for you. Your '*personal shopper*' will escort you and your garments to the ground floor. No need to pay, it's on us."

"But I must have a smart business suit too. I cannot get one that fits me in Moscow. I need a suit so I can look good."

"Tony, take him to the suit department. Get him whatever he wants." Then turning to Alexander, Director Jones said, "I'll be in touch."

The group dispersed as they exited the changing room. Alexander's KGB bodyguards caught up with him and Tony in the suit department. They were more concerned with how they were going to claim their purchases on expenses than the security of their boss.

★

Lying in bed that night, Alexander Orlov did what he did best, he went through all the options and permutations his encounter with the American Secret Service presented. Was it all just a setup for something as yet hidden? Was he heading for a fall? Was it the KGB up to some of their old tricks? If the latter then he was in real trouble if they knew about him and The 400. Thoughts, thoughts, thoughts. What to do? What to do? He would sleep on it. This was not something to be decided in haste.

★

After breakfast, as Alexander packed his cases in preparation to check out of the hotel, he noticed a note on the floor in front of his door. It must have been recently pushed underneath, he was certain it had not been there thirty seconds earlier. Alexander ran and opened the door, he looked both ways down the corridor, nobody other than room maids were to be seen. He asked the nearest room maid about the note. She looked at him like he was crazy and replied, in Spanish, that she had never seen the note before. She shouted in Spanish to her colleagues, asking them if they knew anything about the note. They hardly took any notice, they simply shook their heads and got on with their work. The next guests would be checking in shortly and their rooms had to be ready.

Walking back to his room, Alexander read the note. It said, '*Travel to the airport alone.*'

After checking out of the hotel, Alexander said goodbye to the concierge, thanking him for the help and advice he had given him during his stay. When they shook hands, Alexander passed the concierge a $100 bill. He said he hoped Alexander's stay was enjoyable and he looked forward to welcoming him at the hotel again in the future. As Alexander exited the hotel a taxi was standing in the rank waiting for him as usual. As his KGB bodyguards went to put their luggage in the trunk Alexander told them to take the next taxi as he had to pick up some last minute gifts for his wife. They shrugged their shoulders in the knowledge that the American Secret Service would do and excellent job of ensuring Comrade Orlov's safety and went to the hotel bar for an eye-opener.

"Airport? Right?" Shouted the taxi driver over his shoulder.

"Yes, the airport."

Within seconds of Alexander taking his seat in the back of the taxi the in-car telephone buzzed. The taxi driver said to Alexander that the call was for him and he should pick up the receiver.

"Hello, who is this?"

"Good morning Mister Orlov, it's Director Jones, we met yesterday."

"How could I forget?"

"We can talk openly, the driver is one of my agents and if you close the sliding window he won't be able to listen in on our conversation. I should mention that this call is being recorded and…"

"I understand. What do you want?"

"I imagine you've been thinking about our meeting yesterday? Yes? Well, we were short of time then but we have lots of it now. I've arranged for a traffic snarl-up on the bridge but don't worry, you'll still make your flight."

"I repeat. What do you want?"

"The driver has a package for you. If all goes well with our conversation he will hand it to you, its contents are very important."

"What is in the package?"

"Your future Mister Orlov. In it you'll find a notebook containing security protocols for our communications. You'll be told how to use it once you're back in Moscow. The protocols are unique to you. Keep them safe as without them you're lost. The package also contains the deeds to several properties here in New York City and the key to a safety deposit box. You'll be given account and access details after the job is finished. The safety deposit box contains keys and account details for six other safety deposit boxes, each containing eight gold ingots."

"Are you working for The 400? Maybe you are one of them? Or one of their agents… a familiar perhaps?"

"Me, one of The 400? Or one of their agents?… just like you Mister Orlov? No Mister Orlov we are not The 400." Director Jones paused, Alexander could hear paper shuffling in the background, "We know all about General Secretary Kirilenko planning to unleash Terror on the people in the Soviet Union…" Director Jones hesitated, unwilling to share all she knew, "In the past, we made the mistake of standing aside when the Soviet Union invaded Europe. That was a huge mistake. At the time, the United States was trying to find a diplomatic solution but we all know how that went. We will not stand by and see history repeated. We are going to do all we can to help our erstwhile allies."

"I do not see how I can…"

"Please Mister Orlov, you are our Director of The Network in the Soviet Union and unless you cooperate we'll be forced to abandon you to your fate at the hands of the Central Committee."

"How do I know you will not do that anyway?"

"Why would we when you are playing such a vital role in all this? We want you to keep on playing your role but with a few minor adjustments."

Director Jones told Alexander that she knew about The 400's plan to take over the running of the Soviet Union after Lev's phony revolution. She said she knew that through The Network he was behind most of the Soviet Union's problems; food shortages, irregular pay for Soldiers and bureaucrats, work share and work relocation schemes, job dilution and job-sharing, populations consolidation and resources balancing and so on. Alexander smirked inside, she had given him credit for things he had no hand in, they had been brought about by good old fashioned Soviet incompetence. Finally, she told him she knew about him subverting Vasily Dobrovski, the Presidium member responsible for planning the Terror. Though Director Jones did not say so she also knew that Alexander and Lev had recruited Red Army Officers and planned to have them lead the revolution, or if not lead it then not attempt to stop it or stand in its way.

Then came the price Alexander would have to pay for the inducements he had been offered. On the face of it, it appeared not to be so very great a price. Whereas The 400 wanted revolution in order to gain control of the Soviet Union, Director Jones wanted a political revolution. She said the American government desired fundamental change at the top; "*a change of personnel and a change of political direction toward democracy. A political change as much as anything*," was the way Director Jones described it.

Alexander asked what it all meant in real terms. Director Jones said that the people The 400 wanted at the top after the revolution would be substituted for the people the American government wanted at the top. She described it as a win, win, win.

"Everybody wins. The 400 gets what it wants; the opening up of consumer markets in the Soviet Union; the people of the Soviet

Union win because they will not be subjected to Terror; and the world wins through the restoration of democracy to billions of people."

'*Billions*?' thought Comrade Orlov. "There are barely one and a half billions in the entire Soviet Union," he muttered.

"Our time's up. Are you going to continue work for The Network? The 400 never need know. Are they offering you what I am offering or are they doing their usual pie in the sky? '*Don't worry, we'll look after you*'... promises, promises, promises."

"I need time to think..."

"Mister Orlov, you've had all the thinking time you need. It's time to decide. The question is simple. Are you going to work for The Network to ensure the right outcome for the revolution. I'm sure you can tell The 400 some tale of woe when things don't go according to their plan. They won't care too much because they'll be getting what they want and you'll be safely ensconced in Russia so you'll be safe. Your answer please Mister Orlov." Alexander never liked to give an answer without cogitating for hours, sometimes days, but here he was, all alone and in the hands of the American Secret Service. They could do anything to him and nobody would...

"Okay, we have a deal. That is how you say it is it not?"

"Yup, that's how we say it '*pardner*'. When the driver hands you the package he'll also hand you four computer discs. The team in Tula will need them for their attack on the KGB's HQ in Moscow." Alexander was thrown by Director Jones' mention of the Tula cell and the attack they were planning on the KGB's HQ. He was wondering what else she knew and how much was guesswork. He concluded that she knew enough for him to take her offer seriously.

Their conversation over, Director Jones called off the snarl-up on the bridge and traffic flowed freely again. Alexander's KGB bodyguards barely made it in time to check in for their flight back to Moscow.

Disc Doctoring

During his flight back to Moscow Comrade Orlov thought about his discussions with Secret Service Director Jones. He was not totally comfortable with having the US government for a partner and reneging on the deal he and Comrade Kirilenko had made with The 400. '*Perhaps there is a middle way?*' He thought half way across the Atlantic. Comrade Orlov concluded that the American government wanted to back the revolution because then China would be sandwiched between the Soviet Union and the USA; which it could then, no doubt, subvert. The 400 was a simpler matter. They were in it for the money and always had been. They just wanted to have people running the Soviet Union they could do business with. People like Lev and Maxim Kirilenko. Comrade Orlov's middle way was to develop '*friendly relations*' with both parties and for them to vie for favour with Comrade Kirilenko after he became dictator of the USSR. All he had to do now was to convince his boss that the plan was a good one.

★

Landing at Moscow airport in the dead of night, Comrade Orlov told his KGB bodyguards to make their own ways home. He ordered his driver to take him straight to the Kremlin. Waiting for him in Stalin's old office overlooking Red Square was the General Secretary of the Soviet Union, his boss, Maxim Kirilenko.

"Alexander, my old friend." Such a greeting from Comrade Kirilenko usually meant trouble but in this case it did not. The two men hugged and kiss-greeted Russian style. "Do you bring good news for me from America?"

"Very good news Maxim, very good news. We now have two partners to help with the revolution and win the Soviet Union back."

"Two partners?" smiled Comrade Kirilenko not liking the sound of that one little bit.

"Yes, let me tell you all about it."

The schemers grabbed a bottle of Vodka and made themselves comfortable on an antique English Chesterfield settee. They talked all night and into the next morning about how they were going to play the new situation to their advantage. Had Comrade Orlov been more bold when he first conceived the plan he could have done everything without Comrade Kirilenko but it was risky and so he carefully introduced the plan to make him dictator of the Soviet Union, just like he had always wanted. It would mean eliminating the Central Committee and replacing them with people more amenable to his way of wanting things done but Comrade Kirilenko was okay with that. *'Replace them with people who would not stab him in the back the first chance they got. Obey him without question'*. Comrade Orlov would never admit it but the plan was not really his, it was the brainchild of The 400.

★

Alexander was recruited by The 400 years before he was made to approach Comrade Kirilenko with a plan to rid him of his troublesome Central Committee. It was a calculated risk which had it gone badly there was no fall-back position but, so the thinking of The 400 went, Orlov was dispensable. He waited for the right moment and chose an evening after a fractious Central Committee meeting. Comrade Kirilenko was incandescent with rage at the Commissars of the big six Commissariats. To commiserate, Comrade Orlov and his boss got very drunk together, though Alexander was not as drunk as he made himself out to be. After finishing their second bottle of Vodka, the Chef de Cabinet took a deep breath and began talking and did not stop until he had gotten the whole story out about The 400. At first, Comrade Kirilenko was aghast at the depth of Alexander's treachery but saw the potential of the plan. Finally, he would be rid of those troublemaking CC scoundrels and just like the Soviet leaders of old he would become a Red Tsar and, no doubt, very, very rich into the bargain. Operation Zima was designed to distract the attention of the Central Committee away from the real plan. The Jewish homosexual, comrade Vasily Dobrovski, had been made responsible for the Terror and consequently would carry the can if it went wrong. Being under the command of Comrade Alexander Orlov as Director of The Network, Dobrovski was double jeopardised as he would be executed as the person behind the revolution if it failed. As a Jew and a homosexual it was a no win situation for Vasily Dobrovski. Nobody would protect him, speak up for him or attempt to save him. Which was business as usual in the Soviet Union.

★

As their meeting came to a close, Maxim asked Alexander about the computer discs.

"Show them to me, I want to see them."

"There is not much to see. Nothing in fact. They are just normal computer discs."

"Show them to me! I want to see them!" Alexander showed the discs to Maxim. "How do they work?"

"You put them into the computer and they tell it what to do."

"How do they do that?"

"I do not know. That is what we have Alexei for."

"Can you trust him?"

"I hope so, he has our secrets inside his head." Kirilenko shot Orlov a concerned look. "Do not worry, Alexei is loyal. Besides, we have his family." To add weight to his argument Alexander added,

"People like Alexei are hard to come by and at this late stage we do not have any other choice."

"What is next?"

"We need Alexei to look at the discs and tell us what is on them."

"How does he do that?"

"I do not know," lied Orlov. "Once Alexei tells us what is on them, we… you, can change the instructions for the revolution. Our partners will not be very happy but what are they going to do? What can they do? We will be in Moscow and they will not. They will have to accept the new situation and make deals with you."

"Which I will be happy to make. You must let the Americans and The 400 know that as soon as possible after I have gained control."

"Of course. We do not want to start a war."

"No we do not. Bring Alexei here. He must remain in the Kremlin until after…"

"Maxim, that is a very bad idea. If he goes missing Lev will smell a rat and the whole plan will fall apart. I think we can trust Alexei. We have his family and he is going to be very rich and living in America in just a few weeks' time. Everybody wins."

"About sending Alexei to America… let us not be too hasty." Alexander was not prepared to argue with Maxim on that point and so just agreed with him that they would not act hastily over Alexei going to America after the revolution.

★

The following afternoon Comrade Orlov took Vasily Dobrovski into his office and locked the door behind them. Dobrovski thought his time had come and his days were over. Alexander opened the bottom left hand drawer of his desk, pushed the hanging files to one side, took a black phone from behind a secret panel and placed it on top of his desk. He repeated the process on the right hand side of the desk but this time he took out a peculiar looking device which he placed around his neck and switched it on. It whistled as he adjusted the volume. Then he spoke into the microphone.

Vasily Dobrovski stared in disbelief as he realised Alexander Orlov and the Director of The Network were one and the same person. He had a thousand questions but knew to keep his mouth shut until after he had time to think.

A twin of the phone atop Comrade Orlov's desk resided in the top drawer of Alina Kuznetsova's desk, the NV activist Orlov had recruited from the Vladivostok cell to be Vasily Dobrovski's PA.

★

Comrade Dobrovski had come into work one morning to find Alina Kuznetsova sitting at his PA's desk. He asked her what she was doing there and she replied that his PA, Elena, had been rushed to hospital but unfortunately she died from '*complications*'. Vasily asked Alina what the complications were and to which hospital Elena had been taken. She apologised, saying that she did not know which hospital Elena had been taken to but would find out for him if he wanted her to. He told her not to as he guessed what had probably happened to poor Elena. He blamed the Central Committee for whatever had happened to Elena but they were as suspicious as he was about Elena's sudden death as she was reporting on Dobrovski's activities to several of them.

★

After revealing that he was the Director of The Network, comrade Orlov knew Dobrovski's mind would be in turmoil thinking about the implications.

"You did not even guess?"
"No comrade Orlov, I…"

"Please, call me Alexander… we are compatriots now. We are in this together."

"I… I…"

"It must be a great shock to you but do not worry, your secrets are safe with me which is more than I can say of mine with my wife." Laughed the Chef de Cabinet.

"How long?… how did you?… when did it happen?… I…"

"You are making no sense. Gather your thoughts and we will talk later. The time is near and there is much to do. Do not do anything foolish like go to Bazanov."

"Comrade Orlov, I would never go to a person like him!" said Dobrovski shocked.

"A person like him? Then who would you go to? Hmmmmm?"

"Nobody Coomrade Orlov, nobody. It was just an expression of horror that you might think that I would go to somebody like Bazanov. I hate, loathe and despise that man more than any other person on the planet."

"I can understand why that might be. Nevertheless, do not give me cause to doubt you otherwise you will watch as Andrei pays the price."

"There is no call to threaten me comrade Orlov. I am loyal to The Network."

⋆

It was a risky business making phone calls in the Soviet Union, you never knew who was listening. Even with his point to point scrambler phone there was no guarantee that Comrade Orlov's call to Alina Kuznetsova would be confidential if her office was bugged. He had arranged for one of the people he owned the life of to provide Alina with a device for detecting the radio signals bugs generate so both could be confident their conversations were private.

"It is me. Can you speak?" asked the hollow sounding metallic voice of the Director.

"Yes, I have been expecting your call… the time is close."

"Quite so. We need to make sure Comrade Dobrovski follows the instructions he will shortly receive. Firstly though, I need Alexei to come to Moscow for a little job I have for him."

"He is doing some work for Lev. I doubt he will have time to come to Moscow… besides, he could be under surveillance…"

"I need him to come to Moscow!" insisted Alexander with a coldness that even the voice-altering device could not disguise.

"Why? Is it something to do with computers?"

"Of course it is something to do with computers! Why else would I need him to come here?"

"I am as good as Alexei with computers." Alina said, exaggerating as usual. "What is it you need done?"

'*She has proven herself to be very capable in the past,*' thought the Director. "What do you know about computers?"

"Everything Alexei knows about them." Exaggerating again as usual.

"Do you know how to alter a disc?"

"Yes, of course, that is basic computer work, it is simple to do." If what Alina had just told Alexander was true then Alexei had been pulling the wool over his eyes for a very long time.

"You will come to a meeting this evening. I will bring the discs and a computer and you will show me what you can do." Alexander hung up the call. His temper was up and the next person who upset him would get it in the neck.

After sending Alina the address for their meeting that evening, Alexander considered updating Comrade Kirilenko. '*Why bother? Why disturb him with details of things he does not need to know about?*' Henceforth Alexander would keep his cards close to his chest for his own survival in case things went badly. '*If what Alina said is correct then Alexei is a dead man. Nobody makes a fool out of Alexander Orlov, Chef de Cabinet to Maxim Kirilenko, General Secretary of the Soviet Union!*' Alexander's fragile ego was never very far from the surface of his hideous skin.

At 1800 a cautious Alina Kuznetsova exited the lift on the fourteenth floor of a building just a few doors down the street from her office. The corridor was in almost total darkness. Her senses were on high alert. She wished she had not surrendered her .22 Stechkin to the security guard on reception. A light went on in a refreshments bar at the far end of the corridor. A pretty blonde woman appeared and peered into the darkness. Assuming Alina was there in the blackness she asked if she would like a coffee.

"It will help keep you awake as it is going to be a long night." Alina realised the Director used a voice-altering device but had never suspected he was a woman.

"I thought you were a man."

"I beg your pardon?" said the woman in a breathless laugh.

"All the times we have spoken I always thought that you were a man."

"I think you are confused, we have never spoken."

"But you are the Director."

"No, I am not the Director but he will be with you shortly. Sugar in your coffee?"

"Yes please," Alina replied flatly, feeling stupid and sheepish.

"The Director should not keep you waiting long. I understand there is a lot to do and..." A light flashed on the device the woman was carrying. "The Director is ready for you now in fact. Follow me."

Alina entered meeting room one and found it exactly as Vasily Dobrovski had found it; unlit apart from an angle poise lamp shining in her direction creating a silhouette of the person sitting behind it. At the other end of the table was a computer and four discs, numbered one to four. A metallic voice ordered her to sit down and switch the computer on. It was a type she was familiar with and so had no trouble bringing it to life. After the computer finished its start-up routine the silhouette spoke.

"Put the first disc into the computer and tell me what is on it." After inserting disc number one Alina said, "It is asking me for the decryption code." Alexander retrieved a notebook from his jacket pocket.

"79678479666 9821917."

"Say it again, but slowly so I can type it in," said Alina, exasperated.

"79678479666 9821917." Alina entered the decryption code and the computer responded with "*Welcome*." She thought about the decryption code for a moment and wondered whether it was really just a password. It was the two occurrences of 79 that raised her suspicions. If she was right then the numbers were probably in pairs and the 1917 at the end was too much of a coincidence for it not to relate to the October revolution.

"It worked. I am in."

"What does it say?" Alina did not respond straight away, she was still thinking about the password and what the numbers might mean. "What does it say?!!"

"Sorry, I was distracted for a moment. It is a list of names of Red Army Officers, mostly Generals, and next to them there is a series of numbers."

"They are locations and coded commands."

"It is simple enough to read the disc but I cannot help you with the meaning of the commands without carrying out analysis."

"Do not worry what the commands mean. Write everything down and…"

"Wait, there is more." Alina said after scrolling down the screen. "After the names of the Red Army Officers there are other names… one of them is Lev!" Alina was stunned and shocked at seeing Lev's name in this company. What did it mean? Was it a death list she was looking at? or perhaps those who were to die in the Terror? She was having serious doubts about the Director. Sensing Alina's concern, Alexander decided to take her into his confidence.

"I see you are shocked at Lev's name appearing alongside those of Red Army Generals and KGB Colonels and are wondering what is going on. I cannot tell you everything in case you get captured and tortured or worse… turned. If you betray the cause you will destroy the work done by thousands of good Soviet citizens over decades and turn the sacrifices they have made into dust.

"You probably joined Narodnaya Volya to bring about change in the Soviet regime? Change can create unusual alliances. Some alliances are not what they appear but I can assure you that everybody on the list has been carefully chosen. Inevitably, some of them will be traitors but they each know so little and what they do know in isolation has no value. Everybody will learn what their part in the plan is at exactly the same time. The coded commands they will be sent will direct them to carry out predetermined actions. Each carries a notebook similar to this one," the Director waved his notebook in the angle poise's cone of light, "which contains a list of commands. Nobody will know what they are required to carry out until the very last minute. All commands will be sent simultaneously by computer and the recipients will then act as one to overthrow the state. Afterwards, the Soviet Union will be reborn under new leadership. We will resurrect Lenin's vision of a workers' paradise, for all the peoples of the Soviet Union." Alina heard the words but they sounded hollow and false to her. She thought the Director might believe them but she was not swallowing the story.

"Thank you for taking me into your confidence Comrade Director. I will not let you down." While listening to Orlov's little speech about a shiny new Soviet Union Alina's subconscious worked out the key to the password. It was made up from the decimal values of ASCII characters plus the year 1917 at the end; 79 equals ASCII capital O… 67 capital C and so on. Being ASCII, October was spelled out in American not Russian.

"I am sure you will not," replied Alexander, his words laced with the familiar threatening tone used by people of power in the Soviet Union. Everybody knew what the tone meant; '*the lives of your family are in your hands.*'

"There is a great deal to write down Comrade Director. It would be easier if I had a printer..."

"A printer?"

"Yes, a printer... to connect to the computer."

"Why? What do you mean?"

"I can print off the lists as they appear on the screen." Alexanders blood boiled, Alexei had pulled the wool over his eyes farther than he had previously thought. There was now absolutely no chance of him going to America after the revolution as his reward for all the work he had done. Alexander was now planning to entertain Alexei in Lubyanka. Putting thoughts of Alexei to one side, Alexander pressed a button on an intercom which showed a red light. A female voice answered.

"Yes?"

"Bring me a printer for the computer." Then to Alina, "While my assistant brings a printer, tell me everything of what is on the discs." Alina loaded the discs one at a time. Alexander believed he knew what was on them but only had Alexei's word for that and now his word was no good.

The lists on the discs were much the same in terms of recipients but most of the coded commands appeared different on each of the discs. '*Why are the commands different on each disc?*' thought Alina.

The Director's assistant eventually wheeled a printer into the room and parked it next to Alina. She apologised for its unwieldy size but assured the Director that it was the best printer she could find at that time of night. He made no comment about the printer but asked her to bring in a large pot of coffee with milk and sugar on a tray with cakes, "*chocolate cakes... and some cold meats and bread too. Do not go home tonight, I have something I need you to do later.*" Alina connected the printer to the computer and loaded each of the discs for printing. The Director compared the differences in the coded commands while waiting for the last disc to print out. He stopped reading for a moment and asked Alina if it was difficult making new computer discs.

"If you mean manufacturing computer discs, I have no idea, but if you mean preparing them for use in a computer then…"

"The latter," growled the Director. Despite her earlier thoughts of being careful what she said Alina told the Director it was a simple task to prepare a disc.

"It is a relatively simple task to prepare new discs, Comrade Director."

"Good, I want new discs, ones containing the names and the commands I want on them."

"But why go to all the bother of creating new discs when all you have to do is edit the existing discs?" The kopek dropped with Alexander and again he realised just how far Alexei had pulled the wool over his eyes. Eyes that soon would see no more.

"You can do that?" asked Alexander, grinding his teeth.

"Yes, did Alexei not…"

"No, he did not! Show me how it is done."

"I do not want to overwrite what is on the discs so I will just copy the contents of one disc onto another disc and after that I will change its properties to enable me to…"

"Just do it!" shouted Alexander. He hated dealing with technical people because they could tell him anything and he had to believe what they told him as he knew no better.

After creating a copy disc, Alina turned the screen half way round so the Director could observe her changing whatever he ordered her to change; recipients' names, locations, command codes… anything. After seeing how easy it was Alexander thought about what Alexei had put on the discs. He realised he could not rely on them and he would have to go over all the printouts and… '*No,*' he thought, '*I only have to analyse one print out to know if he is a traitor.*' Comrade Orlov would make the changes on the printouts and have Alina create a new set of discs for the start of the revolution. He would destroy the originals… '*maybe*'… he just could not let go of that which he did not understand. '*I will keep them hold of them just in case.*'

"As you have finished printing the information on the discs you may leave. I will study them and contact you in the next few days. Be prepared to do whatever I order you to do. Tell nobody of what has passed here tonight. I have eyes and ears everywhere and will find out if your tongue is loose."

"Please Comrade Director, there is no need to threaten me, I am loyal to the cause." But which cause she did not say and Alexander noticed.

As soon as Alina left the room, Alexander grabbed the printouts and relocated to another building for security's sake. '*I have much work to do,'* he thought. He had to ensure that everybody who should be on the list was on the list and check that their locations, computer designations and coded commands were correct for Maxim's new direction for the revolution. This was no small task. Alexander's pocketbook contained the master coded commands. Each recipient had different coded commands for each command. For example, if two Red Army Generals received coded commands to arrest NKVD Officers, Political Commissars or KGB Agents the command code would be different in each case though the execution of the order was the same. Therefore if anybody was a traitor they could not use their own codes to decipher anybody else's coded commands. Putting one with the other was a mammoth task. Had Alexander known how to operate a computer he could have edited the lists straight to the discs but he did not know and so had to write everything down by hand.

Once Alexander got on with the editing it was not so bad. A check on the names revealed that there were only a few people to add or remove plus Alexander added some people of his own to ensure that people key to the uprising were shadowed. They would be closely protected because if they fell the revolution would fail. Next came the computer locations. This was a little more complicated because he had to be accurate otherwise the command messages would not get through. Then there were the actual commands. In themselves they were straightforward but as the same command used a different code for each recipient it was a laborious task to cross reference them with his own master list of command codes.

⋆

By 0700, Alexander had almost completed his task but he was feeling tired and knowing he could not make any mistakes he decided to go home and get some sleep. He went via the Kremlin to report progress to Maxim. Alexander used to be able to get by with very little sleep but since his New York trip all that had changed. That trip took a lot out of him and for the first time in his life Alexander felt old. By Soviet standards he was old, sixty, but he possessed an iron constitution and could put many of the Central Committee to shame with his energy but he was feeling weary and thought about retirement after all this was over, '*maybe in the USA?*'

Alexander had in mind that his meeting with Maxim would be short. When he walked into Maxim's office he seemed nervous and appeared reluctant for his Chef de Cabinet to go home to bed. After a few minutes, Maxim put his arm around Alexander's shoulder and told him his beautiful young wife was missing.

"Missing? How could she have gone missing?" Howled Alexander. "She was at the dacha, surrounded by security guards. How could she have gone missing?"

"She went to visit one of her girlfriends in the early hours and as it was so close by she insisted on going alone; saying that she would be no more than ten minutes."

"Who told you this?"

"Vronika's friend, the one who was staying at the dacha with her. She called about four hours ago."

"Why did you not tell me immediately?"

"I thought… I thought she would have turned up by now. I am sorry my old friend, I realise now that I should have called you."

"Who do you think is behind it? The KGB… Luka?"

"You know how it is. This sort of thing happens all the time to those associated with high ranking officials. It is the way things are. We will stop this sort of thing after the revolution." Alexander knew this to be nonsense, this sort of thing had always gone on and would continue to go on… '*always*'.

"What shall we do? Wait for some demand?"

"That is what we need to discuss. It is too much of a coincidence that this should happen now, just when we are about to light the blue touch paper for the revolution. I need to know Alexander… does anybody else… could anybody else, know of our plans?"

"No. I am certain that nobody else knows. How could they? Nobody has any idea what will happen until the computers send the commands. Even those on the lists do not know what is going to happen until they receive their orders."

Maxim said he did not want to appear heartless but they had urgent matters to discuss and he would ride over to Alexander's dacha with him. Alexander told Maxim of the events of the previous twenty four hours. He seemed pleased with progress. Their '*business*' talk over, Maxim felt he should comfort Alexander in his sadness and anger.

"How could something like this happen…"

"Please Maxim, as you said, it happens all the time in the Soviet Union, you know that and I know that. What I want to know is who is responsible. Who was it who failed to protect my wife and who was it that abducted her?"

"We will find her my friend, we will find her. And I will punish those responsible!"

"I will check the Lubyanka personally."

"I would not do that if I were you. Things are not very good with Bazanov at the moment. If he finds you in his Lubyanka he might not let you out again."

"The sooner we start the revolution the sooner we can be rid of Bazanov and the others and I can get my Vronika back."

"Alexander, my friend, I was thinking that some of the weaker ones should be saved. They would be forever in my debt and their supporters will not rise up against me after the revolution." Alexander noted Maxim was back to the '*I*' and the '*me*', it seemed it was no longer the '*we*' and the '*us*'. "I want to see the final list of names and commands before they…" Maxim was lost for words, he had no computer-speak.

"Before they get put onto the discs?"

"Exactly. I want to see the final lists before they get put onto the discs." Alexander smelled a rat. "When will they be ready?"

"I need to sort things out here first."

"I understand but when will the lists be ready?"

"I will have them for you by this time tomorrow."

"Very good. Ah, we have arrived. I wish you all the best of luck in finding your wife and dealing with those responsible for abducting her."

"And those who allowed it to happen?" added Alexander with malice in his voice. Maxim had never seen this side of him and made a mental note to keep a closer eye on his Chef de Cabinet in future.

As the convoy of cars drew up to the dacha, Maxim asked Alexander if he wanted him to leave some of his Kremlin Guard to help with the interrogations. He replied that he did not. He said he had everything in hand.

Entering the dacha, Alexander saw Vronika's '*best friend*', the one he had recruited in the torture cell at the Lubyanka. She gave him the slightest of nods to let him know that the job was done, Vronika was in a place of safety. The countdown to revolution had begun and Alexander did not know where it would end. He wanted his wife to be safe in case things did not go according to plan and so had arranged to have her '*abducted*'. Given his wife's propensity to blab secrets he had simply told her that things were getting hot with the Central Committee and being concerned for her safety he said it was best if she disappeared for a few weeks. The less she knew the better. And so Vronika went into hiding. Alexander did not know where she was but he held the key to finding her if he needed to.

★

After a short sleep, Alexander finished editing the lists. He met up with Maxim the following day to review them before making a call to Alina on the secret point to point scrambled telephone. The discussion was short. He ordered her to meet him at 1800 a different location to their previous meeting. When she turned up she was bundled into a car and driven to the original location. She understood why the Director had taken this precaution. '*He does not trust me.*' From the basement carpark, Alina rode the lift to the fourteenth floor. It was just as it had been two days previous. The same blonde woman asked the same question, '*would she like some coffee*?' There was no hanging around this time though, it was straight into meeting room one.

The Director was sitting behind his angle poise lamp. At the other end of the table was a computer, four discs, two screens and a pile of computer paper. One of the screens was pointed toward the Director.

"There are the lists and discs. Time is short, the work must be completed tonight."

"Two screens? You do not trust me?"

"It is not a matter of trust. It is a matter of accuracy. I need to ensure that the commands are correct."

"Who will load the discs into the computer?" Alina asked knowing full well who would be doing it. It would be Svetlana and Grigori as all those who had gone before them were dead.

"That is none of your concern."

"But what if something goes wrong Comrade Director? What if there is a problem? I know all about computers. I could help. I should be there." Alina was nothing if not persistent and ambitious.

"I will think about it."

"Thank you Comrade Director," replied Alina in her sweetest most subservient voice.

"Give this to your boss tomorrow." The Director threw a small black button across the table to Alina. "After he gets over the shock, you will hand him a printout of the computer discs and you will tell him that he has to make sure that all the people on them must be in their places in one week; no longer; one week. Maximum." After a moment a nervous Alina spoke.

"But Comrade Director, he will have me arrested!"

"I can assure you, Alina Kuznetsova, having you arrested will be the last thing on Comrade Dobrovski's mind. Now, get on with the editing and be quick. I do not want to be here all night."

★

After reading the lists, Alina realised that after the revolution it would be the Svetlanas and Grigoris who would be running the new Soviet Union and she wanted to be a Svetlana. It would be their kind who would stand atop Lenin's tomb and watch the Red Army as it marched past saluting them. They would be presented with medals. They would be the ones making the speeches. They would be the specially invited guests at parades all over the Soviet Union. It would be they who would be interviewed by Pravda for their heroic stories. Their faces would be on Malenkytels all over the Soviet Union. Billboards would carry their images in heroic poses. They would be Heroes of the Great Patriotic Revolution. It would be they who give late night talks to Pioneers over camp fires telling how they lit the fire of revolution by inserting discs into computers. They would be hailed as heroes wherever they went. Alina now understood that everything would change yet nothing would change and saw her chance to grab greatness by being at the centre of things when the revolution began.

★

The following morning Alina was at her desk when Vasily Dobrovski arrived, late as usual. He hardly paid her any notice, "*Coffee*" was all he said. Alina rose from her seat and followed Vasily into his office. Reaching for his mail he turned to her for less than a second then repeated "*Coffee*" before adding, "*What are you doing in here*?" Since Alina's arrival following the tragic and unexpected death of his PA he had never liked her. Alina reached inside her purse and palmed something from it. She stared at Vasily and wondered what his reaction was going to be to the object in her hand. She was still not entirely convinced by what the Director had said about Comrade Dobrovski having too much on his mind to have her arrested once she had shown him the little black button. The more she thought about it the more ridiculous it seemed but she had no choice, she had to go through with it.

Alina gave Vasily a blank stare then opened her hand to show him the little black button nestling on her palm. He almost collapsed and had to lean on his desk for support while desperately thinking about everything he had ever said in her presence, '*Had he been indiscrete*?'

"You? You! How could it be you?" cried Vasily in disbelief.

"I have a message for you from the Director."

"You… you have a message for me?" spat Vasily enunciating each word crisply.

"Yes," was all Alina said in reply, enjoying the moment.

"From the Director?" he asked with venom in his voice.

"Yes and listen to it carefully," then adding for effect, "your life depends on it." Alina smiled inside at her power. '*Maybe she was not so different to them after all*'. "I am going to give you a list. You are to study it and make sure that everybody on it is where they should be within one week."

"But I have no power to do anything like that."

"Yes you do. You are responsible for Operation Zima and as such you have the power to order those people named on the list to go where they need to be. There is a lot to do so get started. I have begun preparing the orders, all you have to do is sign them and send them."

"But then what? What will happen when they get there?" Vasily became frantic as the magnitude of it all hit him.

"Courage comrade, courage," said Alina in a whisper, patting Vasily's shuddering shoulders. "These are the days we have all worked so long and so hard for, let us face them together side by side with our comrades."

"But what if it all goes wrong? It will be traced back to me!"

"Do your job right comrade and pray it does not go wrong," scolded Alina. "If you had seen what I have seen you would have more faith. Now… get to work!" She ordered.

After Vasily checked the names and locations on the lists, he discovered that most of them were already in place. There were only forty four orders that needed to be made to transfer Officers, Agents and Operatives in preparation for Z day.

★

That evening after Vasily returned to his luxury apartment overlooking the Moskva River he told Andrei everything and let him decide for himself whether he was going to run or stay. Andrei told Vasily he would never leave him and that if he had to die he would do so at his side. On hearing Andrei's response, Vasily started shaking from head to foot and apologised to Andrei for putting his life in danger. Andrei held Vasily's hands and whispered in his ear, "Courage my love, courage" and making the sign of NV.

The Tula Cell

Air travel in twenty first century USSR had become more commonplace year on year. According to official government figures, 0.067% of the Proletariat had, by the first of January 2016, flown in a non-military aircraft. The Congress of People's Deputies were against proliferation of air travel except for military, security and political representatives; such as members of the Congress of People's Deputies. They, the Central Committee and the Supreme Soviet, demanded that Soviet citizens taking their winter and summer breaks, interim holidays or attending celebratory marches, travel by train. The Soviet Union was very proud of its rail network despite much of it being in the hands of local warlords who demanded a tribute be paid to them for every train passing through their territory. One of the NKVD's responsibilities was to eliminate such practices but many citizens suspected that the NKVD was on the gravy train.

★

Despite there being very few Soviet citizens who had ever flown in their entire lives, Svetlana and Grigori, unlike Vladimir, were seasoned air travellers. They had only taken the Trans-Siberian express to Pioneer Camp because, according to Svetlana, '*it would be romantic*'. According to the rules, they should have caught the train anyway but such rules do not apply to the Svetlanas and Grigoris of the Soviet Union.

The flight from Vladivostok to Tula was an adventure in itself because only small or military aircraft were allowed to land there.

This occasioned Svetlana and Grigori changing planes four times and refuelling twice along the way. They, along with the other passengers, had to chip in money to buy fuel. This was normal according to the pilot though Grigori reckoned she was in on the scam, along with the ground staff and the companies selling '*Kerosene Blend*', '*whatever that was*'. Food was an '*optional extra*' but experienced air travellers were well self-catered for with their dried salted fish, bread, cold meats, cheese, blinis, caviar and Vodka, despite alcohol being free on the plane. Several of the passengers had not flown on such small aircraft before and consequently they had not stocked up for the journey. They sat hungry throughout the flights and while hanging around in cold café-less airport lounges, if they could be called that, inside small dingy unheated buildings.

Following orders to be cautious, Svetlana and Grigori were careful not to make eye contact with the foodless passengers lest they felt obligated to share their food with them. They told themselves, and each other, that as they were on a secret mission they could not take the chance of mixing with strangers; '*who knows who they are or what they were or what they could be? They could be anything*!' However, they did put a little picnic together for a small child as she was obviously so very hungry. The justification for giving her the picnic was to prevent her from crying from hunger during the journey. It was really Svetlana's idea to give the child some food and Grigori just went along with it.

Throughout the flight, Svetlana and Grigori communicated in code, practising what they had learned in the Pioneer Camp, about what to do if they landed in Tula and found they had been betrayed or compromised. They were carrying NV documents laced with neurotoxic poison so if the worst came to the worst they agreed that they would follow through on their suicide pact, so they said at least.

The weather when they were coming in to land at Tula airport was dreadful. Rumours circulated amongst the passengers that the plane was being diverted to Moscow. Svetlana and Grigori looked at one another wide eyed. How were they going to get back to Tula to rendezvous with their cell? The plane circled the airport three times while being bounced up and down and side to side by the blizzard. The pilot came on the intercom, "*we are going to land at Tula because we do not have sufficient fuel to make it to anywhere else… not even Kaluga.*" Returning to Ryzan was out of the question for the same reason. Grigori thought about where the fuel was that they had paid for back in Ryzan? He was certain the ground staff had short changed them but that did not really matter right then. It was land in Tula or… nothing, there was no other option.

★

Anyone who has flown on a plane that is in trouble will immediately associate with the vacuum like silence that seizes hold in the aircraft cabin, as was experienced by the passengers of Ural-Air 4 that day. Ears become numb to sound. Engine noise goes unheard as minds are focussed on survival. Not wanting to communicate the fear they feel nobody makes eye contact. Passengers try to appear as calm as possible and give reassuring hand squeezes to loved ones.

The passengers knew their chances of surviving a plane crash were miniscule, as did their pilot. They had seen the news reports about airplanes crashing on landing. The news cameras showed pictures of burned out wreckages and scattered remains of the aircraft. Passengers' belongings could be seen strewn on the ground. Reporters walked amongst the debris for maximum effect spouting their hackneyed phrases; "*terrible accident,*" "*tragic loss of life,*" "*an air tragedy,*" and so on. Cameras homed in on children's shoes, or a toy, or some item of child's clothing to drive home the horror to their viewers. Reporters were careful not to disclose too much information about the passengers, better the Proles be appalled by the tragic loss of life.

★

Ural-Air 4 received several warnings not to attempt a landing. The pilot called the control tower and advised them that she had no option but to land as they were out of fuel. Over the pilot's radio came a warning for her not to land until after an approaching military transport had landed. The air traffic controller said the plane was, "*coming in hot*"; jargon for an emergency landing. '*What the hell does he think our situation is?*' thought the pilot who called the tower again to request immediate clearance to land explaining as Ural-Air 4 was running on fumes.

"Ural-Air 4, Ural-Air 4, do not, I repeat, do not attempt to land."

"The engines are sputtering. They are not getting any fuel… I am running on fumes!"

"Ural-Air 4, an Ilyushin 8 is coming in fast and low on your port side… get out of the way! Now!"

Ural-Air 4's pilot took immediate evasive action which panicked the passengers further. They were now past the numbed silent phase and were into the screaming, shouting and running crazily around the airplane phase. Fortunately, the pilot's door was locked otherwise some of them would have stormed the cockpit.

The pilot's voice came over the intercom. She pleaded with the passengers for calm and told them she had a plan to get them on the ground, hopefully in one piece. The plan, she said, was to land in a field behind the control tower. She swore that making a tail down landing was their best chance of surviving a '*controlled*' crash landing. Knowing no different the passengers accepted what the pilot said. Out of the portside windows the passengers saw the Ilyushin 8 touching down. For a moment it looked as though the plane had made it when the landing gear collapsed causing the wing to hit the ground and the fuselage to spin, in doing so the entire right hand side of the plane became engulfed in flames. Ural-Air 4's passengers saw the faces of the Ilyushin's passengers through the windows of the doomed plane. Those who knew how to do so prayed and those that had never prayed in their lives copied them. They continued their praying as Ural-Air 4 made its final approach to the field the pilot had chosen to land in.

Ural-Air 4's pilot's hands were firm but responsive to the plane's control gear. At one hundred and twenty feet she reached for the landing gear switch before gathering her thoughts and slapping the back of her errant hand twice. "*No wheels... idiot!*" She stared dead ahead, ignoring the terrifying sight to her left. At forty feet she switched off the fuel supply; the plane immediately lost altitude. Pulling back hard on the controls the nose went up and the tail went down. Just as she had planned.

The plane's tail touched down with no more than a whisper, hardly disturbing the recent dusting of snow. Small billows of powdered snow swirled in the vortex behind the plane. There was a slight bump as the plane's fuselage hit down. The snow was soft and yielding and the landing freakishly smooth. The propellers didn't suffer any damage until they hit something hard under the snow causing Ural-Air 4 to flip over onto its top. Now upside down, the passengers were hanging from their seats. With visions of the Ilyushin horror in their minds, they unclipped their seat belts, fell to the ceiling and ran to the rear door. The first person to reach it was a teenager who opened the door at his first attempt. As soon as the door was opened the passengers spewed out of the plane as if fired by a cannon and ran as fast as they could to get away in case of an explosion.

Realising they had just defied death, the passengers were ecstatic with jubilation; hugging and kissing one another and whirling around in a mad triumphal dance. "*Where is our pilot?*" Svetlana yelled. She was nowhere to be seen. Then one of the passengers pointed to the windscreen of the cockpit. There was a large red splat in the middle of it. "*Who will rescue our brave pilot?*" Nobody moved until Svetlana made tracks back the crashed airplane. Grigori held her hand but she pushed it away.

Entering the plane there was a familiar yet unfamiliar smell. They assumed it was fuel; "*Kerosene Blend*" recalled Grigori. He said they should leave. Svetlana ignored him and made her way through the wreckage to the cockpit. There she found the pilot, upside down and still strapped into her seat. She had a deep cut on her head and was unconscious but alive. Svetlana pulled hard at the seatbelt release mechanism until it gave way and then shouted at Grigori to make himself useful by grabbing the pilot's feet while she took her arms. They barely made twenty feet from the plane when, with a massive whoosh, it exploded and went up in flames. The passengers cheered Svetlana's heroism and crowded round her and the pilot. By this time a number of military personnel were on the scene. A Major said ambulances were on their way.

★

The passengers from Ural-Air 4 were taken to what they were told was a '*holding area*' beneath the airport's terminal building. With its cells and metal loops built into its walls they thought it looked like a prison. The pilot was taken straight to hospital under guard. Inside the holding area the survivors of the Ilyushin 8 aircraft were being brought in. The Ural-Air 4 passengers wanted to speak with them but were prevented from doing so by an NKVD Officer. Svetlana asked the Officer if she and her boyfriend could leave as they were unhurt and wanted to continue with their vacation before they had to return to university in Moscow.

"Are you in a hurry to leave?" asked the Officer using his interrogation voice.

"Now that you mention it, we are."

"You will not be permitted to leave until you have given a full account of the reckless behaviour of the pilot. She ignored instructions not to land. Her incompetence and negligence caused the Ilyushin to crash." Svetlana was shocked and disgusted by the NKVD Officer's accusation but she knew this game. It is the Soviet blame game. Somebody had to be sacrificed and it looked as though it was going to be the pilot of Ural-Air 4.

"I can tell you that our pilot," Svetlana knew she had to choose her words carefully, "was not on the same flight path of the Ilyushin. Our plane ran parallel to the airstrip as we were aiming to land in a field."

"Are you an expert in the protocols of flying?"

"No, I…"

"What is your name… and his name too," said the Officer pointing at Grigori. "Is he your boyfriend?" Grigori stepped forward.

"My girlfriend's name," Grigori had never actually called Svetlana his girlfriend in public before, she smiled, "is Svetlana Anna Panshina and mine is," Svetlana held her breath, "Grigori Andreivich Rabinovich. I am the nephew of former KGB Colonel Vasily Zaytsev, now Commissar of the Western Frontier Gulags." '*Oh no!*' thought Svetlana. She was not convinced that it was such a good strategy using Dyadya Vasya's name like that.

"Your uncle bears the name of a hero of the Great Patriotic War. May I ask…"

"No, you may not. Here is my party card if you doubt my credentials." There in black writing on a green card with a red border was Grigori's party card, his uncle's endorsement below his name. Svetlana had never seen a party card with a red border before and by the look on the NKVD Officer's face neither had he. '*Another Jew*,' thought the NKVD Officer. "I see. Do you think your uncle's name affords you special treatment?"

"No, of course not," smiled Grigori. "I am simply concerned that you should at least know who you are dealing with. That is all. Now, armed with this information, you may choose how you wish to proceed."

"I will still need a statement… from you both."

"My girlfriend was about to give you a statement when you interrupted her with your unnecessary question about her knowledge of flying protocols. Neither she nor I are familiar with such protocols but we have eyes and are intelligent enough to have understood what went on. If you are looking for a scapegoat do not look to our pilot! She performed a miracle when she landed in that field and all you want to do is…"

"I think the Officer has the picture comrade. Let us give our statements and leave… if that is okay with the Officer?"

"That is all I ask," grovelled the Officer.

The passengers of Ural-Air 4 were handed pencils and paper and ordered to write an account of the crash landing in the field and the events leading up to it. '*Then they were free to leave*,' they were told. Svetlana objected to writing her statement in pencil and asked for a pen. She was told no pens were available. When they were leaving the terminal building Svetlana asked Grigori if he thought the NKVD would alter their statements. He replied that he thought they probably would. She asked him who he thought would get the blame for the Ilyushin crashing. He said he thought it would probably be their pilot. She said that was unfair, especially as so many Ilyushins crash; "*surely the authorities should investigate why this is the case!*" Grigori looked at her and said, "*Do you mean the same authorities who are making fortunes out of meeting production targets to build new Ilyushins? And before you say anything else, Ilyushin is one of the businesses my father supplies parts to. He is also on Ilyushin's management board and a member of the government committee for air travel.*" Svetlana said she was certain that Grigori's father's appointments constituted a conflict of interests. Grigori agreed and walked on, beckoning Svetlana to hold hands.

★

Checking into their hotel, Grigori looked out around to see if anybody was paying them attention. Everything looked normal, nobody seemed interested in them. Svetlana got the usual looks from men but that was to be expected. Once in their room Grigori looked out of the window onto the wintry street below. There were just people going about their daily business. Svetlana asked Grigori if he thought there might be shops nearby that sold "*good clothes, especially good boots*", as they had lost all their possessions in the plane fire. Grigori called reception to inquire about shopping, mentioning he had a party card. He realised there would be no special shops for the children of the elite in Tula; they were only in Moscow, Leningrad and a few other cities around the USSR but he hoped there might be a shop where party members got '*special*' treatment. The receptionist said he would provide Grigori with a map and mark suitable shops on it for him.

Grigori went to take the map from the receptionist and was surprised when he held onto it. They made eye contact. The receptionist pointed at the map saying, "*this store will have all you need. I recommend you go there.*" The receptionist tapped the inside of Grigori's wrist with an extended forefinger as the two shook hands. It was an NV sign. With a slight, almost imperceptible nod of his head, Grigori removed the map from the receptionist's grasp and stuffed it into his jacket pocket. The NV sign did not go unnoticed by Svetlana but she kept silent about it until they were on the street.

"It looks like we were expected."

"I should hope so. I did not want to go wandering around Tula looking for our cell. Who could we trust? Who knows who we might bump into in this military town?"

Four people sidled up next to the pair as they made their way to the clothes shop, matching their pace along the sidewalk. Surrounded, Svetlana and Grigori were herded into an office building. Inside, the group took a lift to the eighteenth floor. It was the tallest building in Tula. Nobody spoke until they left the lift. The leader of the group wanted to know about the plane crash. Grigori assumed they wanted reassurance that the people they had with them had not been substituted by the KGB at the airport. Grigori gave the man the short version of the plane crash story followed by prearranged NV signs. The leader of the group returned the confirmation signs to reassure Svetlana and Grigori that they too were genuine.

The giving and receiving of signs is a practically fool proof way of ensuring that you are dealing with the right people. If a sign is misgiven, it could mean any number of things from '*I am being watched*' to '*kill me I am an imposter*' but that would be an extreme case as it is invariably better to keep your enemies alive so you can stay close to them and they you.

The leader directed Svetlana and Grigori to enter a room with a huge oblong table at its centre. At the far end of which was sat a figure silhouetted by the light from an angle poise lamp. The silhouette spoke, inviting them all to take a seat at the other end of the table. There was something about the silhouette's voice, '*it was distorted and metallic sounding*'. The group of four did not seem to think this was odd so Svetlana and Grigori accepted the voice for what it was, assuming its owner needed to remain incognito. Grigori thought it might be Lev but if so then why was he… he would have other guesses at the identity of the silhouette during the meeting. None of which was even close. The silhouette briefed them on their mission to break into KGB HQ, access the Colossus Mk XIV computer and load the discs he slid along the table to them.

The self-appointed leader of the group grabbed the discs to show he was in charge of the mission. He took the group over the finer details of the plan. They would travel to Moscow separately, including Svetlana and Grigori, where they would live separately and after their training they would not meet up again until the day of the mission. Grigori said that might look suspicious. The silhouette disagreed, saying that in a city of so many millions who would notice if one person travelled without another or did not keep in the other's company, adding, "*six people travelling and living together makes surveillance easy. You have your orders and you must stick to them.*" Then he shoved six envelopes along the table and told them to take one each. The money in the envelopes was to cover their financial needs in Moscow, including some cash in case they needed to bribe their way out of a difficult situation, bribery being rife throughout the Soviet Union. Before the silhouette left the group he wished them every success with the mission and promised that after the revolution there would be a special place for them in the new regime.

The silhouette departed the meeting via a door at the rear of the room. With their view of the silhouette's back framed for a moment in the open door, they noted his physique and wondered if it was a disguise. The leader of the group called everybody together and spread a map out on the table as he passed around notebooks, ordering everybody to only write notes in their assigned code. Having individual codes has advantages and disadvantages. One advantage being that if more than one person was taken at the same time it would take their captors a while before they realised they were dealing with two unrelated codes. A disadvantage is that unique codes leave a trail back to an individual.

It was Svetlana and Grigori's job to load the computer discs into the Colossus Mk XIV's command consul and run the programmes which would send instructions to NV activists to start the revolution, or so they had been told. It was everybody's job to make sure they got to the command consul. Neither Svetlana nor Grigori had operated a Colossus Mk XIV command terminal before and they hoped the terminals they had practised on in Vladivostok were the same as it otherwise the revolution would be over before it had begun.

★

There was a lot for the team to go over in the four days they had before leaving Tula to travel to Moscow. They had to practise the timing of the raid on the KGB's HQ over and over again and again. None of them was yet ready to become martyrs to the cause so self-preservation was high on their lists of priorities. The leader of the group, Valeri Demidov, referred to the raid on the KGB's HQ as, "*Our daring and heroic raid on the headquarters of the much hated and despised KGB thus striking the first blow in the liberation of the oppressed Peoples of the Soviet Union.*" This little speech of Valeri's changed minutely during each rendition as though he was practising the best words to use; '*for some future victory speech at a rally perhaps?'* each of the others thought.

★

Prior to the arrival of Svetlana and Grigori, the Tula cell were on their toes looking out for spies or anybody who might have them under surveillance. They were suspicious of everybody, especially if they saw the same person more than once. Even more so if they were spotted at the same location. Each day, Valeri collected the team's descriptions of suspicious people and wrote them on the wall of the warehouse they were using to train for their mission.

<u>Male number 6</u>. *Age, about thirty five [there was disagreement about the man's age as he appeared both much older and much younger in the other descriptions]. Height, five foot seven [similar disagreement on the man's height]. They could not even agree on the colour of the man's eyes, hair or even the clothes he was wearing.*

Valeri suggested it might be different men, observed in the same place at different times. After a few days the list was so long, caused so much argument and wasted so much time that the group decided to abandon it as a bad job.

The principal reason for the group failing to produce an agreed list of potential spies was due to the policy of zero unemployment in the Soviet Union. Those who were '*technically*' jobless had to attend various locations at various times which gave the impression of full employment. In a place like Tula, with virtually no employment outside the military, most people followed routines, hence there were lots of candidates for spies as their job was hanging about in the same place and would only move on after a '*colleague*' replaced them.

As with most situations, that which is right under the nose often goes unnoticed. The group, following protocol, arrived separately each day at the warehouse which was situated at the end of a dead-end street. '*One way in, one way out.*' On their way to and from the warehouse they passed an office at the corner of the street. As each walked past the office's glass doors the security guard waved to them, bid them good morning as they arrived and good evening when they left. The security guard walked stiffly with a cane and the group thought he was probably an ex-Soldier, a veteran perhaps, who had been pensioned off by the military in this military town.

Four times each day, the security guard made a phone call to his handler to report comings, goings and suspicious activities. After every report the security guard's handler would order him to "*write everything down and send it to me.*" He regularly exaggerated so-called suspicious activities to keep his job secure. It was part of the security guard's duties to take photographs of everybody who passed his door. As a keen amateur photographer, the security guard developed the film himself and handed the prints and their negatives, along with a report, to a KGB courier who took them to Moscow. KGB couriers rode motorcycles but in the winter months they flew to Moscow. Given the dangers of flying in the Soviet Union, as well as those on the road, the life expectancy of a KGB motorcycle courier was not very great. On the whole they preferred to fly as they were warm and got free food and alcohol on the plane.

★

The warehouse which the Tula cell was using to train for the mission was vast. Looking down onto the storage area were two floors of offices and a canteen, accessed by a metal staircase. Both upper floors held caches of hidden weapons and secret bunkers for people to hide in. If the building was ever stormed by the KGB or NKVD they would suffer great loss of life.

In the centre of the storage area was painted an outline of the new computer wing at the KGB's HQ. The wing had been added four years previously to house the KGB's latest computers, their operators and air-conditioning plant. NV had acquired the architectural drawings for the computer suite just two months after it was built. Doors and windows were marked on the painted outline complete with notes written next to them; *type 42 lock; door opens inwards; window hinge to RHS*. Sections of the outer wall of the wing and the computer rooms themselves had been reproduced in plywood to make the layout as realistic as possible.

A training programme had been devised for the attack on the computer suite at the KGB's HQ to get everybody working together as a team to give them the best possible chance of success; even though they only had four days before they had to leave to travel to Moscow.

Pinned to a notice board in the warehouse was the plan for the attack on the KGB's computer suite at their HQ in Moscow:

1. <u>Everybody to travel separately to the Rendezvous Point [RVP]</u>. *Once arrived, we will give and receive newly devised NV signs to confirm we were not compromised. If compromised the mission will be aborted.*

2. <u>Gain access to the grounds of KGB HQ</u>. *Scale the outer wall using rope and grappling hooks fired from a compressed air launcher.* <u>Note</u>: *we have twenty seconds to climb the wall and drop down into the inner courtyard.*

3. Guards. *Whenever unavoidable guards must be killed. Preferred method is the single loop garrotte. Second method is close-in head shot with suppressed Markov 9mil. Last resort is to cut the guard's throat to prevent them raising the alarm.*

4. Positions for executing the mission. *Computer room, Svetlana, Grigori and Irina. Hallways, Valeri, Georgi and Maria.*

5. Accessing the computers. *Svetlana to load discs and follow the instructions on the screen. If there is a problem accessing the computer Svetlana will be allowed five minutes to solve it or the mission will be aborted.*

6. Making our escape. *Georgi will remain in the courtyard to provide cover until everybody is over the wall. Maria will remain on top of the wall to cover Georgi while he climbs the rope. If we were unsuccessful we will meet to work out what went wrong and what we plan to do about it.*

Valeri estimated they would have twenty minutes maximum from the time they started scaling the walls of the compound to completing the mission and leaving by the same way they had arrived. None of the others thought very much of his plan.

"If we fail will the Terror go ahead?"

"Yes."

"That is it? There is no fall-back plan?"

"No."

"What about blowing up the computers?"

"How will that help? Orders have already gone out for the Terror to start. What is on the computer discs will change everything."

"How?"

"I do not know, we must have faith in the discs, what other choice do we have?"

If they did not send the same message simultaneously to either end of the Soviet Union, Velikobritania and Vladivostok, then the Terror would begin. It was all or nothing. They each felt the burden of the weight of the responsibility they now carried.

*

The evening before training was due to begin, Valeri received a visit from the NV Commander of the Tula region. She entered his safe house guarded by an NV cell. Valeri knew its leader as Sonya but she went by many other names, among them Alice. The Commander said Sonya had brought her a message from Lev. It told of the Terror; when it would begin and where it would begin and NV Tula's role in leading the uprising against it. Unbeknownst to all, Lev had sent identical messages to NV commanders right across the Soviet Union, Tula was not so very special after all. Alice then told Valeri the terrible tale of how she had come by Lev's message and introduced him to the only surviving member of cell NV4R, Vladimir Vakhnenko. The Commander ordered Valeri to take Vladimir to Moscow in place of the person she had promised him. "*Besides, he has vital information to pass on to the leadership,*" she said knowing NV's leadership was no longer there and the promised person too precious for her to lose.

I was taken to a safe house where I was to stay when not training for the assault on the KGB's HQ. Before I left Valeri's apartment that evening he gave me directions to the warehouse where the training was taking place and told about the security protocols I must follow at all times.

Next morning I got up, ate a meagre breakfast, left the safe house and made my way to the warehouse. As I neared it I could not believe my eyes. Svetlana was right in front of me! I wanted to run up to her and greet her but it was against the security protocols. The direction she was travelling in led me to believe that she too was going to the warehouse.

★

Following the addition of Svetlana, Grigori and Vladimir to his reports about the group in the warehouse, the security guard's handler ordered him to plant microphones there so he could find out what was going on. Not wanting to do something like that in the least, the security guard tried to convince his handler that it was far too risky, "*the building is hard to gain access to… it will arouse suspicion. It is probably being watched by some radical group… Narodnaya Volya perhaps.*" The handler insisted the security guard plant microphones in the warehouse and said some would be despatched to him.

Our security guard cursed his handler knowing he would never see his family again if he disobeyed orders. He considered contacting the Tula branch of Narodnaya Volya to tell them all about him being forced to spy on them because the KGB had his family. The reason he chose not to was simple; if he went to NV they would kill him because they could not afford to let him live. In future he would only tell his handler the bare minimum to satisfy him sufficiently to keep his family alive and live in the hope that one day he got the chance to free them or kill his handler. In any event, spying on the Tula cell did not sit well with him. '*I hope the microphones do not get lost in the post,*' he thought with a cunning smile.

★

As I walked into the warehouse Svetlana and Grigori did a double take. It was funny the way they looked at me, looked away and then looked at me again. Svetlana ran over and covered me in kisses, the last one on the lips lasted for over ten seconds. It was my third kiss. I really enjoyed it especially as I saw Greg did not like it one little bit. Valeri told us to calm down and to concentrate as we had so little time left before we had to leave for Moscow. I whispered that we would talk later. '*I would tell them everything and I wanted to know all about what they had been doing.*' Grigori tried his best to look disinterested but I knew he was as eager as me and Svetlana to get the full story.

Our training was punishing. We began first thing every morning with hand to hand combat training. Valeri and his cell were far superior in this to Svetlana, Grigori and me, though everybody admired Svetlana's garrotte and knife work. Grigori was not a natural warrior so he just practised basic self-defence, concentrating on arm locks to incapacitate anybody who might grab hold of him. By the end of day four Grigori was competent at using the flat of his hand to hit an opponent on the nose or throat, both moves being deadly if delivered correctly. I, being a member of a boxing club back in Budyonovsk, already possessed the instincts, skills and movements of a fighter and so easily absorbed the things I needed to know to kill an opponent with my bare hands.

For our second session we practised scaling the twenty foot perimeter wall of our plywood KGB Computer Suite. Our target time was twenty seconds to get all seven of us over the wall and down into the '*courtyard*'. An impossible task in such a short amount of time. We became so good at this drill that we took on the appearance of an acrobatic troupe. Even Grigori managed this despite his chubby body. We both noticed that during this exercise Valeri showed a lot of attention to Svetlana; too much for my liking. Whenever she climbed the rope, went over the wall or came down the other side, he would be close at hand to help her, usually by placing his hands on her backside and shoving her from behind. We noticed that Svetlana oftentimes laughed and squealed in delight when hoisted by Valeri's strong hands. I hated it whenever they got close together. My objections were on the grounds that I saw myself as Grigori's successor for Svetlana's affections should anything ever happen to him. For Grigori's part, Irina was showing a lot of interest in him so he was not so bothered that Valeri was flirting with Svetlana.

⋆

Our third session of each day was taken up practising entry scenarios into the computer suite and what to do and where to go once inside. This seldom went smoothly and did not bode well for the raid on the KGB's HQ. We practised entering the building through doors and windows over and over again followed by dispersing to locations inside the building. It became clear that no matter where we placed ourselves we could not cover all the approaches to the computer suite to protect Svetlana and Grigori while they loaded the computer discs. Valeri considered contacting the Tula NV Commander for additional resources but ultimately decided not to for security's sake. The fewer people involved or who knew the details of the mission the better as far as he was concerned. I complained about my role of having to '*stand guard*' outside the window of the computer suite, "*I feel useless. Everybody else has something important to do.*" I suggested I would be of more use inside the building covering Svetlana, Grigori and the rest of the team. Valeri rejected my suggestion, insisting they needed an outside man and I was it.

The final session of each day was spent on end to end run throughs of the plan. We rehearsed scenarios where we successfully evaded guards to others where there were four or more guards who had to be '*dealt with*'. Some scenarios called for '*dead guards*' springing back to life to reposition themselves for another encounter. I played the role of a guard in all the scenarios. I was not happy. The biggest unknown was how long it would take for the computer discs to load and the coded commands programme to run. Svetlana said that in her experience they would need at least ten minutes but they should allow fifteen. Valeri said the plan only allowed five minutes but after a smile from Svetlana he said he would bow to her superior knowledge on the subject. Their overt flirting was starting to enrage me. We ran a scenario where Svetlana and Grigori were dead and Irina had to load the discs. I chipped in that as I knew more about computers than Irina we should swap roles. My comment cost me any chance I might have had of having sex with Irina.

★

At the end of the fourth day Valeri brought everybody together.

"Comrades, tomorrow we go to Moscow to face whatever fate awaits us. Once we are there, Irina will pick up the weapons and give them to us just before we…"

"Why can we not have our weapons now?"

"Because, Comrade Rabinovich, anybody found carrying a weapon will be arrested and that will ruin the plan. Do you have any more questions?" spoke Valeri in a condescending tone. Grigori thought it best to keep his mouth shut about his green party card with its red border which permitted him to carry weapons at any time.

"No comrade, thank you for explaining." In the way that Grigori and Valeri spoke to one another it was obvious to all that they did not like each other. The rest of the group said as much, adding that they had to put their differences aside until after the mission was over. Both men shook hands and swore that any differences they might have would be put to one side until after the mission. Neither of them meant it.

"Comrades, the success of the revolution depends on us. We must not fail. Go. Go now and do not look back until we are free!" I was not really sure what Valeri meant.

★

We did not meet up that last evening before we left Tula. There was no '*last supper*' together or '*good luck*' drink we just simply dissolved into the darkness. The plan was for each of us to travel to Moscow separately by car, bus, plane and train over the next twenty four hours. In forty eight hours Tula cell NV6K were to rendezvous by the wall outside the KGB's HQ in Moscow. Once in Moscow, we were to head for our designated safe houses to wait until Z hour. Unbeknown to anybody, Valeri and Svetlana booked into a hotel for the night and travelled to Moscow together the following day.

The Hunt for NV6K

As usual, our security guard sat waiting for the group to pass his building one by one on their way to the warehouse and when by 0930 they had not done so he contacted his handler. The handler said he would contact his boss in Moscow to inform him of the change in the situation but in the meantime he would have his agents come and meet him to discuss matters. Our guard knew what that meant; arrest, imprisonment, torture and his death as well as the deaths of all his family. He regretted not breaking into the warehouse and planting microphones to snoop on the group. '*Had he done so,*' he thought, '*I might have something useful to trade to guarantee my continued existence*'… the security guard's mind wandering broke at the sound of banging on the glass doors of the reception area.

"Open the door!" yelled an irate man rattling the doors wildly. The security guard walked to the doors. Not recognising the man he palmed his trusty old Markov .45.

"Stop shaking the doors! You will break the glass. What do you want?" Yuri yelled at the irate man.

"I have been watching the same people as you have been watching… but at their safe houses. They have left Tula! They must have left in the night."

"I do not know you… how do I know if you are…"

"I am Leonid Ivanov and you are Yuri Sakov. You have been reporting on a group that has passed by here on their way to the warehouse at the end of the street. Three new people joined them in the past four or five days. I have been doing the same as you but at their safe houses. It was not easy, they stayed at different locations… and they would not give me any more resources. I asked for them but they… what do they think I am? Why did they not give me what I asked for? It is not as though they are busy!" complained Leonid.

"Who do you work for?"

"Lieutenant Kaminski of the third Tula section of the KGB."

"You are an informant?"

"Yes," replied Leonid shamefully, "but so are you." Yuri was equally ashamed. The two men felt some sort of bond between them.

"There is nothing for us to do now but wait."

"What, are you crazy?"

"I called my handler just a few minutes ago. He said he is going to call Moscow and speak with his boss and tell him about…"

"Oh no, no, no! That was a big mistake Yuri, a big mistake. Did he say anything else?"

"Yes, he said he was sending some agents to '*discuss matters with me*'. I think I know what that means." After a moment's pause Yuri added resignedly, "I should run away."

"Where would you run to?"

"I have heard that the Keltskaya in Siberia offer shelter to all those who need it."

"That is not what I heard. I heard they kill anybody who tries to get near them rather than risk that person being an agent." The truth was somewhere in between.

"What shall I do?"

"I? We, you mean! What shall '*we*' do! I do not want to have to explain to Kaminski how I lost them. We need to get inside the warehouse and find something that we can trade for our lives."

Yuri placed his crutches and security guard paraphernalia on the shelf of his Security Guard Station and walked out of the office building, sans limp. He knew whatever else happened that day he would not be returning to his worthless job.

"How come you know about me but I do not know about you?"

"You know how things are. Kaminski was told about you and he told me about you and that I had to keep watch on you as well as the cell. It was hard work! I hardly got any sleep, especially this past week."

"You were watching me?" asked Yuri in disbelief. He thought of himself as the kind of person who would notice something like that.

"Yuri, you know what Stalin used to say?" Yuri shook his head. "He used to say '*Trust, but check*'. I was checking on you more than watching you if that makes you feel any better."

"I do not understand the difference."

"Neither do I, comrade, neither do I. It was just orders and I am now trying to make the best of it."

The two men made their way down the dead-end street toward the warehouse. '*What if it is being watched?*' Yuri thought. Who knew who or what was being watched in Tula? He expressed his concerns to Leonid who dismissed them saying that he would know if the warehouse was being watched. '*Really*?' Yuri thought disbelievingly.

*

Stood outside the warehouse the two men sized up the job in hand. Yuri went around the side to see if there were any easy ways of getting into the building while Leonid did a skidding run and shoulder-charge at the front door. It was so sturdy he bounced off it and landed on his back. Dazed, he opened his eyes. The falling snow caused him to blink.

It appeared the only way to get inside the warehouse was either by smashing through the front door or climbing forty feet up an icy drain pipe to break a window and get in that way. Not fancying the forty foot climb, the men agreed to give the front door another go but this time the two of them would shoulder-charge it together. They ran, hit the door and bounced off, ending up lying on their backs in the snow. Leonid said he was sure that the door had given a little and suggested another try. This time the door's frame splintered enough for the two men, once they got back to their feet, to work it loose from the wall. After four minutes of pushing and pulling at the door frame it gave way and they entered the warehouse.

The two men were correct in surmising that the warehouse might be under observation. It was. But not by the KGB. The top four floors of the building opposite the warehouse were occupied by an agency responsible for '*reporting on agricultural production*'. It was a front for Narodnaya Volya's HQ for the Tula region and the break in at the warehouse had been watched by no less than twenty trigger-happy NV operatives.

After Leonid's first attempt at shoulder-charging the warehouse door, bets were laid by the NV operatives on everything from the number of further shoulder-charges they would attempt, to climbing the drainpipe to gain entry or climbing the drainpipe and falling to their deaths, to them giving up altogether and running away. As soon as the door to the warehouse went in they informed the Commander of the Tula Cell that the warehouse had uninvited guests inside. She immediately sent a special envoy to Moscow to let the group know what had happened the morning after they had left Tula. One major concern was why the booby trap bomb had not gone off in the corridor when the door went in.

NV Executive Council members debated their next move. They discussed assassinating the intruders before they found the weapons caches. A cloud of indecision descended over the group. They would have to break cover if they checked on who these men were and being so near Z Day that might prove disastrous. Who were they? What if they were regional security… or worse, KGB? Should they take a chance and just kill the intruders anyway? If they did they would have to empty the warehouse of weapons in broad daylight. That would give them the added problem of finding somewhere to hide the weapons. How much time would they have to clear the warehouse before the KGB arrived? It all seemed too risky. They decided to wait and see what happened next. They could always blow the building up destroying the weapons and the evidence in the warehouse but being so near Z Day that would be disastrous.

The Executive Council hadn't been in a situation like this before. If they ordered the men killed who would do it? Who had the authority to give such an order? After a century of Soviet rule few citizens knew how to make decisions, show leadership or take the initiative. An experienced NV Operative suggested they wait and see how events in the warehouse unfolded. She believed there was more yet to reveal and them knowing what it was might mean the difference between the success and failure of the mission in Moscow. The Executive Council agreed with her and ordered an observation post be set up behind a slit in the curtains in one of the offices on the floor below.

★

"Shall we put the lights on?" asked Yuri.

"Of course we put the lights on. We cannot see in the dark. Unless you have brought a torch?"

"No, I did not bring a torch."

Leonid felt around in the darkness for light switches by slapping his hands against the left hand wall and then the right. He got jittery thinking that something could be lurking in the dark and might grab his hand or jump out at him. He was relieved when he located a bank of switches. As rows of fluorescent lights flickered into life along the length of the warehouse their flashing dizzied both men for a moment. When they regained their senses, it seemed to them that the warehouse was larger on the inside than the outside. They had no answer as to why that might be.

In the inside of the warehouse was an odd looking plywood construction which the pair went to investigate. As they drew close they noticed white lines painted on the floor with the positions of doors and windows marked on the floor. The painted line had a twenty foot high plywood '*wall*' along forty feet of its length. The face of the plywood wall had been scuffed by feet marks and gouges had been made in it, particularly along its top edge. '*Why build a wall when you could just step over a line and be on the other side of it?*'

Beyond the plywood wall a series of plywood rooms and corridors had been constructed without ceilings. Oblongs and squares had been painted on the floor in one of the rooms, some of which had small dots on their lower half. The whole scene was puzzling to Leonid and Yuri. It made no sense to them. What were they looking at?

To try and make sense of it all they needed to get a view of the whole scene. Leonid spotted an open flight of metal stairs leading to the upper floors. At the top of the first flight of stairs was a metal grating landing connecting to a second flight of stairs. At the right hand side of the grating was a door. They could not see much of the upper part of the second flight of stairs as they were hidden behind the shadow cast above the line of fluorescent lights. Ascending the lower flight of stairs the men turned and looked on the scene below. All became clear to them. It was the layout of a building. But what building it was and where it might be they could not make a guess at.

Leonid tried the handle of the door served by the metal grating landing. It was locked. His shoulder was still hurting from shoulder-charging the front door so he asked Yuri to give it a try. Yuri suggested they try the door at the top of the next flight of stairs instead. "*Besides,*" he said, "*there is not enough room to get a good run at the door.*" Leonid agreed with him.

Climbing to the top of the metal staircase Leonid pushed open the door at its summit. He poked his head through the gap to take a quick sweeping look beyond the door. All he saw was pitch blackness. There was no guard rail around the mini-landing outside the door which made both men feel very uneasy. Yuri in particular was not very good with heights. The door's self-closing mechanism shut before they had a chance to properly see into the dark void beyond. Leonid pushed the door open again, this time keeping it ajar using his foot. A little residual light from the warehouse cut a pale slice into the darkness of the corridor. Leonid thought he could just about make out the edge of what looked like a bank of switches on the opposite wall of the corridor. '*Why not put the light switches outside the door?*' he thought.

"Yuri, you go in and switch the lights on," said Leonid as casually as he could. Yuri was not at all keen to cross the pitch black corridor even though it was no more than ten feet.

"I cannot… I have… I have night blindness…"

"Night blindness? There is no such thing."

"There is. When I was in the army I was examined by doctors and they said I had night blindness. I cannot drive cars at night and I…"

"Alright, alright. I will go but if there is anybody waiting in the dark and they jump on me be careful to shoot them and not me." Yuri took this as his cue to cock his pistol. Leonid shook his head.

"You mean to say there was no round in the chamber?" Yuri did not bother answering the question as it was obvious he had not.

Leonid pondered whether it was better to run for the switches or go slowly and quietly, listening all the time for tell-tale noises of people hiding in the dark. '*What if the switches did not turn on the lights? What if, when he got to them, they were not the right switches? What if there were other switches that he had yet to discover? What if they'…* "*Are you going or not?*" asked an impatient Yuri. Leonid sprang forward into the dark and on reaching the switches he pressed as many as he could. The lights in the corridor flickered on all along its length. There had been nobody waiting in the corridor to ambush him after all. Leonid gave a nervous laugh and said to Yuri. "*You are a coward.*" The corridor was at least a hundred yards long with all its doors on one side. "*Let us check a few rooms.*" Yuri nodded.

The men advanced cautiously along the corridor, guns in hand pointing the way ahead of them. They stopped at the fourth door they came to. Leonid turned the door knob and the door creaked open. He could tell by the stiffness of its hinges that it had been some time since it had last been opened. The room was in complete darkness except for a thin strip of light describing the outer edges of a large window covered by a shutter. After checking the corners of the room as best he could, Leonid entered led by his gun. When he got to the window he grabbed a metal bracing bar and released the shutter. As it swung open under its own weight light flooded the room. It had stopped snowing. The sky was a brilliant blue and the weak sun low in the winter sky dazzled both men.

In the building opposite the warehouse the people observing events through the slit in the office curtains noticed that one of the shutters had suddenly sprung open and two men could be clearly seen at the window. One of them was lighting a cigarette. The leader heard two snapping clicks, one on either side of her head, as bullets were loaded into chambers. She turned to look at the snipers, shook her head and pointed to the street below. Four cars had pulled up at the warehouse and going by their make and colour they were NKVD snatch vehicles. Four NKVD Soldiers emerged from each car with several of them speaking rapidly on two-way radios with God knew who.

"Where are the weapons hidden?" asked one of the NV observers.

"Somewhere on the second floor… I think." The conversation was joined by a handful of NV operatives.

"Get hold of somebody who knows. If the weapons are discovered we will not be able to join the big party in two days' time." An operative entered the conversation.

"We cannot take the risk. Put silencers on the rifles and shoot both the men at the window right now. When the NKVD find them we should blow the whole place up. It will look like the warehouse was booby-trapped."

"But the weapons! What about the weapons? We need them!"

"We cannot afford to compromise the Moscow mission. Shoot the men now and as soon as the NKVD are inside the building blow it." Other operatives joined in the argument.

"No comrade do not blow the building up."

"I agree with Ilya, let us wait and see what happens. If we do not like what we see then we can blow the building."

"But they will see what is in there."

"What will they see? An obstacle course? A children's playground? A set for a movie? What will they see? They will not recognise it!"

"We cannot take that chance. Blow the building. Now!"

"No!" chorused the majority keen to keep the weapons hidden inside the warehouse intact.

"Okay, tell me, how will we get at the weapons now that the NKVD has arrived? Answer me that," said the NV operative keen to blow the warehouse up.

"We will go in at night… or in the middle of the day… or at any time we like… perhaps when the revolution starts? Who knows, they might hear what is going on and join us… or surrender. We have to take a chance that the weapons are not discovered because without them Tula will not be able to play her part."

A fifth car pulled up outside the warehouse. Out of it stepped a fully uniformed and heavily medalled NKVD Colonel, barking orders on the move at the Soldiers. In response they donned gas masks, cocked machine pistols and stood to attention in two lines of eight to receive their orders before entering the warehouse. It was clear to the NV observers that these NKVD Soldiers were disciplined, seasoned, professionals. The Soldiers moved inside the warehouse, covering each other in four '*advancing-last-man-of-four*' squads. Keeping tight to the inside walls of the warehouse, the Soldiers checked high and low as they watched their corners for any movement. An NKVD Officer touched the shoulder of the Soldier in front of her and pointed toward the metal stair case. The Soldier nodded his understanding and tapped the two others in their squad. The four man squad ascended the staircase while being covered by the other four man squads. The Soldiers were totally silent as they advanced up the metal staircase in their rubber soled boots and metal free fatigues.

Having entered fourteen rooms, Leonid and Yuri were confident that the upper rooms were uninhabited, despite them not gaining access to the first floor. In their eagerness to find something they might trade for their lives they missed every clue as to the locations of NV's weapons caches.

On the staircase the NKVD squad had reached the metal grating landing. One of the Soldiers pressed the door's handle before miming to his compatriots that it was locked. The Officer signalled to him to blow the door and a small plug of plastic explosive was inserted into the lock. The explosion blew the door off its hinges and the NKVD squad rushed into the corridor which they illuminated with lights attached to the ends of their machine pistols.

On hearing the explosion Leonid and Yuri stared at one another through saucer-sized eyes. Leonid went to the office window to check the street below. He saw five of what were obviously NKVD snatch cars. He called Yuri over to see the cars for himself and while he was peering out of the window Leonid shot him in the back of his head. He then ran as fast as he could to the door leading to the stairwell, opened it and shouted to whoever it was in the building.

"Hold your fire! Do not shoot. My name is Leonid Ivanov. I am a special agent working for Lieutenant Kaminski of the third Tula sector KGB. I have just shot a spy. I am going to throw my gun out and then I am going to walk through the door with my hands up. Do not shoot me!" the NKVD Officer shouted in reply.

"Do not attempt to come down the stairs until you are ordered to do so. Do you understand?" Leonid eased the door open and kept it ajar with his knee.

"Yes!" Leonid shouted as loudly as he could. After throwing his gun to the floor of the warehouse he placed his hands on his head and stepped onto the landing. The NKVD Officer shouted for him to kneel down. Leonid complied. Looking toward the voice he saw four high power torches illuminating him from the metal grating landing below and several others from the other side of the warehouse.

"If he moves, shoot him!" came the order from the NKVD Colonel standing at the warehouse's entrance.

"Please comrades, do not shoot me. I am unarmed."

"Stand up!" barked the NKVD Officer. Leonid stood. "Walk toward me… slowly… one stair at a time. If you make any sudden moves I will shoot you dead."

"I understand. I am very nervous. Please do not shoot me."

Leonid slowly made his way, one stair at a time, toward the NKVD squad on the landing below. As soon as he was within reach of them, two Soldiers pulled him from the stairs and slammed him hard down onto the metal grating landing. Leonid yelled in pain. Due to the grating the fall cut his face in a dozen places. The NKVD Soldiers handcuffed Leonid and dragged him backwards on his arse down the metal stairs, smashing him hard onto the concrete floor of the warehouse. He felt his head crack and saw stars before passing out.

In the building across the dead-end street from the warehouse the NV observers had witnessed Leonid shoot Yuri. The bullet passed right through his head and continued on through the window, leaving behind a star shaped crack surrounding a blood, bone and hair spattered hole. The debate was back on about whether or not they should blow the building. A vote was taken. By a majority of one the vote was not to blow the building immediately but if the NKVD discovered any of the weapons caches then it would definitely be blown up. One of the NV snipers asked how they would know if any of the weapons had been discovered. "*Simple,*" came the answer, "*they will remove anything they find and we will see them do it.*" The answer satisfied everybody though nobody wanted to ask the obvious next question.

★

Two days earlier, KGB Major Artur Arsenovich Popov was sitting in his warm comfortable office on the fourth floor of the KGB's HQ in the Lubyanka. The higher the floor the higher rank of its occupant and the deeper the pile of carpet. Major Popov was carrying out his most favourite winter task; reports writing. He had created a reports writing backlog to guarantee he would be indoors during the worst month and a half of the Soviet winter. He never rushed writing his reports, they had to be accurate and worded in such a way that he could not be open to criticism or worse… blame. The report he was working on was, strictly speaking, two reports, concerning events at the Pioneer camp outside Vladivostok. The first part of Major Popov's report was about his "*highly successful interrogation of several fanatical militant students who had arrived at the Pioneer camp in the guise of Camp Counsellors.*" To appear competent, massage his ego and satisfy his fantasy-fuelled, cruelty-crazed lust, he exaggerated the tortures he had used on the students; sparing no gruesome detail, imaginary though they were. At the end of this section of his report, the Major recommended that his subordinates from the Vladivostok inquisition be transferred to distant outposts. The last thing he wanted was for them to return to Moscow where the truth of what really happened there might come to light and kill his career if not he himself.

Major Popov was cogitating the second part of his Vladivostok Pioneer Camp saga; one in which he would claim to have quashed a rebellion while citing subordinates for acts of cowardice and recommending them for the firing squad. He smiled at the image of the firing squad his imagination conjured up while flexing his typing fingers to commence his next work of fiction. Before he had typed a single word he was called into an urgent briefing by his commanding Officer. Until recently she had been a Major, just like him, but had recently been promoted to Colonel, and in the process she had become Popov's boss. Major Popov had always hated Major, now Colonel, Eva Petrova, with every fibre of his being. To him, her being promoted was just like being back in Bishkek, overlooked for everything good that was being handed out, '*especially promotions!*'

When Major Popov entered the briefing room he was surprised to find it overflowing its fourteen hundred seating capacity. Colonel Petrova was standing at the front of the room alongside a General who she introduced as General Yashkin to the audience. '*Bitch. Look at her, who the hell does she think she is?*' The General gave a short speech about the importance of "*vigilance in these difficult and dangerous times with revolution in the air...*" before handing over to Colonel Petrova to continue the briefing. '*What is that old fool talking about?*' thought Major Popov. '*Revolution? Rubbish!*' Even though he knew it was not. Major Popov believed he now knew how Major Petrova had gotten her promotion. '*She is having an affair with that old fart of a General! It is so obvious! She got her promotion on her back! Bitch!*'

Colonel Petrova thanked General Yashkin for his inspiring words of introduction to the briefing and asked a junior KGB Officer to turn off the lights and switch on the projector.

"Responsible Workers, esteemed comrades, specially invited guests... brother and sister Officers." At Responsible Workers, esteemed comrades and specially invited guests, Major Popov looked about the room by the light of the projector's beam and recognised several Central Committee members in the audience as well as Vasily Dobrovski who he also recognised for some reason.

Maxim Kirilenko's Chef de Cabinet, Alexander Orlov, was also in attendance. Naturally, he recognised Luka Bazanov, Commissar of the KGB, by sight.

"As General Yashkin stated, these are difficult and dangerous times for our beloved Soviet Union. We are all under threat. Even as we sit here, groups of dissidents are planning to destroy our workers' paradise by bringing violent and bloody revolution onto the streets. Chief amongst these groups is Narodnaya Volya. We have all heard of that name since we read it in our history books at school but let me assure you, Narodnaya Volya is back and they are very real." Shaking of heads indicated disbelief in much of the audience, accompanied by some audible scoffing, '*I think the bitch must be drunk,*' thought Major Popov even though he knew NV was real. "My section has been monitoring Narodnaya Volya and we estimate they have a following numbering in the millions, perhaps the tens of millions, and they are preparing for war." Some shouts from the audience suggested the Colonel was creating something out of nothing to boost her career. "Accordingly, this KGB facility, and thousands like it across the Soviet Union, is now on high alert." Murmurs from the audience. "Intelligence recently obtained by my deep-cover Agents indicates that a popular uprising is likely within the next two to four months." This assertion produced noises of backsides shifting uncomfortably on seats. "In response to this unprecedented threat to our great nation… our workers' paradise… the Central Committee has produced a plan to annihilate the traitors, wreckers, saboteurs, anti-Soviet elements and anybody else who would attack our beloved Soviet Union. Their plan will crush them all!" Waves of loud applause echoed round the room; nobody wanted to be accused of treachery, for that is what it would be not to loudly cheer anything by the Central Committee. "Before I hand over to our specially invited speaker, Comrade Vasily Dobrovski, I will show you the faces of the enemy so you will know them. These pictures were obtained very recently and are of a terrorist cell at work in Tula, right on the very doorstep of our beloved capital city.

It is believed they are preparing an attack on the Kremlin." Gasps and shouts of indignation from the audience, some of them were genuine.

Speedily, one after the other, faces were flashed onto the screen. The forty fourth face grabbed Major Popov's interest. It was a face he would never forget; Grigori Andreivich Rabinovich. The next face was that of Svetlana Anna Panshina. Next came the face of the pup, Vladimir Vladimirovich Vakhnenko. Major Popov's immediate thought was to go to Tula and arrest Comrade Rabinovich along with the others as a prelude to bringing down the Commissar of the Western Frontier Gulags, Vasily Zaytsev, Grigori Rabinovich's Dyadya Vasya. '*Imagine,*' he thought, '*a terrorist whose uncle is a Commissar? How shocking!*' The Major mock-tutted aloud which attracted an annoyed stare from his KGB comrades, all of whom had him down for a fool and a shameless self-promoter. The Major's '*thoughts*' session continued, '*If I make the arrest myself and expose a Commissar as the uncle of a traitor everybody will see my true value… my quality… my true worth, and maybe I will get a much deserved promotion. Who knows, I might even end up as Petrova's boss… now, that would be nice.*' At that thought the Major smiled a snake smile.

After the picture show, which ended with Lev's face, Vasily Dobrovski took to the stage and asked the junior KGB Officer to load his slides into the projector.

"This first slide shows a map of the republics and the conquered nations in various colours. You will see from the key at the side what the colours mean. In short, they mean trouble. And what is the Central Committee going to do about this trouble? We are going to smash it before it gets worse." Loud cheering for the Presidium member.

"For the last several years I have been working alongside General Secretary Maxim Kirilenko… and my Central Committee colleagues," Dobrovski added so they too would be for it if Operation Zima failed, "on a plan to deal with the trouble-makers destroying our beloved Soviet Union. For decades, under successive leaders, we have become more and more soft… more and more weak… more and more tolerant… but no longer! In Maxim Kirilenko, we have a strong leader, a leader determined to return the Soviet Union to its former glory. In the days following the Great and Glorious Revolution, Lenin… the great father of our great nation… knew how to deal with wreckers, saboteurs and anti-Soviet elements. He brought them Terror… he brought Terror to all those who threatened to destroy our beloved workers' paradise. He sent them and their treacherous families to the Lubyanka or he put them in front of firing squads or had them dragged off to the Gulag to be worked to death as the price for their treachery. Those strong actions brought peace and security to the fledgling Soviet Union. In Maxim Kirilenko we have a leader who will restore peace to the Soviet Union by bringing Terror upon all those who would see her on her knees!" Rapturous applause, without any stage management. "The Terror will start simultaneously at either end of the Soviet Union in Velikobritania and Vladivostok. Once begun it will not stop until it has cleansed our lands of all the vermin. Our glorious fighting forces will crush them all. You will see on the next slide how it will work. Next slide! Operation Zima, as it is called, will start within the next month." Surprised looks from all around the room as there had been no leaks about it. "Taking the lead will be the NKVD with the Red Army following in their wake to occupy cleansed zones and ensuring there is no backsliding. Next slide! Once the NKVD's work is done in Velikobritania and Vladivostok, their forces will move toward the centre of the Soviet Union… cleansing areas as they go… seeking out and pursuing those trying to escape justice by running. The traitors will be caught in the middle and crushed." Comrade Dobrovski clapped his hands together once loudly causing the audience to jump. "No mercy will be given to them. Next slide! This map shows the facilities that have been built to support Operation Zima; thousands of holding camps for the Gulag have been built; thousands of torture houses have been built; thousands of internment camps have been built; thousands of ethnic concentration camps have been built!" More rapturous applause. "The plan has been approved by the Central Committee so you can be confident it will work." Ecstatic applause!

Vasily Dobrovski continued his presentation, providing his audience with the details of their parts in Operation Zima. Long before Comrade Dobrovski finished his presentation, Major Popov had drifted off into his scheme to destroy Vasily Zaytsev and execute his smart mouthed nephew, his female companion and the pathetic shrimp linguist, Vladimir Vakhnenko. Popov ground his teeth at the thought of how he was going to make them pay for the humiliations he had suffered at their hands.

After the presentation was over Colonel Petrova remained in the company of those who mattered to her career. While listening to her superiors waffle on about nothing in particular, out of the corner of her eye she caught sight of Major Popov trying to attract her attention. Colonel Petrova did not hate Major Popov but she neither liked nor respected him. She flicked her head in the direction of the door as a signal to Major Popov that he should leave the room. He stood his ground and smiled at her, demonstrating he had no intention of leaving the room until she came and spoke to him. The Colonel fast-trotted across the floor, grabbed the Major by his lapels and dragged him to an ante room.

"What do you want, Popov? How can you not see that I am busy? I still have important matters to discuss and I cannot do so with you hanging around!"

"Apologies Comrade Colonel but I think I should let you know that I recognised several photographs of the people in the presentation."

"I should hope so!" responded the Colonel exasperated with Popov.

"Yes… indeed… but I know of three of them personally. They are students studying languages at the University of Nationalities here in Moscow. They are suspected of being NV activists. After seeing they have linked up with a terrorist cell in Tula at this critical time I should travel there immediately to interrogate them. I guarantee I will find out from them what is going on in Tula." Major Popov was careful not to mention that one of the '*terrorists*' was the nephew of Vasily Zaytsev, Commissar of the Western Frontier Gulags, he kept that information to himself. Colonel Petrova saw an opportunity to get rid of the troublesome Popov for a few days, '*who knows, with any luck he might not return.*'

"Good idea, Major Popov. But first check with the local KGB to see if they are monitoring that particular cell. If they are then liaise with them before taking any action. I do not want any jurisdiction problems… do I make my meaning clear?"

"You do. I will leave for Tula straight away."

"No, you will finish your reports and you will have them on my desk for my approval before you go anywhere!" Major Popov inwardly cursed Colonel Petrova and also himself for his tardiness in not keeping up with his reports. He returned to his desk and began typing while leaving it to a Lieutenant to contact the Tula KGB to do some digging about the cell. The Lieutenant was eventually directed to a Lieutenant Kaminski of the third Tula sector of the KGB. He asked him what he knew about certain terrorist cells operating in Tula. Lieutenant Kaminski replied that he presently had several terrorist cells under observation, including one that rendezvoused at a warehouse in the southern end of the city daily. After the Lieutenant faxed photographs to Lieutenant Kaminski it was soon clear that the cell Major Popov was interested in was the one attending the warehouse each day.

Major Popov did not want anybody else arresting the nephew of a Commissar of the Western Frontier Gulags, stealing his glory, so he ordered Lieutenant Kaminski to maintain surveillance but not arrest the cell until after he arrived in Tula. Kaminski understood immediately that the Moscow Major from the Security Commissariat at the KGB's HQ wanted to grab the glory for himself and he was not so foolish as to stand in his way. The Lieutenant agreed not to do anything to jeopardise the Major's plan. Though Major Popov had not yet met Lieutenant Kaminski he decided that he liked him... '*liked him a lot.*' After receiving the confirmations from Tula, Major Popov could only think of the rewards coming his way, not to mention promotion to, at least, Colonel. He thought he might even get a Commissar job out of it!

★

When Leonid came round he found himself strapped to a wooden chair, his hands secured behind his back with handcuffs. To make sure he was fully awake the NKVD interrogator slapped Ivanov's face hard, forehand and backhand, four times.

"Hey! Hey! Stop hitting me! I am awake! Why did you do that? Why am I in handcuffs?"

"Who are you?"

"I told you who I am. My name is Leonid Ivanov. I am a special agent working for Lieutenant Kaminski of the third Tula sector of the KGB."

"What is so special about you... special agent Leonid Ivanov?" The NKVD Soldiers mock-laughed at the interrogator's jibe.

"I have... I had... I had special responsibility to watch an operational NV terrorist cell... and the man upstairs... the one who I shot... and report everything back to Lieutenant Kaminski personally."

"Why did you shoot the man upstairs in the back of the head? Why did you shoot him at all? You could have just arrested him."

"When I heard the explosion I panicked. I thought the cell had returned and some of the things the man had said to me made me think he was a double agent working for Narodnaya Volya."

"A double agent working for Narodnaya Volya?" Responded the interrogator sceptically. '*They do not usually go in for double agents as they cannot be trusted*,' thought the interrogator.

"Yes, a double agent. You see, he was watching the same NV cell as me and reporting their movements to his handler who then, I understand, reported everything to a KGB Officer in Moscow and then he…"

"And who is this KGB Officer in Moscow?" asked the interrogator sarcastically. Everybody thought Leonid's story too far-fetched.

"I do not know." Even if Leonid had known the identity of the KGB Officer in Moscow he would not have admitted it as to do so could make him appear to have more information than a person like him should have. Better to keep his mouth shut and let things unfold when Lieutenant Kaminski showed up. "When Lieutenant Kaminski shows up he will clear everything up for you."

"Why will Lieutenant Kaminski show up here?"

"Because I am late reporting and he will come looking for me."

They did not have to wait long for Lieutenant Kaminski to show up. The NKVD Colonel who had led the raid on the warehouse took Lieutenant Kaminski to one side and asked him what he was doing at the warehouse as this was to be his operation. Lieutenant Kaminski smirked and told the NKVD Colonel that he was mistaken, adding that a KGB Major from the Security Commissariat in Moscow was on his way to Tula to arrest the terrorist cell operating from the warehouse. The Colonel asked Lieutenant Kaminski the name of the KGB Major from Moscow. "KGB Major Artur Arsenovich Popov, Deputy Security Commissar for Universities, Trades Unions and Veterans Associations." Though the Colonel outranked the Moscow Major he knew better than to tangle with somebody from the KGB's Security Commissariat.

"Ah yes, I know of Major Popov… I have heard of him," lied the Colonel. "I am sure we can…"

"Good, then you will be able to reacquaint yourself with him when he gets here. His plane should be landing at Tula airport right about now."

Half a dozen KGB agents then marched into the warehouse to back Lieutenant Kaminski up. The Colonel knew when to back down and after a brief, face-saving, discussion he handed the warehouse, the prisoner and jurisdiction of the dead body of Yuri Sakov over to Lieutenant Kaminski and ordered his NKVD squads back to their cars.

KGB Major Popov and his entourage arrived at the warehouse an hour after the NKVD Colonel had left it. He greeted Lieutenant Kaminski with a hearty Russian triple-face-kiss to demonstrate to everybody that Kaminski was his man in Tula. A calculated move designed to keep everybody vying for Popov's attention and looking over their shoulders. After a briefing on the situation from Lieutenant Kaminski, with excerpts from special agent Leonid Ivanov about the people he had been tailing having left Tula, KGB Major Popov turned to examine the plywood structure sitting in the middle of the warehouse. He asked, to nobody in particular, what it was. No response. He asked again but louder.

"Comrade Major, we have not yet had time to properly investigate… but it looks like a plan or a layout of a building… somewhere," responded Lieutenant Kaminski grovellingly. This was just how Major Popov liked his subordinates to act.

"I agree," replied the Major pleasantly, not wanting to undermine the Lieutenant in front of his squad for his inane and obvious observation. On the inside he was thinking, '*I can see that much for myself you idiot!*' Taking the initiative, as he saw it, the Lieutenant ordered two of his KGB Agents to ascend the stairs to get a better view of the structure and report back.

"May I suggest something, Lieutenant Kaminski?"

"Most certainly Comrade Major," replied Lieutenant Kaminski maintaining grovelling mode.

"Instead of sending your Agents, we, you and I, should climb the stairs to get a better view of the structure and see for ourselves what it is?"

"An excellent suggestion Comrade Major. Shall I lead the way or…" Major Popov gestured with a wave of his hand for Lieutenant Kaminski to lead the way.

"Have your Agents checked the entire building for anybody hiding?"

"They have Comrade Major," lied the Lieutenant not wanting to look foolish in front of the Moscow Major.

'*Not entirely useless then,*' hought the Major.

Reaching the metal grating landing below the second section of stairs the KGB Officers surveyed the scene laid out below them. It was obvious to them both that the structure was probably the layout of a wing of a larger building. What seemed odd was the closeness of the wall to the building itself, '*but then again,*' thought the Major, '*the builders might not have been working to scale.*' Arriving on the metal plate landing at the top of the second flight of stairs both men kept their backs pressed hard against the wall as there was no guard rail to prevent them falling to the ground. The Major asked the Lieutenant what he thought the building might be and where it might be. He had no answer to either question, mainly because he was paralysed with fear at the thought of falling from the platform. There was something about the building layout that was familiar to the Major but he could not put his finger on it. Before returning to ground level the Major asked the Lieutenant if he had a camera. The Lieutenant shouted down to his Agents asking if any of them had a camera. One of them replied that she had a camera in her car and went to retrieve it. When she returned she was ordered to take photographs of the structure from various heights between the two landings. Major Popov ordered the Agent to have the film developed immediately, adding that she must hand the prints and their negatives to him personally. As the Agent was leaving the warehouse the Major shouted to her to make sure the prints were eight by ten.

"Where do you think this building could be Comrade Lieutenant?" asked the Major again.

"It could be anywhere, Comrade Major."

"No, Lieutenant Kaminski, that is where you are wrong. The people who built it have left Tula, probably to carry out their mission, so we can be certain that the building is not in Tula. What is clear is that this warehouse was a training ground for an attack on this building… that much I am certain of."

"What sort of building could it be?"

"Looking at its outline, its dimensions, its structure and the height of its walls it has to be a State building."

"You think they are going to attack the state? They will never get away with it! Who would be so foolish as to do such a thing?"

"Assuming it was indeed NV activists who built this then it stands to reason that Narodnaya Volya…" Uncharacteristically, Lieutenant Kaminski cut into the Major's deliberations.

"Narodnaya Volya? Surely not! They died out long ago," spoke the Lieutenant playing stupid to bolster the Major's ego.

"Well, comrade Lieutenant, they are back," responded Major Popov angry at being interrupted, "but this time they are on the other side of the fence." After a minute's silent contemplation of his faux pas the Lieutenant sheepishly asked.

"Do you think the building could be in Moscow, Comrade Major?"

"Yes I do. I do think it is in Moscow. It has to be Moscow… where else could it be? Nowhere… it has to be Moscow! I need to find out which building it is. I will have my Agents look out for the people who were here and they will tell me all I need to know."

"The ones in the photographs your Lieutenant sent me?"

"The same. I will have one of them brought in for interrogation." Major Popov smiled at the thought of interrogating Grigori Rabinovich.

"Just one Comrade Major… not all of them?"

"Better to take one and keep the rest under surveillance… see where they go… what they do… who they meet. From the one I will get to know their plans. I can arrest the others at any time…" A thought flitted across the Major's mind which he gave voice to, "when they attack the building perhaps? That way I will be hailed as a hero. Major Artur Arsenovich Popov, hero…" After a brief pause he continued his daydream, "To make sure everybody knows it was me who caught the Tula cell I will have a Pravda reporter with me when I swoop to take them." In these situations the Major often talked too much. It was his way of letting subordinates know how great he thought he was.

"Do you know when they will do it? When they will attack…"

"It must be soon. They would not risk hanging around in case they get picked up. I think it most likely that the attack will be in the next couple of days." Seeing an opportunity to get himself out of Tula and into KGB HQ in Moscow, Lieutenant Kaminski sidled up right next to Major Popov and half whispered.

"You know, Comrade Major, having seen the structure the terrorists have built and having had my Agent follow them for weeks and reporting all of their movements and habits to me, I think I might be of some use to you in Moscow."

"Let me think about it, Lieutenant Kaminski, let me think about it." Which both men knew to be code-speak for '*you will not be coming to Moscow*'.

As everybody prepared to leave the warehouse the Lieutenant turned to two of his Agents and ordered them to remain behind to guard the building. He told them they would be relieved in twenty four hours. Across the street from the warehouse the NV observers noted that no weapons had been removed from the warehouse and so did not blow it up. Instead they made plans to dispose of the two guards who had been left behind and retrieve the weapons caches in good time for the big party. Little did they realise that NV6K was being hunted down and its leader would soon be in the hands of the KGB.

★

Major Popov instructed his assistant to transmit the photographs of the Tula seven to his Agents with orders to watch out for them at every road checkpoint and bus and railway station in Moscow and to check security footage of air passengers arriving from Tula over the past twenty four hours. The terrorists were to be followed to find out where they were staying and one of them was to be delivered to the Lubyanka for interrogation. Whenever the Major ordered anybody to be delivered to the Lubyanka for interrogation it sent a thrilling shiver down his spine. He wanted to insist on Grigori Rabinovich being the one snatched but decided not to in case the operation went wrong and blame could be laid at his feet. No, better to let the Agents make the decision, that way if anything went wrong it was their responsibility. That was the way things were done in the Soviet Union.

Major Popov flew back to Moscow with the photographs of the structure in the warehouse safe inside his briefcase. On arriving at the KGB's private landing strip near the centre of Moscow he was handed a message, it read. 'All terrorists have been located and followed back to their safe houses. Their leader has been taken to KGB HQ Lubyanka for your interrogation.' Major Popov cracked his knuckles in anticipation of the joy to come.

The Interrogation of Valeri Demidov

Colonel Petrova was surprised and disappointed to see Major Popov back at his desk so soon as well as irritated that he was in one piece. She hoped he might have been caught up in an incident involving the notorious Tula branch of Narodnaya Volya.

"Good…" the Major checked his watch; it was that marginal time between late afternoon and early evening, "afternoon Colonel Petrova. How was your day?" Smiled an unusually cordial Major Popov. Colonel Petrova was highly suspicious of this alteration to his usual sour demeanour and wondered what lay behind it.

"How did events in Tula go?"

"Excellent. They could hardly have gone better."

"You arrested the terrorists?"

"No… not exactly… not in Tula at least." Major Popov was being deliberately obtuse.

"Do not play games with me Major. Make yourself clear at once."

"Very well, Comrade Colonel, one of the terrorists is, at this moment, sitting in a torture cell in the fourth sub-level handcuffed to a metal interrogation chair awaiting my presence."

"One of the terrorists? What about the others? I understood there were at least six of them."

"They are all… under surveillance." The Major could hardly contain himself.

"And?"

"And I will begin interrogating my prisoner as soon as I have finished writing my report for you on events in Tula."

"Do your report after interrogating the prisoner. I will accompany you." The Major had not foreseen this offer.

"Very well but you might not want to accompany me."

"And why is that?"

"Because I understand that Vasily Dobrovski is in a meeting with Comrade Bazanov's security advisors and if you are with me then you cannot be with him and that means leaving him in the hands of…"

"Why are you being so helpful?"

"You are my commanding Officer and I am your most loyal subordinate." Colonel Petrova's suspicions were now boiling over but she could not miss the opportunity of snatching a career elevating meeting with Vasily Dobrovski.

"Very well, but if anything significant comes from the interrogation you are to inform me immediately no matter who I am with or what I am doing. Do you understand?"

"Yes Comrade Colonel, I understand you perfectly," replied Major Popov smiling his best snake smile.

Making his way down to the fourth sub-level Major Popov admonished himself for goading Colonel Petrova in the way he had but something inside him had always made him say too much. He did not want her anywhere near his prisoner. Not being able to '*get promotions on his back like she had*' he was confident that promotion would come after he had foiled a terrorist plot to destroy… he did not yet have the last word of his sentence but he was convinced he soon would.

⋆

Valeri Demidov was restrained hand and foot with Lubyanka bracelets to a metal chair bolted to the concrete floor of a torture cell. It was one of over a hundred such cells on the fourth sub-level of the KGB's HQ in the old, and much extended, Lubyanka. A canvas hood had been placed over his head and tied tight at the neck. It was stiff with blood and infused with the stench of wet and dry vomit, sweat and snot. So, here sat Valeri Demidov, leader of NV6K, under the blindingly bright white lights of a sound proof torture cell. He did not hear the door glide open as Major Popov and one other slipped silently into his three by two cell but he felt the blow on his canvas hood that broke his nose. Had he not been chained to a metal chair and that chair not bolted down he would have ended up on the rough concrete floor but that was cold comfort.

Without speaking a word, Major Popov ripped Valeri's shirt open and his assistant cut his underwear away with a knife, leaving several deep slices in his buttocks. Next, Valeri felt the pinch of saw-toothed bulldog clips snap onto his nipples and testicles. Pushed over onto a single buttock, something long, icily cold and metallic, was inserted into his anus. He knew what was coming next. He was prepared for it. He had been trained to expect it… in training he had been subjected to it several times in preparation for this day.

With the first zap of electricity Valeri lost control of his bladder. Along with the second, more intense, more prolonged zap, came the unmistakeable stench of burning flesh. Once you have smelled that smell you never forget it. So far there had been no questions but Valeri was not going to ask why that was, he just took the zaps again and again and again in screaming, lip-biting, tongue chewing, blood-drenched, silence. "*There is worse to come for you,*" spoke a disembodied voice from behind Valeri.

Something arrived into the cell on squeaky wheels which gave off a lot of heat. Valeri felt the heat all the way down the left hand side of his body. It was unbearable on his naked body. He knew it was a furnace. '*It is a portable furnace,*' thought he in terror. Next, Valeri heard irons raking furnace-coke on a metal grill. The light in the cell was switched off and the variable illumination coming from the furnace played a light show on the canvas hood like the flickering screen of an outdoor Bolshoitel. "*Remove his hood!*"

With his hood removed, Valeri saw a white hot point of light coming toward his face. His entire focus was on that white hot point of light, nothing else. "*His right eye first.*" On hearing those words, Valeri turned his right eye as far as he could away from the white hot point of light until he felt his neck was about to break. "*Okay, his left eye instead.*" Valeri reversed his evasive manoeuvre.

"I can see that you are brave, Comrade Demidov, but even the bravest of men feel pain. There is more than one type of pain though, is there not? The pain of torture can build resistance to interrogation in some people. Sometimes, the more the pain, the more obstinate they become. Withholding information becomes like a game to them, it can even give them pleasure… pain can transform the mind. Then you die and when you are dead you are of no use to me. So, Comrade Demidov, what to do? What to do? Would you like some water?" The Major waited for the slightest sign that Valeri accepted his offer of water but none came. "Give him some water. If he will not take it willingly force a tube through his teeth and down into his throat… make him take it! Break his teeth if you have to."

After ten minutes' struggling and gurgling, a cup's worth of water was forced into Valeri's mouth and down his throat. It was cooling and so good despite its copper and iron taste. He had spat out the first mouthfuls but the Major's accomplice put her hand over his mouth until he choke-swallowed the cooling liquid.

"I do not have time to play games with you, Comrade Demidov, my attendance is required elsewhere. You see I have your mother in the cell next to yours. She probably knows nothing about your scheme… but she can feel pain… and she will feel pain if you do not tell me all." Major Popov smiled and added, "Imagine… just imagine, for a moment… your mother spasming after being zapped with electric shocks and then treated to the irons of the furnace. She is old, frail, starved and weak… she will not last long." Valeri knew that no matter what he told the Major it would not save him or his mother, the KGB sadists would simply carry on and on long after he had given them everything.

"Though I have had you brought here, I have allowed your compatriots to run free for the time being." Major Popov checked for a reaction from Valeri but there was none. "Let me tell you this comrade… I have been to Tula. I have seen what you did in the warehouse there. I have photographs of it. I know there are seven of you and I know where they are staying. They are all in separate NV safe houses… if they can be called that. They are being watched and as soon as they make a move I will know about it. I can have them picked up any time I wish."

"Then what do you need me for?" spat Valeri defiantly.

"I want you to fill in the last piece of the puzzle for me. I want to know what the target is… where the target is." Valeri laughed. "Did I say something funny Comrade Demidov?" Valeri realised the game was up, his interrogator could not simply have guessed their number… or Tula… or the warehouse… or that they had split up into different locations.

"If I tell you the target, will you let my mother go?"

"Of course," lied the Major. "But you, comrade, what at about you? What do you want, Comrade Demidov?"

"I will tell you what I do not want. I do not want to be an informant… or your agent. I know I will die as soon as I tell you…"

"Die? What makes you think I will let you die? No, no, no, Comrade Demidov, much better to keep you alive for a long, long time. The others will die but you are far too useful. I have checked the records, Comrade Demidov, you are an interesting fellow."

"Let my mother go and I will tell you the target."

"Very well, but if you lie I can easily have her brought back."

"Also, you will have to release me so I can rendezvous with the others or they will know they are walking into a trap."

"I do not think so, Comrade Demidov," said Major Popov with a laugh. "If you do not turn up at the rendezvous the others will carry on without you. That is how you work. Now, where is the target?" Valeri laughed again. "You have an irritating laugh, Comrade Demidov, do you know that!"

"You want to know where the target is? Okay, I will tell you. The target is here."

"Where?"

"Right here… KGB HQ Lubyanka. We identified a weak point in the security right next to the computer wing. Entry will be made there and explosives planted in the ducts nearby to destroy the electrical supply cables." Thinking on his feet, Valeri's mind was clear and his plan cunning.

"Why? Why is that the target? It makes no sense."

"The timing of the explosion is set to coincide with the start of the Terror, which is also the same time as the start of the centenary celebrations… it has been one hundred years since…" Major Popov was shocked that Valeri Demidov knew the start time for the Terror but hid his surprise well for him.

"Yes, yes, yes, I know all about the centenary celebrations! But why are you going to blow up the electrical cables of the Lubyanka? Is it some kind of foolish protest? I do not believe you!"

"No, comrade, it is not a protest, it is a starting pistol."

"For what?"

"Revolution comrade… violent and bloody revolution!"

"You are crazy. Do you think I am going to fall for…"

"In just over twenty four hours the whole of the Soviet Union will be lit by the bright fire of revolution."

'*Twenty four hours!*' If that was true, then it was only a day and not months before the revolution would start. '*They said it would be at least four months before the Proles would rise, they said that the Terror would stop them.*' "I do not believe you!"

"The Proletariat will rise up and slaughter all those who have sought to destroy our workers' paradise. We are going to stop the Terror!"

"If what you say is true then why are you telling me, Comrade Demidov? If it is true then you have just ruined your plan. You have…"

"But comrade, it is far too late to do anything about it. Take my advice comrade; run… run as far and as fast as you can… a great storm is coming and it will wash you away!" Major Popov looked deep into Valeri's eyes and what he saw in them frightened him enough for him to leave the torture cell.

Ambitious as he was Major Popov was no fool. Even if Valeri Demidov was only telling a half-truth this was far too big a thing for him to stay quiet over, even at the risk of sharing this information with his hated Colonel. Then if it all came to nought she would be in the firing line and not him. That way things might work out even better than Popov's original plan… he could hope so at least.

★

Exiting from the lift on the top floor of the Lubyanka, Major Popov saw Colonel Petrova walking slowly along the corridor toward him. She was trotting alongside Vasily Dobrovski; her head turned toward him, her eyes looking up adoringly as she pretended to cling to his every word. She was all smiles and coyness, that was until she spied Major Popov. He gave her a look and nodded his head toward a side room before entering it. After excusing herself, "*for a moment*", from Vasily Dobrovski's company she joined Major Popov in the side room, slamming the door shut behind her. She was wearing her furious look.

Unperturbed by Colonel Petrova's open hostility to his presence, despite her requesting his presence in certain circumstances, Major Popov quickly briefed her on the events in the torture cell.

She thought for a moment and decided there was little to lose by telling the Major what she knew about the Terror… which was due to start in a little over twenty four hours. "*The exact same time that Valeri Demidov said the revolution was going to start.*" It was enough to convince the Major and the Colonel that there was something in what the prisoner had said. Colonel Petrova ordered Major Popov not to speak to anybody else about this, claiming that she did not want to start false rumours on the eve of the Terror, but he knew differently… she was, just like he was, glory hunting. Then Major Popov had a brainwave. He could still be the hero. He decided he must speak further with Comrade Demidov… alone.

Vasily Dobrovski had not moved an inch since Colonel Petrova had left his side as in her absence he had been immediately surrounded by career climbers. She elbowed her way through the knot of people surrounding Comrade Dobrovski to retake her position next to him and whispered, "*Can I have a word in private?*" He nodded his head in the direction of the room she had just emerged from. "*Anything to get away from these greasy pole climbing grovellers.*"

"Comrade Dobrovski, important information I have just received indicates that there is the possibility… a strong possibility… of revolution starting in the next twenty four hours." Comrade Dobrovski was shaken by this news as he had been spreading rumours to the contrary.

"And what is the source of your information?"

"A Major under my command interrogated a terrorist called Valeri Demidov. He claims that he and his terrorist cell plan to attack this building tomorrow night and blow up its electrical cables. He says that blacking out the Lubyanka is the signal for the revolution to start in Moscow. I am sure you understand what that would mean, comrade… we would not be able to use the computers to warn our forces in response to any uprising. I can hardly…"

"I must see this prisoner for myself."

"Comrade Dobrovski, that is highly irregular, nobody outside the KGB is allowed to… I will need to clear this with Comrade Bazanov."

"Colonel Petrova… Eva…" added Vasily with a smile, "I sit on the Presidium for Operation Zima. Please allow me to see the prisoner," spoke Dobrovski politely but firmly. All the Colonel had to do was contact Luka Bazanov, Commissar of the KGB, and Comrade Dobrovski would be ejected from the building. She weighed the balance and found in favour of Vasily Dobrovski. She had a long standing hatred for Luka Bazanov after he raped her when she was a junior Officer. He said it was an initiation ceremony… '*how many others have there been like me*?' she had thought every day since.

★

When Colonel Petrova and Vasily Dobrovski entered the torture cell they found Valeri Demidov and Major Popov talking together, drinking Vodka and smoking. Though the Major stood to attention, Comrade Demidov did not acknowledge their presence. The Major knew Comrade Dobrovski should not be in the torture cell but was smart enough to keep his mouth tight shut.

"This is the man?" asked Presidium member Dobrovski.

"Yes, Comrade Dobrovski." The Major and the Colonel answered in chorus, looking annoyed at one another as each wanted to be Comrade Dobrovski's lapdog.

"Comrade Demidov, you have told your fine tale, no doubt, to cause confusion… spread rumours and to keep yourself alive. Well, it will not work with me. I have information from the highest levels that revolution is…"

"Run Comrade Dobrovski Presidium member of Operation Zima, run…" Vasily was shocked that the prisoner knew about Operation Zima and that he was connected with it, "revolution is here… revolution is everywhere… it is already upon us. Actually, there is little point in you running. Where could somebody like you hide in the whole of the Soviet Union? Where could somebody like you find sanctuary? Who would risk themselves to save the skin of somebody like you Comrade Dobrovski? Where will you go when millions take to the streets… they will find you… they will find you all."

"But if we stop you blowing up the electrical cables then…" interjected Colonel Petrova.

"Blacking out KGB HQ is just a signal for central Moscow… there will be hundreds, thousands, like it all over the Soviet Union set to go off at the same time to start the revolution and once it starts there will be no stopping it."

"The Red Army will not stand for it!" screamed Colonel Petrova an inch from Valeri Demidov's face.

"The Red Army is with us comrade!" rounded Valeri.

"The NKVD…"

"The NKVD are hated by everybody… the people, the Red Army… the KGB. The NKVD will suffer the most." They knew what Comrade Demidov said about the NKVD was true. Demidov's only lie was a clever one. They could not know that the real target was the computers in their Lubyanka bunker. Colonel Petrova beckoned Vasily Dobrovski into the corridor. Major Popov followed, not wanting to let them out of his sight or hearing.

"We should pretend to let the terrorists have their little way. If what Demidov says is true then the lights going out in the Lubyanka will bring the traitors out onto the streets where we can…"

"Kill them! Yes, comrade, we will kill them!… slaughter them all," sputtered Major Popov anxious to play a part.

"Silence Popov!" ordered the Colonel. "If we allow the Tula cell to gain access to the Lubyanka we can arrest them before they get to the cables. We can then switch the Lubyanka's lights off and when the terrorists emerge out onto the streets we will switch them back on again, letting them know they have failed. Panic will ensue and…"

"What about the rest of the Soviet Union?" said Major Popov ignoring his orders to remain silent. "Stopping a revolt in the middle of Moscow is one thing but how are we going to prevent revolution from spreading throughout the USSR?"

"Computers is how we will stop them." Both the Colonel and the Major made to interrupt Comrade Dobrovski but he raised his hand for them to remain silent. "Allow me to explain. Your agents will lay in wait for the terrorists and prevent them from blowing up the electrical cables. Once they have been arrested we will use the computers to send messages to Political Commissars and Red Army Generals all across the Soviet Union. It will be instantaneous. The first message will alert the Political Commissars to what is going on. A second message to Red Army Generals will instruct them to crush revolutionary forces wherever they find them. The Generals will contact their Political Commissars to check that their orders are genuine. Once the Red Army is on the move nothing can stop them."

"Yes, we will control events! We will crush the rebellion! We will all be heroes of the Soviet Union!" stammered Major Popov feverishly. He imagined the Order of Lenin being pinned on his proud puffed-out chest as he spoke. "But what if Demidov is lying?"

"If he is then we will know as soon as we switch the lights off as nobody will come out onto the streets."

"In that case I will execute him personally. Nobody will be any the wiser. We will keep everything to ourselves. No harm done. Our reputations will not suffer any damage whatsoever."

The gang of three retired to a nearby sound proof interrogation room to work out the details of their plan to '*single-handedly*' save the Soviet Union. Two of them were thinking of the glory and rewards to come, the other about how he was going to warn the Tula cell that they were walking into a trap.

★

"Yes, yes, Comrade Dobrovski, it is a great plan, fool proof!" fawned Colonel Petrova trying to convince herself that the scheme would work. “But who will send the computer messages? I cannot as I do not know how to use a computer.”

“I also do not know how to use a computer,” added Major Popov.

“I will take care of it.”

“You know how to operate a computer, Comrade Dobrovski?”

“No, but my PA does and she is totally loyal to me. She will do as I tell her as she knows what will happen to her family if she disobeys or betrays me. She should send the messages to the Generals and the Political Commissars. We can trust her.”

“What if we are wrong and the terrorists do not proceed with their mission without Demidov?” asked the Colonel nervously. “We should release him so he can make the rendezvous, we still have his mother so he will not do anything stupid.”

“That is not necessary comrades. I know how these terrorists work,” said Major Popov trying to sound knowledgeable and confident. “They will rendezvous at a predetermined time and place. In the event any of them is picked up they will have a contingency plan. This is an important mission so they will not abandon it, they will proceed no matter what.”

“But what if you are wrong, Major Popov? What will you do then?”

“Simple, Colonel Petrova,” replied the Major his voice dripping with smugness, “we will… I will turn off the lights myself and then turn them back on again after the revolutionaries have come out onto the streets.”

“How will you know what time to switch off the lights, Comrade Major?”

“Again simple. The revolutionaries will be expecting the lights to go off around ten minutes after the terrorists enter the building,” guessed the Major, “so I will switch the Lubyanka’s lights off ten minutes after they enter the building. As I said, simple.” The Major smiled a smug smile. His overt smugness irritated the Colonel.

“And where will they rendezvous?” asked Colonel Petrova determined to make the Major appear foolish in front of Comrade Dobrovski.

"In my experience," replied the Major puffing out his chest, "they will meet up close to their target… here… the Lubyanka. My Agents will follow them when they leave their safe houses and radio me when they are on the move." Colonel Petrova thought the Major was perhaps not as stupid as she had thought but shook that thought from her head, '*no, he is as stupid as I think he is but even idiots have good ideas every once in a while.*'

"That makes sense," said Vasily Dobrovski, before adding. "I have an idea. To ensure the terrorists proceed with their mission, my PA will go to the rendezvous and declare herself an operative of NV with information about Demidov's capture and offer to take his place. She can say she overheard me talking about it with the Central Committee… she will say that Demidov died before giving the details of their mission away."

"No, it is too risky," said the Major seeing his thunder being stolen.

"What risk?" snarled Dobrovski rounding on the Major. "If they do not go for it then arrest the terrorists and switch off the lights without them ever entering the building." The Colonel was getting nervous. She did not want this amateur, Dobrovski, messing things up as it would be her life if things went badly.

"What if the terrorists do not believe your PA and they kill her?" spoke the Colonel trying to sound concerned for the safety of Vasily's PA.

"Why would they kill her? She will be delivering important information to them. They will go for it. I am certain they will go for it." Comrade Dobrovski was desperate to get his PA to the rendezvous with the Tula cell to give them the best chance of success.

"I agree with the Major," said Colonel Petrova.

"I am confident that my PA will prove useful as an insider…"

"As you are so insistent in involving your PA, Comrade Dobrovski, she may come along as a consultant." '*That,*' thought Colonel Petrova, '*should satisfy Dobrovski.*' "I will arrange for a computer operator to be present to send the messages and that is final," said the Colonel.

With time running out, Vasily Dobrovski would have to think of another way of letting the Tula cell know what was happening.

★

The following morning, back in his office, Vasily Dobrovski was cursing his PA for being late on this of all days. When he heard the door to her office open he rushed in to see her. "*You need to contact the Director urgently. One of the Tula cell has been taken… and he has talked. They need to change their plans.*"

Vasily Dobrovski recounted the events of the previous day to his PA. She appeared only slightly perturbed by what he told her. Given the facts of the situation, she was of the opinion that Valeri Demidov had played it just right. His lie was plausible plus the two KGB Officers were keeping their cards close to their chests instead of sharing their information. Alina said she thought things were as perfect as they could be under the circumstances. She declared that the Director had always instigated their contact but she would try calling him on the scrambler phone hidden in her desk draw.

A few miles away Alexander Orlov was in a meeting with Maxim Kirilenko when a buzzing sound emanated from a drawer in Alexander's desk.

"What is that?" asked Maxim Kirilenko.

"Trouble… probably big trouble. I have never received a call on that phone. To be honest I did not even know it could…"

"Are you going to answer it? I would like to know what sort of trouble it is." Alexander put a device around his neck, switched it on, spoke a few words into it and then adjusted the sound output. The voice-sound that came out of the tiny speaker sounded metallic, hollow and totally unlike that of Alexander Orlov. Maxim Kirilenko had never seen this device before and wondered what other secrets his Chef de Cabinet had hidden in his desk drawers.

"Who is this?"

"Director, it is I, Alina Kuznetsova, assistant to Vasily Dobrovski, speaking. He is here with me." There followed a minute of silence where Alexander considered his options. He concluded they were limited as this must obviously be an exceptional circumstance.

"Speak," was all he replied. With that, Vasily Dobrovski grabbed the phone from his PA and gave the story of the previous twenty four hours. "Comrade Kuznetsova, what is your assessment of the situation?"

"I agree with Comrade Dobrovski, Comrade Demidov did the right thing. His lie was quite brilliant. This way the Tula cell will be allowed to gain access to the computer rooms. We must warn them…"

"That is impossible."

"We must try something… anything… what about…?"

"Stop. I will contact the Tula Commander to see if she can be of any assistance."

"Does she have anybody in Moscow who can help?"

"Probably. I will contact her and call you back… stay at your desk and wait for my call… do not leave your desk." Alexander hung up the call.

"You cannot contact Tula… the KGB will be listening." Spat a panic ridden Maxim Kirilenko.

"It will not matter if somebody listens in. They will not have time to realise what it is they are listening to."

*

At the same time as the conversation between Vasily Dobrovski and the Director was taking place, a phone rang in an office on the top floor of the building overlooking the warehouse in the dead-end street in Tula. An NV operative picked up the receiver. Before she could say anything she heard the word '*Cobra*'. She put her hand over the mouthpiece and whispered, "*Get the Commander…*" to a colleague, adding by pointing at the telephone and miming,

"*Cobra.*" The Commander entered the office at pace and grabbed the telephone.

"Wolf five five." The correct response having been given the caller continued in plain language.

"I went to 131 to warn Valeri that the warehouse operation was compromised. He was not there and was nowhere to be found. I went to the other safe houses and located the other operatives. They are all accounted for. I did not say anything to them about '*Fox*' being missing. I suspect he has been picked up. I await your orders." Cobra hung up the call.

The Commander summoned her inner council and informed them that Cobra had reported Fox was missing. They were discussing their next move when the phone rang. They looked at one another in silence. An operative picked up the receiver. A hollow metallic voice, calling himself the Director, asked to speak to the Commander.

"Wolf five five," spoke the Commander and waited for the correct response.

"Bear nine two. I have something for you."

"If it is news about Fox being missing you are too late. I have had a report about him already from Cobra." This news took Alexander back a little but he quickly recovered his composure.

"Very good… I was right to appoint you Tula Commander. Given the hour, I am breaking protocol and ordering you to contact NV6K, let them know of Fox's situation and order them to proceed with the mission."

Comrade Orlov conveyed the situation to the Tula Commander, emphasising that NV6K must proceed with the mission as though everything was normal so as not to give the game away. The Commander replied that Cobra would brief them within the next couple of hours.

★

In a cold, dimly lit, surveillance bunker on the outskirts of Tula a junior KGB Officer sat wide eyed after listening to the telephone conversations he had recorded. He was transcribing them, annotating with remarks such as '*the one calling himself the Director spoke in a strange sounding voice, I think he was using a voice altering device.*' The junior KGB Officer wanted to finish his report and hand it in to his supervising Officer as quickly as possible. He smelled a promotion for this fine piece of work of his.

The junior Officer's supervisor happened to be passing his station and noticed he was writing and not listening. Her curiosity aroused, she asked him what he was doing. He told her he was writing up two telephone conversations he had just been listening in on and briefly described them to her. He became loud and excited the more he spoke so she held a finger to his lips to quiet him down. She was a well-known flirt and told him he was "*a very clever boy*" while tousling his hair. He became instantly aroused. She leaned in toward him pulling his head forward and rubbing her breasts against his cheek. Then, with the middle finger of her left hand, she stroked the nodule of vertebrate at the top of his spine, above which is cartilage connecting it to the skull. She leaned in even closer and while whispering and blowing into the junior Officer's ear she slid the business end of an eight inch stiletto dagger along the length of her left-hand-middle-finger until it was hovering over the nodule of vertebrate. While kissing the junior Officer on the cheek she forced the stiletto through the cartilage and into his brain. The wound was so small and there being no blood or outward sign of entry nobody would suspect foul play. Death was instantaneous. The supervisor grabbed the junior Officer's notes before calling attention to his sudden collapse, "*I think he has had a heart attack.*" She shouted, "*He was under a lot of pressure because he was not very good at his job. You! You there! Take his place! This is a great opportunity for you. Do not disappoint me!*"

The supervisor left the surveillance bunker and made her way to the tall building overlooking the warehouse at the bottom of the dead-end street. On reaching it she gave and received the correct NV signs and was admitted to the top floor. When she entered the Commander's office a meeting was in progress. A vote had just been taken. It had been unanimously decided to kill the two KGB Agents guarding the warehouse and retrieve the weapons caches in preparation for the big party. The supervisor advised the Commander that she had set the timers in the surveillance bunker for 1605, the changeover of shifts, yielding twice the number of KGB Agents blown up in the ensuing explosion.

Countdown to Revolution

We join the end of a meeting of the Presidium of Operation Zima which the entire Central Committee was '*invited*' to attend. "Do your duty comrades as soon we will light the blue touch paper," said Maxim Kirilenko, mustering all the confidence his voice could manage. "You have your orders… now carry them out. The great Terror begins at the stroke of midnight." Having finished speaking, Comrade Kirilenko stood, collected his papers, and walked out of the room without a backward glance. Everybody else then rose and left the Kremlin, each thinking how they could benefit from the situation while ensuring blame for any mistakes could not be attached to them. Most were also thinking about how they could rid themselves of Maxim Kirilenko; '*it is time for a change,*' they thought.

★

At either end of the Soviet Union, NKVD Soldiers stationed in the northern reaches of Velikobritania and the area surrounding Vladivostok moved into position to await the signal to launch the Terror. Everything was ready; the torture houses were fired up and ready to go, the gates of the internment and ethnic concentration camps were opened in readiness for their guests, the trains to transport millions to the Gulag were in sidings and stations. The clock was ticking down in Velikobritania as the dawn of a new Soviet era was about to begin.

Final briefings were under way right across the Soviet Union. The NKVD would lead the Terror and the Red Army would occupy the cleansed zones. Red Army Generals were unhappy with this arrangement as they knew from experience that the NKVD would do a poor job and when their Soldiers stepped into the vacuum after the NKVD had moved on they would be left to deal with the aftermath. A task that would be all the more difficult as, according to intelligence, the peoples of Velikobritania and Vladivostok were expecting them and they were organised and well-armed. Rumours began to fly that the NKVD were only planning on swooping in to pick up named targets and leave the real fighting to the Red Army. The Generals sensed it was going to be a bloodbath with massive losses on both sides; brother fighting brother, son fighting father, neighbour fighting neighbour, vendettas running rife, civil war... leading inevitably to violent and bloody revolution. The Generals hoped the signal from Lev would arrive in time. Some thought the signal was a hoax devised by the KGB to flush out anti-Soviet elements in the Red Army. '*What will we do if the signal does not come*?' Thought others.

★

Lev was sitting in quiet contemplation in his hideout in Leningrad, a city always a haven for subversives. He chucked back the last mouthful of cold coffee from his tin cup and walked into his operations centre. All faces turned toward him. Complete silence took over the room as Lev prepared to address them.

"Brothers, sisters... comrades, citizens of the Soviet Union, our time is near." A few excited yells quickly died away. "This is not a day of celebration but a day of mourning. A day of mourning for the souls of comrades who will not be with us to share the victorious dawn. People will come to know this as a bloodless revolution but blood will be spilled... blood will be spilled. Pray God that it is little. Our brave comrades will have sacrificed themselves for the future of our motherland. They will have sacrificed themselves for the glory of this great nation and the revolution. They will have sacrificed themselves for our workers' paradise at the birth of a new Soviet Union. They will have sacrificed themselves so we might live in peace and harmony. Do them honour. Make them proud. Do not let them die in vain. Pray with me." Some openly prayed while others closed their eyes in respect of the faith of those praying. Lev crossed himself at the end of his prayer and coughed to signal the prayer had ended. "Soon," spoke Lev in a quiet, barely audible, voice, "the forces of the NKVD will be on the move. Their mission? To unleash Terror on the ordinary citizens of the Soviet Union. Their aim? To bite out the heart of the revolution before it takes its first beat but they will not succeed! At the given hour I will send a message to our comrades… our Red Army fighters. The message will be simple and when they receive it they will know what to do. You know what to do. Now return to your Units and prepare them for the fight of their lives… a fight for their lives! God be with you."

"And with you great leader." Came the chorused response as the room piled out. Nobody spoke as their heads were full of thoughts of glory, immortality and mortality.

★

According to protocol, Cobra went to a hub-house after her call to the Tula Commander. It was less than an hour after she arrived that the phone rang. An operative picked up the receiver. "It is for you." She said to Cobra. Listening carefully to her instructions Cobra repeated them back to Wolf five five in slang-code to confirm her understanding and received the correct NV code word in affirmation. She was good to go.

Seeking access to safe houses is always tricky despite Cobra having visited each of them in the previous twenty four hours. If the protocols were not executed correctly and NV signs not delivered and received anything could happen, including summary execution. Cobra was a seasoned professional and took nothing for granted. Following the protocols to the letter she was readmitted to the first safe house on her list. She requested a private room because what she had to say was not for the ears of anybody but Irina, Valeri's second in command.

"I am Cobra. I have spoken with the Tula Commander about Valeri."

"What about him?"

"Do not interrupt. I will let you know when I have finished… then you can speak. The Tula Commander ordered me to travel to Moscow to inform Valeri that the mission has been compromised, the KGB has seen inside the warehouse." Irina was bursting with questions but held her tongue after a glance from Cobra, "I went to Valeri's safe house but he had not shown up there. I reported this to the Tula Commander. An hour later she called me and ordered me to deliver a message to the remaining operatives." Irina held out her hand, "A verbal message."

"Shall I write it down?"

"No, of course not!" Cobra gave Irina a look that made her feel like an idiot. "It is a simple message. You are to proceed with the mission despite Valeri not showing up at the rendezvous point… carry on as though nothing has happened. The KGB will be waiting in ambush in a corridor next to some electrical cupboards. They believe the mission is to destroy the electrical cables to black out the Lubyanka as a signal to start the revolution." Irina could hold her tongue no longer.

"Why would they think that?"

"Because that is what Valeri told them." Irina was rocked by this news. '*Valeri had talked? Was he a coward? A traitor?*' "He was picked up and taken to the Lubyanka as soon as he arrived in Moscow. While he was being interrogated and tortured he formulated a story around the truth because you are all being watched. As soon as you leave here to rendezvous with the others you will be followed. Let them follow you. Do not try to lose your tails or do anything stupid. You will be allowed to continue with the mission because, I repeat, Valeri told the KGB that its aim is to turn out the lights in the Lubyanka as a signal for the revolution to commence."

"He told them about the uprising too?"

"He knows what he is doing. Had he done otherwise you would have all been picked up and the codes would not be sent." Alina was shocked that Cobra knew about the codes. '*Who else knows about them?*'

"This sounds very… very convenient… the timing of it and all. How did all this find its way to the Commander?"

"Good question. The only answer I can give is that she must have some contacts close to the top. That should not surprise either of us."

Not totally convinced by Cobra's story Alina rationalised that she had nothing to lose by believing the KGB already knew there were others and they were watching their safe houses. The uncomfortable truth was she had to go along with what Cobra had told her.

"What next?"

"I will disguise myself before leaving here to repeat the story to the others. I am to emphasise to you that it is vital to the success of the revolution that you deliver the codes. They must be delivered at all costs… even at the cost of your own lives." Alina could tell by the cadence in Cobra's voice that she had no idea what the codes were or how they were to be delivered. This gave her some assurance that she was telling the truth.

"Shall I go with you to make sure that the others believe you…"

"No, nothing must change, everything must stay the same, everything must appear normal otherwise you will be picked up. Just go to the rendezvous as planned and for God's sake try to act natural. Good luck."

"Good luck to you too." With that Cobra tied her hair back with a dark ribbon, put on spectacles, changed her clothes in the blink of an eye and was out the back door in a flash. She had obviously done this sort of thing before.

Over the next hours Cobra delivered her message to the other members of the Tula cell NV6K. Each received it with varying degrees of incredulity but, as with Alina, they rationalised that if they were indeed being watched they had nothing to lose by believing her story. The most difficult to convince was Vladimir. Cobra viewed him as baggage as far as the mission was concerned and was in two minds as to whether or not to dispose of him and take his place as part of the mission cell. She decided she was better employed observing the rendezvous in case there were any problems that needed reporting back to the Tula Commander and so let Vladimir live. His luck was still holding out.

★

The six arrived on time at the rendezvous point. At first they did not know what to say about Cobra or Valeri. They hid their own thoughts about continuing with the mission under the circumstances and the likelihood of success if they did so. Vladimir spoke first.

"Shall we wait to see if Valeri shows up?" The others looked at him as though he was an idiot. They did not mean to, it was just their nervousness making them jumpy. Svetlana spoke next.

"I suppose we all had a visit from Cobra?" All heads nodded, "She was insistent that we go ahead with the mission. She said that the Tula…"

"I could take Valeri's place… his position, you know, inside the building…"

"No Vlad, we need to stick to the plan, that is what Cobra said." Svetlana spoke as kindly as she could so as not to hurt Vladimir's feelings knowing he wanted to be more involved. "You are our outside man. We are relying on you to…"

"Enough, we all know our parts… we just need to get on with it. The longer we hang around here the more chance we have of getting picked up. Vladimir knows his part and we are sticking to the plan. Okay Vlad?" Vladimir gave a single, slight, nod of his head. "We do it how we practised it. Irina, hand out the weapons."

NV6K walked in two groups of three to the wall guarding the computer wing of the KGB's Lubyanka HQ. Everything was still. All was quiet. Too quiet. With the total absence of anybody in the entire area they understood Cobra had told the truth; they were being allowed to complete the first part of their mission.

*

Concealed inside the Lubyanka, Colonel Petrova, Major Popov and Alina Kuznetsova were waiting in the almost complete darkness of the corridor adjacent to the electrical cable cupboard, along with twenty KGB Agents, for the Tula cell to arrive. Intent on grabbing the glory of arresting the terrorists personally, Major Popov whispered to the four KGB Agents closest to him to follow him. Colonel Petrova hiss-whispered to the Major asking him what he thought he was doing. He lied when he replied that he was going to reconnoitre the area to make sure the terrorists were sticking to their plan. The lie sounded plausible so the Colonel said he had her permission to proceed. The Major and the four KGB Agents slunk out of sight before entering the computer room via a service door to await the arrival of the Tula cell.

*

Practice makes perfect but when the last practice was forty eight hours previous plus there was the additional pressure of doing the job for real and the fact that they knew they were being watched by the KGB and the fact that Valeri had been taken and the fact that he had… excuses aside, performance anxiety took hold of Grigori when he attempted to operate the air powered gun to launch the climb rope over the wall of the Lubyanka. KGB Agents observing Grigori's pathetic efforts walkie-talkie chatted that somebody should volunteer to lend him a hand. A click followed by a crackly voice ordered everybody to maintain complete silence. At that moment Vladimir stepped forward.

★

Feeling this was my chance to shine, I stepped forward, grabbed the grappling hook air gun off Grigori and launched it over the wall. It gripped first time. I lifted myself up on the rope to ensure it had grabbed properly on the other side of the wall and returned to my place in the line. Svetlana smiled at me. I was a happy man.

Grigori held the rope fast as one after the other the six climbed up the rope. There were no guards in sight in the inner courtyard which was to be expected given what Cobra had told them. Grigori was last to climb the rope and while sitting atop the wall he thought he caught sight of someone moving about in the computer room. He pondered for a moment. Should he say something to the others? Was this all just part of the new plan? Fear gripped him, he hesitated and almost turned and fled but he held his nerve and joined his compatriots in the courtyard.

The six, their senses electric and on high alert, moved with purpose toward the fourth window along from the right. Maria slid a flat flexible steel jemmy along the joining edge of the window until it shorted across the contacts of the alarm system. Next, she took a thicker jemmy and slid it in between the locking mechanism of the window and its retaining clasp. It sprung open, just like in practice. The six felt better, more confident, now that they had the window open and no alarms were blaring. Svetlana stared at Vladimir with a look that said, *'stay here, do not go follow us into the computer room.'*

I felt disappointed as I had planned to follow on behind the others into the computer room believing they could do nothing about it if I did.

The inside team climbed through the window and entered the computer room. Maria and Georgi went to their cover positions, Svetlana, Irina and Grigori went toward the computer and were about to remove the discs from their backpacks when a torch shone on their faces.

"Comrades!... especially you Comrade Rabinovich... do not move!" The Major then shouted to the Colonel, "I have arrested three of them in the computer room, the others are guarding the corridor." Svetlana and Grigori recognised the voice of Major Artur Arsenovich Popov and shuddered.

"Surrender! Surrender or you will die," screamed Colonel Petrova at the top of her voice. Maria and Georgi immediately took cover. They shucked a round into the chambers of their Markovs and Maria shouted back to the Colonel.

"Comrade, do not try to stop us from doing our duty to the good people of the Soviet Union. We are the revolution and we are here. Please comrade, lay down your arms. Join us!"

"This is your last warning." The Colonel shouted again. "Surrender or you will die!"

"If you do not surrender immediately I will shoot your comrades," shouted the Major. He waited for ten seconds and fired a shot. "That is the end of Comrade Rabinovich!" He yelled holding a hand over Grigori's mouth to keep him silent. "The women are next!"

"You have thirty seconds to consider the hopelessness of your situation," screamed the Colonel. "Throw out your weapons. Surrender! Come out with your hands above your heads or you will be shot." With those in the computer room already taken, Georgi and Maria knew they had no option but to surrender, hopefully to live to fight another day.

"Comrade," yelled Maria, "we are coming out, do not shoot." When Georgi and Maria emerged with their hands above their heads Colonel Petrova shouted to them.

"Where is the other one?"

"There is just the two of us." The Colonel then shouted to Major Popov.

"There are only two here, there were supposed to be six altogether, where is the other one?"

"I do not know. I am sure I saw three people going to the corridor." While hiding in the darkness the Major had become confused as to who had gone where.

"Where is your missing comrade?" shouted the Colonel.

"We do not know. We are telling you the truth, we do not know where he is."

"Kick your weapons away and walk toward the light. Do not make any sudden moves or you will be shot."

Maria and Georgi kicked their weapons away and walked toward the light as ordered. They made only three steps before they were seized from behind by KGB Agents skulking in the shadows and handcuffed with their hands behind their backs. One of the Agents laid into Georgi with vicious kicks and blows, nobody attempted to stop her. She carried on until she had beaten Georgi senseless. The Colonel shouted to the Major that she was going to turn off the lights in the Lubyanka to signal to the revolutionaries that the Tula mission had been successful. Everybody inside the Lubyanka had been forewarned that the lights would be going out and they were prepared for it. The Colonel asked the Major's opinion on how long the lights should be left off for. He replied that as soon as the revolutionaries were out on the streets they should be turned back on again.

When the prisoners were assembled together in the computer room Major Popov knew exactly who was missing. It was the language student and justice evader, Vladimir Vakhnenko.

"The missing terrorist is called Vladimir Vakhnenko. Tell me where he is or…"

"I think he ran past us… I think he ran somewhere inside the building. He could be anywhere by now," said Maria, hoping Vladimir had already gotten away and was informing Cobra of what had happened.

"Alert the guards, search the building… start with the lower floors…"

"He might be attempting to rescue Demidov," suggested Colonel Petrova. Walkie-talkies were shouted into and Agents took to stairwells.

The moment Alina Kuznetsova entered the computer room Svetlana and Grigori's hearts sank. They knew the game was over. She, however, completely ignored them and walked past them to inspect the mainframe's exec consul. She did nothing to alert Major Popov that she recognised Svetlana and Grigori. Alina, of course, knew the Tula cell's true mission and what was in Svetlana and Grigori's backpacks. Her conundrum was how to get her hands on the discs and transmit the codes to the rebels in the Red Army without Major Popov realising what was going on.

"It seems suspicious that these two went to switch the computers on. What were you planning to do? Write a letter home?" sneered Major Popov.

"I can show you how computers should be used." Said Alina producing a disc from her briefcase. "In case of an emergency, Comrade Dobrovski ordered me to put instructions of how the rebels are to be dealt with onto this disc. To type them individually would have taken hours. All we have to do is send the instructions via the computer to Political Commissars and Red Army Generals. It will take less than a minute."

"Very good comrade, well done." Major Popov intended telling everybody the disc was his idea.

All that was on the disc, however, was an infinite loop FLF function designed to eat processing time. Alina '*accidentally*' dropped the disc onto the floor and then fumbled about under the mainframe exec consul pretending to try to find it while tampering with Svetlana's backpack. Major Popov was not so stupid as not to see through Alina's desperate ploy. He smashed her on the back of her head with his pistol, sending her sprawling across the floor. Two KGB Agents each grabbed an arm and yanked Alina to her feet, almost dislocating her shoulders in the process. An Agent came running, breathless, into the computer room.

"Valeri Demidov has escaped Comrade Major..."

"Vakhnenko must be involved somehow. All of you! Go! Find them and bring them to me. Go! Go! Find them!" With that, Major Popov was left alone to guard his prisoners. He did not feel he needed any assistance as they were all handcuffed and most had been severely beaten. '*They might meet with an accident*,' he mused, '*why not? Who would blame me? They tried to overcome me... yes, they tried to overcome me.*'

"How are you with computers, Comrade Major?" grunted Alina Kuznetsova spitting blood from between her teeth. "With the revolution begun how are you going to send messages to the Political Commissars and the Generals in time for them to do something about it?"

"It is not a problem, somebody will be brought here very shortly to do it. Tell me traitor... what about Comrade Dobrovski, is he a traitor too? Is he involved in the revolution? He was very insistent that you should join the Tula cell and when I refused him permission he mentioned your computer skills and how useful they could be to us. Tell me what you know."

"I know this," replied Alina in a low voice. "Vladimir Vakhnenko did not run inside the building to release Valeri Demidov."

"And how do you know that?"

"Because, Comrade Major, he is standing right behind you with a Markov 9 mil pointed at your head."

"Do you think I am stupid? Do you think I am going to fall for that old trick?" spat the Major in his signature mocking tone of voice. The next instant a single loop garrotte slipped over the Major's head and pulled tight around his throat. He tried in vain to grasp it using both his hands but it was too late, the garrotte was already tight to his skin.

"The keys! Where are the keys to the handcuffs?" I shouted. Grigori shouted that they were on top of the exec console. I led the Major by the garrotte to the exec console. Reaching out with my free hand I grabbed the handcuff keys and unlocked Grigori's handcuffs. Grigori then released everybody else.

Svetlana and Grigori grabbed the discs from their backpacks and inserted them into the drives. Alina, Georgi, Irina and Maria grabbed machine pistols and took up position in the corridor that led from the computer room. I asked what I should do with Major Popov. Grigori said to kill him. Svetlana screamed out aloud that I should not. A shout from Alina was in agreement with Grigori. I had never killed anybody before, none of us had. Looking around the computer room I spied a long threaded bolt screwed into a girder that had been bent upwards for a makeshift coat hook. I dragged the tip-toeing, struggling-for-breath, Major toward the bent bolt and reaching it I wrapped the cord of the garrotte around it several times. The bolt was so high off the ground, and the remaining cord so short, that the Major had to remain on tip toes to prevent the garrotte from cutting his throat. I moved away from Major Popov but kept my eyes and my Markov 9 mil on him. In a way I actually felt sorry for the Major. I was about to ease the tension on the garrotte when I was ordered by Irina to guard the service door to the computer room. I picked up a machine pistol and took up my position, ignoring the plaintive, choking, grunted, pleas from the Major to have the garrotte loosened.

After loading the discs, Svetlana and Grigori monitored the loading sequence. A message appeared on both of the screens at the same time; '*disk failure: error 1309: fatal error reading disk. Retry <Y/N>.*' They both pressed Y several times but with the same result: '*disk failure: error 1309: fatal error reading disk. Retry <Y/N>.*' They simultaneously shouted for Alina to come to them. When she saw the error message on the screens she laughed thinking, '*I should have taught them how to deal with disc format errors.*'

"What the hell are you laughing at?" bleated Grigori.

"Do not panic Comrade Rabinovich, it is a simple problem to

solve." Alina logged into the operating system of the exec. A number of options appeared on the screen, the fifth being disc format. Option eight of the sub-menu was a list of disc formats. Alina selected the third option on the list; 8" 1420k TD. "Okay, try it now."

Everything loaded as it should. Strings of commands scrolled up the screen. A message appeared asking; '*Are you sure you want to proceed with the transmission of the selected files? <Y/N>?*'

"Who should do it?" asked Svetlana to nobody in particular. "Pressing Y will change history. It will be the end of so many people. It has to be done…"

"Alina, it should be Alina. Without her we would have failed."

"Alina," shouted Svetlana, "we have decided that you should have the honour of…" Svetlana's words were cut off by bursts of machine pistol fire. Without hesitating, Svetlana pressed Y. The exec console went active. Line after line of commands rushed up the screen, each line ending with the words; '*Transmission successful.*' The green read lights on the disc drives flashed so fervently they gave the impression of being permanently on. The lights on the communications stacks flashed rhythmically to a cadence of revolution.

"It is working! It is doing it!" shouted Grigori after the second screen started displaying return messages; '*Confirm received, will comply.*' Then suddenly the transmissions stopped: A message came up on the exec console: '*EOF reached. Eject disk <Y/N>?*'

Pandemonium was breaking out in the computer room and the corridor leading to it. Bullets were flying and ricocheting everywhere. Irina lay on the floor in a spreading pool of blood. She moved an arm. Georgi grabbed her by the foot and dragged her back behind the protection of the exec console. A hand grenade rolled along the corridor floor toward the computer room, everybody took cover. It was a fragmentation grenade. They were lucky to survive the explosion as well as they did, though everybody was now wounded. Realising they had achieved as much as they could by successfully transmitting the computer files Svetlana screamed out, "We surrender. Stop shooting. We surrender." The shooting stopped from both sides.

"Put down your weapons and place your hands on your heads! Stand where we can see you and do not move." In response to this order, several bursts of machine pistol fire erupted from multiple locations, wiping out the KGB Agents.

"Irisha… Georgi… Masha… it is me, do not shoot."

"Valera? Valera!" They yelled in unison.

"Yes, it is me… Valeri, none other!" Valeri kicked away the KGB's barricades to join his Tula cell compatriots.

"Valera, Irisha needs help urgently!"

"This place has its own hospital, it is up on the first floor. Go and find a doctor and bring them here. Tell them that you are a member of the new Ruling Council and if they refuse to come shoot somebody… just not the doctor."

"Just like the old Ruling Council," answered Svetlana acidly.

"Exactly. Now go, hurry, I do not want my life's love to die today." Hearing Valeri refer to Irina as his life's love shook Svetlana. She had no idea they were close but she had no regrets over the night they had spent together in Tula.

Walking across the devastation of the computer room Valeri saw Major Popov strung up by a garrotte. His eyes were full of fear and dread. Suddenly, shooting resumed in the corridor as KGB reinforcements arrived to take back the computer room. Valeri grabbed the Major and told him the revolution was already under way and there was no point in anybody else dying. He asked the Major to order the Agents to stand down. He said he would. Valeri placed Major Popov in handcuffs before he cut the garrotte, leaving him to fall to the floor.

"This is Major Popov. I am with the freedom fighters. They say the revolution is already under way and I believe them. Comrades, leave this place… go home to your families… save them and save yourselves. Lay down your weapons and…"

"Comrades, do not listen to him, Major Popov is a traitor. Kill him! Kill them all! Do not leave anyone alive," screamed Colonel Petrova from the corridor. Multiple bursts of rapid machine pistol fire and the smell of cordite filled the air. Everybody inside the computer room took cover behind the computer stacks. The Tula cell returned fire as best they could but they were pinned down. I slipped out of the computer room's service door. I had a clear line of sight to the side of the KGB's barricade. There were six Agents. They were joined by another two. As I was taking aim one of the new arrivals shot Colonel Petrova in the back of her head and held the other KGB Agents at the point of his machine pistol. "*Long live Lev… long live the revolution… long live Narodnaya Volya*!" The two new arrivals disarmed the KGB Agents and shouted into the computer room that it was safe to come out, "*Colonel Petrova is dead and her lackeys are disarmed.*"

Ever cautious, Valeri ordered everybody to stay under cover, saying he would show himself to make sure it was safe to come out. The remainder swore that if Valeri was attacked they would fight to the death to avenge him. For some reason Major Popov swore this oath too. The Tula cell stared blankly at him. He ignored their stares and stood shoulder to shoulder with them. They guessed his game.

*

Immediately Lev received the message from KGB HQ he put his plan into action. His inner council were at his side. They contacted the leaders of NV Units right across the Soviet Union, thousands of them, who in turn contacted thousands upon thousands of others who themselves were in contact with millions upon millions of Soviet citizens whose loyalty to Lev and NV had been cultivated over many years. An order was passed down the line that everybody was to tune into a radio broadcast to be given by Lev at midday at which they would receive instructions on what they should do next.

Lev personally contacted two dozen Red Army Generals to inform them that the revolution had started. He told them what he expected from them. Concerned that several of them would not hold their nerve Lev made calls to NV operatives close to them. He gave orders that they were to assassinate the Generals they were shadowing and take over their commands.

★

Maxim Kirilenko was sitting alone in his Kremlin office nursing his fourth stiff whisky of the night when news of the transmission of the computer messages from KGB HQ was handed to him by Alexander Orlov. '*Why has he written down what he could just as easily say?'* thought Maxim. *'Maybe he is creating an official record to save himself should things go badly*?' Maxim felt vulnerable. He regarded comrade Orlov with deep suspicion. All manner of things flooded into his head. Pangs of regret over starting the whole business chewed at his stomach.

"Is this really good news Alexander?"

"You doubt it? Of course it is good news! The revolution has begun and soon, very soon, all your enemies will be dead. You will be the first General Secretary to rule as a Tsar since Stalin. The Russian people need a Tsar… the Soviet people need a Tsar, a strong Tsar to govern…"

"What shall we do next?"

"The plan. We must stick to the plan. You must order the arrest of the Central Committee, starting with Luka Bazanov. Then you must appoint somebody who is loyal to you to immediately take over the KGB. We cannot afford to let them get ideas of their own."

"And who do you suggest for the job, Alexander? Yourself?"

"No! No! No! Comrade General Secretary, I am not at all suitable. The best person from the list is the homosexual Jew, Dobrovski. Besides, if it all goes badly we… you can point the finger at him as being behind these… treasonous plots. It was he who arranged the Terror. It was he who met with Valeri Demidov. It was he who conspired with… not important. It was he who grabbed control of the KGB. It was not us. It was not you, it was him! Him! Him! Him! It was all him." Maxim Kirilenko smiled at Alexander's words, then half-joked.

"You have been spending too much time with Americans. What happened to you Alexander? What did they do to you my old friend?"

"I… I see. Very funny. Very funny. At least you seem more relaxed now. So? Dobrovski? Bazanov? What are your orders?"

"Call the Captain of my Kremlin guard. They are to round up and arrest every member of the Central Committee. I want Bazanov dead. See to it."

"And Dobrovski?"

"I will call him on your special phone, but without using the device so he will know it is me, and tell him about his new job. I will order him to go to KGB HQ immediately and take over there."

During Maxim's conversation with Vasily Dobrovski he learned of the radio message to be broadcast by Lev at midday. "*That was not part of the plan,"* he gasped. *"What the hell is he playing at? What is going on?"* General Secretary Kirilenko rampaged around the Kremlin in a manic tantrum kicking everyone who came within range. Finally coming across Alexander Orlov he dragged his Chef de Cabinet all the way back to his office and locked the door behind them.

★

Vasily Zaytsev, Commissar of the Western Frontier Gulags, usually slept like a baby. It was not his conscience that gave him fitful sleep that night, it was anticipation of his part in things to come.

In the small hours Comrade Zaytsev got out of bed and checked his computer. Nothing. He went into the kitchen and made a pot of coffee. The noise woke his guards as well as the kitchen and household staff. They were very surprised to see their boss up so early. They had always regarded Comrade Zaytsev as fat and lazy and, '*come the revolution he will be first up against the wall.*'

As Vasily and his entourage sat shivering in the kitchen a lackey strolled in and handed him a piece of paper covered in what the lackey thought was gibberish. The first thing that came to Comrade Zaytsev's attention was command 20.

"Let us all get something warm inside us on this cold morning… so far away from our beloved Russia. I will treat you to a drop of the good stuff from Shotlandiya." Vasily returned to the kitchen with a couple of half empty bottles. "I will pour," he insisted. '*Bastard,*' some thought, '*giving us the dregs from half empty bottles.*' But it was excellent whisky so nobody refused. "What is it they say here? Cheers! Down the hatch!" With that toast everybody slugged down their drams in one. Comrade Zaytsev had been careful to ensure that his body guards were served from one bottle and his household staff from the other. He sat looking at his watch.

"Are you expecting somebody Comrade Commissar?" asked one of his KGB bodyguards.

"No, not somebody… something," he replied coldly.

"What time is it comrade Head Commissar?"

"Time? There is no time to lose," Vasily replied randomly, growing impatient waiting for the poison to take effect. He had made it up himself by soaking NV message paper in a three quarter empty bottle of fine malt whisky, turning the elixir of life into a bottle of deadly neurotoxin poison. He had always been careful to keep it under lock and key to prevent accidental imbibing. After a few more minutes the guards fell like skittles while the household staff sat looking at one another, some staring at their now empty glasses.

"Comrade Commissar… what is happening?" asked a panic stricken cook.

"Revolution comrade cook, revolution is happening, revolution is here! Go to your families and tell them that the long waited for revolution has begun." Vasily made several NV signs and received a surprising number in return. "I am your Regional NV Commander. Now go... go and await your orders. Comrade Lev himself will speak to you on the radio from Leningrad at midday. Mention nothing to anybody of what has passed here." The household staff nodded their heads and left the Commissar's house.

The Commissar of the Western Frontier Gulags made calls to each of his Western Gulag Chiefs of Staff, ordering them to attend an urgent meeting in thirty minutes in his office. Before he left the house Vasily went upstairs and kissed his wife Olga on her cheek, whispering to her that he loved her. In her half-awake state she half heard him but knew what he had said. Going to the boot of his limousine, Comrade Zaytsev and his so-called chauffer grabbed four fully loaded machine pistols, extra magazines and a pair of grenades each. They would be the only ones armed at the meeting with the Western Gulag Chiefs of Staff.

★

In the far north of Velikobritania, in the province known as Shotlandiya, an NKVD Unit arrived at their first location. They were under orders to pick up eleven NV activists for transport to Irlandia. The settlement was a small, sparse, ribbon scattering of single storey houses built from local granite whose inhabitants were likewise made from granite having lived off the scrubby land there for generations. The Red Army was in position a mile outside the settlement ready to occupy it after the NKVD had completed the cleansing of the area. Afterwards, as per the masterplan, the NKVD would move on to the next location leaving the Red Army to mop up residual resistance and occupy the settlement.

As the NKVD column reached the first of the houses all was quiet but when it turned the only corner in the settlement the sight that greeted them froze the blood in their veins. Standing before them stood hundreds upon hundreds of Shotlandski dressed in illegal traditional clothing with their faces and bodies painted blue. The Commander held up her hand to halt the column of Soldiers. In response, the mass crowd of Shotlandski raised up their weapons to the heavens, shaking them violently and yelling a mighty, ear-splitting, war cry which smashed the spirit of the NKVD column. The Commander called forward twenty NKVD Soldiers armed with flame throwers and machine guns. One of her Officers said to her, "*I would not do that if I were you.*" She asked why not. "*Because we are outnumbered.*" The Commander said the Officer needed to learn how to count. The Officer replied, "*Look behind us.*" Turning around, the NKVD Commander saw more than a thousand armed and naked Shotlandski painted blue.

In blind panic the Commander got on her radio and called for backup from the Red Army. "*Commander Ludovitza, this is General Murkov, what is your situation*?" The NKVD Commander relayed the situation to the General and repeated her request for Red Army support. "*I cannot do that Commander Ludovitza.*" She asked why not. "*Because I am under strict instructions from Leningrad to assist with the uprising.*" She asked what he meant. General Murkov replied, "*Comrade Ludovitza, I suggest you surrender. Throw yourself, along with your Officers and Soldiers, on the mercy of those you came to slaughter and hope they will be merciful. Long live Lev. Long live the revolution. Long live Narodnaya Volya.*" There was a click over the radio and the call went dead.

Similar scenes were enacted right across the northern zones of Shotlandiya with the same outcome. The Shotlandski massacred the NKVD while the Red Army stood by and did nothing. In instances where the Shotlandski were outnumbered the Red Army assisted them to slaughter the NKVD. Both parties took to the task with glee.

★

News of the transmission of the computer messages reached Lieutenant Kozlov in Vladivostok. He ripped open his sealed orders, ran to the fourth sub-level of the Security Section and he shouted. "*Comrades! Comrades! Stop what you are doing and listen to me. Comrades, the revolution has begun. It is time for you to take up arms. Long live Lev. Long live the revolution. Long live Narodnaya Volya!*" Lieutenant Kozlov's announcement was met with muted cheers. Ignoring the lack of enthusiasm he continued. "*Comrades, get up from your desks go to the surface and take over the camp.*" Nobody moved. "*Comrades, what is wrong? Why do you hesitate? This is our moment our comrades are relying on us.*" One of the longer standing staff members shouted back that they were afraid that it was all just a ruse and they would be mowed down as soon as they emerged into the parade ground. "*Comrades, follow me. Follow me. If it is a ruse I will be the first to die.*"

Standing, the workers of the fourth sub-level formed up in single files between the rows of desks. As they made their way to the exit they merged into a marching torrent. As they reached the doors of the Security Building they swarmed into the parade ground. Suddenly, powerful spotlights illuminated them. Each waited with bated breath for the machine guns to open up. Instead, they were greeted by thunderous cheers and were dragged to join a parade formed behind massive banners of gold writing on red backgrounds. One read:

THE RED ARMY
PRIDE AND THE GLORY
OF THE REVOLUTION

Another banner read:

LONG LIVE LEV
LONG LIVE THE REVOLUTION
LONG LIVE NARODNAYA VOLYA

There were a great many banners. It was as though this day had been long planned for.

★

The masterplan had been for NKVD to bring Terror to the peoples of Velikobritania and Vladivostok and then move inward from both those extremities toward the centre of the Soviet Union. However, NV Units right across the Soviet Union sprang into action, annihilating the NKVD wherever they came across them. This was not the bloodless revolution that Lev had promised but it was as close as anybody could get over the vastness of half the world's land mass.

The New Order

Midday. Leningrad. Lev, head bowed to his chest, stood silent in front of a microphone in Leningrad's state run radio station. In the control booth were his closest confidants, Markovs pressed hard into the backs of the radio station's production crew. A solitary reporter from Pravda was present to write the story of Lev's speech. The Pravda presses were being held, waiting for her copy. Millions upon millions of citizens all across the Soviet Union and beyond tuned their radios to listen to Lev's speech.

"Comrades… this is Lev speaking to you from Leningrad. I am talking to Narodnaya Volya. I am talking to the Red Army. I am talking to the KGB. I am talking to disparate revolutionary groups right across our lands. I am talking to all the peoples of the Soviet Union. I am also talking to whatever remains of the NKVD… and I am talking to Maxim Kirilenko and his Central Committee.

Yesterday, forces of the NKVD moved against ordinary Soviet citizens in Velikobritania and Vladivostok. Their purpose? To bring Terror to the good citizens of those two great powerhouses of our workers' paradise. Why? Because the Central Committee ordered them to do so. Did they refuse to follow their illegal orders? No, they gladly obeyed them.

In response to this declaration of war by the Central Committee on the good citizens of the Soviet Union, my Narodnaya Volya forces… at the cost of their own lives… stood firm against the murderous NKVD. I am happy to report to you, the good citizens of the Soviet

Union, that my NV forces were victorious in their endeavours… with no little help from our Red Army… I declare them the Pride and the Glory of the Revolution!

For many years, I have been working to free our great nation from the creeping cronyism, tyranny and grasping hands that enslaved us all. Over decades, the Central Committee has been thinking more about themselves, their careers and their own glory than about our nation and its citizens. They have grown rich and fat while the rest of us have starved… starved of work… starved of food… starved of dignity… starved of everything… everything!

How many of you are work sharing… job splitting… work loading? How many of you are suffering job dilution… production relocation to the centre… to Moscow? Any why? Why? All because those we trusted to run our great nation decided to run it for their own benefit… for their own interests… for their own profit. You all know what I am saying is true. Bandits roam our lands, holding trucks and trains to ransom because they have no other way of surviving. Ordinary citizens staged protests to bring inequalities to the attention of those who we entrusted to run the state. But they have deaf ears. You all know what I am saying is true.

Who is to blame for all this? Who are the ones behind all the chaos? The answer is simple. Maxim Kirilenko and his Central Committee! They are the ones to blame. Chaos exists because it suits them and their purposes. They are the ones to blame. It is they who have destroyed our workers' paradise. They are the ones to blame. It is they who ordered the Terror. They are the ones to blame. They wanted to control the Proletariat by Terror. They looked to days past and saw that Lenin himself used Terror. But he did so against Tsarism… those peasants still loyal to their aristocratic, land-owning, feudal overlords. Peasants who knew no better than to fight against the forces that were freeing them. At that time there were other forces intent on keeping power… Kerensky and his cronies… traitors who Vladimir

Ilyich had no option but to destroy. His method? Terror. They were different days… different times… but that did not stop the Central Committee bringing Terror to you… to each and every one of you!

What is to be done? What is to be done dear comrades? We must sweep away the debris of the past. Sweep away the Central Committee and cut off its tendrils. We must clean them all away. I call upon the citizens of the Soviet Union to rise up in solidarity with Narodnaya Volya to cleanse our lands. Remove from power all those who presently have it and fill the void with Councils made up from local citizenry led by my Narodnaya Volya Commissars. They will make themselves known to you.

I call upon all those listening to spread my word and carry out my will… the will of the people… The Peoples' Will… without bloodshed. This is a bloodless revolution. I am not saying that you must forgive and I know how hard it is to forget but I am asking you… pleading with you… begging you… to be merciful… even to those who would not have shown you mercy… or compassion… or humanity. I will not have this, our new beginning, baptised in blood.

I now address the Central Committee. Surrender! Give yourselves up! I promise you a fair trial by an impartial judiciary. Which is more than you deserve and more than you have given others in the past. Do not walk into the streets. They are not safe for you. Stay in your offices. My Narodnaya Volya operatives will pick you up. If you put up a fight I cannot vouch for your safety or the safety or survival of your families.

A new era is upon us and I hereby declare myself autocrat of the Soviet Union until such time that democracy can be established…"

There really is no need to complete the above sentence as it was as worthless then under those circumstances as it has been countless times in the past.

"Effective immediately, I am declaring martial law across the Soviet Union until it is confirmed that all pockets of NKVD and other anti-Soviet resistance have been neutralised and the entire USSR is safe once again. Until further notice, a curfew is in immediate effect beginning at 1800 in each time zone. All citizens, unless they are attending their places of work, must be in their homes by 1800 and will remain there until 0600 the following morning, again, unless they are attending their places of work. Curfew passes for citizens working outside the curfew hours will be authorised and distributed by local NV Commissars only, nobody else. There will be no exceptions. Anybody found breaching the curfew will be arrested and appropriately punished by their local NV Commissariat. Long live the revolution. Long live Narodnaya Volya."

This was an uncharacteristically short speech by the loquacious Lev but he was a man in a hurry, a man on the move, a man on a mission and did not want grass growing under his feet. He had places to go, people to see, enemies to kill, alliances to make and break. A Central Committee to wipe out and Americans to welcome.

In millions of homes right across the Soviet Union, and in certain establishments in the USA, the response from the congregation to Lev's "*Long live the revolution. Long live Narodnaya Volya*" was; "*Long Live Lev… Long Live Lev…*" For eight days after Lev's speech, victory celebrations were held throughout the Soviet Union. People were once again in love with the state. They had their workers' paradise back again. The love was not extended to the NKVD though and in most circumstances they did not give up without a fight. Massacres and atrocities were carried out by both sides with the Red Army finally having the last word by crushing the last vestiges of NKVD resistance. In all, over thirty million died in this so-called bloodless revolution.

★

Maxim Kirilenko and his Central Committee listened to Lev's speech frozen with terror. They remained where they were ordered to wait for the knock on their doors. In the Kremlin, Maxim Kirilenko was apoplectic with rage, fury and indignation. He was lambasting Alexander Orlov for '*talking him into this scheme of his.*'

"Idiot! You... you... you idiot! What have you done! I am doomed. You have killed me!"

"There must be more to it... this must be a ploy by Lev or a ruse... something to placate the Proles during the... transition."

"Transition? What transition? There was never meant to be any transition! After stopping the Terror plot I was to arrest the treasonous Central Committee for overstepping their authority and invite Lev to join me... join me to help run the Soviet Union... in partnership, not for him to declare himself its ruler... its Tsar. The revolution was not meant to be against me..." This last sentence was spoken in a whimper.

"I will speak with The 400... see what they have to say about this."

"What can they say? What can they do? They are thousands of miles away..."

"That is not true comrade."

"Not true? What do you mean by '*not true*' Comrade Orlov?" asked Maxim sensing his Chef de Cabinet was involved in Lev's skulduggery.

"Some of The 400 have been here... in Moscow... in the Kremlin... for some months now."

"Why was I not told about this? How did... what did?..." Comrade Kirilenko was utterly speechless. In his puzzlement he looked a thoroughly dejected and beaten man.

"I am sure this misunderstanding will be cleared up in no time." A knock reverberated on the door of Maxim Kirilenko's office. He did not invite anybody to enter but they did so anyway.

"Maxim Konstantin Kirilenko," spoke the leader of the arrest party, "by order of Lev and the Governing Council of Narodnaya Volya, you are under arrest. You will follow me."

"Where are my Kremlin Guard? Why are they not here to protect me?"

"They laid down their arms and surrendered. They are free to go where they will." '*Not one of the bastards was willing to fight for me… to die for me… after all I have done for them. Bastards!*'

"Where are you taking me?"

"To a place of safety." Comrade Kirilenko knew what that meant. "Both you and Comrade Orlov are named on the arrest warrant. You are both to be removed from the Kremlin by covered truck to avoid retribution by the Proletariat." Comrade Orlov was shaken at hearing he was also being arrested.

"On whose authority are you arresting me?" he protested.

"See for yourself." The leader of the arrest party passed Alexander the arrest warrant signed by Lev. His name was double underlined. He realised there was no use in protesting any further.

"You did not answer my question. Where are you taking me… us?"

"You are being removed to the Lubyanka to be interrogated." They both understood what interrogated meant in that place. Alexander and Maxim were ready to tell everything without the need for torture but there was a price to pay for who they were and what they represented and they had to pay that price. They had to be seen to pay the price so stories of the horrors inflicted upon them could be told and retold over and over again around Pioneer Camp fires.

Comrades Kirilenko and Orlov had heard about the tunnels below the Kremlin but had never visited them until now. They walked in grooves worn in the dirt floor by the dragging feet of the condemned. Kirilenko's knees went watery and let him down as he stumbled over the uneven ground. Crawling on his hands and knees he noticed a crudely cut hole leading to a chamber with tiled walls, sloping concrete floor and gutter at its end. From his experience of constructing execution rooms in his youth he recognised it for what it was. "*At least I am not going in there,*" he muttered without a thought for Alexander Orlov hobbling along in front of him.

At the end of the corridor Maxim and Alexander joined a small group of Kremlin staff waiting in the dark for the lift to arrive. After a ding announced the lift's arrival its double concertina metal doors flew open and the group was herded inside with the aid of rifle butts from behind. The lift stank of everything unimaginable. The floor was wet and slippery. Several of the group added to the floor's wetness. At the thought of his wife a tear came to Alexander's eye. At least she was safe. She was in hiding thanks to her husband's fake kidnap caper. '*At least she is safe.*'

"It is no use crying comrade."

"Perhaps he is crying for the fate of his beautiful young wife. I have seen photographs of her. She will make a fine whore."

"Are we going to pick her up?"

"No, Kiril is going to do it. He said that if he finds her he is going to keep her to himself for a while. I told him that if he finds her he should share her out."

"You mean keep her for you!" The guards in the lift laughed aloud.

Forced from the lift into the inner courtyard of the Kremlin, Maxim Kirilenko, his Chef de Cabinet and the clutch of Kremlin career climbers were thrown onto the back of the waiting lorry and its cover dropped over them. They were driven across Red Square to the Lubyanka to await their appointment with the interrogators.

★

As things turned out, Vronika was not found by Kiril or anybody else. After everything died down she was advised by friends to renounce her relationship with Alexander and divorce him. She knew that would be what Alexander would want her to do and so she did; she divorced Alexander. A few weeks later, Vronika took up a position working for the Chiefs of Staff in the Kremlin, eventually marrying her ex-husband's replacement in Lev's government.

★

As former General Secretary of the Soviet Union, Maxim Kirilenko, was being frogmarched from his Kremlin office, Lev was on an express train bound for Moscow. He had learned his history well and knew that this was his most dangerous time. Having overthrown the regime, he was expendable. If he was going to be assassinated it would be before he got to Moscow. Accordingly he was protected by no less than five hundred body guards and NV operatives were positioned every five hundred yards along the line from Leningrad to Moscow. The journey was redolent of Stalin's trip to Potsdam all those years ago when he resolved to abduct Truman and Churchill and declare war on Great Britain, changing the world forever. The sense of history being remade was not lost on Lev. Helicopters flew above Lev's train to announce his progress and well-wishers could wave as it zoomed by. Tanks were stationed at every level crossing and on every bridge along Lev's route. He was better guarded than the Romanov Jewels in their bomb proof cases in the Hermitage.

★

Lev arrived at the Leningradski railway station to tumultuous cheering from half a million Proles. The number reported in Pravda the following day was five million. The scenes were reminiscent of Vladimir Ilyich's arrival at Petrograd's Finlandski station in 1917. Like Lenin, on arrival Lev gave a rousing speech. The crowd were mainly NV activists and supporters. At Lev's orders, certain others were '*actively*' prevented from welcoming him back to Moscow. The round-ups resulted in the various ethnic and other concentration camps being filled to overflowing. He did not want an assassin in the crowd or a sniper on a roof. The people holding the high ground were NV Special Forces, nearly all of whom were ex-

Spetsnaz. Dozens of decal-less black helicopters hovered overhead, watching the watchers. Troops wearing black balaclavas leaned out of helicopter deck doors shouldering rifles mounted with telescopic sights assisted by laser dot guidance. Floors above the third floor of every building all along Lev's route to the Kremlin were emptied of workers and replaced by Troops dressed completely in black and bearing no insignia of battalion or rank.

A parade was organised in Red Square to greet Lev's arrival at the Kremlin. As he stood alone atop Lenin's tomb thousands upon thousands of Soldiers twenty helmets deep by forty long marched past him. They saluted their new leader in perfect synchronisation. Next came tanks with their guns held high in salute to Lev. Next came the armoured divisions, Lev was not very impressed by them. Finally came the pride of the Soviet war machine; missiles. Missiles of all types and sizes. Lev was like a child in a candy store. Small clustered missiles for bringing Terror to internal enemies, mid-sized missiles for bringing down aircraft, larger missiles for attacking enemies at the Soviet Union's borders and finally came the nuclear ICBMs. The crowd cheered and clapped loudest for them.

After the parade passed Lev did what he liked to do most of all; give a speech. Credit where credit is due Lev was a fine orator. He spoke until it was almost dawn. By then, many of his audience were dead on their feet but they knew they could not leave while Lev was still speaking. To do so would be disastrous for them. They had to tend to nature where they stood. Lev did likewise but he was well prepared for it.

Though exhausted, sleep was the last thing on Lev's mind. He had an empire to run and run it he would… starting right then and here. He marched at pace into Maxim Kirilenko's former office, swept all the papers from the desk onto the floor with a single flourish of his hand and sat on Maxim's chair. Lev wriggled to get comfortable but could not. He rose and booted the chair away and shouted for another chair to be brought. As the chair's replacement was smaller than the rejected chair Lev gave the original chair a second chance. '*Maybe it was not so bad after all.*'

First order of business, sign proclamations giving himself absolute power. Second order of business sign death warrants to get rid of the old order and settle personal vendettas. Third order of business, order medals to be struck and named in his honour. Fourth order of business, form an inner council of advisors; '*some of the old lackeys will do nicely.*' Fifth and final order of business for day one, arrange a conference with his sponsors… for, say, four weeks hence. '*That will give me time to tidy the old place up a bit and burn the trash.*'

Business for day one done, Lev called for a daybed to be brought to his office. '*Just like Stalin had,*' he thought with a smile. When it arrived he marched everybody out of the room and closed the doors to his office behind them. They were ordered not to disturb him, "*not even if Lenin himself rises from his tomb.*" Lying on his daybed Lev took to his thoughts. '*The Red Army is eating out of my hands… the KGB are keeping their heads down and working hard at appearing loyal… good idea of mine for Dobrovski run to it, for the time being at least… NKVD, smashed to pieces… the Proles?… who cares about them? Who cares what happens to them?*'

Over the following week, Lev left his office only twice and that was to attend march pasts by adoring Proles as they saluted while he stood atop Lenin's tomb. From day seven others began appearing on top of Lenin's tomb with Lev; faceless, nameless, unknowns. One day Grigori's father stood next to Lev; on another day, Svetlana's.

⋆

On day sixteen of Lev's supremacy the Tula cell was brought to meet him at the Kremlin. They were being honoured with Lev's specially struck medals as Heroes Of The Soviet Union – First Class with a cluster of Five Red Stars; henceforth they would have cities, roads, factories, schools, universities, just about anything named after them.

"Comrade Lev," chimed a Kremlin flunky, "these are the young heroes from Tula who transmitted the computer message to…"

"Ah yes, you are the ones who lit the touch paper! Sit down. I recognise a couple of you. You… I sent you to Tula with Olga? Yes? How is she?"

"She is dead Comrade Lev. She died in a torture house along with Sergei and Vitaly." I did not say how they had died, as technically they all died at Alice's hands. To my great shame I had not thought about Olga, or the others, in weeks and now here I was standing in front of Lev unable to tell him how they had died.

"That is a great pity, I knew Olga well and liked her very much. She is one of many who fell during the years of our struggles." Lev patted me on the shoulder. "Her name will be commemorated on a monument in Tula and in her home city of…" Lev paused to look to his left.

"Cherepovets, Comrade Lev, she came from Cherepovets," said a researcher with an odd accent. I thought, '*If I did not know better I would say she spoke Russian with an American accent.*'

"Yes, Cherepovets… Cherepovets," spoke Lev as in a trance. "If not for you our wonderful, courageous, daring, young people," a Pravda reporter captured every word for later editing by Lev before his words went to print, "we would probably not be standing here today. It is only fitting and proper that you each receive my highest honour. I will personally present you with your Hero Of The Soviet Union medals at today's workers march. You will have the honour of taking the salute atop Lenin's tomb standing right next to me."

"Comrade Lev," interrupted Valeri, "Comrade Vakhnenko deserves special mention. If not for him our mission would have failed. There would have been no '*lighting the touch paper*'… no starting gun… no revolution."

"Oh, really?" Lev did not seem interested in the slightest with what Valeri had said. "Come, follow me, all of you, it is time for the ceremony." Before Lev left his office he whispered something to one of his aides. The aide gave me a look I did not like.

"Pedro will accompany you Comrade Vakhnenko." The aide said to me.

"Pedro?"

"Hola."

"I have never met anybody called Pedro before."

"There are lots of Pedros where I come from," laughed Pedro.

"Where is that?"

"I understand you speak Spanish."

"Yes and several other languages too." I thought Pedro's Russian was terrible.

"Good, we'll speak Spanish."

"We have to speak Russian otherwise we will get into trouble."

"Not anymore you won't. From now on you can speak any language you want." I felt lucky that I could already speak Spanish and I enjoyed talking with Pedro. We spoke Spanish all the way to Lenin's mausoleum. He did not ascend the steps with me but walked away talking with some people who looked remarkably similar to him. They even dressed alike.

There we all were, '*Tula Cell NV6K*', standing alongside Lev and important dignitaries on top of Lenin's tomb, taking the salute of the workers marching past. Grigori pointed and whispered that one of the dignitaries was his father. I do not know why but I did not think that strange at the time, I simply accepted it as fact.

Each medal ceremony was very brief. I think mine was the briefest. Afterwards Lev gave an uncharacteristically short speech and then invited Svetlana, Grigori, Alina and Valeri to give speeches. They must have known ahead of time that this was going to happen as they had each prepared a speech. Svetlana's speech was wonderful. It was inspiring, heroic and full of hope for the future. Grigori's was not bad either. Before Valeri went to make his speech the aide who

Lev had spoken to just before we left his office whispered something in his ear which obviously disturbed him. At first he shook his head but then after another whisper he nodded. Valeri's speech was full of praise for others, which was typical of him, but there was not one word of mention about me and my, according to Valeri, heroism in saving the mission. I was perplexed and went to talk to Valeri after the ceremony but he was quickly spirited away along with Svetlana, Grigori and Alina. After they had all departed I was left standing alone atop Lenin's tomb in the midst of a bunch of strangers. Nevertheless, I felt lucky that I was in Red Square having done my duty for the cause. My feeling of luck was not like my usual feeling of luck, it was somehow manufactured internally and forced to the surface. I had no control over it.

Uncertain of what I should do next I left Red Square and found myself walking toward the University of Nationalities. I wondered if I could stay there until I found some accommodation. Just before I reached the university somebody shouted my name. I turned to see the aide who Lev had whispered to.

"Vladimir. Where have you been? I have been looking all over the place for you." I was not in a good mood.

"Why? Why were you looking for me? What do you have to say to me? Why am I being treated so badly?" I was feeling hurt that my so-called friends had left me without so much as a backward glance.

"Vladimir, my friend, how can you say such things? You are a decorated hero of the Soviet Union. You stood right next to Lev on top of Lenin's tomb and everybody saw you receive your medal from Lev himself. Everywhere you go people will know that you are a Hero Of The Soviet Union and you will be treated as such. Come, my friend, tell me what is wrong?"

"Why was I left behind after the ceremony…"

"Left behind? You were not left behind, my friend. You were… overlooked. Yes, simply overlooked. Everybody was busy talking to one another and… well, you know… they were… preoccupied. Tell me Vladimir, what is it that you want?"

"I want to go back to my university to finish my course and graduate. Simple as that. Can you arrange that for me?"

"Of course I can but the universities are staying closed for the time being. I tell you what. I will arrange for a flight for you back to Velikobritania so you can be with your family and friends. Take a holiday, you deserve it! As soon as the universities are open again you can return to finish your studies. How about that?" My lucky feeling was back and this time it was the real thing.

"That sounds great." I said feeling very much relieved inside. "I would like to see my friends before I go though."

"Of course Vladimir, of course. Come with me."

We returned to the Kremlin. I was ushered into a room where a drinks reception was being held. Everybody was drinking champagne and eating little sandwiches. I looked around the room and saw Svetlana. She, as usual, was surrounded by men. I walked past the group she was with and she caught sight of me.

"Vlad! There you are. We were looking all over for you. Where were you?"

"After the medals ceremony and the speeches I…" I felt too embarrassed to continue. "I liked your speech very much."

"Thank you. What happened to your speech? Too shy?"

"No, I was not asked to give a speech."

"Well, maybe next time," said Svetlana trying to sound encouraging. She knew what type of person I am, always in need of encouragement. She said once that it was a sign of immaturity… or was it insecurity?

"Next time? What do you mean '*next time*'?"

"Here, take a look." Svetlana handed me a sheet of paper with cities and dates printed on it. "Here are the places we are going to make speeches in. It is very exciting. Lev says people like us are the future of the Soviet Union. You can make a speech…"

"I am going back to Budyonovsk for a while… until the universities reopen, and then resume my studies."

"The universities are closed?"

"So I was told by…" I looked round for the aide but he was nowhere to be seen, "you know? The man Lev whispered to before we… he was with us on top of Lenin's tomb… he spoke with Valeri before he made his speech. You must have noticed him."

"No, I cannot say that I did. Oh look, it is Pedro. Have you met him? Between you and me I think he is from America."

Svetlana, Pedro and I talked for ten minutes before being joined by the others from the Tula cell. One by one they drifted away until I found myself alone once more. Determined not to let it get to me I wandered around the room, attaching myself to the outskirts of various clusters of people. I was astonished to hear they were talking different languages. Most of them were speaking American. When I joined in their conversations they stared at me until I stopped talking.

Before the reception ended Lev's aide found me sitting on the edge of a table, drinking champagne and eating some very tasty food wrapped in pastry. He asked me to follow him and we left the reception. Once outside the room he handed me a ticket for a flight bound for Stolitsograd early the next morning. He suggested I get a good night's sleep and handed me a voucher for a hotel next to the airport.

★

I was going home! I could already see the headlines in the Budyonovsk Ekho; '*Hero Of The Revolution returns to the city of his birth! Demands for Budyonovsk to be renamed Vakhnenkograd.*' I went straight to my hotel room and took a shower. While singing with my horrible, tuneless, voice in the echoey shower, I wondered whether hotel rooms were still bugged. There was one way to find out… '*I will say something and see what happens.*' '*I will prepare speeches for my arrival in Englia. In them I will boast about the part I played in the revolution… about my part in the success of the revolution… how I single-handedly saved the revolution and without me there would not have been a revolution.'* I shrank away from my musing. '*No! I must not be boastful,'* I thought, *'but I must have a speech ready. I will have to give a speech as soon as I get off the plane.'* I stayed up half the night writing speeches for all occasions and circumstances. Most of all I was looking forward to making a speech at school number 8 in the Leninski Distrikt. How proud the teachers and pupils will be of the '*old boy*' who saved the revolution. '*Let them all see how well the former student has done for himself.*'

★

"Hey Lev, you gotta minute buddy? We need to discuss something urgently," said one of the new people beckoning Lev into his private office and then closing the door behind them. "I've been going over the figures and sorry to say pal they just don't add up. Something needs to be done… and fast or we're broke."

"What needs to be done?"

"We were thinking that some radical changes need to be made to the population base otherwise it'll be generations before we recoup our outlay and get the Soviet economy on track. You know, Lev, we feel we were misled about the true state of things here in the good old USSR. It's far, far, worse than we were ever told… or ever even imagined."

"I say again… what needs to be done?"

"Let me get back to you on that one. I'll have something for you before the next session of the Ruling Council. In the meantime here's a list of Ruling Council members that need swapping out… replacing if you will. Alongside each of their names you'll find the names of their replacements. It'll make it easier getting things passed if we go with this new team."

"Are they 400?"

"No, not directly, we never take a front seat, you know that."

"What about Misha?"

"She won't be involved. I can assure you she will never be allowed to interfere. Being from Romanov blood she has far too much baggage to approach this opportunity with a clear head."

"Good. We do not want the Proles rallying around her."

"Yeah, you're right, Lev, you're right. I'm glad to see we're in agreement. As I said, I'll get back to you before the next session of the Ruling Council. In the meantime, any problems, you know who to call." The new person opened the door signalling to Lev that their talk was over and he was to leave.

The next session of the Ruling Council of the Soviet Union.

The Ruling Council members sat impatiently in the thousand seat auditorium waiting for Lev to appear. Though he was always late for meetings he was highly intolerant of tardiness in others, invariably lambasting latecomers. He seemed to delight in it.

After nearly an hour, First Citizen Lev, General Secretary of the Soviet Union, sauntered into the auditorium reading whatever page he was up to in the pile of documents he was carrying. He looked around the echoing vastness of the room and checked attendance before sitting himself down behind Maxim Kirilenko's old desk, he hated people referring to his desk as Kirilenko's old desk. Lev hammered his gavel on the well-dented spot on the corner of the ormolu decorated Napoleonic writing desk to call the session to order.

Without even attempting to disguise the contempt he felt for his audience, Lev sarcastically remarked how good it was to see so many Ruling Council members present. Those with careers, not to say their lives, hanging by a thread, shifted uncomfortably on their seats. The Recorder for the meeting was Lev's Chef de Cabinet, Valeri Demidov. Comrade Demidov demanded silence to read out the order of business; which was superfluous as there was only one agenda item; Operation Zima; AOBs were not permitted under Lev.

"Operation Zima is on the agenda today, so let us get down to business. I now hand over to First Citizen Lev. Comrade Lev, you are invited to take the floor." Lev walked round his desk to stand in front of the microphone in the middle of the stage. The old NV school of the Ruling Council had expected a lengthy agenda that day so they could begin addressing the various ills of the new Soviet Union but it would not be so that day.

"Brothers, sisters, comrades, citizens… we have struggled so hard and for so long but today we stand on the threshold of greatness in these momentous times." Lev paused to take in his audience for a second time. "This day, you have the chance to make the changes necessary for the good of all citizens. You all know what I am talking about! We are beset by problems left to me by the previous administration… challenges to be overcome. I believe we can cure the sickness that lies at the heart of our motherland." Another pause, this time for dramatic effect. "The patient is dying! But today I stand before you with a solution to all our problems… all our ills." '*Solution? Not suggestions? Will there be a debate? Will there be a vote?*' "You will have noticed some new faces in the front rows of the council. Most of them will be unfamiliar to you." '*They are all unfamiliar to me… and me… and me… and us.*' "I have made some changes to the membership of the Ruling Council. Why, I hear you ask, are changes necessary? It has been brought to my attention that some on the Ruling Council were putting themselves before their duty to our great nation… putting their needs ahead of those of our citizens… to feed their greed… their ambitions. I call them wreckers, saboteurs, traitors, scoundrels, self-serving profiteers… you know the type.

"What is to be done?… What is to be done? What is to be done about the scoundrels who would put themselves before the greater good? No punishment is too harsh for such vermin." All bar the new faces were wondering where this was leading. None of the old NV school was now sitting easy in their seats. "I recall the words of the great Stalin when he said, '*trust... but check*'... yes, trust, but check, and so I checked. And what I found disgusted me. How could the men and women I fought alongside... who I saw at their best and worst... have done what they did... and all for personal gain. It was deeply, deeply, shocking to me. The former members of this Ruling Council who used to occupy the front rows, those who were among the most trusted of you, have been sent to the Lubyanka for their own protection because when what they did is made known they would not be able to show themselves in public without being ripped to pieces at the hands of an angry mob.

"These people... these people who we entrusted to help us to make our nation great again only sought to fill their pockets. Instead of bringing dignity and work to the peoples of the Soviet Union, all they thought about was shameless profiteering. I feel somewhat responsible..." cries of *"do not blame yourself comrade Lev", "it was not your fault", "they had black hearts",* "Thank you... thank you all for your kind words of support but I will carry this burden with me for the rest of my days... I have let you down... I let Narodnaya Volya down and I let the Soviet Union down. I feel the only honourable course of action for me to take is to resign." More shouts of support for Lev but not being enthusiastic in all quarters he cast a glance to see which sections of the Ruling Council were not pleading with him to stay on as General Secretary. Then, one of the new faces stood.

"Comrade General Secretary, I am sure I speak for us all when I demand that you stay on as our leader. Your resignation would diminish the Ruling Council... diminish the Soviet Union and would not serve the needs of the Proletariat." Rapturous applause came from the rows of new faces which, with them standing and turning to face the rest of the assembly, spread throughout the auditorium. They all knew this game and how to play it.

"Comrades... I thank you for your understanding and forgiveness... I will work hard to reward your trust in me... I will never let you down again." A pause for effect and a moment of pretended contemplation. "Comrades, after this vote of confidence in me and my leadership, I feel I have your support for what must be done to address the damage caused to our beloved Soviet Union by the traitors who were in our midst. Let me talk frankly. We… the Soviet Union… have been asleep for decades… since the passing of Stalin in fact. Since his time we have been in continuous decline; and why was that? The answer is simple but the remedy is not. As a nation, we grew over-bureaucratised and our economy fat and inefficient… over decades our citizens developed a sense of entitlement which was unsustainable. We got used to expecting everything to be handed to us on a plate… everything we wanted… without working for it. We reached out our hands and the state filled them with luxuries." Lev paused to momentarily stare at his feet, he thought how shiny his shoes were. "Comrades, our economy, I think you will agree, is incompatible with the demands of our great nation. Today, throughout the Soviet Union, there is work-sharing, job splitting, job dilution… industry, production and output has been relocated to the centre… to Moscow. The conquered nations and outlying republics are suffering because they were left behind… they have no work… they waste their lives in a haze of alcoholism… drinking cheap Vodka… supplied to them by the state to keep them drunk! What a waste of life… but more importantly, what a waste of resources." Lev paused to stroll around the stage, taking his audience into his unblinking, soulless, shark-like, eyes. "And this abominable situation is compounded by lengthy holidays… workers, ordinary workers! get three months paid holiday… minimum!… a year! No economy can stand that. It is madness… madness!" All bar the front rows of delegates looked down in shame.

"Look at China… look at America… they have only two weeks' vacation a year… maximum! Something needs to change comrades and soon or all we have fought so hard for will be lost in the blink of an eye." A question from one of the new people sitting in the front row.

"How can we save our Soviet Union comrade? Tell us… please tell us." Asked the planted sycophant.

"To cure our beloved Soviet Union we must take our medicine. The medicine needs to be effective… it will not be sweet and it needs to be taken immediately… in very large doses… before it is too late! Comrades, we are standing on the brink of an abyss. One wrong step and we will fall into its depths."

Old school NV delegates gasped when they saw Lev remove sheets of paper from his jacket and begin reading from them. He had never previously relied on notes of any kind.

"I prepared some notes to make sure that I am understood and not misunderstood or misquoted by my friends at Pravda." Lev turned to his left and smiled. The in-house Pravda reporter sat her pen and notebook on the floor. "Dear friends… comrades… we all know the truth of the situation. The Soviet Union is on her knees and has been for decades." Lev paused to take the audience into his steely gaze once more, "What is to be done? Whatever is to be done is up to us to do it. Nobody else, it is our responsibility as the Ruling Council! Today, in the Soviet Union there are simply too many people for the economy to support and until our economy strengthens we need to take drastic action. For our economy to grow and become strong we must trade with America and China… we must gear up our banks and financial institutions to be competitive with America and China so we can grow an economy capable of sustaining our population. Why is it necessary to have an economy? Why can we not just keep going as we are? The answer is simple. The old Soviet Model simply just does not work. We have to accept it as fact, the evidence is irrefutable. The Soviet Model is against human nature. It is against mankind's competitive instincts and it feeds his innate idleness… the Soviet Model feeds his inner demons of despair, defeat and desperation. Our workers ask themselves why they should work hard if the person standing next to them is lazy. Our workers ask themselves why they should work hard when they see party officials getting more than them. Our workers ask themselves why they should work hard when they see people driving Merkovs and wearing denim. Our workers ask themselves why they should work hard when they see relatives of party officials getting the best jobs. Our workers ask themselves why they should work hard if they do not directly benefit from their efforts.

"Comrades, the Soviet Union is broken… you know it is… it has been broken for decades… the light of hope in the eyes of our citizens went out years ago. There is no need for them to work hard… there is no need for them to seek shelter… there is no need for them to put food on their tables… there is no need for them to put clothes on their backs… the state does all that for them… the state does everything for them. We treat our citizens more like pets than people. They have no incentive to work… to improve… to better themselves and their lives. They do not even have an incentive to go on living. We must give them a reason to live… a reason to get out of bed in the morning and go to work for the glory of the Soviet Union… but for themselves not just the motherland.

"Today, comrades, there are half a billion too many people living in the Soviet Union. What is to be done about them? Carrying them is dragging us all down. Here is how we will make the Soviet Union great again:

"To build an economy to compete with America and China we must embark immediately on unprecedented road, railway, telecommunications and other infrastructure projects. Such projects might appear to solve the problem, and to a degree it does, except that we cannot afford to pay for them and therefore we make use of Gulag labour as it is free. It is somewhat ironic that the Gulag was expanded for the Terror but now it works in our favour.

"Next, you will appreciate that we lag far behind America and China in technology. Do you realise that in America there are telephones that can be used in cars? They can be used to call anywhere in America… anywhere in the world if they wish! Nearly all Americans have computers in their homes! Most American homes have more than one Malenkytel… they call them televisions. All, yes all, American televisions are colour… colour… not black and white… colour! Everybody has them! Even ordinary workers have them and what do we have?

"Next. Production. The production coefficient of Soviet workers lags way behind the production levels of comparable American or Chinese workers. Even China is ahead of us! Even Canada is ahead of us! Even the republics of South America are ahead of us… including the socialist ones!…"

Lev listed item after item, making point after point, for over two hours. Then came the remedy… the medicine.

"Production must be matched to local populations and skill bases, without exception. No excuses. The Gulag labour force will be increased by ten million per month over the next twenty months, after which time it will be reviewed. Dissidents, trouble-makers, saboteurs, wreckers, traitors and scoundrels will be rounded up and removed to transit camps to be dealt with. From there they will either be transported to unpopulated regions or sold to China; they always have a need for people to support their agrarian economy to feed their billions." Lev paused to look around the auditorium for any reaction to his *'remedy'*, there were only blank expressionless faces staring back at him. They knew this game. "Treaties and trade agreements will be signed with America and China. The United States of America has agreed a funding programme to enable the Soviet Union to finance factories and infrastructure to get our economy going. It will not be easy as so little of what we have is of any use in the modern world. The target is to have an economy at least ten percent the size of the United States within three to four years.

"You might be asking yourselves, '*how will we bring about these changes and how can we afford them*'. For the first part, I will bring forward legislation to deal with trouble-makers. For the second part, most of those occupying the front rows are consultants for American industry while the remainder are involved in investment and financial institutions."

Lev asked if there were any questions. A solitary figure toward the back of the auditorium took to her feet. Lev asked her to wait until a microphone was passed to her so everybody could hear what she had to say.

"Comrade Lev, this is a very exciting programme that you have outlined for us today. You said that you are going to bring about programmes to deal with trouble-makers. What do you mean by this? How are you going to do it?"

"You ask a good question," replied Lev using a phrase he had picked up from the new people. "Thanks to the preparations made by the previous administration to bring Terror to the masses, I will use that infrastructure to deal with trouble-makers, wreckers, saboteurs, anti-Soviet elements and counter-revolutionaries. Terror is all they understand! NVPSK forces are about to execute Zima V2 in Velikobritania and Vladivostok. They will wipe out all those opposed to the new way. After clearing those places of radicals and criminals they will work their way toward the centre of our glorious nation, cleansing as they go. When they meet in the middle we can all be confident there will be no more trouble."

Question answered, Lev left the auditorium accompanied by forty of the new people. The remainder stayed behind to check the political reliability of old school NV Ruling Council members concerning Lev's plans. They were not so much checking political reliability more identifying trouble-makers. Within forty eight hours over four hundred of the old NV Ruling Council members were arrested for anti-Soviet, counter-revolutionary, activities, put on trial and executed the same day. By the next meeting of the Ruling Council its number had been reduced to four hundred; new faces all.

⋆

The American companies backing Lev's changes were in fact fronts for the CIA and the investment and financial institutions were owned and operated by The 400. After an absence of a century The 400 had finally returned to Russia.

The machinery for Terror remained in place from Kirilenko's time. Nothing had been dismantled or decommissioned; not detention camps, not ethnic concentration camps, not torture houses, not slave labour camps… nothing! Switching on the machinery of Terror was as simple as switching on a light and Lev did not hesitate to flick the switch for his American masters.

Home Again

As I exited the plane in Stolitsograd I expected to be met by massed throngs of people to welcome home this hero of the revolution but there was nobody. Exiting the airport building I expected to be greeted by dignitaries standing at the head of parades waving banners, just like they had in Moscow, and with thousands of cheering people lining the pavements, but there was nobody to welcome this hero of the Soviet Union home. It was raining as usual. I asked an airport worker for directions to the railway station. He pointed and said, "*Follow the signs.*" It was in the early hours of the next morning when I arrived back in Budyonovsk. It was still Budyonovsk, not Vakhnenkograd as I had hoped and dreamed it might be. But I was happy to be home. I felt lucky that I had gone through all I had gone through and survived. I was alive.

The second I entered our little family apartment, with its three by three Khrushchev kitchen, I felt at home; it was as though I had never been away. Thoughts of heroism and glory flushed themselves from my mind. I no longer thought of myself as a hero and stopped expecting to be treated like one. I did not mind… well, I did mind but what could I do? Despite the lack of hero worship I still felt lucky inside. I was back to being the same old happy go lucky person. I even heard somebody on the street shout, "Look, *happy go lucky Vladimir is back!*" It sounded something like it anyway.

★

Weeks after the reception in the Kremlin for the Tula heroes the universities were still shut. During that time, according to the media, the Tula cell went travelling the length and breadth of the Soviet Union giving rousing patriotic speeches to workers and activists alike. They took salutes at march pasts and were presented with medals wherever they appeared. They became very adept, very slick, at speech making. As the weeks rolled on only two of the original Tula cell remained on the speech trail, Svetlana and Grigori. Alina hung on in there somehow. Things were turning out for her just the way she hoped they would. She had done well for herself. The three were told that the others were "*just not the right sort of image to project.*" None of the three seemed to care much about what had happened to the others, they were far too absorbed in the opportunities their new lives gave them.

Vladimir read about the exploits of the '*Tula Heroes*' every day in the Budyonovsk Ekho. There were always articles telling of the heroic parts they played in the revolution. There was never any mention of Vladimir or the part he had played or that without him the revolution would have failed. There were pictures too. Vladimir thought Svetlana looked more beautiful than ever, "*She is very photogenic. Grigori is getting fatter.*" He had noticed how, one by one, the Heroes got fewer in number until they were only three.

★

There being no sign of universities reopening anytime soon, I had to find work. Everybody in the Soviet Union must work. It is one of the big rules. Mum spoke to her boss and he spoke to a friend and through a friend of hers I got a good job, a responsible job, in the languages section of the Security Commissariat. One of the big rules at work is that nobody is allowed to write a diary. I had never thought of writing a diary before and as I did not see the harm in keeping a record of things I began one, "*It might be fun.*"

★

Day 1

My name is Vladimir Vladimirovich Vakhnenko. Welcome to my diary. I have never written a diary before so I am not sure what to write in it. If I keep to the same topics every day I will be able to compare the entries to see if there are any changes. I will not write about anything to do with my work because I am politically reliable and not a wrecker or a saboteur nor am I anti-Soviet or a counter-revolutionary. In fact I am a highly decorated Hero Of The Soviet Union – First Class with a cluster of Five Red Stars. I was presented with my medal by Lev himself during a ceremony in Red Square in Moscow. I am very proud to have received our nation's highest honour.

Today I got up at 0500. Ate a cold breakfast in the dark. The power went out four times before I left the apartment. My journey to work was normal. It took one hour and fifteen minutes.

★

Day 2

Today I got up at 0500. Ate a warm breakfast in the dark. The power went out twice before I left the apartment. My journey to work was normal. It took one hour and fifteen minutes.

★

Day 3

Today I got up at 0500. Ate a warm breakfast. The power went out only once before I left the apartment. My journey to work was normal. It took one hour and fifteen minutes.

Yesterday I called the University of Nationalities in Moscow from work. The person on the other end of the call would not identify herself but she told me that the university was still closed and that no date had yet been given for it to reopen.

I should not have made the call from work as I could get into trouble for doing it.

I cannot stay here. I do not like the work. I do not like what is going on.

★

Day 4

Today I got up at 0500. Ate a cold breakfast in the dark. The power did not come on before I left the apartment. My journey to work was normal. It took one hour and fifteen minutes.

I swore not to write about anything that goes on in work but I must. My diary is the only one I can talk to about it. If I talk to anybody else it will be the end of them and me.

According to the documents I am translating, whole areas of Budyonovsk have been '*cleared*'. I do not know what that means exactly but I can guess. I think it must be connected with the large numbers of people being sent to the Gulag.

In the north western region of Velikobritania more than four hundred thousand people have '*relocated*' in the last ten days; men, women, children, old, young. That is KGB speak for arrested in the night and taken away for processing. Some of the documents I am working on refer to '*Category One types*' being '*removed to torture houses.*'

There were not as many people on the bus this morning and I noticed there are far fewer walking in the streets. Nobody says anything because we are scared to talk to one another. This is due to the '*increasing number of denunciations*' as reported in the Budyonovsk Ekho.

⋆

Day 5

Today I got out of bed at 0500. I did not sleep at all last night. I am very tired. I ate a cold breakfast in the dark. The power did not come on before I left the apartment, I am not sure if it came on at all yesterday. There were only twenty people on the bus this morning. The journey into work still took one hour and fifteen minutes.

I must find another job. I cannot bear to stay at the Security Commissariat. Everybody is staring at me. I am scared of what they might be thinking. I hope I have not said anything which might be construed as treachery but when did that ever stop Soviet style justice? Do they know about my diary? No, surely they cannot know about it.

⋆

Day 6

I did not go to bed last night, I sat up all night in a chair instead. I did not eat breakfast. The power did not come on before I left the apartment. I left for work at the usual time. There were sixteen people on the bus this morning. The journey into work still took one hour and fifteen minutes.

Yesterday, when I arrived back at the apartment, I noticed there were lots of new people moving into the apartment block next to ours. I tried to attract the attention of some of them so I could introduce myself but they would not look at me. I do not know what happened to the occupants of apartment block Novydom 8. I heard it said that "*Good Russian people are moving into the apartments.*"

Mum said I should go to bed. She said even if I did not sleep I would rest my body if not my mind. At 2249 I took her advice.

★

Day 7

I had a great sleep last night despite the nightmares. Nightmares usually wake me but not so last night. I slept right through them. More than that I actually took part in them. I was in my nightmares. I had heard about people who can enter their dreams to participate in them but until last night I did not believe it possible. I am looking forward to my sleep tonight.

I got up at 0500, as usual, ate a warm breakfast and had a hot shower. The power stayed on and did not go out even once. That is the first time I can recall that happening since before I went away to university. My journey to work was normal. There were only ten people on the bus today. The journey still took one hour and fifteen minutes.

Everybody in the office seemed much more relaxed today. Nobody stared at me. A section of cubicles on the other side of the office was dismantled during the night. I do not know where the Agents went. I wonder what they will do with the space? I heard they were going to put a table tennis table there and a sofa and coffee machine. That would be nice but I doubt it will ever happen.

Maria Morozova, Political Commissar of the Fourth Budyonovsk District Security Commissariat, ordered me to put the story of my heroism in saving the revolution down in writing. She said she will fill in the blanks. I do not know what she meant by that and I did not ask. She said my story will be held at the Soviet Central Archive in Moscow for future generations to read about the part I played in the revolution. I was so happy that my part in the revolution would finally be recognised. I worked through my breaks and lunch to finish my story as quickly as possible and get it sent off to Moscow. Moscow, how I miss Moscow.

When I arrived back at the apartment block after work the doors of the apartments on the top four floors were open. They were empty. I do not know where their occupants have gone. In the evening, I heard noises and looked out of the window and saw people moving into the empty apartments. They seemed very happy. They were saying how they finally had somewhere nice to live at last. "*Good homes for good Russian people*," was what they said.

★

Hello. My name is Anna Malinova. I found Comrade Vakhnenko's diary when we moved into our new apartment. It is much better than our old apartment. It has a Khrushchev kitchen, not a useless Malenkov kitchen and it is all ours. We do not have to share it with any other families. I made friends with four girls on my floor. They moved in on the same day as us.

I promise to write every night. Goodnight diary.